#scandal

Also by Sarah Ockler

#sca

ndal

BY SARAH OCKLER

Simon Pulse
New York London Toronto Sydney New Delhi

SIMON PULSE

An imprint of Simon & Schuster Children's Publishing Division

1230 Avenue of the Americas, New York, New York 10020

This Simon Pulse paperback edition June 2015

Text copyright © 2014 by Sarah Ockler

Cover and spine photograph copyright © 2014 by Tyler Stalman Photography (couple), Creata/Thinkstock (house and tree)

Also available in a Simon Pulse hardcover edition.

All rights reserved, including the right of reproduction in whole or in part in any form.

SIMON PULSE and colophon are registered trademarks of Simon & Schuster, Inc.

For information about special discounts for bulk purchases, please contact Simon & Schuster Special Sales at 1-866-506-1949 or business@simonandschuster.com.

The Simon & Schuster Speakers Bureau can bring authors to your live event. For more information or to book an event contact the Simon & Schuster Speakers Bureau at 1-866-248-3049 or visit our website at www.simonspeakers.com.

Cover designed by Regina Flath

Interior designed by Ellice M. Lee

The text of this book was set in Perpetua.

Manufactured in the United States of America

10 9 8 7 6 5 4 3 2 1

The Library of Congress has cataloged the hardcover edition as follows:

Ockler, Sarah.

#scandal / by Sarah Ockler. — 1st Simon Pulse hardcover ed.

p. cm.

Summary: When pictures of Lucy kissing her best friend's boyfriend emerge on the world of social media, she becomes a social pariah after the scandal rocks the school.

ISBN 978-1-4814-0124-1

[1. Scandals—Fiction. 2. Social media—Fiction. 3. Best friends—Fiction. 4. Friendship—Fiction. 5. Love—Fiction. 6. High schools—Fiction 7. Schools—Fiction] I. Title.

PZ7.O168 Aah 2014

[Fic]—dc23

2013045348

ISBN 978-1-4814-0125-8 (pbk)

ISBN 978-1-4814-0126-5 (eBook)

For Alex,
because . . . ZOMBIES!

#NOTEVENCLOSE

If a picture is worth a thousand words, a picture tagged on Miss Demeanor's Scandal of the Month page is worth about a million. Especially when the story all those words tell is an absolute lie.

Well, mostly a lie.

The part about falling asleep in his arms is sort of true. I don't remember the details about the horse, or how it got into the living room exactly, but judging from the smell that morning, that part's true too. And yes, the Harvard-bound debate team captain definitely cannonballed into the pond wearing only tuxedo socks and silver fairy wings. *Everyone* got shots of that.

But there's no way the other stuff happened.

Not like the pictures are saying it did.

A SPECIAL MESSAGE TO LAVENDER OAKS SWORDFISH ON THE OCCASION OF PROM

MISS DEMEANOR

2,002 likes 👍

92 talking about this

<u>Friday, April 25</u>

It's prom weekend, fishes, and you know what that means: Sex! Scandal! And . . . glitter?

Yes, glitter, as you'd expect from Lavender Oaks's first-ever Mythical Creatures Promenade. I'm not sure what that even means, but everything's better with sparkle, so let's raise a glass to the planning committee for spreading a dash of pixie dust on an otherwise pedestrian tradition. Cheers!

For those of you who haven't planned the ruination of

your innocence at one of the many after-parties, may I suggest popping by the east field for the school-sponsored medieval joust and mutton roast? Principal Zeff assures me that while the lances are made of foam, the horses and meat (mutually exclusive, despite recent legislation) are the real deal.

Chain mail not your thing? Rumor has it the (e)lectronic Vanities Intervention League is hosting a postprom reenactment of the fake moon landing on the grassy knoll, but they don't believe in Facebook; we can neither confirm nor deny reports. Still, if anyone spots any (e)VIL club members at the dance, snap a few pics. I'd love to see those girls rock an updo with their tinfoil hats.

Team Tinfoil Hat pics aside, don't forget to upload and share your juiciest weekend shots here on the Miss Demeanor page, tagged #scandal to enter my Scandal of the Month contest. This is it, kids—the very last #scandal before graduation. Make it count! Winners will be immortalized with a blinking gold star and, of course, eternal humiliation. Can't put a price on that!

Speaking of fame and glory, today we crossed the

magic number: 2,000 fans! But it's no time to rest on our überpopular laurels. Millions of Americans have yet to profess their loyalty. I'm saying! So do your part and tell a friend, tell an ex, tell a nana to hit that thumbs-up button!

On a serious note, a message from Students Against Substance Abuse: Driving dry is hella fly. The SASA president will personally monitor the punch bowl for suspicious activity, and the VP has the smoking lounge on lockdown in case you have any nontobacco smoking plans. With all that glitter and gossamer, something tells me you won't need hallucinogenics to have a funky trip, anyway.

While you're out bustin' a move in your satin and sequins tomorrow, I'll be home reclining in my zebra-print Snuggie, knuckles-deep in a box of Fiddle Faddle. Not very mythical, perhaps, but I've got a date with *Danger's Little Darling*, and after last week's killer episode, I can't wait to see what Angelica Darling has in store. God, I love me some Jayla Heart. That saucy starlet's the hottest thing to ever come out of Lav-Oaks. Don't believe me? Check out her fan page, the Jayla Heartthrobs. 200K fans? There's a girl who knows how to bust a move.

In closing, a Facebook message even Team Tinfoil Hat can't protest: Have fun this weekend, fishies. Be safe. And don't forget to smile for the spy satellites!

xo ~ *Ciao!* ~ xo
Miss Demeanor

THE ROAD TO HELL IS PAVED WITH GLITTER

Say . . . *magic pixie dust!*"

Inside the bedazzled Lavender Oaks gym, a photographer blasts me and Cole with the flash of a thousand suns, and the words "terrible" and "mistake" appear in neon bubbles before my eyes.

Dear formerly respectable self: How many lines *will* you cross tonight? Wearing a dress. Riding in a party Hummer. Striking a pose next to a horse festooned with a plastic unicorn horn.

Prince Freckles is normally reserved for the horseback riding elective, but the Mythical Creatures prom committee lassoed him into mascot duty. He doesn't seem to mind his makeshift pen—roped-off section near the bleachers, hay on the floor—but the costume is another story. Sequins? Clearly not Prince Freckles's personal style best.

"Short straw?" I whisper.

He flicks a pink ear in my direction and lets out a pathetic snort. *Don't let the other horses see me like this.*

The camera flashes again, and I wish on some of that magic pixie dust to spirit us both away, far from cowpoke Colorado and the ankle-deep hay and the too-tight hair ornaments.

Sadly, if my fairy godmother's on the scene, her gossamer-winged butt is parked at the punch bowl, and my wish floats up to the disco balls unfulfilled.

"Aww, cutest couple *ever*," the photographer says with a final blinding flash.

Cole winks at me across the speckled horse. His copper-green eyes shine with so much fire my chest hurts, and right before I basically *die*, he gets dragged off by the guys in his band and my half-stalled heart sputters back to life.

Close call, it warns. *Pat-pat-pat.*

"I can't believe they got an actual unicorn. Miss Demeanor will fa-*reak* when she sees this." My friend Griffin and her soul-mate-of-the-hour, an elf-costumed kid named Paul from Saint Paul's Prep, enter the pen. Griff shakes out her dyed platinum curls and tries to snap a selfie, but the phone her parents got her in Helsinki is so complicated, she can never work the camera.

The real photographer takes over, and I find a seat on the bleachers to watch the show of Paul ogling Griffin's succubus dress, a midnight-blue sheath with a sewn-on devil's tail and a deep *V* down the front. Cute and pointy Legolas ears aside, Paul's getting the Tarts of Apology tomorrow—Griff's method of breaking hearts at the corner table at Black & Brew Café. Bad news goes down better with pastries, she always says.

She has a lot of theories. It's exhausting.

Griffin lets out a high-pitched squeal as Paul palms her ass, and the tea-rose corsage near my shoulder tumbles to my lap, scattering petals on the way down. I scoop them into a pile, their edges already curling.

Prom impostor.

It's Saturday night. I should be home slaying online zombies and sneaking people food to Night of the Living Dog, not playing dress up in the land of make-believe. Because fact-check time, for anyone keeping it real:

1. Prince Freckles isn't really a unicorn.
2. Cole isn't really my date.
3. This poof of a dress isn't really my style.
   Vintage rockabilly halter, butter-white

chiffon with black cherry print and a bloodred sash. It's so pretty I'm practically allergic.

From the horse pen, Griff squeals again, and my gaze darts to the doors behind her. Maybe the Hummer's still in the parking lot, still shooting iridescent orbs from its rooftop bubble machine. I can sneak out, catch a ride home. In less than an hour I'll be out of this pinup gear, sucking down a Dr Pepper and roasting undead hordes with a flamethrower.

My fingers squeeze invisible triggers. . . .

"Don't tell me my last-minute date's already bailing." Cole's back, crouching in front of me with a smirk. Normally he keeps a little scruff on his face, but he cleaned up for the occasion, and the late-spring sunshine has left his skin tan and smooth. Kissable. "What's wrong, Luce?"

I heft four thousand layers of chiffon over my black thigh-high boots, the only part of the ensemble that's mine, and crush the fabric in my fists. "I'm a wedding-cake topper."

"Not even." Cole takes the wilting corsage from my lap. "You look, um, *really* nice." He leans in close, messy hair tickling my nose. He smells like outside, like campfire and ripe apples, and—

Hey! Prince Freckles's sequined-covered stomp says it all: *Don't even think about it!*

With a heavy sigh, I flick a lone rose petal from my lap. I'd love to follow the horse's advice, but it's too late. Don't even think about it? I *have* thought about it. Every day. For the last four years.

We've never kissed, never cuddled, never been anything more than capital-F Friends. Cole Foster broke my heart anyway. Like the perfect dress and the flowers that refuse to stay put, the only boy I've ever loved belongs to Eliana Pike.

Ellie.

My best friend.

"Thanks for filling in tonight." Cole's breath glances my shoulder as he works to reattach the corsage. Beneath his touch, my heart flops like a beached fish, and I turn my face away from his gaze.

Perfect. How am I supposed to survive an entire night of dancing if I can't even manage eye contact? Honestly, the whole arrangement is getting to be a serious problem.

"Not a problem," I say.

Get it together, Luce. Ellie's in bed with the superflu, missing senior prom—the event she looked forward to more than anything the whole three years she's been with Cole. All I'm missing is a little online carnage.

Please go with him, Lucy. You're my surrogate! You have to send me pictures all night long!

Never one to say no to Ellie, I've been following those orders all night. *omg u & griff r stunners*, her last text said, after she reviewed the series my parents snapped in our driveway. *u r totes keeping that dress!* She's been texting for the play-by-play ever since.

"You sure you're okay?" Cole's gaze sweeps the black cherries bodice, and for a moment there's something in his eyes, something more than the usual mischief.

When he looks up again it's gone, and I'm suddenly naked, a transparent idiot full of impossible fantasies. There was never anything in his eyes, and here I am still pretending, stunt-doubling like some Goth Cinderella who can't accept the fact that everything turns to dust at midnight.

People are looking at us now, whispering and curious as news of Ellie's predicament makes the rounds, but it's hardly a scandal. By Monday morning she'll be back in Cole's arms, the dress replaced on its hanger like the whole dark fairy tale never happened.

I take a steadying breath, a reboot on the pity party. Maybe it was crazy to say yes when Ellie asked, but I *did* say yes. I made a promise, and it's Cole's prom too—he deserves to have fun.

I won't let either of them down.

"Totally sure." With a fresh smile, I rise from the bleachers and grab Cole's hand, shaking off my reservations. It's just a dance. A few hours, a few pictures, then I'm back in zombie-slaying heaven. "Rent-a-Princess at your service."

As soon as Ellie's better, I'm totally putting her in the hospital.

The gym is stacked to the rafters with the fanged, the furred, and the feyed, everyone sparkling and fabulous in a strobe-light haze but me, who decided becoming Ellie for the night was mythical enough, and Cole, who didn't want me to feel left out.

After I snap a few decor shots for Ellie, Cole navigates us through a sea of fist-bumping vampires—*Where's Ellie, bro? What's up with you and Lucy, bro? If you're done with Ellie, bro, can I hit it?*—and spins me onto the dance floor.

Good timing. I have a superlow bro-speak threshold.

Cole mimics my scowl, holding the pose until I laugh. "I know you'd rather be shooting zombies," he says, "but we're not leaving until you have eight consecutive minutes of fun. I'm timing you."

I poke my auburn Texas-style updo—when Mom heard I'd be promming it up tonight, her inner debutante could not be leashed—and secure a loose bobby pin. "I'm having fun."

"Great," Cole says. "Now I have to bust out my *River-dance* moves."

"You can't *Riverdance* to rap mash-ups, *bro*."

"This isn't just any mash-up. It's 'Reckoner's Encore.'" Cole's a drummer in a band called Vanitas—my suggestion, after their inaugural gig in Cole's garage last year—and now he mimes the beat with invisible drumsticks. "I *rock* this shit."

"Take it away, Irish."

"Ye of little faith!" Cole folds his arms over his chest, jumps up, kicks his heels together, and lands without falling.

"Um . . . did you really just . . . ?"

"I'm really just getting started." His grin is wide and genuine, and when another baseline thumps through the speakers, he doesn't miss a step.

Three, four, five songs pass, and Cole's moves get crazier and more daring, like he has this whole reserve inside, waiting for a chance to make me laugh. He twists and bobs, sings made-up lyrics in my ear, taps beats on my hips, and for an entire hour I ignore the camera flashes around us, the endless buzz of Ellie's texts from the phone inside my sash. Following Cole's lead, I dance and twirl and laugh as if this feeling will last forever, as if it's always been mine to hold.

Then the dance tracks fade into a ballad, slow and full of longing, and I picture Ellie, curled up with a bowl of soup and her stuffed companion Hedwig, her voice a watery echo.

I want you guys to have so much fun for me. . . .

"I'll be back." I slip out of Cole's embrace and weave through the battlefield, avoiding Griff and Paul's grind-fest, dodging packs of drunk vampires and duck-faced, selfie-snapping fairies until I'm out of sight.

Most horses would revolt, or at least poop on the floor, but Prince Freckles is a pacifist—probably how he got saddled with this crap gig in the first place. While the rest of the Lav-Oaks horse fleet is undoubtedly prepping for tonight's jousting tournament, my equine-American bestie is alone in the pen, unsupervised, bearing his shame without complaint.

"Brought you a treat." I hold out an apple pilfered from a cheesy *Twilight* display by the punch bowl. The fruit disappears in a single bite, and across his gray-speckled rump, I catch sight of Olivia Barnes.

The cute but mousy girl from my advanced art class is constantly asking about Cole and Ellie—how long they've been in love and is it the capital-L kind or just lowercase? With Ellie down for the count, the little Jezebel finds the courage to ask Cole for a dance, and they're off, swaying and bobbing like a boat in the smoke-machine fog.

My stomach goes all pretzely, and I force my attention back to Prince Freckles.

We're no longer alone.

"Lucy?" Kiara Chen saunters toward us in a silver floor-length dress, face painted with teal swirls, her glossy black hair studded with starfish. "Can you take my picture with the unicorn? Like, superfast? And then I'll send it to my mom?"

She's way too jittery for such a beautiful mermaid, but I—equal-opportunity ally to creatures both land and sea—slip the phone from my sash and comply.

"My parents wanted pictures," she explains when I hand her the phone. At lightning speed, she taps in a number and sends the files. "My club is strict about . . . you know. Cameras and texting and stuff."

Her eyes are darting around like there's a spy on her fishtail, and now I get it. Kiara is vice president of (e)VIL, this whackadoo conspiracy-theory club that wants to rid the world of technology or Facebook or something. I'm betting if her crew caught her posing for digital pics *and* sending them through cyberspace, they'd execute her. In a super old-school way, like a guillotine.

Kiara returns my phone. The instant it touches my hand, it's buzzing, the number unfamiliar.

"Must be your mom." I read the text out loud. "'Adorbs! Instagramming it for Nana. See you after the dance, sweetie! DVRd *DLD* for you!'"

Kiara goes the color of Bella Swan's apple. "*DLD*? Um . . . I mean, I've never seen it. Mom's the Jayla Heart fan in our house. That's her name, right?"

"That is, in fact, her name." I give her a teasing smirk. Jayla Heart, class of 2007, bounced to Hollywood right after grad, eventually scoring the lead on *Danger's Little Darling* and becoming the pride and joy and tabloid scandal–magnet of Lavender Oaks. "If you're gonna cheat, there are *much* better shows."

"I'm not—"

"Your secret's safe with me." I pat the horse's rump. "And Prince Freckles is a vault."

She thanks me, smiling and relieved, but before we start braiding each other's hair and making sleepover plans, Cole shows up, and Kiara disappears.

"Making new friends?" His hair flops into his eyes, doing nothing to hide his adorable grin, which is all, *If you love me and you know it clap your hands!*

"Everywhere I go." *Clap-clap.*

"Mermaids and unicorns can't save you," he says. Prince Freckles and I look up simultaneously, and Cole pats his jacket pockets. "Since I'm carrying your lipstick, your eyeliner, your license, and your house keys, I'm thinking you at least owe me a slow dance."

"'Nothing Compares 2 U?'" I fumble with the sash, smoothing nonexistent wrinkles. "Way to rock a breakup anthem at prom, Lav-Oaks."

"Don't get any ideas. You can't break up with me until midnight. Your contract is specific." Cole untangles my hands, and for all his earlier jokes, suddenly there isn't a funny thing left on earth.

I rest my head on his chest. Just as my ear finds his heartbeat, his breath catches, his fingers trailing lightly down my neck.

An electric shiver races to my toes, and *wow*, mystery solved. *This* is why I sent two previous boyfriends packing after a month of lackluster make-out sessions, why every one of Griffin's football practice oglefests and Ellie's attempts at fixing me up with Cole's friends are epic fails.

All along I've been holding out for *this*, the airy buzz spinning through my body as Cole presses closer. *Butterflies.*

No matter how fleeting, the darkest part of me knows it's worth it. Knows I'll hold on to this for the rest of always, and as long as the song keeps playing, I don't have to let go. . . .

"Lucy." Cole's breath is hot in my ear, and I wonder if

he feels it too, this current between us, charged and impossible. "I think—"

"Excuse me to interrupt." There's a nudge at my elbow, and I turn to see Marceau, our pant-worthy foreign-exchange student. Devil horns crown his shoulder-length brown hair. "May I borrow this dance?"

Cole hesitates, fingers pressing ever so slightly into my back, but with Marceau looking on, the spell between me and Cole is already broken, and later he'll call Ellie and murmur her name into the phone, whispering that prom was just a dance without her, that Rent-a-Princess was no substitute for the real thing.

"Sure, I'd love to dance." The lie is thick on my tongue as I take Marceau's hand and follow him into the crowd, far away from Cole and the dangerous things coiled inside me.

Marceau is a familiar face in the halls of Lav-Oaks, but we don't have any classes together. I know he's from a far-off land where they say football instead of soccer, which he plays here as goalie, and Griff mentioned last week that he recently broke up with this spazzy sophomore due to irreconcilable differences over their Facebook relationship status.

"I'm Lucy," I say, in case he doesn't know me with the same level of Wikipediac detail. "Last name Vacarro."

Last name Vacarro? Apparently we're on a cop show now.

"Tell me something, Lucy last name Vacarro." Marceau's

lips are full and soft, his voice like hot chocolate. I should probably take the devil horns as a warning, but I just smile, like, *Keep saying your words to me, beautiful boy with gourmet accent!*

"Why do they call us Swordfish?" he asks. "I have inquired. No one can say."

"It's our mascot," I say. "Like the Denver Broncos? We're the Lavender Oaks Swordfish."

Marceau frowns, revealing a small dimple in his chin. "Yes, but in the mountains, where is a fish?"

"We have mermaids," I say, remembering Kiara. "And fish sticks in the cafeteria sometimes. Does that count?"

"I do not know this fish stick. It frightens the soul." He gives a mock shiver and spins me out, yanking me back just before I crash into Cole's best friend, John, Vanitas's singer and guitarist. He's here with his on-again-off-again girlfriend, Clarice, president of Students Against Substance Abuse. She's had it out for me ever since I discovered the gateway drug of black nail polish in seventh grade, and beneath her chunky black bangs she eyes up my boots with her typical glare.

"Diggin' the boots, Vacarro," John says. He's wearing fairy wings over his tux, and a smudge of glittery guyliner stands out against his dark brown skin. Clarice has the same costume, but it looks better on him. "Hot!"

Clarice makes a clucking sound and yanks him into a crowd of yard gnomes. Or possibly Snow White's dwarves. Hard to tell with all the fog and strobe-light action.

Marceau is quick and confident on his feet, but after our third turn around the gym, my boots revolt. Marceau escorts me to the refreshment table—legit *escorts* me—and kisses me good-bye on the cheek, his amber eyes sparkling.

Me to Ellie: *danced 3 songs w/ marceau. le yum. 2 late 2 join french club?*

Ellie: *!! eff french. try mile high club w/ that hottie, u vixen! rawr!*

"*Someone's* got a crush," Cole teases. I didn't even see him walk up.

"What?" I shove the phone behind my sash so fast I get, like, sash-burn. "I don't have a crush. Ellie and I were just—"

"I was talking about *him*." Cole nods across the gym toward Marceau, who's joined up with the gnomes and a leprechaun couple in matching green tuxes. They've all got their phones in the air, filming the outrageousness from above. "He's been checking you out all night. Asked me earlier if we were together."

"What did you tell him?"

Cole's eyebrows shoot up, and I rush to explain. "I mean, you didn't tell him I liked him, right? Because—"

"*Do* you?" Cole's eyes are fierce and fiery, the smile gone from his lips.

Is he . . . jealous?

High above, a glitter cannon explodes, and a huge canvas banner of Jayla Heart flutters beneath the basketball scoreboard, vomiting sparkles on our heads.

"I don't," I whisper. "Like him, I mean."

It takes a second for the world to start spinning again, and then it's like, *Welcome back, Cole's smile! Oh, how we've missed you!*

"You're off-limits, anyway." Cole brushes glitter from my shoulder. "I told him you're my favorite groupie."

"You wish! Drummers don't get groupies; singers do. Ask John."

"Drummers get *all* the groupies. And for your 411, I'm an excellent singer." His green eyes lock on mine, and right as I'm about to pass out from lack of oxygen to the brain, Cole nudges my arm. "I'm ready to blow this disco inferno. You're crashing at the cabin tonight, right? Ellie told you about the party?"

Party?

"I'm . . . I can't. I have to go home." Faking it through dinner and dancing was hard enough. Besides, Ellie *didn't* mention it. Apparently the Rent-a-Princess list of duties stops just short of "attend intimate all-nighter at my boyfriend's secluded mountain cabin."

"Your parents don't trust me?" Cole says. "I'm totally trustworthy." He holds up his fingers, Scout's honor, but he knows my parents adore him—always have. When he and Ellie hooked up, Mom was all sad-faced and, "Huh. I always thought *you* two would get together, sugarplum. I didn't even know Ellie liked him."

"There's an *Undead Shred* tournament," I explain. "My crew's counting on me. You have to stay together or you die. Or get incapped. That's slang for incapacitated, which you get when you don't . . . stay together." I shut my eyes, wondering if that useless fairy godmother is around. After five seconds I'm still standing here mortified, so . . . nope.

"I know incapped," Cole says. "I've dabbled in the undead arts before."

Mortification be damned. I open my eyes and cast a suspicious glare. "Did you just say 'dabbled in the undead arts'?"

"Don't hurt me." Cole holds up his hands in surrender. "Point is, using zombies as an excuse to ditch me? That's beat, Vacarro. What kind of prom date are you?"

"The beat kind, obviously."

Cole's mischievous grin rises once again, custom-made by the fates to be my complete undoing.

"It's just a party," he whispers. "What's the worst that could happen?"

FRIENDS DON'T LET FAIRIES DRINK, WAX POETIC, STRIP, AND SWIM

Inquiring minds want to know, Lucy Vacarro." Griffin discovered the video function on her phone, monster created, and now she's filming us in the Fosters' bathroom. "How far *are* you willing to go as Ellie's prom surrogate?"

I pause mid–eyeliner application and frown playfully at her reflection in the mirror. Somehow she ended up with Marceau's devil horns. "Brunette Griffin was nicer."

"There's no denying that Cole *is* adorable."

On the countertop, my phone buzzes with Ellie's number, a call instead of a text. There's a fire in me, guilt and desire, and I bury them both. The party hasn't even begun, and it's already my worst idea ever. Even though it was Cole's idea.

I rearrange my face into something like this: *Cole? Adorable? Whatev.* "True," I say. "Yet irrelevant."

"I have a theory about you two." Griff scopes out the buzzing phone, but when I still don't answer it, she continues. "It's not like anyone would find out if you . . . you know. Fulfilled Ellie's postprom duties."

I slip and nearly blind myself with kohl. "What is *wrong* with you?"

"Whoa, girl. I'm kidding. Obviously." Griff watches me a second longer in the mirror and narrows her eyes. "I know that look."

"There's no look."

"You *like* him!"

My face burns. "Are you drunk already?"

"Luce. You're getting a little—"

"I'm getting a little nothing, because I don't like him. And please stop documenting everything I say. It's creepy."

"Having closeted sexy-time thoughts about your best friend's boyfriend is creepy. Just be honest for once. It's so *obvious.*"

I go to smack her arm, but she dodges, still wielding her phone like the paparazzi. It almost makes me feel sorry for Jayla Heart, whose Hollywood shenanigans grace the gossip rags weekly. "Turn it off."

"These are the moments of your life, Lucy Vacarro.

You should *thank* me for documenting them." Griff has the movie announcer voice going, free hand framing my face, like, *Action!* "If it's not on Facebook, it didn't happen. You know that, right?"

"You're so gross right now. You know that, right?" I leap on the subject change. "They're a corporation. They're probably tracking us."

"Now you sound like (e)VIL." Griff scrunches up her nose, same face she made at dinner when Paul explained where veal comes from. "Those people have no lives. It's sad, really. Even sadder than your gamer marathons." Griff turns her phone into a mock controller, frantically thumbing buttons.

Securely off the Cole innuendos, I return to my eyelining. "You'd so lose your life in the zombie apocalypse, blondie."

"At least I have a life to lose. Did you see mermaid chick—"

"They have no *Facebook*," I say. Kiara, an antitechnology mermaid with a secret tech life? That has to count for something. "For all we know, their lives are fascinating."

Griff snorts. "Their idea of fun is reading old newspapers and looking for codes."

"And *your* idea of fun is sleeping with half the school and getting on Miss D's scandal page. So?"

Her smile drops down the sink, and my heart follows.

"Sorry. I didn't . . . That came out wrong." I don't know why I'm all defensive about (e)VIL. Before tonight, I never talked to any of them. And it's not like Kiara and I are suddenly making plans to search for extraterrestrial life together.

This whole unrequited Cole thing is fracking my brain. I shouldn't even be here. It's obvious Ellie didn't want me to come to the party, and I'd rather not spend the night disproving Griff's little theories—they're not exactly wrong.

I meet her eyes in the mirror. "Griffin, seriously. I don't know why I said that. I'm sorry. It's—"

"Whatev. Not like you're lying." She slips the devil horns from her head and sets them on the sink with a casual shrug. Something wounded flashes across her face, but then it's gone, replaced by her cool, sexy confidence. "I'm hot. What can I say? And I do loves me some boys."

I conjure up a smile to match, but it's not about her hotness or how many people she hooks up with. When it comes to Griffin's conquests, the tally is her business. I just hate how it changes her, how her revolving bedroom door is a constant topic for the fans congregating on Miss Demeanor's page.

Griff is like a piece of clay that never makes it to the kiln. Last week an ashtray, next week a vase, each new guy ushering in a personality and hairstyle to match. She's been hanging out with me and Ellie for two years, but whenever we start to get close, the new Griff shows up and we have to learn her all over again.

Oh, I'm over that now, she says. *So yesterday.*

She smooths her curls before the mirror, tendrils licking her shoulders like white flames. "Do I look okay?"

"I wouldn't change a thing." I hold her gaze, but all she's got left is her nothing-can-touch-me smile.

"Except for maybe Cole's undying love for Ellie?" she says.

"Griffin! I don't—"

"You should tell him. Or maybe . . ." Her lips curl into a smile, dark and devious.

I hate when she gets like this, but guilt nudges me to play along. "Maybe what?"

"*I* could tell him." She taps her chin with a glossy red fingernail. "That might be fun for everyone."

"You wouldn't."

"Drinks?" she says. "Paul's a pro on the blender." She flicks off the lights, and before I can remind her that she hates frozen drinks because they give her brain freeze, she's gone.

The two-story timber-framed "cabin" is tucked into a grove that backs up to forest service land, miles from civilization.

I've only ever been here with Ellie, and now it feels odd without her, like the place was redecorated and I just can't figure out what's different.

Also, I don't usually hang out in the foyer behind the floor-to-ceiling curtains, peering out the front windows like a shut-in.

That makes ten. I sip my sweet "Piña Paulada" and count another set of headlights bouncing up the dirt path. Olivia, the art girl Cole danced with earlier, hops out of an SUV with her friends Quinn and Haley, a trio of winged sprites in blonde, brunette, and red. Disappointment settles in my stomach.

Want some whine with that cheese? Here goes: My hair hurts. My feet are killing me. Griff's ignoring me. Cole's been looking for me, but whenever I see him I disappear, hoping against the odds Griff hasn't carried out her pseudo-threat.

The doorbell rings—Olivia and company—and I think about the *Undead Shred* tournament I'm missing, the rush that comes with tossing a Molotov cocktail and bolting to the nearest safe room. My online crew's gonna freak when they hear I ditched them for a party. Half of them are in college or older, way beyond high school ridiculousness.

That's what rocks about it. As long as you can kill walkers and keep the team safe, you can be anyone you want in the gaming world. Princess. Warrior. International girl of mystery. Unlike in the real world, where everyone can see you bumbling around like an idiot in a dress, live and uncut.

A prom party! What was I thinking?

Cole. That's what I was thinking. And in the hour I've been here, I've done nothing but avoid him.

Maybe . . . I could tell him . . . fun for everyone . . .

My phone buzzes again just as Cole passes behind me to collect the car keys from Olivia's friend, and my neck prickles. Ellie didn't leave a voice mail before. Her texts are getting impatient.

where r u? y no more pics?

at cabin, I type. *cole playing host. but zzzzz! party is snooze-fest w/o u!*

She replies instantly: *u went to party? thought u had game stuff 2nite?*

I hesitate. Another text follows: *hello, u h8 parties. what's going on?*

last minute decision, I type. *no worries. prolly find a ride home early. u mad?*

A few minutes pass before she responds, my breath fogging the window as I wait.

just surprised, she finally says. *& cranky w/ super big bird flu. sux.*

:-(wish u were here, el.

me 2, my goth princess. so where's frenchie? u in total amour yet?

The window is cloudy, and with my free hand I trace a heart in the fog. Ellie's next text arrives before I respond.

u better b! i'm living vicariously, watching TVD reruns & eating crackers in bed. send more pix! esp. if frenchie shows! maybe he'll take u home?

"Duuuude."

The word floats on a moss-scented current, and I turn toward the source, ducking out from behind the curtain. Clarice's substance-abusing nemesis, a kid who earned the nickname 420 in middle school, blinks from beneath the rim of a dingy orange hat. The rest of his mythical creatures attire consists of tuxedo pants and a black T-shirt with a picture of a Gelfling that reads, *I thought I was the only one!*

Conversing with 420 is like playing Mad Libs, but it's more entertaining than cuddling with the drapery and faking my way through Ellie's texts, and anyway, I love *The Dark Crystal*.

"What's up?" I say through a too-bright smile. Cole passes behind him, scoping out the foyer and the living room beyond, but he doesn't see me.

"This place is like . . ." 420 blinks. I give him my full attention.

"A mountain oasis?" I ask helpfully.

He shakes his head and giggles.

"Retreat-like?" I say. "Cozy?"

He closes his eyes.

"Woodsy," I press. "Outdoorsy. Secluded?"

Time passes. Mountains erode. Streams merge into rivers. Six new species evolve, and I'm pretty sure this kid just fell asleep standing up.

"Good talk, 420." I leave him to contemplate the mysteries of the Foster cabin and relocate to the kitchen. Chips and dip, rescuer from social ineptitudes great and small!

"That kid is *wasted*." Clarice scowls at me over the munchies table as if I'm responsible for 420's life choices. "I can't believe they're letting him graduate—"

"Attention, attention! I've got a song in my *heaaaaart!*"

Clarice and I turn toward the sudden commotion in the living room. John, the only member of the class heading to Harvard, is standing on the coffee table in nothing but tuxedo pants, a turquoise cummerbund that matches Clarice's dress, black socks, and his silver wings.

"Perfect." Clarice abandons a plate of apple slices and cheddar and marches into the living room, her wings stiff and commanding. Why she's so concerned about 420 when her own boyfriend has already stumbled into the karaoke stage of debauchery is a mystery, but so are most

relationships in Lavender Oaks, and I follow her angry footsteps, switching on my video capture for Ellie.

John's thumbs hook behind the wing straps stretched over his muscular shoulders. "'These are the *tiiiimes* to remember,'" he sings. "'And they will not last *foreverrrrr*.'"

Cole's nowhere in sight, but across the room, Marceau tips his beer bottle toward me and smiles. I didn't see him arrive, and I'm surprised at the flutter in my chest. In the wake of my inappropriate Cole-fantasizing, I grab on to the feeling like a lifeboat. Even though we're landlocked, as Marceau astutely pointed out, but still. Flutter! Not Cole! Progress!

"Hey," I mouth over the crowd, holding up my frosty glass of yellow-white slush. Marceau winks.

I send Ellie a quick text—*frenchie has arrived. let the panting and/or pantsing commence*—then flip back to video as John continues.

"Four score and four years together," John says. "We've endured countless tornado warnings. Sex-ed assemblies with Mrs. Frockton." John puts a hand on his bare chest and shudders.

One of the vampires I saw at the dance makes a gagging sound. "Givin' me nightmares, bro!"

Everyone laughs, but John holds up his hands to quiet the crowd.

"We've survived Kincaid's British lit class," he continues. "The questionable safety of Merton's chem labs. The questionable safety of cafeteria hamburgers." John clenches his stomach, then rockets his fist into the air. "Despite my best efforts at delinquency, my pretty face has yet to appear on Miss Demeanor's scandal page. You don't have to protect me, D! Obama took the pressure off when he became the first black prez. The second one has more room to cultivate a shady past."

"You're shady as hell, bro," one of the vamps says.

John flashes a crooked grin. "I'm saying! Miss D, if you're here, you lovable scandalmonger, come forth!"

"It's totally Lucy, right?" Griff giggles from her perch on Paul's lap, and everyone roars at the ridiculous joke. The chill between us thaws, and across the room she returns my smile, making a heart with her hands.

"Fine," John says. "If the real Miss D refuses to self-identify, I dedicate this next scandal to Lucy. Hot-ass chick in your hot-ass boots. That thing on video?" He points to my phone, and I give him the thumbs-up.

John goes all Shakespeare in the Park on a rendition of that rage against the dying light poem by Dylan Thomas, which has nothing to do with graduation as far as I can tell, but his performance is partly musical and beyond compelling.

"Do not go gentle into that good night!" John's voice is

thick with emotion. Everyone cheers, and in a moment of passionate abandon, he rips off his cummerbund and flings it into a bowl of Doritos.

"That's enough," Clarice says. She tries to wave him down from the coffee table, but he shakes his head. She's fuming. "You're such an asshole when you drink!"

The crowd *oooh*s.

"Don't you yell at me!" He unbuttons his pants. More cheers.

"You'd *better* not be taking off those pants," she warns. "I'm serious. You take off your pants, we're through."

"Don't you yell"—John looks from Clarice to his crotch—"at my pants!"

The room erupts, taking up the chant as he ditches the offending pants.

"Don't you yell, at his pants! Don't you yell, at his pants! Don't you yell—"

"Consider yourself dumped," Clarice says. "You hear me? It's over!"

"Okay, then. As I was saying." Unaffected by his sudden breakup, John stands in his striped boxers and holds up his hands for everyone to settle down. "Do not go gentle into that good night. Go . . . *swimming!*"

He hops off the table and stumbles out the sliding patio doors behind him. Everyone but Clarice whoops and rushes to follow, Griffin dragging me by the arm, Cole catching up behind us, and by the time we reach the pond in the backyard, John's naked, save for the fairy wings and black socks.

The last thing I see before closing out my video is a great brown ass cannonballing into the water, camera flashes lighting up the sky like an electrical storm.

"There goes the second black president of our great nation," Cole says.

"Newly single, too." I snap a few still shots as he bobs in the water. "Think he'll really run for office?"

"If he does, those pics will be pretty tweet-worthy."

"They're already tweet-worthy," Griff says. "We're uploading them for hashtag scandal." She tries to take a few shots of her own, but quickly gives up and stumbles back toward the cabin. "Paul!" she shouts, loud enough to wake the entire forest. "These lips won't kiss themselves!"

Cole nods toward my glass, mouth curved in a smile. "I lose track of you for one hour, and look what happens. How many is that?"

"Three. I'm fine. Don't worry."

"I *am* worried, Lucy dear." His sleeves are rolled up now, no more jacket and tie. His bare forearm is warm around my neck. "As your date, I'm obligated to hold your hair back if you yack. That's one aspect of our relationship I'm not interested in exploring."

"Feeling is mutuual, dude."

Cole rubs his shaggy head. "I don't have quite enough hair."

"It's the principle." I slip out from under his arm and chug the rest of my drink, trying not to shiver at the double-whammy alcohol burn and brain freeze. When I look up again, Cole's face is serious, eyes flashing with sudden intensity.

In all the commotion, I forgot I'm supposed to be dodging him, and now that we're alone, nowhere to run, fear shoots through my limbs.

"I have to talk to you." His words spill out in a rush.

I'm going to kill you, Griffin Colanzi.

"Luce, I'm not—"

"Duuuude." Out of the darkness, 420 lumbers forth, clutching the bowl of cummerbund-spiked Doritos. The effort of trying not to laugh turns his face red. "I might be hallucinating."

Beneath Ellie's dress my legs tremble.

Cole says, "Good for you, man."

"Yeah." 420 rocks back on his heels. His eyes go big. "I mean, no! There's something on the deck. It's eating the bird feeders." He grins like a jack-o'-lantern and wanders off toward the pond, still babbling. "Unicorn or some shit."

THERE'S A UNICORN ON THE DECK (AND OTHER STATISTICAL ANOMALIES THAT SHOULDN'T BE PHOTOGRAPHED)

420 was not, in fact, hallucinating.

"There's a unicorn on the deck," I say. "Is this happening?"

"Spence must've kidnapped him." Cole guides Prince Freckles down the steps, cursing Vanitas's bassist. "His truck's the only one with a horse trailer. Fuckin' cowboy."

"Couldn't stay away, huh, buddy?" I rub Prince Freckles's snout and scrutinize his face for signs of distress, but he seems fine. His glittery horn is bent, and when I unhook the chin strap, I swear he moans in relief.

Cole ties the leads to the railing. "I'll get him something to eat. Want anything from inside?"

"I'm good." I climb back on the deck and pet the horse over the railing. He nuzzles my hand, content.

"Be right back. Don't go anywhere, Luce. I really need to talk to you."

The mountain air cools fast, but between the drinks and my nerves, I don't feel the chill.

I really need to talk to you. . . .

Even the gentle presence of the horse can't slow my thoughts, my mind spinning webs of awkward possibilities. *I don't like you that way, Lucy. I'm flattered, but I have a girl-friend. How could you do that to Ellie? Maybe you should just go home. . . .*

Then, from possible to impossible. *I've always sensed something between us, Lucy. . . .*

My phone buzzes with another text. I know it's Ellie. It's like she can read my mind, hear the twin echoes of guilt and longing in my heart.

having fun w/o me? :-(what happened w/ frenchie?

so so, I text back. *lost frenchie in the mix—stay tuned. u'd be bored here, girlie! lots of debauchery, not much convo.* I send her the John video as proof.

Ellie's always up for a party, but she prefers them low-key and intimate, the kind of drinking that evolves into intellectual arguments about oppression or sexism or unfair labor practices. John's often her most engaging opponent, but our illustrious debate team captain is currently shivering on the couch in nothing but a wool blanket, a stitched-on herd of buffalo grazing across his shoulders.

The backyard has cleared out. If anyone noticed our four-legged party crasher on the march back inside from the pond, no one thought it odd, and by the time Cole returns with carrots for the horse and a beer for himself, we're alone.

The bottle hisses as Cole twists off the cap. He leans on the railing kitty-corner from me, casual and cool. Crickets count the seconds I wait for him to speak, to give me a chance to deny Griff's allegations, but he just sips the beer.

Beyond the sliding doors at the other end of the deck, the living room is a tangle of dancing bodies. I can't see Griffin, but Paul's lounging on a recliner, and John's gone horizontal on the couch, still wrapped up like a burrito. A new playlist starts, mixing with the whir of the blender, and the dancing bodies slow to a rhythmic sway, everyone snapping pictures and videos, still howling about John's swim.

"Most of them will have to check their Facebook status tomorrow to see if they had fun," I say.

Cole laughs, but he doesn't look at me, just sets the bottle on the rail with a *thunk*. "Remember the time we got busted stealing mugs from Pete's Kitchen?"

Sophomore year. The three of us dared one another and thought we'd gotten away with it, but the manager had seen Ellie and Cole stuffing mugs under their coats. He nabbed them at the door. We spent the next two hours at the diner, me sipping coffee at the counter in a fresh mug, the stolen one undetected in my bag, while Ellie and Cole bussed tables to avoid calls to parents.

I still have my Pete's souvenir. Beige with dark blue letters and a thick handle you can barely get your fingers around. It's on a shelf in the studio Dad set up for me in the basement, holding my small paintbrushes. Every time I look at it, I picture Cole, the stained apron around his waist, hands caked with coffee grounds and old mashed potatoes.

"*You* guys got busted," I remind him now.

"No shit, troublemaker. No one ever suspects you."

"I have a nose ring," I say. "People *always* suspect me. I'm just better at hiding the truth. It's called *stealth*, bro. Get some."

"Nah, there's something else. Like, this quiet confidence thing. You're all, *Don't mess with me, candy-asses.*" Cole makes a tough-guy face that quickly dissolves into a smile. "God, I love that about you."

Sparks ignite in my stomach. I wish I'd asked him for another drink, something to cool the heat swirling inside me.

Cole takes a swig of beer and looks up at the crescent-moon, hazy and cloaked in soft gray clouds. Beyond it, a tiny white point glows brighter than the rest.

"Is that a planet or a star?" I ask.

The invisible pull of his stare evaporates as he turns to look.

"Planet," he says. "Venus. And those stars just above the tallest ponderosa? Cassiopeia." Cole moves closer and takes my hand, his palm cool from the beer. He stands behind me and lifts my arm, traces an outline in the sky above the tree line. My bare shoulders graze his chest, and I have to fight the urge to turn around, to seek out his heartbeat again.

"Makes a W," he says.

Prince Freckles snorts. *Dinner* and *a show? You guys are the best!*

"I have a star map," Cole explains. The beer bottle dangles from his fingers, cool against my leg, too close. "Dad's teaching me astronavigation on our treks this summer. Corny?"

"Not corny." I lower my head slowly, eyes drifting from Cassiopeia back to earth, and I finally turn to face him.

His eyes fill with sadness as he studies my hair, my skin, my mouth like this is the last time we'll ever see each other, five seconds left before the earth explodes. His lips are full and pink and I'm wondering what they might taste like and then, with the horse looking on and Cassiopeia watching from the night sky, Cole presses his mouth to mine.

Every cell in my body collides, a million tiny explosions across my skin.

The swirl behind my belly button deepens, and when I close my eyes, the sky shatters and the stars fall, pinpricks of white-hot light landing on my shoulders like glitter.

Cole's mouth is cool and sweet, apples and beer. I lean closer and wrap my arms around his neck. His hands are on me, one tangled in my hair, one pressing the bottle to my back, and I'm lost.

Spinning, falling.

Four years.

Hungry. Desperate. Amazing.

Four years.

Unforgettable.

Four years.

Completely, entirely, line-crossingly wrong.

In an instant the haze clears.

I push him away and meet his eyes.

"Luce—"

I shake my head, fingers grazing my lips. "This isn't— we can't."

"I'm sorry." Cole drags the back of his hand across his mouth as if to erase me. "I didn't mean . . . Sorry."

I nod slowly as he backs toward the sliding doors, bathed momentarily in soft yellow light from the living room. He nearly plows into Olivia, just standing there with her perfect pink wings and chestnut-colored pixie cut, all adorable and annoying.

"We're playing cards and . . ." She hesitates, watching with wide eyes as Cole slips past her and disappears inside. "I need a teammate."

"I suck at cards," I say. With a shrug, she's gone.

I wasn't the one she'd come looking for.

The music keeps going. Laughter on the other side of the doors. Blender. Bottles clinking. Crickets and breezes and the soft nickers of the horse, all of it marching on.

But for me, everything stops. An instant, heart-stilling pause on the playlist of my life. My pulse thuds in my ears as I hit rewind and relive that moment again and again, the forbidden want squeezing me with an ache both deep and endless.

You look really nice. . . . A slow dance . . . What's the worst that could happen? . . . I love that about you. . . . I didn't mean . . .

"There you are, Lucy last name Vacarro."

I look toward the doors, but it's only Marceau. He joins

me on the deck, stands at the railing where Cole stood just minutes ago.

"I was looking for you," he says. "I missed on you."

"I *missed* you."

His amber eyes shine in the dark. "We are the same."

I open my mouth to correct him, but swallow it. I can't trust my words, and I grab my phone off the railing and absently scroll through the pictures, my mind still tripping all over Cole. Behind my ribs, in the hollow place where my heart used to be, a smooth black stone rattles against the bones.

Four years.

From the first time I saw Cole in the woods behind our neighborhood, the week after the Fosters moved into the house around the corner from ours, I've been thinking about him. Dreaming. He was there with Spike, his Dachshund, and he crouched in the dirt to let Night of the Living Dog sniff them out, and when he said my name and smiled I saw the whole future of us. Homecoming games. Movie nights. Study sessions. Prom, tonight, all that dancing. Kissing.

I never said anything—not to anyone—and now he's with my best friend, and in a few months he'll be in Boston, and she and I will be roomies at UCLA, and my chance will be gone forever.

Is gone.

Was gone, end of freshman year when Ellie asked him out and he answered.

Yes.

It's nobody's fault but mine. I stood by and let my dreams fade into missed opportunities, and I have no right to hunt them down. No matter how good that kiss felt, no matter how long it lingers.

"Lucy?" Marceau smiles again, crooked and sexy, full of flirt.

I have to get over Cole. No more obsessing about a guy who belongs to my best friend. I have to let him go.

I step toward Marceau and give him a damsel sort of look, and he slips his hands behind my neck, guides me the rest of the way. His kiss is gentle and tentative, the opposite of Cole's, and even though nothing changes inside, I close my eyes and try to make it so. *Marceau. Marceau. Marceau.* No attachments. No betrayals. No regrets. No—

"Are you *kidding* me?" Cole's voice shatters everything.

Marceau and I unlock. Cole is wide-eyed and blurry, his hair untamed.

"Did I do the wrong thing?" Marceau whispers. His arms stiffen around my shoulders.

Before I can answer, Cole turns on us and dodges back into the house.

"I do not understand," Marceau says. "He said he is not your boyfriend."

I force a smile. "It's just a misunderstanding. Be right back."

"Lucy! Darling!" Griffin rises from Paul's lap and captures me in a tipsy embrace.

"Have you seen Cole?" I ask.

Her eyebrows shoot up. "What's going on?"

"We just . . . I need to talk to him."

"Baby, come back!" Paul paws at her dress. "My lap is cold."

"So much for the grace of the elves, you rotten scoundrel." Griff smacks his hand and rocks forward on her toes. Behind her overkissed lips, her breath is warm and sharp. "If something happened with Cole, you better tell me—"

"Or what, Griffin?" I snap.

She pulls back, unsteady on her feet. "I just think—"

"Don't think. Go back to your make-out marathon with Legolas and stop worrying about me and Cole." I grab her shoulders and steer her into Paul's lap, ignoring the hurt on her face. The time for apologizing is tomorrow, when we're both sober. Right now I have to find Cole.

I march through the kitchen and almost crash into Olivia, who seems to be making a career of being where she shouldn't. Her arms are loaded with Mike's Hard Lemonades, and she giggles at our near collision.

"Sorry!" she says. The tips of her ears are pink beneath her pixie cut, and her blue eyes look frightened. Something tells me this is her first unsupervised party. "Ohmygod, Lucy! Are you okay?"

"Do you know where Cole is?" I ask.

"Upstairs," Olivia says. "He seems, like, out of it. Oh, do you think he broke up with Ellie? Maybe?"

Hope drips from the end of her question, and I let the silence hang between us, waiting for her to make the implied threat real. *I saw you kissing him. I'll tell everyone. Ellie will hate you.*

She looks at me over the bottles, blinking and confused, not so threatening after all. Before she can take another breath, I rush past. Marceau is still outside and Griff's probably never speaking to me again and Cole's upset and there's a horse on the deck and sparkly fairy wings all over the place and the entire night is reaching postapocalyptic proportions of mythical madness.

If I were online right now, I'd lay a flamethrower to this whole shit.

But reality calls.

I gather my chiffon and trudge up the stairs. Cole's in the hallway, dragging a vampire and a winged zombie out of the bathroom by the arms.

So much for reality.

"It's a bathtub," Cole snaps. "Not a motel."

"Chill. I got this, bro." Vampire loops his arm around zombie girl, who's clinging to a plastic baby bottle that says LIQUID BRAINZ—inauthentic on about five different levels—and together they stumble down the stairs.

Cole drags a hand through his hair and turns to face me. His eyes are glassy and red, and I can't tell if it's from the beer or the creature-wrangling or something else entirely.

"I assume you're not here to help with make-out patrol," he says. "Unless you're waiting for the room? Where's your boyfriend?"

"I just . . . You seemed pissed, and I didn't want . . ." Blood simmers beneath my skin, but I can't stay mad. I can't stay anything.

That kiss wrecked me.

"What happened out there?" I finally manage.

Across from the bathroom, he clicks open another door and nods for me to follow, all the hard edges of him replaced with something soft, something scared. "I've been trying to get this out all night."

After what happened on the deck, his bedroom feels like a crime scene in waiting. The sight of his pillows sends a warning through my head.

Danger! Danger! Danger!

"I need to tell you something," he whispers, and his earlier words echo. *What's the worst that could happen?*

Everything presses in. Ellie's last-minute favor, the dance, the kiss, Marceau, Miss Demeanor, Griff, Prince Freckles, Olivia, John's midnight swim, my throbbing feet, the syrupy drinks. My head spins, and suddenly I don't want to talk. I don't want to smell Cole's outdoorsy scent and look at his soft lips and pretend the kiss didn't happen. I don't want to hear his voice, to feel his hand on my shoulders as he tells me about the stars.

"Take me home?" I ask. "I can't stay here."

Cole presses his forehead against the doorframe. The sound of his defeated sigh loosens something forbidden in me.

Four years.

I step closer.

Four years.

I reach for his fingers, brush them with mine. Fear. Guilt. Hope. Shame. All of the above.

He pulls me through the doorway, both of us stumbling. He closes the door behind him, leans up against it. Everything in me trembles.

"Cole . . ." My breath is as shaky as my knees. "What are—"

"Ellie and I broke up."

THIS BED AIN'T BIG ENOUGH FOR THE THREE OF US

Things haven't been good with us," Cole explains. We're standing in his room in the moonlight, door bolted, so much for the *danger danger* stuff. "Not for a long time."

"No way. Ellie would've told me." I close my eyes and the floor tilts. "If my best friend's relationship was falling apart, I'd definitely know."

Wouldn't I?

Ellie didn't ask about Cole in her texts tonight, didn't mention how cute he looked in the tux, but I assumed she was texting him directly, sending him the usual puppy-eyed love notes.

I squeeze the dress in my fists. She was so excited the

day she found it; she dragged me and Griff to this vintage store in LoDo to see it. If only she hadn't gotten—

"She's not actually sick." I open my eyes at the realization. The room stops moving, but Cole's rubbing his jaw, his nonanswer all the confirmation I need.

"I can't do this," I say. "Please take me home."

Even before he shakes his head, I know it's impossible. We've been drinking, and anyway, his car isn't here. He'll have to borrow John's and take me in the morning.

Resigned, I flop on his bed, springs moaning and creaking, something scratchy poking my thighs. I reach under the fountain of chiffon and yank out a pair of fairy wings.

Perfect. I just ass-pancaked my fairy godmother.

Cole sits next to me, but I can't look at him. I need to stay sharp, clearheaded. Looking at him only makes me replay that kiss. It was hard enough when I just imagined it, but now that I've had the real thing, I'll never get him out of my head. And if it's true about him and Ellie breaking up—

No. No, no, no, no, *no*.

"Why did you kiss Marceau?" Cole's voice is laced with betrayal. "You said you didn't like him."

"Why do you care? I don't have a boyfriend. I can kiss anyone I . . ." Guilt makes my words evaporate. When

I speak again, it's a whisper. "Ellie's your girlfriend—at least, she was. My best friend. We cheated on her."

The confession floats and curls between us like smoke, and my gaze drifts out the window to avoid it. The moon has shed its hazy coat; a white crescent shimmers above the ponderosa pines. Cassiopeia is hidden, and if she can see us from her perch in the sky, she isn't saying a word.

"Look," he says. "I'm not trying to justify it, okay? Things with me and Ellie are over. I don't know what she told you, but it's true. Why do you think she bailed tonight?"

The floor wrenches sideways again, and I put my hand on the dresser to steady myself. The walls are too close, the air thick with an earthy tang. There's a baseball hat on the dresser, orange and dingy, a peeling pot leaf decal that's basically scratch-and-sniff.

"Looks like 420 stopped by," I say absently.

"Luce, look at me. Please."

His voice cracks. I want to look, but I can't. Is he telling the truth? Whose idea was it that I go in Ellie's place tonight? That I wear her dress and corsage?

Why didn't I just say no to her for once? I could be home slaying zombies, lips unkissed. Rules unbroken, lines uncrossed.

Friendships intact.

"She'll never talk to me again," I whisper.

"It's not your fault. It was my mistake."

My head jerks up.

"Oh . . . *kay*," he says. "Not a mistake? I mean, it *wasn't*. I just—"

"No. I mean yes. You're right. We were caught up in the moment."

"And a little drunk."

"And a little drunk." *Yes, yes.* I nod, but my stomach twists with guilt. And disappointment. Which triggers more guilt. A whole ocean of it now, prickly hot waves crashing between my shoulders. I stand again and pace the floor, excuses blowing away in the storm.

I can't keep this from her.

A fresh wave sears my skin, but that's the truth. Maybe Cole made the first move, but I didn't stop him. Not until after I kissed him back. Even now, moments ago outside his bedroom door, I wanted . . .

On top of the dresser there's a crack. I slide my thumbnail into it and run it up and down, avoiding 420's hat, imagining I'm carving a trench. Soon I'll reach the clothes inside. Then the floor. The party below. The earth. The molten hot thing in the middle that keeps it all spinning.

"Is that why you invited me to the party?" I say, acutely aware of the bed behind us. "Rebound girl?"

Outside, clouds skirt back over the moon, darkening the room. Cole touches the red bow at my back, his voice a pale whisper to match the sky. "Not even close."

"T-shirts are in the top drawer," Cole says. His parents asked him to keep everyone out of the other bedrooms, so we decided to crash together in here. Far from ideal, but there's nowhere else to go. I'm spent, and I can't face anyone downstairs. Definitely not Marceau. Especially not Griffin.

She'll know.

"I'll be back," he says. "Just need to make sure no one's driving."

"Tell Griff I'm . . . just tell her I'm passing out and we'll talk tomorrow. And please apologize to Marceau."

Cole's jaw twitches.

"I totally ditched him," I say. "Just . . . tell him I have a headache."

His eyes soften. "Do you want Tylenol?"

"I don't *have* a headache, Cole."

He sighs and unlocks the door.

"Wait, I can't." *Breathe, Lucy.* I offer him my back. "I need help with the sash and zipper."

The floorboards groan as Cole takes three steps toward me. The air shifts, campfire and apples and beer, and then there's a tug at my waist as he works out the bow Mom so expertly tied. I wind the red sash around my hands to keep from fidgeting. To keep from touching him.

Knuckles brush between my shoulders as he grips fabric with one hand, zipper with the other.

"There's a hook at the top," I say. "You have to undo it first."

He's slow and delicate, like he's afraid to do the wrong thing, to touch me. The tiny metal hook releases. The zipper opens, tooth by tooth by tooth, my back exposed to the chill in a long, narrow *V*, and I give in to a gentle shiver.

"Sorry," he whispers. One hand is still on the dress, fingers just beneath my left shoulder, breath tickling my neck, agonizingly close. He swallows. Twice. His other hand drifts to the curve of my hip, and Griffin's words haunt me.

It's not like anyone would find out.

"Thanks." I slide past him to the dresser, my bound hands clutching the dress to my body. "Check on Prince Freckles? And grab my phone? I left it on the deck."

Finally alone, I open the drawer and dig out a pair of basketball shorts and a shirt from Estes Park. *Bears love people!* it says, right under a bear chasing a stick figure. *They taste like chicken!*

I lay Ellie's dress facedown on the bed and zip it up,

remembering again how excited she was to find it. I was just playing dress up tonight, a Cinderella doll, but she loved this dress. She called it *the one*, her eyes glowing with possibilities about how the big night would unfold.

How could she fake something like that? Why didn't she tell me?

When did we start keeping secrets?

Four years ago . . .

I drape the dress over the footboard, hang those stupid fairy wings over the post, remove the chandelier earrings Mom lent me, pull on Cole's shorts and shirt, and shake the pins from my fancy Texas hair.

By the time I crawl between the forest-green sheets, the transformation is complete. I'm no longer a princess.

Just a girl with a twisted-up heart.

I turn on my side and glue my eyes to the wall, to the calming ocean-blue paint. It doesn't matter what Cole said, how long he and Ellie have been drifting or how much blame he takes. Ex or not, I'll never be able to forgive myself.

The kiss was over almost as soon as it started, but my feelings weren't.

Aren't.

And that's the worst offense, because for the first time in four years . . . I think maybe he likes me too.

Cole slips back into the room, shutting the door and

sliding the lock in place behind him. Dresser drawers open and close. Buttons, zippers, legs sliding out of pants. Dress shirt tugged from arms, dropped to the floor. Shorts pulled up. Keys on the dresser, clicks and clangs, and then a camera flash like lightning.

Say . . . magic pixie dust!

"Sorry," he says. "Trying to set your phone alarm. John gave me his keys—we'll head out at nine."

The air cools when he lifts the sheets, mattress moaning under his weight. He flops around for a minute, finds the right spot. The sheet falls back into place, tickling my arm as it lands softly between us.

Music and laughter filter through the floor from the living room below, and on the dresser, my phone buzzes with a text, then another. *Ellie.* I squeeze my eyes shut and try to slow my breathing, convince them both I'm already asleep.

"Luce? You okay?" Cole whispers.

The bed is small—only a twin—and he's shirtless and there's hardly any space. I've never shared a bed with a boy before—just friends or otherwise—and now my skin involuntarily seeks his warmth, his touch. In the narrow gap between us, I feel Ellie's presence, watching us with tears on her cheeks, holding out for an explanation that just doesn't exist.

I inch closer to the wall without answering his question.

"We'll take off first thing." He leans over and kisses my shoulder, lips warm through the *Bears love people!* shirt, and Ellie vanishes. "Everything'll be better in the morning."

The bed creaks as he settles back onto his side. I focus on emptying my head. Counting sheep. Ten. A hundred. Drifting.

Somewhere far, far away . . .

"Lucy?" His fingers trail through the ends of my hair and I shiver. He finds a stray bobby pin, drops it to the floor.

Ping!

It's impossible to hold on to my resolve; like my fairy godmother wishes, I feel it floating away, breath by breath.

Sheep. Count the sheep, Lucy. One, two, three . . .

The bed moans again. Cole rolls toward me.

"For the record," he whispers, "if you ever got sick, I would totally hold your hair back."

THE MURDEROUS LITTLE HARLOT
ALSO KNOWN AS MY SISTER

Are we okay?" Cole asks when we pull into my drive-way the next morning.

It was a groggy thirty-minute drive, and now Cole's looking at me through heavy-lidded eyes, hair rumpled and adorable, and for a heartbeat I imagine us waking up together in his bed, smiling instead of shamed, lingering in postprom bliss instead of making small talk about the trashed cabin. Spence the horse-napper and Prince Freckles were already gone, but the rest of the place was still full of the drunk and the damned, everything smelling suspiciously equine.

Cole smiles before I respond, and all I can think is, *I should be looking at that smile over pancakes and coffee. . . .*

"No." I blink away the fantasy. "I mean yes. Call when you find my cell? I forgot my license and stuff in your tux, too. Oh, and I couldn't find my earrings. And I left some hairpins in your bathroom."

I basically forgot everything that wasn't attached to my body, all in my haste to disappear before Griff woke up. I'm pretty sure she was wasted last night—too drunk to remember our run-in—but there's no way she would've just sent me out the door in Cole's clothes this morning, all bed-headed and guilty-looking. Not without the grand inquisition.

"Hairpins?" Cole says.

"I'm dead if Mom finds out I lost them. The earrings, not the pins. The cell, too."

"Should I call you on the missing phone?" he asks.

"Stop trying to make me laugh."

"Never," he whispers. The familiar mischief is back in his eyes, and I allow myself a smile. "Lucy . . ." Cole taps his fingers on the steering wheel, and my smile vanishes again, a ghost in the morning sun. "I don't know what to do, either, okay? It's not like I don't care about Ellie. I don't want to hurt her. It's just . . . it's over. What happened with us . . ." He sighs, his gaze tracking a robin in the grass before finding its way back to me. "We'll figure something out. We'll go to her house and—"

"I have to do it," I say. "Alone. I want her to hear it from me." Even if she lied about being sick, about her reasons for skipping prom, I can't keep this from her.

Images of Ellie and Cole swirl in my mind, all our high school highlights blending together: listening to Vanitas in Cole's garage practically every weekend. Fishing trips to the cabin. My parents and me taking care of Spike when the Fosters went to Italy last year. Dad teaching me and Ellie how to drive stick in his old five-speed Accord. Ellie getting her UCLA acceptance letter the day after I got mine, both of us jumping up and down at her mailbox, planning out our future.

Ellie, my best friend. And Cole, a spark burning in my heart, always bright and silent, always just a dream.

Until last night.

In the cramped space of the car, Cole rubs his eyes and I trace circles on the window and all I can wonder is, *Why can't I have them both?*

I reach for the door handle.

"I know it's weird." Cole touches my hand, pulls away again. "I get it. I just don't want things to be—"

"They're not. We're fine. I mean, not *we're*, like *we*. Just you. And me. Separately. Anyway, I'll talk to Ellie tomorrow. I'll go over there before school." I smile and duck out of the car, grab Ellie's dress from the backseat.

Cole's touch lingers on my skin, my wrist, my fingers after I close the door, but I don't turn back, not even when his car rolls down the driveway and zooms into the street.

Category-five disaster.

I'm still in the bear shirt, and the basketball shorts are so long on me they cover part of my boots, which really tie the whole ensemble together. My hair is a roiling sea of bent red-brown waves, my lips ache with the ghost of last night's kiss, and as I drag myself up the walkway to the house, I notice our front door is *wide* open.

A beautiful blonde crosses her arms in the doorway, flashing her cosmetically whitened smile like an evil queen, and behind her, Night of the Living Dog barks in warning.

Who's the fairest of them all?

Angelica Darling.

Also known by legions of rabid fans as Jayla Heart.

Also known by Mom and Dad as Janey Vacarro.

My sister.

"Jesus, you look like hell," she says. "Come inside and tell me *all* about it."

Thrashing computer-generated zombies is my go-to relaxation technique, but even the battle against the undead can't keep my mind off Ellie and Cole.

It doesn't help that my sister showed up a month early

and announced over postprom brunch that she's staying the *entire* summer, which left my parents choking on their zucchini frittata with utter joy while I glared at her, like, *Damn! Give a girl a warning shot!*

Lav-Oaks flew her in to do the commencement speech—Principal Zeff swore me to secrecy on that special surprise—but that was supposed to be it. Three days, in and out. For my parents' sake, I could've faked my way through three days of nod-and-smile.

But the whole summer?

Before today, Jayla and I hadn't spoken in almost a year. *Ambush.*

On account of my prom-induced exhaustion, I scored several hours of alone time after brunch, but Mom and Dad are all about the forced sisterly bonding, and now Jayla's standing behind me, her polished face and buttery blond highlights superimposed over the onscreen carnage.

"Why can't you, like, paint your nails or go to the mall like a normal girl?" she asks.

Not a second too soon, I ice a charging zombie with my machete, splattering the screen with blood.

Jay flops on my bed, tossing aside a few stuffed ghouls. "Sometimes I worry about your mental health."

Click-click boom!

The shotgun works well for a few zombies at a time,

but the corpses I wasted give rise to a howling horde. They remind me of the fairies flitting around the gym last night, and I'm all, *Say hello to my little flamethrower, bitches.*

I roast them like marshmallows. A few slip past, grab me. "I'm hit!"

"Miss me?" Jayla asks.

"Fuck!"

"Lucy!"

"I'm black-and-white! *Nononononooo!*" I frantically work the keys, but it's no use. My gamer crew is being all permafrosty about my tournament bailout, and I'm way too distracted for a solo campaign. "Happy now, Jay? I'm dead."

"Good. Come talk to me. It feels like forever since we talked."

Allow me to translate.

"Like Forever": from the Germanic "Like Forever," last summer, after my disastrous visit to her posh pad in Malibu, cliché as it sounds. After I switched my flight to come home a day early. After Cole and Ellie picked me up at Denver International and I spent the night at Ellie's so I wouldn't have to lie to Mom and Dad about the change in my itinerary.

"Lucy, come on." She bats her baby blues. Really, I couldn't make this stuff up. "Tell me about prom. Mom said you looked amazing—like a real girl."

"Let me guess. This is you apologizing?"

Jay tugs a thread on one of my ghouls, ducking my gaze. "It was a year ago. Can't we let it go?"

"That's what I thought."

"Live in the moment for once. It's done. Anyway, I'm turning over a new leaf."

I choke back a snort. New leaf? Allow me to translate again.

On her weekly televised drama, Jayla plays a scheming, conniving killer whose questionable morals are justified by such original backstory as a string of cheating boyfriends, an absentee father, and an alcoholic mother who sleeps with Angelica's friends.

In real life, my sister's questionable morals have no such justification.

DANGER'S DARLING A DANGER TO HERSELF, the latest tabloid smear campaign said. SATURDAY NIGHT VIXEN VAMPS IT UP IN VENICE BEACH. That one had a picture of Jay draped over some tattooed six-pack of a dude, her eyes big and glassy, leather skirt riding up her thighs. I found a whole stack in the recycle bin last weekend, still bound in plastic ties like Mom had stolen them right off the delivery truck.

Mom's convinced the tabloids lie.

I narrow my eyes at her. "You're up to something."

"I have time off before shooting for next season, so I

thought I'd see what's shakin' in the Mile High." She scans a series of zombified celebrities tacked to the wall over my bed, a pen-and-ink project I sketched a few months ago for art. "Obviously not much."

I'm no detective, but it doesn't add up. If my sister has time off, why would she spend it here? She has a beach house on Martha's Vineyard. Boyfriends on every continent. She and I are totally on the rocks, and even her calls to my parents have been supershort, Jayla always phoning in an obligatory hello from the middle of some important shoot and, *Oh, sorry, gotta run!*

I watch her across the room, searching for a crack in the facade, but she's so tan and smiley it's hard not to get caught up in her current. Hard not to believe her, every explanation made logical by her luscious lips. Hard not to miss her when she's up close and personal again.

I blow a breath into my bangs. It's *always* like this with Jay, like the "Itsy Bitsy Spider" song she sang during our childhood baths. When that girl laughs, up comes the sun and dries up all the rain.

And then the hurricane hits, right when you least expect it.

"Oh," she suddenly squeals, "I totally have to show you something! You'll *die* of sweetness!" She smashes against me in the computer chair. "Make a hole. Make a hole."

I scootch over and swallow the lump in my throat, soaking up the essence of her latest signature scent. Pears, this one smells like. Crazy, expensive, diamond-studded pears.

Her fingers *click-clack* across the keyboard as she navigates to her Facebook fan page, the Jayla Heartthrobs. Two hundred thousand fans, growing steadily by the hour, I'm sure. Every picture has hundreds of likes and comments. *Hundreds.*

My research is hardly scientific—already established, not a detective—but I spy a distinct correlation between Jayla cleavage exposure and number of fanboy likes.

"Congrats on being the last thing thousands of adolescent boys think about when they get into bed at night," I say.

"Isn't it awesome?"

"In a gross and illegal way, sure."

She tries to smack me, but I duck. Video games have seriously honed my reflexes.

Jayla replies to a few messages with Xs and Os, and in the pale glow of the screen I study the curve of her jaw, the berry-hued lips, the salon-shaped brows. Even without the money, she's always been a stunner. But for the first time since she became famous, she looks older, way more than the seven years she has on me.

"Don't you start filming the next season in the summer?" I ask.

"We're shooting in the fall this time."

"But you—"

"Here's the one I wanted to show you." She taps a French-manicured nail against the screen. "'Dear Jayla Heart. You have *my* heart. I turn eighteen in two years. If you're still single, will you marry me?' Isn't he the sweetest thing ever?"

I roll my eyes. "Like high-fructose corn syrup."

"How many marriage proposals have *you* gotten, little miss smug?"

I clap my hands and give her a radiant smile. "Golly, I don't know. Maybe Mr. Right is waiting for my response right now!" I lean across the keyboard and sign in to my dusty-ass Facebook profile, barely giving it a glance.

"Eww." Jay scrunches her nose. "You have the same number of Facebook friends that I have on my hair and makeup team alone."

Whoosh! That's the sound of my rekindled sisterly affection evaporating. "Guess that's why my online marriage prospects are so slim," I say.

"I get that you're not a party girl, but you should be all over this. You don't even have to do your hair to hang out online."

My hand shoots to my head. "I do my hair."

Jayla snorts. "Seriously, Luce. Facebook is, like, twice the friends and half the effort."

"You think?"

Jayla doesn't get it. I didn't abandon social media because I don't want to make an effort. I just couldn't deal with the we're-so-in-love, aren't-we-adorable status updates from Ellie.

Ellie.

Without my phone, I have no idea what's going on with my friends. For all I know, Cole's already confessed everything. Or Griffin's sharing her theories, taking revenge on me for snapping at her last night, for leaving without saying good-bye. And I'm hiding out at home, a phoneless coward, not one word closer to figuring out what I'm supposed to say to Ellie tomorrow.

I jam my thumbs into my eyes to erase the images of last night, and when I blink it all away and look at Jayla again, she's shaking her head, her face all, *WTF?*

"Are you *trying* to make everyone hate you? Or is this, like, a call for help?" She squints at the pictures loading on my page. There's one of a girl in a pink lace bra, dress pooled around her waist. She's kneeling on the floor, arcing backward and drinking from a Mike's Hard Lemonade bottle that's stuck between her boobs.

Caption: *Sweet little Olivia puts the HARD in Mike's Hard Lemonade! #scandal*

Dread fills my insides. "Is that on my profile?"

"Not cool. People don't like their drunken shame

spread all over the Internet." Jayla's voice is machete-sharp. "Trust me."

"Move." I bump her out of the chair and slide closer to the computer. Olivia's acrobatics are part of a whole new album on my profile, created two hours ago. "PROMiscuity," it's called.

Someone must've gotten into my account, but how? My password is supercomplicated, and I've never given it to anyone, never signed in at school or at anyone else's house. I'm hardly ever on Facebook anymore. The only way someone could upload photos to my account is by hacking it, or by uploading directly from—

Oh shit. My phone!

I didn't *forget* my phone—someone swiped it last night. And whoever did it snapped a bunch of drunken shots and uploaded them to my Facebook profile, tagging them so they'd show up on Miss Demeanor's page for the #scandal contest.

It's one thing for people to post their own dumb stunts. But whoever did this made it look like *I* posted them, and Jayla's right. It's not cool.

I click through the photos with shaking hands. Funneling? Strip poker? The vampire bros smoking out of a . . . What *is* that contraption? Who the hell let Prince Freckles into the living room, and why is Margo Hennessy making out with him?

The album has already been shared and reposted dozens of times. Hundreds, maybe, everything tagged to Miss Demeanor's page, the damning shots mixed in with pictures from earlier in the night—ones I *do* remember: John in the pond. The blinged-out gym. Group poses in front of the party Hummer. Cole nervously pinning my corsage the first time. Paul sucking on Griff's earlobe in my front yard, one hand creeping on her boob. My parents sitting in the Hummer, just for fun.

And then my heart sinks.

Kiara, posing with Prince Freckles.

See no (e)VIL, photograph no (e)VIL! What Kiara's friends don't know won't hurt them . . . but it might get the little traitor kicked out of her favorite club! #scandal

I promised her I wouldn't say anything, and now it looks like I broadcast it to the whole school.

"Explains why you're all death-warmed-over tonight," Jayla says.

I click to the next incriminating shot. Me and Marceau on the deck.

"Yum." Jayla raises her brows, suddenly more impressed than accusatory. "Well played, little sister."

Doing my best to maintain international relations, ooh-la-la! Despite this passionate embrace, Marceau's lips were no match for my date, Cole Foster! #scandal

I blink back tears, my throat tight and dry, fingers trembling.

Click.

Worst fears.

Confirmed.

Me and Cole, standing beneath the stars, lips locked in a five-second, totally accidental, three-hundred-percent mistake of a kiss.

Click.

Ellie's black cherries dress draped over the end of Cole's bed, pink wings casually tossed on top.

Click.

A bare foot. Two. Four. My hair spilled across the pillow. And Cole's arms wrapped around me tight, our bodies an indiscernible tangle beneath a knot of dark green sheets.

Who needs costumes to create such magical, mythical memories? #scandal

FRECKLES PLEADS THE FIFTH

MISS DEMEANOR

2,742 likes 👍

601 talking about this

<u>Monday, April 28</u>

Good Monday morning, fishies! How y'all feeling?
Here's a tip: water. Lots of it. Your still-throbbing heads
will thank me!

In the time-honored tradition of prom-goers since

humans first crawled out of the pond with the dinosaurs (and/or appeared on the earth exactly seven days after it came into existence four thousand years ago, give or take, depending on your beliefs, all of which I publicly support while whispering about you behind closed laptops), many of you undoubtedly engaged in a few rites of passage this weekend. Before we continue, please join me in a moment of silence to mourn the collective loss of innocence.

. . .

Bee-tee-dubs, thumbs-up on keeping your names out of the police blotter, kids! Always a proud moment when my esteemed Lav-Oaks colleagues avoid embarrassing legal trouble (and associated fees). Trust me on this little nugget: The last thing Mommy and Daddy want to do is dip into your college fund for bail money. Awkward for everyone, please pass the hard lemonade!

While we're on the not-entirely-unrelated topics of hard lemonade and awkward shit your parents don't know about, thanks for oversharing those delectable prom and party pics! We have our work cut out for us as we try to determine the most #scandal–worthy moments.

The girls lacrosse team dancing in their underwear and dragon wings at Red Rocks? The entire prom court tossing their collective cookies on the steps of the state capitol building? Ms. Zeff, out-jousted by the physics club president? Like I always say, ladies. When it comes to dueling lances, it's not the shape or the size that matters, but the velocity of the projectile and the angle of the trajectory!

As for the bash at that undisclosed mountain locale, wowza. Someone's putting Angelica Darling to shame! Good God (and by God I mean inclusively God, Goddess, Buddha, Allah, Mother Earth, Zeus, universal force, and any and all past, present, and yet-to-be discovered deities), tell me there's more to this tale than meets the bloodshot eye. Despite intense bribery of the sugar cube nature, Prince Freckles isn't saying a word.

Start talking, peeps. Miss Demeanor is always listening.

xo ~ *Ciao!* ~ xo

Miss Demeanor

HOW MANY TARTS DOES IT TAKE?

*P*lay dumb, Lucy. You never even saw those pictures.

So goes the strategy my self-appointed publicist devised last night. She wouldn't even let me change my Facebook password or delete any photos. "You'll just look more guilty," she said, like, straight from her *How to Duck and Cover in a Shit Storm* manual.

Of course, this morning's *CelebStyle* features a close-up of Jayla in the Denver airport terminal, all Louis Vuitton bags and angry middle fingers and white leather napkin trying not quite hard enough to be a dress.

J-HEART'S HIGH TIMES IN THE MILE HIGH!

So much for duck and cover.

I snatch up the remaining copies from the newsstand at

Black & Brew while the barista bags my order. Ellie might be ignoring my desperate e-mails, but no way can she stay all deep freezy if I show up on her doorstep with coffee and Tarts of Apology.

Doubt is a hard lump in my throat, but I swallow it down, pay for the breakfast and tabloids, and make my way to Ellie's neighborhood on foot. I timed my arrival for after Ellie's moms left for work, but as I step onto her front porch and press the doorbell, my body vibrates with fear. Maybe it would've been better to have witnesses. . . .

"What do you want?" Ellie's face appears behind the screen. Her eyes are red and puffy, her chocolate-brown hair wrapped in a messy topknot.

My words bail, and I shove the carton of coffees and paper bag forward, hoping they convey everything. *I'm sorry. Can we talk? Don't hate me. Tart? Coffee? Still friends?*

She scrutinizes the bag.

"Chocolate raspberry," I manage. "And white chocolate kiwi?" The last part comes out uncertain.

"You must be *really* sorry." She opens the screen door and steps out, blocking my entrance into the place I've considered a second home for six years. "Again. What do you want?"

"I just . . . I thought we could talk and . . . Can we go inside?" I maneuver the coffees and pastries and inch closer to the doorway. She doesn't budge.

"I trusted you." Her voice breaks on the last word. I open my mouth to answer, but everything in my head twists and tangles.

I didn't mean to. I care about him. We were drinking. I totally meant to. I've loved him forever. I didn't want to go to prom. I'm glad I went to prom. I hope you still want to do our summer road trip. And college. And you lied to me . . . .

"You should probably just get to school," Ellie says.

"What about you?"

"I'm staying home to enjoy a delicious breakfast." Ellie grabs the bag and the carton with both coffees, and before I can choke out another word, the door slams shut.

"So not how it looks," I whisper, but my best friend is already gone.

With twenty minutes to go before homeroom, the sprawling Lavender Oaks campus is a ghost town, save for a small knot of students gathered on the front steps. Absent Kiara, the now four-membered (e)lectronic Vanities Intervention League marches in a circle around their leader in his wheelchair, wordlessly pumping their poster-board signs.

MAKE LOVE, NOT STATUS UPDATES!
REAL FRIENDS DON'T NEED BATTERIES!
GET YOUR HEAD OUT OF THE CLOUD!

Franklin Margolis, valedictorian and editor of the school newspaper, lurks behind them. With a pen, he pokes at his curly moptop, observing the protest a moment before scribbling something onto a yellow pad. Not sure why he bothers with the journalism gig—everyone ditched the *Lavender Oaks Explorer* when Miss Demeanor hit the scene last year—but if his unwavering dedication to the fashion disaster of jeans plus sport coat is any indication, Franklin is a determined trend-bucker.

The group disperses as I approach, reassembling at the far end of the parking lot to greet the incoming cars.

I dig deep for some enthusiasm and call out a "thanks!" across the quad. (e)VIL might be whackadoo, but they get it. Facebook is out of control, and though my account exposed Kiara's fling with technology, maybe—in a secret-hand-shake-on-the-grassy-knoll kind of way—they're on my side.

Unlike Griffin, who's suddenly yanking me through the school's front doorway.

"What the hell, Lucy?" she says. "I've been calling and texting all weekend. I thought you were dead."

Play dumb play dumb play dumb . . .

"I saw the pictures," she says, forcing me to meet her eyes. Confusion battles rage on her face, barely concealed, and I cringe at the memory of her Paul-maul pics. "Where's Cole?" she demands. "What's going on?"

"Nothing. I didn't . . . I didn't post that stuff."

"It's your Facebook." She's wearing the baby veal face again. "You were flirting with Cole all night, and—"

"Griffin. Why would I post pictures like that on my own page? Like, totally busting myself? That makes no sense."

She snorts. "Unlike making out with Cole and spending the night in his bed? After you made out with Marceau, who by the way was sniffing around your locker earlier, all starry-eyed and 'Where is Lucy Vacarro?' *That* makes sense?"

"I'm just saying I didn't upload the pictures."

"Sorry, Luce, but the evidence is kind of stacked."

"Someone swiped my phone," I say, and Griff's scowl is like, *Yeah right.* "What happened to innocent until proven guilty?"

Franklin and his nosy yellow pad pass through the doorway, eyeing us with detached politeness.

Griff crosses her arms and presses her back to the maroon lockers, waiting. When Franklin's gone, she says dryly, "Okay, prove."

I don't deserve her trust, but the sudden lack of it stings.

"Don't go all blackout on me now," she says at my silence. "You were acting crazy all night, and now Ellie thinks I knew what happened and kept it from her, and she's . . ." Griff's white-blond curls seem to tighten with their own rage, and she shakes her head to untangle them. "I was *kidding* about you and Cole hooking up. I never thought you'd—"

"The kiss just . . . it happened. And Ellie . . ." Everything inside me burns. I want to ask Griff if she knew they'd broken up, if Ellie had said anything to her before prom, but the accusation in her eyes silences me.

Three days ago, I had two best friends. We weren't perfect, but we were mostly close. And now?

"Listen, Luce." Griffin folds her arms again. "Ellie wants her dress back."

Last year the administrators had the bathroom at the end of the art wing painted orange, and they wired it with a commercial-free XM feed from the easy-listening station. They said it was to "discourage student loitering, smoking, and socializing," which they believed its tucked-away location made all too easy.

Instead, it became the default emo hideaway, private and cold, our daily little miseries set to the smell of bleach and their own tearful soundtracks.

Lav-Oaks is a silver linings kinda place.

A place where Phil Collins is now cautioning me with dire emphasis: *Oh! Think twice . . .*

"Lucy?" Griff's head prairie dogs over the top of the adjacent stall.

"What if it wasn't?" I say. *'Cause it's another day for you and me in paradise . . .*

"Educated guess. I heard your ugly-cry." Griff climbs down and barges into my stall. "I didn't mean to get all *Mean Girls* out there, okay? I'm just shocked."

I yank a strip of toilet paper from the dispenser and blow my nose.

"I was on the phone with Ellie all night," she says. "She's a complete mess."

"Did she say anything about Cole?"

"Hmm." Griff presses a finger to her lips. "Liar, cheater, dickhead. Some other names I had to look up on Urban Dictionary."

"He told me they . . ." It's a weak excuse before the words are even out, and I let the rest—*broke up*—die. A wave of sadness rises up, and I ball another wad of toilet paper around my hand, blot my eyes until it's too black to do any good. "I suck for putting you in the middle. If you bail on me, I get it."

Griff tears a fresh hunk of paper from the roll and hands it over. "I'm a lover, not a bailer. I just . . . I don't know what to do, honestly. I *am* in the middle. You guys are my best friends—no way I'm taking sides."

"Does this mean you believe me about the phone?"

She rolls her eyes. "You think?"

I blow my nose again. Translation: Thanks.

"Who would do this?" Griff asks. "It's not like the whole world was at Cole's party. We knew everyone there." Griff shakes her head. "It makes no sense."

I close my eyes against the flicker of faces, everyone at the party a suspect. Olivia, her friends, Clarice. Miss Demeanor's always looking for a scandal, and she could've been there too—no one knows her true identity.

The warning bell rings, T minus one minute to homeroom and widespread eternal damnation, and outside the tiny world of our stall, the bathroom door swings open and closed, the wave of hallway chatter cresting and receding.

"Lucy?"

Cole.

I make a grand effort to erase my mascara tracks, but it's no use. My eyes are so puffy I can hardly see, and my heart races at the thought of facing Cole again, at the memories of this weekend. At Ellie on the porch in her bathrobe, the door slamming before I found the strength to apologize.

"I'm going to homeroom," Griff says. "I'll tell Mrs. King you're sick." Her smile is small and dim, but it seems genuine, and I follow her out of the stall. She throws an icy glare at Cole.

To me she says, "See you in calc," and then she's gone, leaving me alone with Cole and a real crooner of a song about making brown eyes blue.

Cole's eyes, neither brown nor blue, have lost some of their sparkle, filled instead with worry.

"Margolis saw you head down this way," he explains. "I wanted . . ." *To kiss you again.* "I had to see if you were okay." His hands push through his hair, which has reached epic levels of sticking-outness, and I curse my beating heart for being so obvious.

"I didn't post the pictures," I say. "My phone—"

"I know." He's pacing, almost frantic. "I just found out, like, an hour ago. John and I crashed at the cabin last night. We were cleaning all day, didn't even check our phones. This morning in the car he was all, 'Dude, the Internet exploded.'"

"Did you call Ellie?" I ask.

"She's straight voice mailing me. Oh, I found some of your stuff." From a low side pocket in his olive cargo shorts, he pulls out a Baggie with my earrings, hairpins, license, makeup, keys.

"No phone," I say.

"No phone." He pinches the bridge of his nose. "This is insane. Ellie must be freaking."

I fill him in on my Black & Brew breakfast fail, and my stomach churns with fresh nerves. I backed down this morning at Ellie's when I should've spoken up. When I should've fought harder, made her listen to the explanation and apology she deserves.

"I can't believe she found out on Facebook," Cole says. "And you . . ." His voice softens as he meets my still-puffy eyes. "You shouldn't have to deal with . . . I mean, your Facebook's a war zone." Cole jams his hands into his pockets, shorts tugging low on his hips. "No one said *jack* on mine—just the tags . . ." He trails off.

"I'm the girl. It's just how it is." I turn on the water and try my best to clean my smudged face. Purple smoky eye on the day of my public stoning? I've had better ideas.

Behind me, Cole sighs. "Doesn't make it right. I was there too."

"I could always join forces with Team Tinfoil Hat." I tell him about the protest (e)VIL organized for me, but instead of laughing, he cringes.

"They're not . . . Luce, they're protesting *you*." Cole yanks a crumpled yellow flyer from his back pocket and hands it over.

LUCYGATE!

ONE MORE EXAMPLE OF HOW OUR NAR-CISSISTIC OBSESSION WITH SOCIAL NETWORK-ING VIOLATES PRIVACY, DESTROYS INTERPER-SONAL RELATIONSHIPS, AND WILL ULTIMATELY CAUSE THE DOWNFALL OF FREE SOCIETY.

CAPITALIZING ON STUDENT INDISCRETIONS TO BOLSTER ONE'S POPULARITY AND INCREASE THE SURFACE AREA OF ONE'S ELECTRONIC FOOT-PRINT IN THE CLOUD IS NOT OKAY. WANT TO DO SOMETHING ABOUT IT? JOIN (E)VIL FOR OUR PRESUMMER PLENARY. NO CELL PHONES. ASK ASH HOLLOWELL FOR DETAILS, FACE TO FACE.

CLOUD FREE, THAT'S HOW WE ROLL.

"They were giving them out in the parking lot," Cole explains.

On the back there's a Sharpie sketch of what can only be me—red hair, black boots, the dress—taking pictures with a giant phone. The whole thing is covered by a huge red circle with a slash.

No Lucy.

"Their drawing skills suck." The flyer reeks of mark-ers—they must've pulled an all-nighter to make them by hand. I pitch it into the trash.

"Hey." Cole slips his hand behind my neck, a once-friendly gesture that in the wake of our kiss is everything but. "They can say whatever they want. Far as I'm concerned, this is between you, me, and—"

"Well, isn't this precious." The voice is sharp, laced with scorn.

I didn't hear the bathroom door, but Olivia's reflection glowers in the mirror, her eyes red.

Putting the hard in Mike's Hard Lemonade . . .

"Olivia!" I step back from Cole, ignore the shiver creeping up my spine. "I'm so, so sorry. Someone stole my phone and—"

"Save it." She slips past us and yanks a paper towel from the dispenser.

"It was just a party thing," I say. What my words lack in conviction, they make up for in volume and speed. "It'll blow over, right? Everyone does dumb stuff at parties."

Olivia wets the towel and presses it to her face, muffling a sarcastic snort.

"Think of all the crazy shit people will do at grad parties in a few weeks," Cole says. "No one will even remember your picture."

She reveals her eyes, wild with a deep menace that belies her tiny frame. The spent paper towel, wadded carelessly and chucked too far from the trash can, hits the floor with a *thwack*. "My father saw it. He has an excellent memory."

"The cloud is forever, Lucy Vacarro." The chant echoes behind me.

I slam my locker door shut and whirl around, surprisingly disappointed that the (e)VIL girl taunting me isn't Kiara Chen. Misguided mission aside, Kiara's forced retirement from Team Tinfoil Hat was unfair. I owe her an explanation.

But this particular minion is just a girl whose name escapes me, a jock in a Swordfish warm-up jacket with streaked blond hair and the long, muscular legs of a swimmer. There's an ocean of yellow flyers in her arms.

"Shouldn't you be out looking for Atlantis?" I snap.

Undeterred, she offers a flyer with jazz hands flare, and for the rest of the morning this is me: creeping along the maroon-and-gray walls like a legit zombie hunter, ducking in and out of classrooms and closets, dodging Clarice, Marceau, and a bunch of other randos whenever I spot someone from the party.

Escaping the flyers, however, is not an option. They're a paper virus, traveling across lockers, slipped under doors and desks, stuffed into backpacks and pockets. I can't get through a single exam review without being harassed about "the cloud"—even Griff was snickering about it in calculus when we were supposed to be computing the force of fluid pressure on the marshmallows in Mrs. Smolinski's Jell-O mold.

Unlike our teachers, the Lav-Oaks rumor mill is operating at full capacity, and by lunchtime it's clear that dining at my usual courtyard table with Cole and John— especially with Ellie still out and those flyers covering every flat surface in the Centennial State—is not the way to make this scandal vanish. Instead, I make a date with the only classmate guaranteed to keep his maw shut about the cloud.

Prince Freckles snorts when he sees me enter the stables, but it's a welcome snort rather than a judgy one. I drag the groom's stool to his stall and unpack my lunch, glad to be ignored by the other horses and their soft, peaceful nickering. I'm probably breaking ten different health codes, and the taste of my egg salad sandwich and chocolate pudding cup are muted by the hay-and-animal smells, but the company is worth it.

"So you survived your first Lav-Oaks prom," I say. "Golf clap for you, buddy. That's no easy feat."

Speak for yourself! Prince Freckles paws at the dirt, hooves still coated with golden glitter.

"At least you lost the horn. It wasn't doing you any favors." I laugh when I remember the magic pixie dust photographer, the whole stupid setup with the pen and the hay and the fake disco lights. Ellie would've died—she would've convinced the photographer to let us do bestie poses on the horse, Ellie and Griffin and me riding bareback in our prom night finery like a triple Xena, slightly more princess than warrior.

It wasn't meant to be. If Ellie had been at prom, I would've spent my Saturday night with the undead instead of with the very-much-alive Cole Foster, absent the Xena pics but still in possession of my phone and my secrets and my best friend. The most important person in my life.

I have to fix this.

"Here's some advice, horses." I rise from the stool. In their stalls along the wall, the animals prick their ears, swat invisible flies with their tails. "Don't ever get on Facebook."

Prince Freckles whinnies. *Also maybe let's not fall for our best friends' boyfriends.*

"You're getting a little too smart." I hand over the last of my lunch, an apple he gladly devours, and nuzzle the velvety gray patch between his eyes. "See you tomorrow, buddy."

I'm back in the main building a total of thirty seconds, supremely mellow after my equestrian lunch date, when the death knell of the intercom buzzes through the halls:

"Lucy Vacarro, please report to Principal Zeff's office."

THE PAL IN PRINCIPAL

Is that *hay?*" Jayla drops all pretense of composure and crinkles her nose as I enter the office. She's perched on a chair across from Zeff's oak desk, and beneath a floral headscarf and sunglasses that cover half her face, she looks like a kid playing dress up.

I cross my arms over my black tank top. "What are you doing here?"

"Have a seat, Miss Vacarro." Zeff motions toward the adjacent chair. "I understand your parents are out of town. Your sister kindly rearranged her schedule so that we might discuss the situation in person."

Out of town?

Kindly?

Schedule?

"Situation?" I ask. *Play dumb play dumb play dumb.*

Ms. Zeff looks from me to Jayla, then back to me.

Normally I like Zeff. She's been principal only five years, so she's not all jaded and hateful yet, never invents reasons to bust us. She's only about ten years older than Jayla, and just as pretty, with shoulder-length wavy brown hair and honey-brown eyes. Decent, I usually say when my parents ask about her. Cool.

But for the first time in my life, I'm standing in her office, looking across the polished expanse of the desk, my throat constricting in a decidedly not cool way.

"Would you like a chocolate chip cookie?" she finally says, holding out a plate of them. "I find difficult conversations go better with treats."

I wonder if she got that theory from Griff, or if Griff got it from her. Either way, I flop into the chair like a noodle and reach for a cookie, first bit of good news all day.

Soon enough, I realize my grave error. Effing oatmeal raisin.

"I understand you attended quite a party this weekend, Miss Vacarro." Ms. Zeff slides the cookie plate behind her monitor and pulls out a stack of yellow papers, (e)VIL's handiwork.

"It's okay, Lucy." Jayla removes her sunglasses and

eyes me with practiced compassion. "This is a safe space."

"Really?" I shoot flaming eye-daggers at her. To Zeff, I explain, "It was just a few friends."

"I see." She thumbs through her papers and tugs a white one from the bottom. "Do you know what this is?"

I lean forward to read the title. "'Lavender Oaks School District Cyberbullying Policies.' Cyberbullying?" My pulse ticks from trot to gallop. Yeah, it sucks that someone took my phone and posted smarmy pics, but I don't need the principal fighting my battles. Miss Demeanor would probably create a special place in fan page hell for that. "I'm not being . . . It's not a big deal. Not like that."

"I've seen the pictures," she says. "It's a big deal."

I break the cookie in half and shove in a bite, forcing myself to chew.

"I want to show you something." Zeff's fingers fly over the keyboard; she turns her monitor so all three of us can see it together.

Facebook.

Ick. Ms. Zeff's not supposed to exist outside this building. Spying on her profile feels like catching my parents making out on the couch.

"I'm giving you a peek at my personal life," she says,

"because I want you to understand that social networking can be a positive—"

"Jayla Heartthrobs!" Jayla squeals when she sees her own face under the likes list. "And *Danger's Little Darling*! Yay!" She narrows her eyes at the screen. "Who's Miss Demeanor?"

"She does the Scandal-of-the-Month stuff," I say when Zeff doesn't respond. "No one knows who she is." I raise my eyebrows at Zeff. "You're a fan?"

"It's important to monitor the school grapevine, yes. But I never comment. There's a line, Miss Vacarro, and adults need to—"

"Coach!" Jayla's still beaming over Zeff's likes, another match made in social media heaven. "You like Coach bags!"

"And *Fifty Shades of Grey*," I say. Awesome. Now I'll have to look straight into the sun to burn *those* images out of my retinas. I shove in another bite of cookie. The oatmeal turns pasty on my tongue.

"Weird." Jayla's nose crinkles again, ragingly adorable. "All your friends are babies."

"What? Oh, no!" Ms. Zeff laughs. "They just *have* babies. Like, constantly."

"But you're practically *my* age," Jayla says. "Way too young for friends with kids."

"Tell my mother that. Excuse me a moment." Zeff takes to her keyboard, sounding out words as she responds to a message that just popped up. "Grayson. Is. Adorable," she type-says. "Love. Those. Tantrum. Videos." She smiles at us. "See? You post things from your life, and you encourage your friends to do the same, and it's a nice, tasteful way to share important moments without having to overcommit."

Another message pops up, wondering if Zeff "watched the bathtub one."

"Watched. Them. All!" Zeff rolls her eyes playfully as she types. "New parents," she explains to us. "They're quite . . . enthusiastic. Anyway, it's pretty nonthreatening as long as everyone stays respectful. Respect is the key to successful social media interactions."

Watching her feed scroll by, baby after crying baby, I realize two things: One, the Facebook profiles of new parents are an excellent form of birth control. And two, Zeff isn't concerned about my being bullied.

She thinks *I'm* the bully.

"Ms. Zeff, I didn't post those pictures," I say. "From the party?"

Her professional smile melts into a frown that says, *I want to help you, but first you must help yourself by telling the truth.* "Technically, we're supposed to go through the antibullying manual together."

"But I'm not a—"

"There's a manual?" Jayla asks.

"We take it seriously, Miss Heart." Her eyes drift back to the monitor, suddenly huge with shock. "Unlike my *mother*, who takes *nothing* seriously ever! Can you believe this? She just posted something about my father staring at a woman's ass." She deletes the offending message and bangs out a clipped reply: MOM, YOU'RE VIOLATING MY PERSONAL SPACE AGAIN.

She turns her attention back to us. "What I meant to say . . . Lucy, the school doesn't need another scandal, and—"

"Ms. Zeff?" Her assistant buzzes through the speaker phone. "Sorry to interrupt, but I've got your mother on line one. She says it's important."

"Excuse me, ladies." Zeff picks up the phone and mutters into the receiver, eyes still trawling her Facebook messages. "Hi. Yes, I'm just . . . I understand, but take it up with Dad. You live in the same house, for the love of . . . Okay, but don't post it on my page. . . . Of course I love you, I just can't . . . No, I don't want to say hi to . . . Hi, Daddy. No, I'm fine . . . School's great—I'm actually in the middle of . . ." She meets my eyes briefly, then glances back to her monitor. "Miss Demeanor? How do you . . . ? Just click unlike. There should be a button and . . . What's blinking? No. Listen, Dad, we'll talk later, okay? I'm in a meeting with . . . Hanging up now. Love you too. Bye. *Bye!*"

Zeff suddenly looks exhausted, like she was the one whose Facebook was scandalized and whose best friend is probably breaking up with her and whose principal is reading *Fifty Shades* and pushing stale oatmeal raisin cookies under the guise of easing difficult conversations.

"Here's the deal, Lucy," she says firmly. "Since the harassment didn't happen on school computers or during school hours, and it's not a hate crime, I can't legally do anything. But I've already received calls from parents, and the *Explorer* editor wants an official statement for the paper. . . . Things could escalate if we don't nip it in the bud."

"But I'm not the—"

"Isn't it butt?" Jayla says. "Nip it in the butt?"

"Bud, Miss Heart. Cookie?" Zeff offers the plate again, but I decline. Fool me once. "Here's what's going to happen," she says. "I'd like you to delete all the prom photos from your profile and issue a formal apology. If you could post a little something about what you've learned from—"

"Someone stole my phone and—"

"I really thought it was butt." Jayla nibbles on her sunglasses, clearly vexed.

"It would go a long way, Miss Vacarro," Zeff says, "if you showed remorse toward the students who were impacted. Olivia Barnes was especially scandalized—she's been in and out of the counselor's office all morning."

I swallow the oatmeal-coated lump in my throat. "I feel awful about Olivia, but I was scandalized too. I mean, why would I post incriminating photos of *myself*? No one sees how crazypants that is?"

"Teenagers do a lot of things in the heat of the moment," Zeff says. "Unfortunately, the combination of camera phones and social networking ensures that a momentary lapse in judgment is never forgotten."

"But I didn't—"

"Miss Vacarro." She holds up her hands, like, *Stop, in the name of love!* "It's clear you were at the party, and regardless of who posted the photos, you made some poor choices this weekend. You'd be setting a good example all around if you'd simply accept some responsibility here."

"Ms. Zeff," Jayla says, finally back on planet earth, "poor choices aside, surely you can see that Lucy is the one being bullied."

"I understand there are some shades of gray, ladies."

Eww.

"No shades," I say. "I straight up didn't do it."

"I want to believe you. Both of you. Lucy, your academic record is perfect; your artwork speaks for itself. And, Jayla, I'm a huge fan. I wish I'd been on staff while you were a student here."

"Thank you," Jayla says, and I'm just waiting for the "but."

"But the fact is," Zeff says, "the pictures originated on Lucy's profile. You're welcome to report the incident to Facebook, but the school doesn't have the authority to . . . to . . ." Her eyes slide to the monitor, to a new message from Mom.

She types out another angry missive—MOM! BOUND-ARIES: NOT JUST FOR NATIONS!—and merges back into our conversation, multitasking like Jayla drives. I'm seriously getting whiplash.

"Legally I have no authority," she says. "But if I deem that this scandal is disrupting the educational process or that students are being bullied on school grounds as a result of the photos, I could pursue . . . disciplinary action." Zeff has the decency to look distressed, but not distressed enough to stick up for me.

"The sooner you apologize," she says apologetically, "the sooner this will go away. Isn't that what we all want?"

She's nodding, nodding, nodding, and soon Jayla's nodding, and then my head's bobbing too. Zeff's right—I *do* want this to go away. I'm not trying to stand up to bullies or make a federal case or be (e)VIL's poster girl. I'm trying to duck and cover, get my friends back, forget this whole thing ever happened.

Most of it, anyway.

I'm resigned to the Facebook fates. "Fine. I'll do it."

"That's my girl." Her smile returns, and she rummages in her desk drawer for a late pass. "Now that we've settled that, where are you off to next?"

"Ms. Zeff? With your permission," Jayla says, enjoying the faux-thority these school-sanctioned dramatics have enabled, "I'd prefer to take Lucy home early so we can discuss this as a family and determine the appropriate next steps. In addition to posting the formal apology, of course."

"Oh, of course." Ms. Zeff's eyes are kind, foolishly trusting. "And, Lucy? I know it's hard when you're not as social as your peers, but there are more positive outlets for your frustration. Your art, for instance, can be a great stress reliever. Or hot yoga. My sister has social anxiety—it's really helped her."

"I'm not socially anxious." Socially annoyed, sure, but I doubt there's a hot yoga for that.

"Give it some thought." Zeff's doing that nod-and-smile thing, like, *You're already agreeing with me about the yoga.* "And please remember that my door—sorry. Hang on."

Keys are banging again, Zeff spitting out words between clenched teeth. "Maggie. I. Already. Saw. The. Video. Twice. Adorable!" She offers me a forced smile. "Chin up, Lucy. My door is always open. Got it?"

"Got it," I say.

"Great." Zeff's attention is back on her profile, fingers poised on keys, ready to take down the oversharers. "Would you mind shutting the door on your way out?"

ANGELICA DARLING'S ADVICE TO A WOMAN SCORNED FROM A WOMAN WHO DOES A LOT OF SCORNING (AS WELL AS CHEATING, LYING, CONNIVING, BACKSTABBING, AND THE OCCASIONAL POISONING)

There's a sleek white Porsche in the visitor's lot with tinted windows and polished chrome rims, a tricked-out 911 Turbo like the one Angelica Darling drives on the show.

If getting my own scandal was the first sign of the impending apocalypse and getting a Get-Out-of-Jail-Early card was the second, the Porsche is definitely the third.

"You couldn't rent a Camry like a normal person?" I ask.

"Mom thought it was clever," Jayla says, all faux Jackie-O fab in the head scarf. She clicks the key fob to unlock it. "Get in."

"What the fuck, Jay?"

"Ever hear of keeping a low profile? Shut up and get in the car. I don't want anyone to recognize me."

"Ditto," I say. Jayla's been going by her stage name ever since she scored a national shampoo commercial her junior year, and as far as I know, Ellie, Griff, and Cole are the only ones in my class who know she's my sister. But anyone with half a brain cell could do a little digging and connect the DNA dots. Sharing a dip in the gene pool with Angelica Darling? My scandal quotient would skyrocket.

I collapse onto the front seat without further argument, velvety black leather hot on my thighs. Jayla races into the street before I even have my seat belt buckled.

"You know what would be awesome, Miss Low-Pro? If you didn't kill me before we got home. Today sucked enough without dying in a fiery crash."

"We're not going home." She banks around the curves that lead to the highway, pink peep-toes jamming the gas pedal. "We're going to therapy." Her eyebrows wriggle. "Retail therapy."

"Don't be gross."

"Don't be stupid. When your rich sister offers to take you shopping, you say 'how high.'"

"You *must* be high if you think a shopping trip can fix this."

"Shopping is the single most effective way to survive a scandal," she says. "They've done, like, clinical studies."

"I thought we were supposed to quote unquote discuss this as a family?"

"Oh, there's an idea!" Jay downshifts as we merge onto the highway, the engine growling at the change. "Let's be grateful I already dropped Mom and Dad at the airport by the time Zeff called the house, and leave the rest of the parenting to me. Deal?"

"Wait. What? Where did Mom and Dad go?"

"Laguna Beach," she says breezily. "I sent them on a couple's retreat so you and I could bond. No worries—they'll be back before graduation. Oh, they said to tell you bye."

Ignoring my gaping stare, Jayla jerks across four lanes of afternoon traffic and zooms us down the highway, parentless, bound for the only place I hate more than school.

The Lav-Oaks Mall.

"There's something you should know," Jayla says, dragging me by the arm into the Apple store. No one's paying us much attention—I made her ditch the scarf and heels for a Broncos hoodie and flip-flops from Dick's Sporting Goods the moment we arrived—but she's no less dramatic without an audience. "While you were wasting the morning on your education, I was monitoring the online sitch. Your classmates are bastards."

"Brilliant." I yawn. Retail therapy is exhausting. "Will this difficult conversation be the sort that requires a cookie?"

"Just . . . here." Jayla taps a URL into an iPad from the display table and turns it toward me.

My once-desolate Facebook profile has become, in just two days, a bustling communications hub. Most of the tagged pictures are old news—me kissing Cole, me kissing Marceau, me and Cole in bed. There's a new one tagged from Olivia's profile of me and Cole leaving the emo bathroom this morning, and a few others tagged from a new profile named Narc Alert—shots of me moping around the school this morning and another with me getting into the Porsche, Jayla a thankfully unrecognizable blur. *Cole & Marceau just can't compete with this sugar daddy. A girl has needs! #scandal.*

"What kind of disease would, like, legit force me to graduate by mail?" I ask, eyes watering with shame. "And where can we buy a vial of it?"

"Lucy. First of all, don't cry and ruin your Sephora makeover." Jayla rubs her thumbs beneath my eyes to fix the lines. "I showed you this to motivate you. Find your inner lioness, okay? You can't let these people dictate your life. They're piranha. And they don't go away after high school." She closes out the page and returns the device to the table. "Since your principal is obviously pro-piranha—"

"Ms. Zeff is okay." I downgraded her from "cool" because oatmeal-raisin cookies should never, under any circumstances, be advertised as chocolate chip. Also, the fake apology letter she's making me write kind of blows.

"That woman is more concerned with crossing off her little 'how to stop cyberbullying' checklists than doing her job," Jayla says.

"That *is* her job."

"I have a better strategy for you." Jayla leans in close like she's about to go all (e)VIL conspiracy theory on me. "When you post your apology, tell them you're sorry . . ."

Dramatic pause. Raised brows. Deep breaths all around. Aaand . . .

"Sorry you've wasted four years of your life with a bunch of bottom-feeding ass-vampires who thrive on inventing tragedies just so they can suck the blood of the innocent, turning a young woman's private pain into a public feeding trough for a pack of raisin-balled drama-whoring maggots who'd trade in the ashes of their own grandmothers for five seconds of pleasure at the expense of those very women on whom their sham-factory, boob-envying livelihoods depend."

I blink. "Ass-vampires?"

"Well, I'm obviously paraphrasing, Lucy. The point is, they can all just pucker up and suck this—"

"How can I help you, ladies?" The Apple guy must not recognize my sister, because she's flipping the iPads the double Fs, and he's giving us a look, like, *You flip off my merchandise, you buy my merchandise.*

He's also giving Jay's boobs a look, like, *Where have you two been all my life?*

"As a matter of fact"—Jayla squints at his name tag—"*Steve*, you *can* help us. I want the iPad. Two of them. And we're getting my sister a replacement phone since some dirt-snogging jackass stole hers for nefarious sexting purposes. Is that not the great injustice of our time, Steve?"

"Sorry," I tell him. "She skipped her pills this morning. Bad idea."

"Steve!" Jayla snaps her fingers. "Are you helping us, or just staring inappropriately at my junk?"

Steve goes, "Um."

"The activities aren't mutually exclusive, Jay," I point out.

"Helping and harassing?" Jay says.

"Yes!" Steve is the color of hot sauce. "I mean, no. Yes, I'm here to help. How can I be, um, helpful?"

"Give us a minute to confer." Jayla flashes her movie-star smile and shoos him away with a flick of her pear-perfumed wrist. Steve shuffles off behind the Genius Bar, shoulders slumped.

"Too much?" she asks me.

"Gee, you think?"

"This whole thing just has me so riled up," she says.

"Steve?"

"The scandal!" Jayla sighs. "It's so typical. Blame the woman. There's a name for it now, not like when I was your age. Slut-shaming. *Slut-shaming,* Lucy! Like a girl who has sex is vile, but the guy? It takes two to tango, right? Or whatever you guys were doing in—"

"We weren't doing anything." *Tango?*

"The point is, this is exactly like what happened in episode seven, season three," she says, "when everyone thought Angelica slept with her mother's fiancé?"

"Angelica *did* sleep with her mother's fiancé," I say, for one thing. And two, advice from a fictional slut is so not helpful, especially considering that three, I'm not a slut. Not that I'm shaming. I'm just, by even the loosest definition, not one. And four, "Jay, you realize we're not on TV, right?"

"I'm just trying to help." She bumps her hip against the table where the iPhones are tethered. "Here comes our boy *Steve.* Better decide what color you want."

"You don't have to get me a phone, Jay. Or an iPad."

Jayla swats the air. "I said I'd take you shopping. Key word: shopping."

"Key word: this." I twist around to display the bags draped over my shoulder: Urban Decay eye shadow, eyeliner, and mascara from Sephora. Five different kinds of OPI nail polish, plus a bottle of Burberry Brit she found while the counter girls did my makeover. Two pair of Lucky Brand jeans. Gucci sunglasses that cover the entire square footage of my face. A black-and-silver bikini that covers way less.

"I hate how we left things in California, okay?" Jayla's fierce confidence is gone. "You were storming out and I . . . I just didn't know what to say. Not my shining moment as a sister—I get it."

The weight of those memories presses on my lungs, squeezing the air into a sigh. "Jayla, you just—"

"Let me make it up to you," she whispers. "Pick out a phone."

Steve assembles our gear, including cases and accessories and AppleCare plans, and cheerfully swipes Jayla's credit card.

His iPad lets out two short chirps.

"Let's try that again," he says. He reswipes the card twice, no luck.

"Is there a problem?" Jayla asks.

Steve blows on the card, then gives it one more go. *Chirp-chirp!*

He looks sheepish when he tells her the card's been declined. "It's probably a bank error."

I switch my overloaded shopping bags from one shoulder to the other. "It's probably ready to melt."

"My assistant must've forgotten to let them know I'd be traveling," Jayla says dismissively. "They must think it's stolen. I'll call her later and get it straightened out." She fishes another card from her wallet, then changes her mind and swaps it again. "You take debit, right?"

Steve looks from us to the pile of gear, back to Jayla's chest, and taps his head. *Eureka!* "Didn't you say you're a teacher? I forgot to give you the educator discount."

Jayla bristles. "Teacher? I'm the——"

"Best drama teacher at Lav-Oaks," I finish. "Everybody loves her. She's *super*dramatic."

Our total plummets two hundred bucks. The debit card works, and once he sets me up on the new phone— restoring the data from my old one by way of, ironically, the iCloud—we're out of there.

Jayla puts a hand to her forehead and feigns a swoon. "I'm famished! Cantina Blue?"

"Don't you have to call Macie?" I ask. "About your credit cards?"

"Like I don't carry enough cash for Tex-Mex? Come on." Jayla stalks ahead toward the food court, pointing at her wrist. "Hey there, boys and girls! It's margarita-o'clock!"

"And it's, like, so stupid," Jayla's saying. "Steve doesn't know me. He doesn't know my bank account." She downs her second margarita and flags the waitress for a third, and I'm pretty much definitely driving that Porsche home.

I poke straw holes in my virgin strawberry daiquiri. "He saved you two hundred bucks, Jay."

"It's the principle!" She's wearing the pout that made her famous, and if she were a puppy, I'd totally pet her. "He assumed I have, like, financial problems. He didn't even recognize me. He felt sorry for me."

"Maybe he felt sorry for *me* because I have such a pain in the ass for a sister."

Jayla huffs. "It's not too late to return that Sephora stuff."

"Touch it and die."

"You wouldn't hurt a fly."

"A fly, no. A sister, yes." I wield my slush-covered straw like a blade. "I'm a highly trained zombie fighter. Don't mess with me."

Jayla laughs, deep and genuine, and by the time the waitress brings our Mile High Nachos and Sizzlin' Veggie Fajita Rollups, I'm glad she dragged me to the mall. However temporary, my sister's back. Not Jayla, but Janey, and we're snarfing too much Tex-Mex and groovin' to the ranchera music and ordering more margs and then she gets that determined gleam in her eye that means our south-of-the-border soiree is about to head, well, slightly more south.

"Lucy! Lucy! Ohmygod!" Jayla stumbles out of the booth and grabs my hand. "They have a mechanical bull! Come *on*!"

I try to hold her back, to bribe her with the promise of fried ice cream and coffee, but when Jayla Heart sets her mind to public disaster, nothing can stand in her way.

Eight seconds later, I'm shoving quarters into a metal box, praying to the God of Tourist Attractions that my sister has decent medical coverage and that Cantina Blue is void, at present, of Jayla Heart fanboys, *CelebStyle* paparazzi, my Lav-Oaks classmates, and—just to be safe— anyone with a mobile Internet connection.

"Let's do this, Toro! *Yee-haw!*" Jayla squeals as the bull jerks and grinds to life. The quarters get her five minutes and an "authentic" cowgirl hat for the ride, which she's currently pressing to her head with one hand, the other gripping the saddle horn.

A half-dozen men and little kids gather, everyone encouraging her from the sidelines to "hang on" and "ride hard" and "get 'er done, darlin'!" After three minutes, convinced she's got both Toro and her audience entranced, Jayla whoops, tossing her hat in the air. "Go, cowgirl, go—*ohh!*"

In a tangle of arms and legs and flip-flops, my sister is on the safety mat, laughing as the bull clinks to a stop above her.

"Screw you, Toro. Screw all you . . . stupid . . . bulls." Flat on her back, Jayla's flipping off the bull, laughing, and a few more curious heads pop up from the surrounding booths.

One of the busboys has his phone out, thumbs working the screen, probably uploading video to Blue Cantina's Drunken Cowgirl Wall of Shame. Behind me a mother hushes her child, calls for their waitress to bring the bill.

We're about one customer complaint away from an "Everything all right here, ladies?" visit from the manager.

I kneel on the mat beside her. "Time to go, Jayla."

"Call me *Cowgirl*!" She grabs the discarded hat and flings her arms out, two limp noodles around my neck.

"Time to go, Cowgirl. Lose the hat." I get her on her feet and lead her back to the booth. Aware that we're still being watched and possibly filmed, I slap a wad of Jayla's cash on the table and hastily collect our things. We're almost to the exit, me balancing our shopping bags and purses on one arm, my sister on the other, when Jayla goes boneless.

"Lucy! It's horrible!" she wails, a blond puddle on the fake tile floor. "I'm a terrible parent!"

"You're not a parent."

"I'm not setting a good example," she says. "I'm fiscally irrespicable. Sponsible."

With tired eyes, I take in the pile of Jayla, the salsa stain on her thigh, the cowgirl hat–shaped lump inside her hoodie. "Oh, you're an *awesome* example."

"If Ms. Zeff saw me, she'd call social services. They should lock me up and throw away the keys! Do prisons still use keys, or is it, like, electronic? Do you think social services will send me to jail? I'm awful!"

More waterworks.

"Jesus, Jay. How the fuck did you get so wasted?" I set down the bags and loop my arms around her waist. "Help me out here, Cowgirl. I can't—"

"Lucy? Last name Vacarro?"

I stand and turn around slowly, plastering on a festive smile. "Marceau! Hey! I'm . . . um . . . my sister's contact lens . . . Have you been here long?"

Jayla moans from the floor.

Marceau's eyes are warm and kind, and with no more judgment than a playfully raised eyebrow, he says, "Let me help, *chéri*."

He grunts as he hauls Jayla to her feet, letting her use him as a human kickstand while I scoop up the bags. "I'm here with my host mom," he tells me. "She says I'm not allowed to leave Colorado without trying the Miles High nachos."

"Mile High," I say. "Just the one."

"Nacho?"

"Mile. It's the altitude," I explain.

"Welcome to Denver!" Jayla blurts out. "One mile above the sea."

Marceau smiles. It's basically award-winning. "At

home we would say 'one point six kilometers high nachos.'"

Guilt needles the back of my neck. I can't believe he's so sweet. I probably ruined his official prom experience, and now I'm screwing up his official nacho experience, and he's still helping me drag my drunk cowgirl sister to the car without complaint.

"You smell really really good," Jayla says, leaning into Marceau's neck. "My sister should totally hook up with you."

"Aren't you a funny little lamb," I say. "Now be quiet, okay?" I turn back to Marceau. "I know this is . . . crazy. But do you think you could, like, *not* say anything about this at school? My sister's kind of—"

"I'm famous!" she slurs. "Bulls bow to *me*!"

Marceau's still smiling. "I can understand why."

I fumble for an explanation, but I'm pretty sure Jayla just passed out, and Marceau doesn't press. It's likely that he doesn't recognize her—unless his host mom's a fan, he's probably never seen *Danger's Little Darling*.

"So, our secret?" I ask.

He nods once. "My older brother, he is like this one. Party all the time."

We're at the car now, Jayla draped around Marceau like a scarf, me digging through her purse for the keys. Once I've situated the packages in the trunk and myself in the driver's seat, he gently lowers Jayla to the passenger seat, tossing the stolen cowgirl hat into the back. He leans across her to buckle the seat belt just as I move to do the same. Our cheeks brush, his long hair silky against my jaw. Our eyes lock.

Damn. He *does* smell really really good.

Why can't I just like a boy who's not *connected to my best friend?*

With a sigh, I thank him and start the car, and Marceau tucks Jayla's floppy arms against her body and shuts the door. He watches as I reverse out of the spot, the slump of his shoulders the only trace of regret at what just can't happen between us.

Or maybe he's really missing on those nachos.

~Dear Suckers:~ To my Lavender Oaks classmates:

~Even though it totally wasn't my fault,~ I'm ~hella~ very deeply sorry about the photographs that appeared ~through no fault of my own~ on Facebook over the weekend ~after some jackoff stole my phone and hacked into my account.~

I understand that the photographs are inappropriate for posting publicly ~because unlike aforementioned jackoff, I'm not a perv,~ and I sincerely regret any embarrassment, pain, or trouble they may have caused ~especially the~

~~ones that are ruining my own life at this very moment.~~
I assure you that the original photos have been deleted
from my profile. I've also deactivated and replaced my old
phone, on which the photos were taken. The replacement
phone contains neither compromising photographs nor
stored social network passwords. ~~So don't even *think*
about it, ass-vampires.~~

I'd like to encourage other students to follow my example
in ~~flipping you all the double-Fs~~ deleting any remaining
shared or tagged photos from your profiles. ~~Especially
you, Miss Demeanor, you gossipmongering nitwit. It's
kind of your fault this whole thing got started. Scandal
of the Month? Who *does* that?~~

Social networking can be a fun and valuable
communication tool, ~~especially for those who don't know
how to have actual, real-life communications;~~ but only if
we all ~~decide agree~~ commit to treating one another with
respect and dignity, online and offline.

Sincerely,
Lucy Vacarro

~~P.S. Zeff is making me write this.~~

~~P.P.S. My sister says SUCK IT.~~

With Jayla conked out in my bed, I revise the fake apology a dozen times. When I finally post it on Facebook, I tag a bunch of people who were tagged in the original photos, bases covered.

I'm such a spineless jellyfish that I can't believe my jellyfish tentacles have the strength to type, but Zeff's right—this needs to go away.

Mission accomplished, I change into Cole's bear shirt and do a breath check on Jayla. She's alive, out cold, definitely not moving tonight. I shimmy off her jeans and tuck the blanket around her shoulders. She's a little girl lost beneath the bedding, and I crawl in next to her and fold myself around the empty spaces, knowing she won't be here when I wake up.

WHEN THERE'S NO MORE ROOM IN HELL, THE DEAD WILL WALK TO THE HORSE BARN

Rule number one." A whisper from behind sends chills across my scalp. "Never apologize to the masses."

I skipped coffee this morning on account of Black & Brew being dead to me and I'm not prepared for an (e)VIL assault. Yet Asher Hollowell isn't aware of my non-caff status, so here he is, all hush-hush from his wheelchair command post like we're on a code name basis.

"Cool out, Black Ops." I close my locker and turn to face him. "That letter was a direct order from Zeff. In case you haven't noticed, I need to get off her radar."

"What if I said I could help?"

Suspicion engaged. "I'd update my status from 'majorly annoyed' to 'mildly intrigued, but cautious.' So. Who's the artist?"

Ash fidgets with a manila folder in his lap, forehead creased. "Wait. Is that *all* part of your status update, or just the intrigued part?"

Right before I got sucked into this *Twilight Zone* convo, I found another flyer stuffed into my locker, and now I drop it into his lap. "Who's in charge of these?"

LOG OUT AND WAKE UP!
IS LUCY VACARRO <u>REALLY</u> A SENIOR AT LAVENDER OAKS HIGH? OR IS SHE AN ANDROID CREATED BY THE NSA TO COLLECT DATA ON OUR WHEREABOUTS? OUR CONVERSATIONS? OUR UNHEALTHY SNACKING HABITS? OUR PARTIES? DON'T BELIEVE EVERYTHING YOU'RE TOLD! QUESTIONING AUTHORITY <u>ISN'T</u> UNPATRIOTIC—IT'S YOUR PATRIOTIC RESPONSIBILITY!
SHOW US YOUR BIRTH CERTIFICATE, MISS VACARRO!

On the back is another Lucy drawing, still with the poufy dress, only now there's antennae sprouting from my head and dials across my chest.

Ash presses a hand to his standard-issue black T-shirt. "I refuse to apologize for being a true patriot."

"In that case, oh-say-can-you-see your ass outta my way? I'm not getting a tardy on your account."

Ash has impressive instincts, blocking my forward motion with a one-armed spin of his wheels. "I really can help," he says. "But I need something from you."

"You're not getting my birth certificate."

"Forget that. It's . . ." Ash taps the folder. The sound seems to ignite his passion. "Join us! Together we can fight this thing! Strength in numbers—something we're seriously lacking. Uh, numbers, not strength."

I slip the new iPhone from my pocket and wriggle it before him. "Sorry. Automatic disqualifier."

"We have a program for that."

"Program?"

With just a few minutes before homeroom, the halls are filling up, and Asher rolls in tight to avoid the foot traffic. "Like AA for device addicts," he says. "Except it's not actually *anonymous*." Asher laughs. "The regime is tracking your cell calls—how *could* it be?"

"There's a cell-tracking regime?"

He nods solemnly. "Knowledge is power, Miss Vacarro."

"Skank alert! Woop-woop!" Quinn and Haley, Olivia's

prom-night sprites, howl at me as they pass. A few nearby students laugh.

"Don't associate with Juicy Lucy, Asher," Quinn says. "You'll end up on a government watch list."

Haley hums the *X-Files* theme song, both girls erupting into giggles as they disappear into the early-morning mob.

"Did she call me Juicy Lucy?" I say.

Asher's eyes are full of fresh sympathy. "See? Who better than you to speak out about the dangers of social networking? Of online trials in a world where 'like' is a noun and sentencing is passed with the click of a mouse?"

There's a headache creeping in behind my eyes and its name is Asher Hollowell. Also, Asher Hollowell has a point.

Maybe I do have some allies in this. Maybe the Lucy illustrations are supposed to be ironic.

Then again, one time Jayla gave an interview to *#TRENDZ*, this entertainment rag that had posted pics of her doing the walk of shame from her studio intern's place the week before. They promised her a chance to clear things up, but all they did was take her quotes out of context and amp up the scandal.

"I should get to homeroom," I say.

"Then you leave me no choice." Ash opens his folder, revealing an impressively crazy collection: website printouts, handwritten notes on napkins, color-coded Post-its, CIA-style photographs.

"If you don't believe in technology," I say, "how do you even know about my scandal? And where did you get all the stuff in your little folder?"

"It's a *dossier*." He leans in close, lowering his voice. "Know thine enemy, Miss Vacarro. We have people on the inside. Counterintelligence on the vast machine."

"Machine? I thought it was a regime. See, there's your recruiting problem—too many codes and buzzwords. It intimidates people."

He bows his head, procuring with great ceremony a two-page color printout. I recognize the Facebook logo, and when I see the fan page title, my mouth goes dry.

Juicy Lucy: Give Her a Squeeze!

I tap the URL into my phone's browser. The pictures of me and Cole are just thumbnails on my tiny screen, but the fan numbers are a megaphone of suckage. The page just launched this morning, and it already has more than two hundred likes.

"For the record," Ash says, "no one on my team liked it."

"No one on your team has Facebook."

"Technicality." He slips the printout back into his dossier, tapping all the loose papers into place. "Our flyer drawings are *meant* to be shocking—a recruiting technique. The fan page is just cruel. We want to help you, Lucy."

I lean against the lockers. There's a small voice in my head telling me that Ash, unlike *#TRENDZ,* is good people. A little out there, maybe, but not conniving. Not paparazzi.

"Can I trust you?" I ask.

"Is Elvis alive and well in El Segundo under Witness Protection as an FBI drug informant?"

Blink. Blink.

"It means yes," he whispers. "You can trust us."

"What about Kiara?"

He looks at the floor, blood rushing to his face. "Probation. You don't have to worry about her."

"I'm not *worried*. I want her reinstated. I only took that picture for her because her mom wanted it."

"Kiara knew the rules when she signed up," he says.

"It's a rite of passage, Ash. You can't deny moms that kind of stuff."

He rubs his chin, weighing my argument. "Is that the extent of your conditions?"

"Will you put an end to the drawings, too?"

He meets my eyes, hesitates only a moment to let a group of vampire bros pass. Unlike the girls, they don't stop to howl, but they're definitely looking at us, definitely bro-ing it up with a few lewd gestures.

"Fine," Ash says. "Kiara's in, drawings are out. Consider it done."

"Good. Consider it . . . considered." What does one

say in these situations? Affirmative? Roger? Rock on? "Um, thanks. I'll—"

A familiar sight at the other end of the corridor hijacks my brain-train: Griffin has entered the building.

With Ellie.

"You guys! Wait!" I ditch Asher and motor through the crowd to catch up, breathless when I reach them. "You . . . you're back."

"Yeah. Hey." Ellie won't look at me. "I'm not on there, you know. The Juicy page? I think it's awful."

"Of course not." My eyes fill with tears at the defeated sound of her voice, the still-rumpled knot of her hair. "I'm sorry if I pushed you yesterday . . . with the tarts? I just wanted to talk, and . . ."

Her eyes stay fixed on my white Converse, the skeletons I'd been sketching on the canvas all year.

After an eternity of pained silence, Griff slips her arm around Ellie's shoulders, the very definition of support system. To me, she says, "Tell Mrs. King I won't be in homeroom."

In first period calculus, the Jell-O mold has been replaced with Colorado peach "Pi," and Mrs. Smolinski composes a love story on the whiteboard between differential equations and baked goods. This is exactly the sort of academic comedy Griff and I should be secretly texting about, but now that Ellie's back on the scene, Griff's stonewalling me.

So much for not taking sides.

"And the solution is pure elegance," Smolinski's saying, but instead of taking notes, I'm hiding behind my textbook with my new phone, scanning the Juicy page.

Confirmed: Ellie, Cole, Griff, Marceau, and the members of Vanitas aren't on the fan list. But with more than two hundred likes, that still leaves most of my classmates, not to mention a dozen kids who don't even attend Lav-Oaks.

The usual Lucy-bashing pictures are there, plus a shot of me and Asher from this morning—*I'll show you my secret bunker if you show me yours.* My apology note was reposted too, complete with critical reviews such as, *Your example is sleeping with your best friend's boyfriend!* and *u should be apologizing for being born!* and the simple yet classic, *SLUT!*

Maybe I should've used Jayla's ass-vampire speech.

"There's not a problem in the world that calculus can't solve." Smolinski's still scribbling on the whiteboard with furious determination. My phone blinks with a text.

Cole: *saw on fb u got a new phone. hope this is ur 1st text. :-) OH HAI LUCY'S PHONE!*

Me: *u win. ur saving me from smolinski's calc lovefest right now :)* I leave out the part about how seeing his name on my phone makes my insides go all firecrackers.

Cole: *zzzzz. ;-) so . . . u ok? john & i are trying 2 figure out who made fan page. nobody seems 2 know.*

Me:

What am I doing? Ellie still isn't speaking to me. Griffin's being a flip-flopper. The scandal is crossing inter-school district borders. If Cole gets any more involved, it'll just feed the rumor mill and make things harder for Ellie.

Whatever happened between me and Cole, whatever lingers now . . . it needs to go back into hypersleep.

Cole: *please talk 2 me. worried abt u. want to help. :-|*

Me: *i'm ok. gtg.*

This #scandal *so* needs to vanish, but how? The Zeff-mandated apology was a dead end. No offense to Mrs. Smolinski, but advanced math won't help me out of this mess either. Asher's offer flits through my mind, but . . . no. The last thing my rep needs is an affiliation with Team Tinfoil Hat.

I need solid backup.

Otherwise (formerly?) known as my friends.

After dragging myself through the rest of calculus, through British lit and physics, through a brief tearfest with the Indigo Girls in the emo bathroom, I hightail it to the cafeteria to catch Ellie before lunch.

We've got six years of loyal BFF-ship together—how long can she ignore me? Especially on Tater Tot Tuesdays, when we always team up to steal Cole's and John's? We've got a road trip to plan, dorm decorations to pick out. The rest of our lives to map.

Together. Inseparable.

Leave me alone, Lucy!

Ellie's anger hovers like a storm cloud as I trudge to the stables. I hate going all walking cliché two days in a row, but the cafeteria is way behind enemy lines, total red zone. I'd probably get drone striked with Tater Tots.

Lunch bag and sketchbook in hand, I pass the other horses and reach Prince Freckles's stall, immediately relaxed by his presence.

I'm not the only one.

Franklin Margolis is paling around with my equine bestie when I arrive, scoping out the scene and scratching notes onto his yellow pad. His messenger bag rests on a brick of hay just outside the stall.

"What's the scoop, paper boy?" I drop my backpack and plop down on the ground.

Franklin looks neither amused nor surprised to see me. He hesitates, polite smile firmly fixed, probably scanning his journalistic vocabulary for a synonym for *whackjob loonypants* so he can properly describe me in his article.

"Lucy Vacarro. Perhaps you can assist," he says. The

British accent increases his genius vibe the same way Marceau's increases his yum factor. "I'm interviewing the equestrians about prom-night mistreatment. Rather, *alleged* mistreatment. I've yet to locate the rumored golden horn, but it appears that the committee used superglue to decorate the hooves." He nods toward Prince Freckles's feet, still bedazzled with glitter. "Thoughts?"

"I plead the Fifth."

Franklin sits next to me in the dirt, trading the notepad for a packed lunch from his messenger bag. "The truth is I've been looking for you, love. I saw you walk to the stables for lunch yesterday and hoped I'd find you today. And here you are."

"And here I am. Care to tell me why I'm being stalked by the newspaper editor? I'd like to chill on the publicity awhile, if you don't mind."

Prince Freckles lets out an emphatic shiver-snort, like, *I got your back, Lucy Belle.*

"I'm not interested in publicity," Franklin says. Beneath his chestnut curls, his brown eyes are alert and genuine, and he doesn't look away when he speaks. "I'm interested in your story. Obviously I've seen the photographs, the Juicy page. Not a fan, by the way."

"That's what they all say." Admittedly, it sounds better in his accent. Like, more official.

"I don't go in for the online popularity rubbish," he says. "And for the record, I think it's bollocks what they're doing to you over a few regrettable photographs."

"For the record, I didn't post them."

Franklin nods. "Let's say I believe you."

"I believe you," we say simultaneously. I laugh with him, which is unexpected, considering I also just discovered that Jayla put olives in my egg salad. Totally grateful that she made my lunch, but *olives*? What are those Hollywood weirdies doing to her?

"Any idea who did it?" he asks.

I've been over it a hundred times, but I just can't figure it out. *Everyone* at the party was outed by the pictures. Drinking, hooking up, butt shots, smoking—no one escaped unscathed. For all I know, a bear snuck into the cabin, swiped my phone, took the shots, and vanished, uploading the evidence from his underground lair in Wyoming.

It's about as plausible as anything else.

I shake my head.

"Still." Franklin procures a can of ginger ale and a falafel wrap from his lunch bag. "I'd like people to hear your side of the story."

"How? My own friends won't even listen to me."

"A feature interview." He takes a few bites of falafel, expertly navigating the wrap. I'd be wearing it by now.

"Present your evidence. Talk about the dangers of judging without facts. Invite fellow students to engage in a healthy discourse about—"

"That's so cute."

Franklin cocks his head.

"Your blind idealism," I explain. "Faith in our classmates."

"You think they're not capable of intelligently debating an issue in a neutral public forum?"

I bite back a laugh. "Pretty sure all the discourse is happening on Miss Demeanor's page. No offense, but if I want advice from my peers, I'll message her."

"Odd. You don't strike me as the Miss Demeanor type." He wolfs down the last of his falafel and folds up the napkins and wrappers, neatly tucking them back into the brown bag. "Look. You can't ignore this. I mean, you could, but then you'll graduate with this scandal as your last memory, and in twenty years at the reunion, they'll still be calling you Juicy Lucy, because people are cruel and petty and bored. Is that what you want?"

"I have no plans to attend the reunion."

"Just an example. I fail at American irony."

I shove the uneaten bits of my sandwich back into the bag and fish out a granola bar, which is actually a fiber bar. Last time I let Jayla make lunch.

"Thanks for the offer," I say. "But I'm not interested in an interview." Adding more fodder to the fire? In zombie-slaying circles, that's called ringin' the dinner bell, and it's the fastest way to get yourself munched.

"You're certain?" Franklin says.

"I just want to fix things with my best friend. Ellie Pike? She's the one who . . . she's Cole's . . . Cole's the one I . . ." I shake my head to unclog the words. "She's not speaking to me."

"And you think Miss Demeanor can assist?" Franklin asks.

"Maybe. Fiber bar?" I hold it out to him.

"I'm quite regular, thanks." Franklin's brow is pinched. He taps the side of his soda can, eyes meeting mine again. "So you won't grant me an interview, but you'll muck about with an anonymous online gossip?"

"Why not?"

"You've a much better chance at being heard with the *Explorer*."

"Is that a fact?"

"Technically an opinion, but a valid one, which—unlike that horrid gossip column—deserves serious consideration."

Franklin folds his arms, his gaze unwavering. He's good-natured about it, but his utter certainty feels like a challenge, like the noobs who come on *Undead Shred* talking about kicking ass only to march off alone and die.

"Don't judge Miss D. just because she's not all, 'Ooh, I'm the valedictorian and I have important sorts of bloody discourse,'" I say.

"Your English accent isn't half bad," he says with a crooked grin. "Then, it's not half good, either."

"I'm just saying, if you're so fair and balanced, you should support all forms of journalism. Even Miss Demeanor's." I grab my phone and sign into the ground zero of my Facebook account. A few taps later, I'm an official Miss Demeanor fan, dashing off a private message to the great adviser of our time.

From: Lucy Vacarro

Dear Miss Demeanor:

With your finger on the pulse of Lav-Oaks's most popular gossip channel, you likely already know me. I've recently been embroiled in a scandal over some photos taken at a postprom party, in part because of your ongoing encouragement of scandal documentation.

In a sense, one might say you owe me.

No judgments, of course. I realize that you trade in scandalmongering and I'm not one to impede the life choices of fellow students. Still, you're nothing if not fair and balanced, and I thought you might like to know the truth.

Despite all evidence to the contrary, I didn't post those photos, and I didn't have sexual relations with the male subject in those photos. I'd like to clear my name and patch things up with my best friend, who is currently not speaking to me because of this disaster (the male subject was, until recently, her boyfriend).

I'm sure you're aware.

Anyway, word on the streets of Lav-Oaks is that you're the one to go to for advice. So . . . got any for me?

Yours truly,
Vilified and Illified

"Vilified and Illified?" Franklin laughs when I show him the message.

"You know advice columns. It's all, 'Stranded in Sacramento' or 'Heartsick and Hopeless.' I'm trying to be legit."

"The *Explorer* doesn't require you to feign legitimacy. *Illified*, good grief."

I sign out of Facebook feeling slightly less destroyed than I did when Ellie gave me the shove-off. Thankfully, Jayla didn't screw up the chocolate pudding cup portion of my lunch hour, and I hold the dessert up in a toast. "Franklin old chap, I've been called much worse and lived to tell the tale."

He raises his ginger ale, giving me his sly, lopsided smile. "Indeed."

WITH FRIENDS LIKE THESE, NO WONDER ANGELICA DARLING WHACKS ALL OF HERS

MISS DEMEANOR

2,983 likes 👍

788 talking about this

<u>Wednesday, April 30</u>

Today's Wednesday Words of Wisdom—a meme I just made up since it's Wednesday and I'm both wordy and wise—go out to a couple of former friends in the midst of a thorny #scandal, the details of which have been widely publicized.

In such situations of the backstabbing nature, I like to ask, WWAD—what would Angelica do?

Anytime a friend has double-crossed Miss Darling, she's had them killed, a move that in this case is neither an option nor a good idea. Although I sometimes confuse the two myself, this is real life, not television. While real bestie betrayals aren't unheard of, interested parties would be wise to fully investigate the evidence. Ending a friendship is a serious, often irreversible decision, and without absolute proof of betrayal, you could be making a grave mistake.

If you're the wronger, on the other hand, and you're looking to make things right, why not come forth with your honest, heartfelt feelings? If you need a forum in which to carve open that vein, Miss D is your girl, girl. Call me Switzerland, 'cause I'm impartial. Or is that neutral? Either way, consider this an invitation to let your voice be heard!

Speaking of hearing voices, in dramatic times such as this, let's all remember the old chestnut: Assumptions make an ASS out of YOU and UMPTIONS. I don't know who Umptions is, but I'm pretty sure if he were a Lav-Oaks student, he'd focus on more pressing issues, like planning the senior prank. Maybe we could redirect our collective angst into something more productive, such as relocating Principal Zeff's car to the roof or giving the iron Swordfish statue a gender reassignment? Just throwing suggestions out there, people. Class secretary and horse lover Margo Hennessy tells me the official planning meeting is in the you-know-where on you-know-what at precisely you-know-when-o'clock. Unless you *don't* know, in which case you won't know what you're missing.

It's all very meta, and you know what I'm missing? An adult beverage.

xo ~ *Ciao!* ~ xo
Miss Demeanor

IF YOU CAN'T BEAT 'EM, JOIN 'EM, THEN BEAT 'EM AFTER ALL THE JOINING, BECAUSE THEY TOTALLY WON'T SEE THAT SHIT COMING

Must be a slow news week if both the newspaper editor and the gossip blogger are offering me page time. Not to mention Asher's (e)VIL invite yesterday. Way to rally around a crisis, random people I've never talked to before!

After besting my Fruit Ninja score on the walk to school, I flip my iPad case closed and sip my coffee, Black & Brew forgiven on account of my addiction being more important than petty vendettas. Today was another early-to-riser for me, and I enter the building with a clear mission: swap a few books at my locker and slide into homeroom without any confrontations, accusations, or invitations.

It's not that I don't appreciate the sudden support—particularly in light of the explosive popularity of the

Juicy page—but my besties shouldn't need to read my defense in the newspaper or Facebook court. This is a private matter among friends (and, okay, some not-so-friendly acquaintances who got swept up in the photo scandal), *not* some save-the-whales, antisocial-media rallying cry.

Unless I get a free T-shirt and/or Chipotle veggie burrito out of the deal, I'm no one's poster child.

Even though my locker is now covered in posters.

Pay no attention to the woman behind this curtain of mystery and contradiction!

"We tried to get them off," John explains as I approach. Cole's there too, scraping at my locker with fierce determination, drumsticks poking out of his back pocket. They must've had band rehearsal in the gym this morning—Vanitas is playing at the pep rally on Friday.

There's a stack of shredded posters at their feet, but the wallpaperist who did this was serious about longevity. Printouts of the infamous bedroom shot are duct-taped to my locker in layers.

"Creative," I mumble. According to the liner notes scrawled over the photos, I'm a narc, a slut, a home wrecker, *and* an ugly C-word who needs to get some. "Yet inconsistent."

With my back against the adjacent locker, I sink to the floor. Coldness seeps through my ripped denim shorts, through my purple fishnets, straight to my skin. I can't bring myself to look at John, but I apologize about the pond pictures anyway.

"You kidding? That's the funniest shit I've ever done. Don't worry about me." He tilts my chin up to meet his eyes, and I'm relieved by his familiar smile. "Got it?"

I smile in response. Maybe random, sudden support isn't so bad after all.

"Gotta bounce." John tugs on one of my braids and knocks against Cole's shoulder. "Catch up with you later." On his way out, he scoops up the torn posters, pitches them into the trash.

Cole slices at my locker with his car keys, trying unsuccessfully to tear down another layer.

"Leave it," I say. "They'll just put more up later. Obviously someone's determined to humiliate me."

"Us," Cole says. With a key, he points to one of the pictures and taps his pixelated face. "We're in it together."

Inside, warmth tangles with guilt like a weed choking a flower, and I scan the hall for cell phone snipers. A handful of teachers dot the dim corridor, but it's early yet; most of my classmates are still home toasting their Pop-Tarts.

Cole crouches in front of me, head bent close. "Looked for you in the woods last night," he says softly. "No Lucy. No Night of the Living Dog. Spike misses his bestie."

"Yeah, things are kind of crazy at home. My parents are in California and my sister's back for the summer, so there's . . . that."

Also, I didn't want to run into you alone. I'm avoiding you because every time you look at me like that, it hurts. Stop looking at me like that. Don't ever stop looking at me like that.

Cole shifts around and sits next to me, setting his sticks on the floor. Our shoulders are touching and it's all *aren't-we-the-greatest-of-pals*, except for my heart, which is spazzing in a very nonpals way.

"Things any better with you and Jay?" he asks. He was the one who drove Ellie to pick me up at DIA after last summer's California disaster. I didn't share the specifics, but it was obvious we'd had a major fight.

"So-so," I say. "She's . . . trying." I pull my knees to my chest, wrap myself in a hug. "She feels bad about all the scandal stuff."

"Yeah." Cole runs a hand through his perpetual bed-head. "Finally talked to Ellie last night. Five whole minutes."

"That's about five times what she's giving me."

"Pretty sure she hates me more than she hates you," he says.

"If she hated you, she wouldn't have a reason to hate me, because the hater and the hated . . . it doesn't . . . You know that saying? Like, your enemy's enemy is not your enemy, so you—"

"That's it. We're switching to decaf." Cole leans across me and nabs my coffee cup. He takes a swig like we've known each other forever, and only now, in the aftermath of all the sparks, do I realize he's always done it. Every dinner-and-a-movie he and Ellie third-wheeled me on, every botched double date, Cole always ate the fries off my plate, always stole the grand finale bite of my grilled cheese on rye or brownie à la mode. Not Ellie's, but mine, like we had this unspoken fry-sharing agreement, and I never questioned it. It was just our thing, accepted and unremarkable, significant only in the remembering.

"After graduation," he says, returning the coffee. His copper-green eyes are full of light again, the posters behind him dull in comparison. "Deal?"

"What about Ellie?"

"Oh, that girl will *never* go decaf. She's way—oh." Cole stops when he sees my face, T minus one second to eye roll. My knee gets an encouraging squeeze. "Sucks. Like, there's all this sadness in her voice and I'm the one who put it there and it kills me. I mean, I get it. She's fuming about the pictures, fuming that neither of us said anything earlier about . . ." His hand waves between us, *you and me*, *me and you*. "Things. Us. I wish I knew how to make it okay for her. For you. All of it."

My brain is all, *There were* earlier *things? Us things?* Earlier us *things?* But my mouth just goes for the gold with, "Yeah."

"Miss Vacarro. Mr. Foster." Principal Zeff nods curtly as she breezes down the hall, polished and put together as usual. If she notices the posters on my locker, she doesn't stop to investigate, to check whether they meet the "bullying on school property" handbook criteria. "Glad to see you two getting an early start on your education."

Once she's out of earshot, I ask, "How does someone see two scowling kids sitting on the floor and think it has anything to do with education?"

"We're in the building a half hour before the bell," he says. "And we're not smokin' a jay in the bathroom with 420. What else *could* she think?"

"I'm still scowling. You see that, right?"

Cole pretends to erase my grimace, fingertips grazing my lips. "Take it off, because I have an awesome fun idea and you're not allowed to shoot it down."

"I've already had my eight minutes of fun," I say. "Your contract has thus released you from further obligation." There's something dangerous in joking about that night, but it feels normal, too. Easy, like the fry-and-coffee stealing thing. And even though my locker is covered in damning evidence and my lips still tingle from his touch, it's so good to laugh with him, so real, and when he returns my smile, it's all, *Wow. This is what home feels like.*

"We're hitting up the prank meeting tonight." Cole nods, triumphant, like Franklin asserting the superiority of the *Explorer* yesterday.

"Are you pranking me right now?" I ask. "Because in the words of Miss Demeanor, that's very meta."

"Shhh!" Cole presses his fingers to his temples. "I'm pretending I didn't just hear you admit to reading Miss Demeanor, and you're agreeing to my idea instead."

"Dude. We can't show up at a group thing, like, *together.*"

"You're shooting me down, Luce. We talked about this."

"Have you *seen* my fan page?" I bang the locker with my fist. "This crap?"

"Yeah, but we can rise above." He takes one of my braids in his fingers, rolls it absently. "You know that old saying, if you can't beat 'em—"

"Join 'em by giving them more photo ops for the poster project? Good plan."

"That's not . . . Okay. You know that scene in *Walking Dead* when Rick and Glenn go zombie undercover in that dude's guts?" He drops the braid and reaches for the coffee, takes another swig. This time he balances the cup on his knee when he's done, nestled perfectly in a hole in his jeans. "Something tells me you're not getting the 'joining' metaphor here."

"It's possible you've misinterpreted that scene," I say. "Not surprising, coming from a self-professed zombie 'dabbler.'"

Cole raises an eyebrow.

"That scene functions on multiple levels," I say. "From a plot perspective, they needed to get to the truck without calling attention to themselves. By wrapping themselves in guts, they could trick the zombies long enough to get past the horde."

"But what about—"

"Symbolically, it was a spiritual turning point. They had to die a metaphorical death—become zombies themselves, temporarily—so they could be reborn into a world where the dead walk and the living are losing their humanity. It was one of the last scenes where they still treated the zombies as humans, as lives cut short by a freak accident. That's why they checked the dead guy's license before they gutted him and said he was an organ donor."

"Um . . . I still think there was some joining going on."

I shake my head. "Rick didn't willingly lead his man into a horde just so he could show those zombies he was above it all. He did it to save their lives."

"But—"

"If you really want a metaphor, in Rick's new world, death has become life, and the real monsters aren't the flesh-eating zombies, but the living, who've de-evolved to base survival mode because they can't face the reality of death. The reason people are fascinated by zombies isn't the gore, but the fact that we live our lives in a coma, walking around like we're already dead, kept in check only by the systems and laws."

"You've given this a lot of—"

"Rick and his crew struggle not only to survive, but to hold on to their humanity, the only thing that separates them from the literal walking dead. It's not unlike high school, which is a metaphor for the popularity contest of life. So do you want me to go on? I could do this all day." I take back my coffee and down the last of it, and Cole's just grinning, melting my heart into a pile of goo.

He lets out a low whistle as I crush the empty cup against the floor. "I think my decaf plan has merit," he says. "And necessity."

"Unlike the prank meeting."

Cole sighs, and for a few minutes we sit in silence, the school awakening around us: Teachers scuttle to classrooms, lights flick on, cell phones chirp to life. The first wave of students trickles in from the bus drop, and Cole nudges my knee with his, our peace meeting its end.

Farther down the corridor, someone props the main doors open, students and sunshine filing in from the courtyard. The commotion momentarily distracts us, but when our eyes meet again, Cole's focus is intense, unflinching.

"I miss my favorite groupie," he says, and I shiver, hopefully unnoticed. "I can't just pretend it didn't mean . . . You know I'm torn up about Ellie, but what? I'm supposed to act like I hate you just because everyone's talking shit?"

I tip my head against the locker and close my eyes. Maybe he's right. Before all this, it's not like we didn't pal around in the woods with the dogs or swap notes from shared classes. It's not like I didn't pass by his garage in the summer on my bike, hang out while he banged on the drums.

Maybe if we go to the meeting like normal, show them we won't be cowed into hiding by rumors and name-calling . . . maybe that's the key to fixing this mess.

"Come with me tonight," Cole says, triumphant once again. He grabs his drumsticks, taps me on the knee. "We'll sit in the back and make inside jokes about their ideas to laugh at for years to come."

"Gee, you really know how to impress a girl."

"This is A-game stuff. Take it or leave it." Cole rises and stretches out his hand to give me a lift, and I take it. He sees the resigned *yes* in my smile and gives my hand a quick squeeze. "Pick you up at seven. Wear something . . ." He wiggles his eyebrows, backing up toward his homeroom. "Pranky."

"Really thought you'd go with 'gutsy' there."

"Ooh." He points at me with the drumsticks, his smile infectious. "Decaf, Vacarro. Look it up."

Cole, John, and I reconvene at my locker during lunch to finish clearing the posters. For most of the afternoon, other than a few shoulder bumps and the ongoing arctic freeze-out from Ellie and Griff, Lav-Oaks seems content to put the scandal on snooze.

Jayla makes pad Thai for dinner—score—and for dessert I receive a new Facebook alert: a photo essay, making its bid for Pulitzer Prize for Breaking News Photography, tagged to me with love from Olivia on the Juicy Lucy page.

The album is a fifteen-shot series of me and Cole drinking coffee this morning, complete with extensive commentary from my many endearing fans.

OLIVIA: Here they are practically DOING IT in the hallway.

JACKSON (VAMPIRE): Class it up, bro.

JOHN: I'm only joining this RIDIC page to say—stay out of it. Cole & Lucy are my peeps.

SPENCE: Only joining to say—what he said ^ ^

CLARICE: Only joining to say—John, maybe u should worry about your OWN pants (or lack thereof) instead of what's going on in Cole's.

JOHN: Why are u so obsessed w/ what's in my pants?

MARGO: Only joining to say—u guys I totally wasn't
   making out with Prince Freckles in the living
   room. We were having a moment. Lucy I hope u
   die or at least get an uncomfortable rash.

OLIVIA: Bwahahah I'm sure she already has a rash.

JOHN: Srsly? U guys need to back off. Lucy didn't do it.

HALEY: Why should we back off when that skank put
   our private biz online? I'm grounded 4 evs. Sorry,
   no sympathy from the prisoners.

QUINN: If my parentals were on FB, I'd be dead 2. I
   stand with the prisoners. Solidarity!

REN (VAMPIRE): Bros before hos, Lucy. Or whatever
   the chick version of that saying is.

OLIVIA: *fistbumps Haley & Quinn* Fight the power!
   The SLUT power! lol

JACKSON: Some people just like attention. Oh did
   u see pics of me & zombie Farrah? We were
   WASTED, bro. HILARIOUS.

REN: Mmmm. Zombie Farrah . . .

HALEY: Back on point . . . Juicy Lucy, give her a squeeze!

There's another two pages of fascinating conversation,
but before I reach the satisfying conclusion, the chat box
pings with an invite from Franklin.

FRANKLIN: Saw u sign in. Ur not doing what I think
    ur doing, r u?

LUCY: If u think I'm thoroughly depressing myself
    by reading nasty comments from so-called
    classmates on a fan page of their own making,
    then . . . no. Totally not.

FRANKLIN: Watch this video. Always cheers me up,
    esp. at the 2:04 mark.

LUCY: K. Watching now . . . Please hold for
    expressions of cheer . . . .

LUCY: !!! :-) Switching to inbox to message u.

From: Lucy Vacarro

Dear Franklin,

    Baby owls? *Whoooo* knew you were such
a softy? Never before have I seen so much
onscreen cuteness. I say we adopt them for
"research purposes." We can raise them in
the stables—I'm sure the horses won't mind.
Seriously, thank you. It helped. Truly. :)

    Cole and I have decided to adopt the old
standby—if you can't beat 'em, join 'em. Will we
see you at the prank meeting tonight?

                        —Slightly Less Vilified

From: Franklin Margolis

Dearest SLV,

I really am a softy at heart—don't let my urbane sophistication and stylishly unkempt Jewfro fool you. So glad I could make you smile. Sadly, you and your compatriots will have to mastermind your evil plots without me. I'm severely allergic to anything group project. Prince Freckles suggested I might have a superiority complex, and perhaps he's right, because my response to the accusation was, "What do you know? You're just a horse." And he replied, "Neeeaaayyy!"

In any case, hold your head high tonight.

Shall we lunch tomorrow with our four-legged friend? You can update me on the meeting. Off the record, of course.

—Prankster by Proxy

From: Lucy Vacarro

Dear P-by-P,

Lunch tomorrow it is. I'll have a word with Prince Freckles about his manners. He means well, but sometimes he can be a bit blunt.

Off to the slaughterhouse!

—SLV

HORROR MOVIE SURVIVAL TIP: SHE WHO INVESTIGATES NOISES IN THE BASEMENT IN HER UNDERWEAR CARRYING ONLY A FLASHLIGHT SHALL BE DISAPPOINTED AND/OR KILLED

It's weird to show up at a firing squad with mini bundts, right?"

I wasn't planning on group treats, but when I told Jayla about the prank meeting, she agreed with Cole's joining-in philosophy (so much for sticking it to the ass-vampires) and insisted on "making something" for me. Translation: running out to Bundt Heads and ordering six dozen minis, then dousing them with gold sprinkles and presenting them with her usual wide-eyed flourish. "Lucy, I totally made these!"

Now, Cole balances the tower of bakery boxes in one hand, his other hand on my shoulder as we cross the school lot, damned leading the damned. "Unconventional, maybe."

"She's taking the parenting thing too far," I say. "Yesterday I found a fiber bar in my lunch."

"It's important to be regular."

"It's important that we never discuss this again."

"What do your *actual* parents think?" he asks.

"Talked to them yesterday—totally laissez-faire. Mom's thrilled that Jayla's quote unquote taking an interest."

Cole squeezes my shoulder. "You still mad about last summer?"

"Honestly? She's being pretty cool." I tell him about the shopping spree, the cooking, how she covered for me with Zeff. "She even gave Night a bubble bath last night," I say. "Lemon ginger. He smells like tea. He's basically in love with himself now."

"Spike will be all over him," Cole says. "So the infamous Angelica Darling has an actual heart under those perky little . . . clothes!" He twists to dodge my punch, cracking up. "I was gonna say clothes!"

"And I was gonna pelt you with bundts, but since we've reached our destination, you get to live another day. Celebrate life!" I wrench open the emergency exit doors, perpetually unlocked and unalarmed. At the end of the corridor is the entrance to the auditorium, also unguarded. It's unlikely that Principal Zeff isn't aware of the "secret" annual senior prank meeting, but there haven't been any

decent hijinks since the 1972 Swimming of the Burros—
yes, donkeys in the pool—so tonight's assembled brain
trust is low on the threat list.

The aud doors are propped open, seniors being admitted one at a time by an underclassman with frizzy blond
curls and a clipboard. Inside, a few dozen kids are already
bumbling around the aisles, texting and gasping, slack-
jawed, directionless.

Olivia's there, surgically attached to Quinn and Haley.
They stop whispering just long enough to give us the triple
death glare.

"God," I say to Cole, louder than necessary. "Remember when Olivia Barnes was nice?" I'm half joking, more
defensive than snarky, but Cole's face reveals only regret.
He doesn't have to say what's on his mind; deep down, I
feel it too. Olivia was mortified by those pictures, ashamed
to face her own parents, and all evidence points to me. Of
course she's not blowing kisses.

Cole's heavy sigh says, *Maybe this wasn't such an awesome
fun idea after all. . . .*

We press on regardless.

When we reach the doorway, Clipboard Girl shoots
out her arm like a barricade. "You're not on the list."

"We're on the list," Cole says. "We're seniors."

Her eyes narrow. "I know who you are, Cole Foster."

"Great!" Cole shifts the bakery boxes from one hand to the other. "And you are . . ."

"Margo Hennessy's intern." She's wearing a pink tee that says STAFF across the front in red letters, and she points to it with her pen, as if this explains everything. "With strict orders not to let you in. Margo doesn't want any"—her eyes rake my body, lingering on my red platform flip-flips—"disturbances."

Disturbances? Margo's the one who got way past the *I Love You, Man* stage with Prince Freckles and a bottle of her namesake bourbon.

"You're excluding two people from the whole class?" Cole's voice is even, but his ears are red, his shoulders taut.

"Discrimination much?" I say.

"Since it's not a school-sanctioned event, no." Intern steps aside to let a few other seniors enter, no one I know. "And those (e)VIL people can't come either. Margo says they ask too many questions."

"Whatever," I snap. "We'll just . . . go somewhere else and have a private . . . prank party. And we've got six dozen mini bundts, *with* sprinkles, and we're not sharing a single one."

Intern rolls her eyes. "Dial it down, rage-a-holic. I'm not the one who slept with my best friend's boyfriend and posted pictures of it on Facebook instead of, like, admitting it to her face."

"*Excuse* me?" I'm about to say something that'll knock the curl out of her hair, but Cole grabs my arm and pulls me down the corridor, back the way we came. He doesn't stop until we're in the parking lot, and in the low orange sun my anger evaporates.

"Dude." I narrow my eyes at him, barely containing a laugh. "Did we just get bounced from a fake school function by a fake intern with a clipboard?"

He rubs his head with a free hand, hair sticking out like dark tumbleweeds. "Moving on to plan b. Follow me."

"We can't sneak in—they're expecting it. We're, like, official *disturbers* of the peace."

"We came to rise above, Vacarro." Cole's smile, a perpetual invitation to some madcap adventure, captures me in its irresistible current. "Rise we will."

"You're very literal tonight," I say through a mouthful of honey-vanilla bundt cake.

Cole and I have risen above, as promised, and we're watching the sun melt behind the front range, legs dangling over the ledge of the school roof. Zeff surely has a policy against this, but no one saw us climb the fire ladder, and no one knows we're here.

The Lav-Oaks campus is much more peaceful from a distance.

"If we're back on metaphors," Cole says, "I now understand the comparison between high school and the zombie apocalypse." He sticks out his arms and moans, a slack-jawed impersonation of our classmates. "Pranks, praaaaanks!"

"I *wish*. If they were actual zombies, I'd know how to defeat them."

"Makes one of us." Cole scoops out a red velvet bundt from the box, wolfs it down in a single bite. "I could handle basic survival—purify water, build a shelter out of tree boughs. But zombie combat? I'd need serious training."

"Rule number one?" I say. "Stay together. You split up, you die."

"Stay together." He licks the crumbs from his fingers. "Go on."

"Flamethrower is my weapon of choice."

Cole's eyebrows jump. "Really? I always figured you as an ax-to-the-face kinda girl."

"Well, yeah, for really close combat. Shovel works too."

"Shotgun?"

"Totally."

"What about those bottle things where you stuff in a rag and light 'em up?" Cole's arm arcs over our heads, and we both look out across the soccer field, waiting for the explosion.

"Mollies," I say. "Sure." My eyes are fuzzy in the dying

orange light, blurred and content. I don't bother adjusting them. "Bowling ball. Golf club. Wooden leg. Use what you've got."

"Good to know, and by the way, you don't *really* wanna waste the senior class, right, Vacarro?" He elbows me and leans close, breath hot as the sun on my bare neck. "Just in case the spy satellites are rolling."

I exaggerate my laugh to hide the shiver that inevitably follows Cole's closeness. "Of course not, Foster. This is strictly theoretical, Break-Glass-In-Emergency–type stuff."

He shoves in a chocolate bundt, crumbs dotting his gray Led Zeppelin tee. He brushes them off, smiling when he catches me watching, and in the setting sun his eyes give off their coppery glow. For a moment I close my eyes, tell myself it's real. That I called Ellie four years ago, the first day I saw Cole in the woods with Spike, and told her right then: *I think I really like this new boy.*

Cole doesn't say anything else, content to eat bundts and watch the jagged purple horizon, and in the comfortable silence between us, my thoughts drift to Ellie. It's like I can feel her friendship slipping away, and in the death of it, its life flashes before my eyes.

There's this nacho cheesefest of a musical called *The Mermaid of Crystal Cove*, and in sixth grade, our music teacher, Miss Killian, decided we'd perform it. The entire class had to participate onstage, like, singing and dancing.

I was a walrus. I had a bulky burlap costume with paper towel rolls for tusks, and my job was to crawl to the middle of the stage, flap my fins, and recite four lines:

> There lives a maiden in the deep blue sea
> With scales like a fish and a tail like me
> With shimmering shells in her raven hair
> And a coral throne in an underwater lair

Jayla was already in California by then, but she practiced on the phone with me every night for a month, until I could recite it forward and back.

On opening night, when it came time for my fin-flapping debut, I froze.

Miss Killian nudged me toward center stage, but I couldn't move. Stiff and ashamed, I hugged myself with my burlap fins and braced for the dramatic wreckage, for everything to fall apart.

Nothing did. When Killian's efforts failed, she simply shouted my lines from the wings, and everyone kept on singing.

The mermaid, star of the show, found me backstage after. The others had cleared out, met up with their parents for congratulatory ice cream or whatever, but I looked up through watery eyes and there she was, all sea green and silver sparkles, shells in her hair like pale-pink jewels.

"What happened to you?" she asked. "Stage fright?"

I nodded.

"I kept waiting for you out there, but you didn't come."

I shrugged, not sure what to say.

"Well." She seemed to consider my costume, the whole sad little lump of me, and then she said, "My moms are taking me to Cold Stone. They have this ice cream, brownie batter? You're coming with us."

She held out her hand and pulled me up, and just like that, I had a friend. After that, it didn't matter that I didn't shimmer and shine, that my sister took center stage in my parents' eyes, that I never had group sleepovers or birthday parties for fear that someone would find out about Jayla and use me to get close to her or worse, make fun of our family. I made myself invisible, mostly, and that was okay; I was never invisible to Ellie.

That's why I agreed to go to prom. Despite my reservations, I accepted without question. I'd do anything for her, and she'd do anything for me, and the thought of Cole or anyone else coming between us sends a hot blade through my insides.

"I'm worried about her too," Cole says, sensing the direction of my daydreams. His voice is confident but soothing, eyes full of understanding and hope. "She needs time, Lucy."

"Maybe," I say, but my voice floats away untethered, disappearing behind the mountains. Cole knows Ellie almost as well as I do, but he's not a girl. He doesn't know the unspoken rule about boyfriends, ex or otherwise. The line best friends are never supposed to cross.

The pictures told Ellie I slept with him.

I snag another bundt cake, red velvet this time, and nibble along the edge, thoughts ping-ponging from the cabin, the kiss, Ellie, Cole, back to the kiss, our UCLA plans, back to the cabin. It's bad enough that my Facebook profile got everyone at the party in trouble, but the whole school thinks I slept with Cole, that I broke them up. Even people I don't know, like Margo's intern and all the crosstown randos on the Juicy Lucy fan list.

Miss Demeanor advised the wronged party to fully investigate things before ending a friendship. But if Ellie believes that I broke the unspoken rule and then, like Margo's intern said, posted the evidence for her to find on Facebook, there's no way she's going all Veronica Mars on my account.

If I want the truth to set me free, I have to track it down myself.

By the time Ellie and I hit the road to Cali this fall, my #scandal needs to be a distant, cautionary tale, a minor detour on the otherwise long and scenic friendship high-way. My feelings for Cole, sadly but inevitably, will sink into the well of my heart; my favorite memory, my most deeply cherished secret.

"The three of us," Cole says, "have been together too long not to figure this out." He tucks a braid behind my ear, smiling his triumphant smile. The touch lingers on my neck, memories of the kiss feathering my lips. . . .

Behind us there's a rapid *click-click-click-click*, and then a spotlight blinks on, bathing us in an accusatory glow.

I rocket launch to my feet.

Cole's laughing, unfazed, still perched casually on the ledge. "Security lights. They're on timers."

"Now you tell me." Paranoid much? God. My heart's all, *wooo!* Who knew sneaking up to the Lav-Oaks school roof with my best friend's ex and a metric ton of baked goods would be such an adrenaline rush?

"You're thinking again," Cole says. "It's in your eyes."

"I kind of . . . I might have a plan," I say. "For Ellie. Well, not so much a plan as a collection of goals." I return to my spot on the ledge next to him. "Ellie needs proof that I didn't post those pictures and that you and I didn't . . . that it wasn't . . . that it was just kissing. Basically." I take a deep breath, cool the spiraling heat. "But I can't expect *her* to find the proof, right? That's on me."

"Us." Cole's leaning back on his hands, face turned toward the pink sky.

"Us," I say. "So we smoke out the perp, force a confession, clear our names, and expose the . . . dastardly plot?" Undetected, my eyes trace the shape of his lips, the scruff along his jaw. The curve where it meets his ear looks warm and soft. Touchable.

"There's a dastardly plot?" he asks.

"If you guys are plotting," a familiar voice says, "count me in."

"Griffin?" I turn to catch her cresting the top of the ladder. Guilt radiates down my spine as she hauls herself onto the roof, and I immediately scold myself. We're not doing anything wrong up here, anything worthy of guilt.

Are we?

"Ellie's got a movie date with the moms, so I figured I'd crash the prankage, see if I could spice things up. Wrong-o." She kicks off her ballet flats and sits next to me on the ledge. "They're talking about camping. Where's the mischief in that?"

Movie date. How could I forget? Heather and Kathy, Ellie's moms, planned it weeks ago. Girls night out, Heather said, for me and my mom too. They missed their Texas firecracker, Kathy said. Hadn't seen Mom in months.

Ellie teased them about setting up mommy playdates once we left for college.

I fake a yawn, a logical explanation for the fresh tears, and rub my eyes.

"How'd you know we were up here?" Cole asks.

"Followed the trail," she says. "I stopped by Lucy's, but Jayla told me you guys were already here. Staff Sergeant Buzzkill down there gave me the lowdown on your D-list status, so I checked the gym, the art room, the playground, and finally deduced the last possible location. Also, I totally saw your feet. Are those mini bundts?"

"That was . . . thorough." Cole passes me a box, and Griff and I both dig in. Cole takes another one too.

"So what's this about a plan?" she asks, scrutinizing the user-modified sprinkles on her chocolate bundt. "The sooner we put an end to this epic mopefest, the better. I'm all, 'Ellie, just call her!' I'm getting, like, depression by osmosis."

She shovels in the bundt, kicking her heels against the side of the building like it's just another day, just three pals hanging on the roof, chatting about the good times. It's almost . . . nice. Normal. Part of me resents the recent stonewallage, but neurotic BFF jealousy aside, I'm glad she's been there for Ellie. And now she's here with me, no judgments, no told-you-so snark.

"Still working out the logistics," I tell her, "but

CliffsNotes version? We're gonna smoke out the perp, expose the truth, and win Ellie back."

"Sounds like a party." She takes another bundt from the box and shrugs. "I'm in."

"*Salud*," Cole says. The three of us clink our bundts together, not quite as scandalous as it sounds, and down them in a collective snarf.

"But truefax?" Griff says. "I know *jack* about being a detective."

"Holla." Cole gives her a crumb-covered fist bump.

"We're in luck," I say. "I know just the guy."

TIME TO GO KEITH & VERONICA ON THIS BITCH

So that's where you come in."

I just finished updating Franklin on our rooftop plan-hatchery, and now I flop on my bed, phone pressed to ear, a lemon-ginger pooch snuggling beside me.

Franklin's sigh whistles across the wireless wires. "Why does this sound suspiciously like a group project?"

"We're doing all the work," I say. "We just need some pointers. Like, investigative journalism tips. Detecting 101 stuff."

"You've gone Veronica Mars."

"I was thinking Buffy. Well, more like Faith. Dark slayer, side of angst, hold the perk?"

"You're solving a crime, not slaying demons. Veronica is clearly the better analogy." Franklin's still sighing, but we both know that this is the most exciting action to come his way since sophomore year's black Jell-O exposé, which turned out to be the result of Cook Ethyl combining the powdered cherry and lime mixes and not, as we'd all hoped, a school-shutdown-worthy contamination.

"Lucy," he says, "how certain are you that the incriminating photographs were even uploaded from your phone?"

"Positive. I hardly ever used Facebook—only logged on from home and my phone. And the phone is MIA. Cole searched the cabin after they cleaned up, even out by the pond. Someone nabbed it."

There's a muffled groan, followed by the sound of papers rustling and then the unmistakable *click-clack* of a keyboard. "Not that I'm getting involved in these shenanigans, but if I were, the first thing I'd do is compile a list of attendees."

"Cole knew everyone there," I say. "It wasn't a ginormous bash or anything. Maybe thirty or forty?"

"Good, that limits potential suspects. Your last name has two Rs, correct?"

I sit up in bed, startling Night from his nap. He gives me a clipped bark—his version of an eye roll—and trots away, curling up under my desk instead. "This isn't on the record, is it?"

"Of course not." Even his long pauses sound British. "Just jotting a few notes."

I relax. Unlike #TRENDZ, Franklin doesn't seem like the type to trick his sources. He does, however, seem to enjoy taking notes. Must be a detective thing. I grab the iPad from my nightstand and launch the Notes app, pleased to find a non-Fruit Ninja use for Jayla's investment.

"Two Rs," I confirm.

"Great," he says. "Next, I'd compile a report of the entire night, omitting nothing. Where you went, interactions you had, the last time you remember seeing your phone, whether anyone was acting out of sorts—"

"Franklin. Half the people were dressed like fairies."

"More out of sorts than usual," he clarifies. "No detail is insignificant. You never know what dots might be connected from seemingly random occurrences."

I tap a few lines into the iPad. "Go on."

"You'll need visual evidence. Get on Facebook and download copies of the party photos to your hard drive. You'll want to enlarge them and look for background clues: shadows, reflections, people's clothing, time indicators, anything that might offer a hint about who took them, who *couldn't* have taken them, and who else might've been around."

"Shadows, reflections, indicators . . . totally." I thumb it all onto my iPad in a bulleted list. It occurs to me that high school sleuthing wasn't what Jayla had in mind when she bought this, or what Apple had in mind when they invented it, but it's a surprisingly versatile tool. I can only imagine what Veronica Mars could've done with it. She'd be head of the CIA by now.

"Using the attendee list, the report, and the photographic evidence," Franklin says, "you'll narrow down suspects by cross-referencing the guest list with the names of anyone at school who might have a reason to humiliate you and Cole." *Tap-tap-tap* goes his keyboard. "Or a reason to frame you as a narc."

I wince at the word, but it makes sense, and two suspects jump to the top of the list: Olivia and Clarice.

Clarice has always hated me, and Olivia's always had a thing for Cole. She was in the doorway when Cole bolted into the house after our kiss. Moments earlier, she could've seen us, snapped the first incriminating picture. She outed herself with the Mike's Lemonade acrobatics, but that could've been a setup, all part of her master plan.

There's also the vampire-zombie couple that Cole kicked out of the bathroom. People get touchy about interrupted make-out sessions, and they might be gunning for vengeance. Not to mention Paul St. Paul. Griff slipped him the Tarts of Apology Sunday morning; he could be trashing her friends to get even.

And John . . . maybe he's more upset about the career-ruining nudies than he let on, and he only helped me with the locker posters to throw me off his scent. Then there's Spence. Cole was pretty pissed about him kidnapping Prince Freckles—maybe they had an argument. And what about Marceau? I left him high and dry after our kiss, and if I've learned anything from Angelica Darling, it's that scorned lovers make motivated enemies.

That's not even counting all the random people at the party who have no attachment or loyalty to me whatsoever, people who could've just cashed in a last-ditch, out-with-a-bang opportunity on Miss Demeanor's #scandal page. . . .

This investigative stuff is a lot harder than it looks on TV.

"Once you've got your evidence in order," Franklin says, "we'll start interviewing suspects and witnesses."

"Awesome. I'll—did you say *we?*"

"Quid pro quo, love." He lets the comment simmer, still typing. Then he says, "If I help you, perhaps you'll grant me that interview."

Now I'm the one sighing. He's already given me such great advice—I'd love to return the favor. But this isn't a crusade. It's a plan to get my friend back. I'm not Jayla, eager to plaster my life all over the media world, online or off.

"Franklin," I say, "what if I could score you an interview with Jayla Heart instead?"

It takes about a year for him to stop laughing, and then he says, "Even if that were possible, you'd have better luck pitching that to your mate Miss Demeanor."

Little does he know, Jay's in my kitchen right now, communing with her many online fans.

"You're not interested?" I ask.

"In Jayla Heart? Goodness, no. However . . ." Franklin's typing again, fast and furious. "What about a compromise? Something that won't require you to go on record?"

"I'm listening."

"I'll grant you and your team full access to my investigative services," he says. "In exchange, you'll allow me to do a story based on our findings. No direct quotes, no interviews, just facts."

"Investigative services?" I ask. "I thought you didn't do group projects."

"This isn't a group project," he says. "It's a case."

Across the room, Night lifts his head, snapping his jaw in an epic yawn. Without warning, he darts forth like a streak of black lightning and dive-bombs my bed in the most ungraceful way possible. I give him a playful shove. "I'm not made of Snausages, you oaf!"

Franklin laughs.

"My dog," I explain. "He's, like, mauling me. Night! Cool out!" I ditch the iPad and rearrange my legs under ninety pounds of German shepherd. Night puts his head in my lap, not budging, and I lean back against the pillows, closing my eyes.

When I called Franklin tonight, it was just to get a few pointers, some ideas on how to investigate a hacker. I never expected him to get involved—I'm not even sure he realizes what he's signing up for.

"You really want to partner with a known philanderer and narc?" I ask. "Your credibility could take a hit."

"I'm getting a story out of this, love." Franklin's voice is kind but matter-of-fact. "Exposing injustice. Setting the record straight for all concerned. It's what I live for, Veronica."

"Faith," I say. "Dark slayer?"

"Sorry. You have to be Veronica so I can be Keith."

"Keith? Shouldn't you be all, rah-rah Sherlock Holmes?" I laugh. "You turncoat! You're a traitor to your nation."

He gasps indignantly, and I picture his sharp brown eyes, the crazy curly hair. A mad, eccentric genius awash in the glow of his computer screen. "No Keith, no Veronica, no investigation."

I scratch Night's belly. "You won't let it go, right?"

"Not likely, sweetheart." His accent has gone noir. "We're gonna solve this crime, see, and nail the perp to the wall, see."

Night sighs in my lap, and for the first time since the scandal broke, I feel a shred of hope that we might actually solve this thing. That I might actually get my best friend back.

"Here's the deal," I say. "I'll give you Keith and Veronica, and your story, and you promise to never do that accent again."

Franklin laughs. "Looks like we've got ourselves an investigation, Veronica."

LONE GUNMAN THEORY SHOT
TO HELL

Narc! Narc! Narc! Narc! Narc! Narc! Narc!"

The maroon-and-gray corridor grew a mile overnight, and the chant echoes endlessly as I walk to homeroom. No one touches me, but they're throwing wads of wet paper and gum, shooting rubber bands and nasty glares. Their catcalls intensify as I pick up the pace, and the electronic *click-click* of a dozen cameras reminds me of Jayla, swarmed and flashbulbed on her way to some celeb hot spot.

"Narc! Narc! Narc!" from my left. "Slut! Slut! Slut!" from my right, this one led by Quinn and Haley. Olivia isn't chanting, but she's behind them, arms folded, her delicate face twisted into a scowl.

"Slut! Narc! Slut! Narc!" The rhythmic cheer ping-pongs from one side of the hall to the other, swirls into a new refrain. "Slarc! Slarc! Slarc!"

Bouts of laughter roll and froth like waves as I zoom past my locker. There's a fresh batch of posters, and though I'd love to stop and shred them, stopping means facing the mob. It means looking them in the eyes as they call me names and throw erasers at my head. It means letting them see me cry.

Definitely not on my bucket list.

I walk faster still, almost at a jog, ignoring the masses and the spitballs in my hair. Ellie's homeroom is a few doors before mine; we see each other as I pass. Our eyes lock.

She breaks the connection and drops to the floor, digging in her bag.

I offer a belated smile anyway.

This ends tonight.

Cole's making a list of party attendees and Griffin's using her feminine wiles to interview the guys, including Paul St. Paul, even though he's still nursing his broken heart. Jayla's on the case at home, alternating her teen boy fan mail review with careful scrutiny of the Juicy Lucy page for potentially incriminating commentary. Franklin and I are meeting at lunch to review the evidence.

Not even spitballs can chase away the hope, and four

minutes into homeroom, when I discover that an HD video of me cowering beneath the hallway slarc attack has already popped up on the Juicy Lucy page, it only steels my resolve.

With just three weeks until graduation, most teachers have given up on wireless device discipline, and I spend my morning classes examining party photos on my iPad, re-creating the events in a list for Franklin.

By lunchtime I'm ready to rock, and finding Franklin bent over his keyboard in the computer lab is like watching the sun rise after a tornado-black sky.

"Prepare to be wowed," I announce as I drop into the chair next to him. "Or at least mildly impressed." I flip open the iPad cover to reveal my starter report.

"E-mail that to me?" Franklin asks. "We should centralize everything. It's an encrypted file," he explains when he sees my freaked-out face. "I'm the only one who can access it. Promise."

"What about the NSA?"

Franklin considers the question, then shakes his head. "Highly probable they've got more interesting scandals to investigate. And fear not, Veronica." He continues typing. "I won't print anything in the *Explorer* that makes you uncomfortable. You have my word."

Satisfied, I tap his e-mail into the iPad, send the notes

into space. An instant later, he enters a password on his keyboard, and the file pops up on his monitor.

He scrolls through my report. "You left the cabin first thing that morning?"

"I wanted to bail before anyone else woke up," I say. "Didn't want to be there for the 'best night of my life' stories and hangover commiseration."

"Precisely why I skipped prom," he says.

"Yeah, well, it wasn't my idea of a good time either." I tell him about Ellie and the Rent-a-Princess gig. "I know how it looks, but I wasn't plotting to hook up with my best friend's—"

"Hey." Franklin's steady gaze is unchanged. "You don't owe me an explanation, Lucy. We're a team. Can you trust me?"

It's a simple enough question with a simple enough answer. Yes, I *can* trust him. He's trustworthy, and he's been nothing but decent since this whole thing started—even before it started. We've never hung out, but Franklin's just a good guy. No cliquey allegiances, no drama. Smart but never superior. Everyone likes him.

Still, it's been a long time since I let anyone in. Ellie, at the mermaid play. And Cole, because when you fall that hard for someone, trust is part of the package. The last person I got close to was Griffin, and I haven't even let *her* in a hundred percent.

Franklin's waiting patiently, fingers resting on the keyboard.

Still, I don't answer.

He swivels his chair toward me, our knees almost touching. "I know it's difficult," he says softly. "But we've got to review the evidence. Notes, photographs, Facebook comments. It's embarrassing for you. But I mean it, love. No judgments."

My chest fills with fear, but he's right. We can't really investigate this if I don't open up. I have to share the evidence. Let him in. Show him my scars, admit my mistakes.

Last summer, Cole invited me, John, and Ellie on a camping trip with his dad. Ellie's not a roughing-it kinda girl, but she put on her game face. Each day, we took short walks in the woods, played cards, and read books beneath the trees. At night we roasted marshmallows and sang camp songs, and then Ellie and I snuggled in our sleeping bags in the girls tent, trying to outscare each other with ghost stories.

On the fourth day, Cole's father went on a solo hike, and Cole led the rest of us on a trek up Mount Elbert, the highest peak in Colorado. We started before sunrise and hiked all morning. Halfway up, Ellie and I were falling apart. Ellie's knees ached, and I peed on my hiking boots, and at each step above tree line we struggled for breath, desperate to turn back. But Cole and John encouraged us onward, and when we finally reached the summit, we were like the literal walking dead.

Out of nowhere, Ellie threw up her arms and shouted, "Girl power! We made this mountain our bitch!" She launched herself at me in a triumphant embrace, and the two of us laughed and cried, singing Gloria Gaynor's "I Will Survive" at 14,440 feet above sea level.

Then we saw lightning in the distance, a freak storm, a crack of thunder as the clouds shifted over the sun. Cole was all, "Time to go!" We hightailed it down the mountain, chased by thunder and rain, not daring to stop until we got back to camp.

It was the most challenging, exhilarating, and terrifying thing ever.

Until right now.

"I trust you," I tell Franklin. "It's just . . . I haven't told anyone about that night."

Franklin turns back to the computer, pulls up the #scandal album on the Miss Demeanor page. "It's okay. Just pretend it isn't you. Be objective. Ready?"

"I'm ready." I have to be. I have to solve this. For me. For Ellie. For another breathless rendition of "I Will Survive."

Franklin clicks on the photo of me and Cole in bed. I was expecting it, but it still takes my breath away, a rush of guilt and desire and the memory of everything that happened, photographed and not. I close my eyes, trying to decide how much to share, how much to bury.

I muster just enough nerve to explain my argument with Cole after the kiss, all the words that led us to his bedroom, to Cole telling me they'd broken up.

"And after the discussion, you turned in?" Franklin asks.

"First Cole went downstairs to check on things. I asked him to tell Griffin I was crashing and to get my phone." It's coming back to me now, flashes and pieces knitting together. "I left it outside on the deck."

My eyes are still closed, but I hear Franklin typing.

"The picture of you—of the subjects—kissing on the porch," he says, "there's a silver phone on the railing behind them. Is that yours?"

"Yes."

"Was that the last time you had it in your possession?"

"Yes. But I told Cole where I left it and . . ." Memories are coming faster now, fog lifting. Cole's words echo.

Trying to set your phone alarm . . .

"No. He brought my phone upstairs," I say. "It was after I'd gotten into bed. He came in, locked the door . . . there was a flash. He said he was setting the alarm so we could leave early, but . . . yes!" I open my eyes. "Look for a random shot of the dress at the end of the bed. He took it while he was messing with the alarm."

"Saw it," Franklin says. "You said he locked the door. . . . Was it unlocked in the morning?"

"I don't know. Cole opened it first. He was up just before me."

Franklin taps his lips with a pen. Typing, writing . . . there's no note this boy isn't prepared take. "If what you say is accurate," he says, "that leaves three possibilities. One, you or Cole intentionally set the camera timer and took the pictures yourselves. Ludicrous."

I'm not the one who slept with my best friend's boyfriend and posted pictures. . . .

I blink away the image of Margo's intern in her STAFF shirt. "Totally ludicrous. Two?"

"When Cole thought he set the alarm, he inadvertently set the photo timer. But that still means you posted the pictures yourselves, or another person later stole the phone and posted the pictures that you took." He shakes his head. "Scratch that—the simplest explanation is usually the right one. That leaves option three. Most simply, someone saw you in bed, saw the phone, saw an opportunity, and took it."

"For Miss Demeanor," I say.

"Right," he says. "But why would someone go to the

trouble? Even if he or she broke into Cole's room and took the pictures with your phone, that still leaves a lot of steps." He sticks the pen behind his ear, counts down with his fingers. "Photographing the other party guests. Realizing that the phone was linked to your Facebook account. Deciding to upload everything the next morning—presumably sober by then. That level of plotting indicates revenge, not just a simple prank. Someone had it out for you."

"But the lock. It's a slide bolt from the inside." I scootch closer to the monitor for another look at the image of me and Cole, scrutinizing every shadow, every pixel. . . . "The wings! There was a pair of pink fairy wings on the bed. I sat on them earlier and made a joke to myself about squishing my fairy godmother."

Franklin laughs. "Fairy godmother? Good Lord."

"Seriously. After I changed out of the dress, I draped it over the footboard with the wings. The composition looked funny. Like, a fairy tale gone naughty. I kind of wanted to sketch it."

Franklin leans over my shoulder and points to the monitor, the place on the photo where the wings should be but aren't. "Here?"

"They're gone. Even if they fell on the floor, I would've seen them in the morning when I grabbed the dress. Look." I click through the photos and find the one that Cole took accidentally, the bed with the dress hung over it. Sure enough, wings. Pink and glittery.

"The cabin was quiet when I got up," I say, still piecing it together. "I stayed in the clothes I slept in. Went to the bathroom, used some mouthwash . . . I went back and sat on the bed to put on my boots. No wings."

"Could someone have gone in while you were in the bathroom? Where was Cole?"

"He was already downstairs. I was in the bathroom, like, two minutes. I was in such a hurry to get home. I'm telling you, the place was silent. Cole and I were the only ones up, other than Spence, who'd left way earlier. He had to take Prince Freckles back to the stables."

"What happened next?"

"I looked around the dresser for my earrings, and . . . hat! Hat!" I bolt out of my chair, excitement flooding my limbs. It's like a legit investigation now, like we're actually fighting for truth and justice. "When Cole and I first went in, 420's hat was there, but it was gone in the morning."

"Maybe you just *thought* you heard Cole locking the door." Franklin grabs his pen again, pokes at his curls. "Maybe it was something else?"

"I heard it slide and click. I'm sure. When he came back, I was very, like, focused. Everything was amplified." I drop back into my chair.

"A bit shaky," he says. "It's possible you don't recall the exact order of events. To be fair, you were on the piss."

"On the . . . what?"

"Drunk," he explains. "Right?"

"Not *drunk*, but not sober. Still." I'm not shaky on this part. When Cole came back, he opened the door, closed it, locked it, changed clothes, set the alarm, got into bed. The alarm never went off because the phone was stolen in the middle of the night. Same with the wings—they're in the before picture, but not the one with me and Cole in bed, which means someone removed them *before* that photo was taken.

I recap it again for Franklin.

"But you're insisting no one could've gotten past the lock," he says.

"Right." The hat, the wings . . . My eyebrows shoot up with the realization. "They were already in. Must've been in Cole's closet when we got there and waited until we fell asleep before sneaking back out—420 and . . . I don't know. One of the fairies."

"You're saying they hung out in a closet the entire time? Without making a sound?"

"It's a walk-in," I say. "And it's the Fosters' vacation place, so it's not like Cole's got it stuffed with clothes. There's room. And we passed out right away."

At least, for a little while.

"Who was wearing wings that night?" he asks.

"Like, everybody. I think the only girls *not* wearing wings at prom were me, Griff, this one chick dressed like a troll, and Kiara. Kiara wasn't at the party, anyway." My neck burns, but I shake it off. Hopefully Ash reinstated her by now.

"Do you think whoever was in the closet took the photographs? Stole your phone?" Franklin's wearing Griff's baby veal face. I don't blame him; this story's getting weirder by the second.

"No . . . I guess not. If they were worried about getting caught, they wouldn't stop to take pictures. Their mission was to get out without getting busted. And 420 doesn't exactly have the brain cells of a criminal mastermind."

"Another dead end." Franklin rubs his eyes.

"Maybe, but if they were in there until we passed out, they might know if anyone else showed up, either trying to get in or just, like, skulking around the hall. And they can at *least* confirm the fact that Cole and I didn't . . . that while they were in there, things stayed totally . . . platonic." *Totally platonic.* It's a stretch, and the words are black-coffee bitter on my tongue, but I press on. "And they probably left the room separately, just to avoid suspicion. If anyone snuck into the room between their exit times . . ."

"Good point," Franklin says. "They might've seen something."

"One way to find out." I gather my stuff, prepping for my first official interrogation. "Can you meet after school for a debrief? I'll see if Cole and Griff can come."

"Definitely. But . . . you're sure 420 will talk? How well do you know him?"

"We've had some deep conversations, me and the old four-two-oh." I roll my eyes, but it's my first lead. I'm not giving up so easily. "Plus, I have evidence of *his* little scandal. Doubt his burner friends would go all high fives on him for hooking up with a sparkly fairy girl. He'll talk."

Franklin raises an eyebrow. "Blackmail? Didn't know you had it in you, Veronica."

"Don't think of it as blackmail, Keith. Think of it as graymail. Superlight gray. More like pale blue."

DELIVER US FROM (E)VIL

Report from the boy front." Griff barges into the computer lab after school and drops her stuff on a chair. "Did I just say 'report from the boy front'? Don't answer." She pulls her blond waves into a loose knot and continues in a determined breath. "News flash: A boy didn't do this."

"How do you figure?" Franklin asks, perpetually hammering the keyboard. We just finished debriefing on my dead-end 420 inquisitions—during which I was stared at blankly, offered Doritos, and dismissed in a cloud of smoke and giggles—and Franklin is still recording the details.

"I got the attendee list from Cole." Griff unfolds a

crumpled piece of notebook paper, smooths it out over her coral miniskirt. "Where is he?"

"Vanitas has practice today," I say. "We're supposed to text him with an update."

Griff taps the list. "I talked to fourteen guys from Lav-Oaks: John, Spence, the football vampires, 420, a few randos. The vamps ganged up and tried to jock block me, but a few innuendos and a side of cleavage later, they were eating out of my—"

"Griffin." I shoot her a glare. "Stay focused."

"I'm *totally* focused! I have a date with Brian this weekend," she says. "Or Ryan? Brian's the blond one, right? Ryan's the—"

"Thanks so much for the detailed analysis of the football team's hair," Franklin says over his shoulder, "but did you get any actual leads?"

"Sheesh. *Sorry*, Sherlock Holmes."

"He prefers Keith Mars," I say. "Don't ask."

"*Sorry*, Keith Mars." Griff flashes her patented flirty smirk—part fake-insulted and part dare-you-to-kiss-me. Behind Franklin's head, I mouth a "back off." Griffin thrives on a challenge, and the valedictorian would definitely be a new mountain to climb, but we can't derail the investigation on account of her unquenchable hormones.

Her attention returns to the list. "It's so obvious, Lucy.

Yeah, some of those guys put the douche in douche bag, but they're not schemers. It's one thing to make a dumb comment on Facebook. It's another thing entirely to stake you out at a party, steal your phone, take all these incriminating upload-ables, post them on your profile, tag stuff to Miss D, and frame you. Not to mention whoever started the Juicy page." She leans back in her chair and sticks out her chest. "Only another female could pull off this level of backstabby. Right?"

Franklin's still typing behind us. "On behalf of the Y chromosome, I'm offended at your lack of faith in our ability to scheme. However, your point is a valid one. Also, I don't believe 'backstabby' is a word."

"What about Paul?" I ask her.

"Called him at lunch. He's, like, boy-band-lyrics-level angsty over me, but he's not a schemer either. And I was with him all night, after everyone else was asleep in the living room. We were . . . *Anyway*. I know he didn't do it." She waves her hand in the air, erasing her memories of rolling around on the floor with Paul. "This thing has lady rage all over it."

I take her list and lean back in the chair, scrutinizing the names. The guys she's already interviewed have been crossed off, but the last one is circled. "Why is Marceau circled?"

Griff's eyes go wide. "Yes! Another interesting development. He wouldn't talk to me. Got all quiet and dodgy, walked away before I could press."

I lean forward into a cloud of her spicy perfume. "Do you think *he* did this?"

"Jealous lover, crimes of passion." She considers. "He's got the motive. Not to mention a great ass." Griff wriggles her eyebrows. "Still. Despite his qualifications, I stand by what I said. This isn't a boy's scandal."

"Marceau isn't a boy," I say. "I mean, he's a *boy*, but it's different. He's French."

"Canadian," Franklin says. "French Canadian. Subtle but important distinction."

"We have a foreign-exchange student from Canada?" Griff asks. "Who *does* that?"

"Lav-Oaks," Franklin says. "Obviously. So what's his deal? Why so shady, you think?"

Griff laughs. "He's not shady, Sherlock—I mean Keith—just in love with Lucy."

"Shut up! He's not—"

"Franklin. Ladies." Principal Zeff watches us from the doorway, arms crossed. "Just the people who can help."

Griff rises from her chair. "We *are* helping. We're helpers."

"Just wrapping up our final *Explorer* issue," Franklin says. "These two intrepid readers are my sounding boards."

Zeff smiles, her eyes lasering me. "I'm glad you're channeling your energies into something positive, Lucy." Smile vanishes, eyes narrow. "Come with me. All of you."

"They've been doing this at random locations all day," Zeff explains, ushering us across the gym. The prom-night disco balls have yet to be removed; they scatter diamonds of light across our faces as we pass.

"This is the fourth report I've gotten today," she says. "The teachers are nervous, but there's more to this than meets the eye." Zeff shoves open the emergency exit that leads to the soccer and lacrosse fields, and we follow her out. No alarm sounds. "They're asking for Lucy."

We squint in the bright sun. The competitive season is over, but the soccer team still uses the field for scrimmages, and they're out here now, Marceau included, staring at three students dressed in all white, head to toe.

(e)VIL has taken over center field.

"Are those . . . berets?" Franklin asks.

"And let's just go on record in saying that white pants favor few men," Griff says.

Marceau catches my eye and gives a small wave. Before I return it, Griff elbows me.

"Don't lead him on." To Zeff, she says, "I saw those guys in the caf today. They were doing some kind of dance, or a chant, but . . . I don't know. It's better if you tune them out."

"You agree that they're not posing a threat, then?" Zeff

whispers. She's gone all statue, like we're observing rare owls in the wild.

Griff laughs. "They're probably just warning everyone about UFO abductions and protecting yourself from unnecessary probes."

"Are there *necessary* probes?" I ask. Griffin gives me a conspiratorial wink.

Zeff turns to Franklin. "You've worked with them before. Any idea what this is about?"

"You've worked with them?" I ask Franklin.

"Research." He shakes his head. "Thanks for confirming my suspicions that you've never read the *Explorer*."

"Principal Zeff!" Asher calls into a megaphone. "There is nothing to fear. We are gathering peacefully to express our freedom of expression. I mean, to exercise our right to free speech."

Zeff forms a megaphone with her hands. "I. Support. Your. Constitutional. Rights."

"This. Is. (e)VIL!" Asher responds.

"Yes, but . . . evil what?" she asks.

He sweeps his hands before him, indicating their vast group of three.

"Represent!" he shouts.

"Represent!" The other two pump their fists.

Griff, Franklin, Zeff, and I are like, *head scratch*.

Ash raises the megaphone again. "This. Is. A. Flash. Mob."

Zeff turns her hand megaphone into an amplifier for her ear. "A what?"

"Flash mob!" he says. "For Lucy Vacarro and all who've been burned by our cultural addiction to—"

"Mr. Hollowell," Zeff says, waving him toward us, "that all sounds wonderful. Why don't you and your mob friends let the soccer team continue their game, and we'll talk about how we can help one another over here. Sound like a plan?"

Asher pulls his minions in for a conference, then breaks away and raises the megaphone. "We've discussed your demands amongst ourselves and have come to a consensus! We will meet your demands! We're coming over there now!" To the soccer boys, he says, "Please continue, Swordfish, and pardon our disruptive yet socially important interruption." He sets the megaphone in his lap and rolls toward us, leading the others onward.

The soccer team re-forms their lines. Marceau gives me a final, brokenhearted smile, and I curl my fingers in a tiny wave.

"Stop." Griff's breath is hot on my neck. "You're making it worse on him."

Safely back on the sidelines, Asher greets each of us with a curt, official nod. To Zeff, he bows his head and holds out a hand, giving her the floor.

"You tell me," she says. "Seems you've got something important to say."

Obviously thrilled by the invitation, Ash launches into what would be, if there were a few hundred more people around, a riot-inducing speech about the fall of the Roman Empire, the conspiracy of big pharma that's keeping us all sick, something about Homeland Security that I'm not a hundred percent sure on because I zoned out for a minute, and—

"Lucy." Asher crosses his arms, and the other two exchange approving nods. "All down to her."

"Down to who-the-what-the?" I blink. Blinding sun reflects endlessly off their white berets. "Could you repeat the question?"

"Lucy," Zeff says, glancing at her watch, "this sounds like another great opportunity for branching out in a positive direction. And, Asher, I'm proud to see your group testing the boundaries of civic engagement. I trust you'll both resolve this like responsible young adults, without further disrupting the sports teams?" Not waiting for confirmation, she says, "Great. I'll leave you to it!"

And she does.

Asher's (e)VIL membership pitch is a repeat performance from the other day at my locker. Only this time, his minions join in.

"We could really use a rallying point," one guy says. He's got thin, shoulder-length dreads with little shells at the bottom and a silver eyebrow ring. Tens, I think they call him. Pretty sure he's Asher's best friend—I've seen them together a lot.

"You could be our Mockingjay," the other says. It's the blond swimmer who handed me a flyer that first day. Her eyes are bright blue in the sun. "Lead us to take down the corporate social network regime."

"And it's no coincidence, Stephie," Tens says, clearly rehearsed, "that if you rearrange the letters in 'corporate social network' you can make 'Capital' and 'Snow.'"

"And Oreo rocket," she adds with a nod. "Definitely a message."

"Really?" I say. "What's happening here, people?"

"What's *happening* here?" Asher says. "Vanity-based technologies are corrupting our relationships, destroying our souls, and rendering genuine human interaction a quaint relic people won't even be able to reminisce about, because reminiscing would require the very interaction whose demise we're lamenting. *That's* what's happening here."

"I meant—"

"And as someone directly impacted by the shadowy side of friends who let friends Face-frack," Stephie says, "you're in a position to take a public stand on this issue."

Griff giggles behind me. "With great scandal comes great responsibility, Lucy."

Franklin scoffs. "I'm fairly certain that's not how the saying goes."

"Why do you like correcting my syntax so much?"

"That's not syntax. It's—"

"You have control issues," she tells him. "And for your information, I rock an A minus in AP English."

"Guys!" This train is rapidly going off the rails. It's after four, way past time to go home and boot up a little *Undead Shred*. "Asher," I say, "I get some of the stuff you're saying. But I'm not . . . I can't . . . No."

"Please, Lucy?" Stephie asks. Her blue eyes are so sincere, but . . . no.

Asher blows a frustrated breath into his fist. "Truth time," he says. He motions for me to crouch down close, and when I do, he puts his hand on my shoulder. "We're looking for a cause, Lucy. Something to put us on the map before we graduate, something to preserve for future generations of dedicated Lavender Oaks underclassmen."

"You need a legacy?"

"We need new members, especially now. The NSA monitoring our communications. The TSA monitoring our body cavities. Drone surveillance at an all-time high . . ." He looks to the sky, searching. Franklin and Griffin do the same.

"Drones?" Franklin asks.

"Drones." When Ash looks at me again, his eyes are watery from the sun and/or his passion about invasion-of-privacy issues.

"You know the ironic thing?" I rise from the grass and dust off my hands, offering a sincere but apologetic smile. "You guys could recruit a lot more people if you used Facebook and Twitter instead of white pants and mega-phones. All the cool revolutionaries are doing it."

"So I've heard. But listen." Asher winks at me, and my Spidey sense is all, *Whatever comes out of his mouth next, no good can come of it.* "I'm wearing you down, Lucy Vacarro. Trust me. After the pep rally tomorrow? You'll come around. Resistance is futile."

"Dudes wearing white pants is futile," Griff says. But Asher has me locked in his sights like a UFO tractor beam, and Franklin's scratching his head, and Tens and Stephie nod knowingly, and I find myself looking to the sky, just in case.

LAV-OAKS FLASH MOBS NEITHER FLASHY NOR MOBBY

MISS DEMEANOR

3,213 likes 👍

702 talking about this

Friday, May 2

In a series of unprecedented public displays that
weren't actually all that public, everyone's favorite
conspiracy theorists ditched the tinfoil hats yesterday
for berets, igniting several self-proclaimed "flash mobs"
across campus. These megaphoned, white-cloaked

warriors made such lofty demands as: Dismantle the social media regime (boo hiss, tinfoilers, boo hiss)! Boycott smartphones! And . . . some other stuff . . . that no one remembers . . . due to mitigating circumstances of the wardrobe malfunction nature.

(Style tip, public protestors: He who dons white pants should un-don colored underpants.)

Inappropriately dressed as they may have been, (e)VIL's attempts at defending one of Lav-Oaks's own against the tyranny of the Lav-Oaks masses is to be commended. Just not by me, since I exist only online and Team We Hate Social Media won't be clicking my like button anytime soon (that's not a euphemism, kidlings).

So, my massive masses, if you see one of our no-flashy-no-mobby flash mobbers, thank them for . . . whatever it is they're doing, because it probably has something to do with free speech and freedom from oppression and all that inalienable rights hoo-ha that I don't feel like referencing right now because the bathroom where my U.S. Constitution shower curtain and coordinating Bill of Rights liner so proudly and currently hang is a long walk from my bed where I so proudly and currently hang.

Like most things on which I so doggedly report, you'll just have to trust me on this. And, you know. Fight the power and stuff.

xo ~ *Ciao!* ~ xo

Miss Demeanor

THE TRUTH *IS* OUT THERE, JUST NOT ANYWHERE CLOSE TO HERE

Top ten reasons not to bail on the Lav-Oaks senior pep rally:

1. Vanitas is playing.
2. Jayla's making a surprise Angelica appearance and I promised I'd critique her performance.
3. (e)VIL. Ash *did* say that resistance is futile, so here I am, not resisting.
4. Actually, there's only the three reasons.

Inside the highly lacquered gymnasium, I scan the bleachers for a friendly face. Griff's white-blond waves call out from the crowd, but she's next to Ellie, and she turns away when she sees me. Seconds later, my phone lights up.

Griff: *sorry. here w/ ellie. franklin's got u covered.*

Me: *nbd. anything to report on mystery wings?*

After the (e)VIL onslaught yesterday, Franklin and I gave Griff the 411 on 420, and now Franklin's got her working the wings angle, scanning party pics to see if she can match up the evidence and find our fairy. Despite their pseudo bickering on the soccer field, she seemed more than eager to take his assignment.

Griff: *nothing yet. got my eyes on olivia tho—girl's def hiding something. more soon. agent colanzi out. xo*

The sight of Olivia's name makes my blood simmer. It's still hard to imagine anyone would willingly post such an incriminating photo of herself—she looked seriously wrecked in the emo bathroom that first day—but I can't shake the feeling that she's involved. Not just in the obvious ways—the Juicy Lucy posts, Operation Mean Girl with Quinn and Haley—but something deeper, more sinister.

Or maybe I've been spending too much time with Ash Hollowell.

I drop the phone into my pocket and lower my sunglasses to look for Franklin. When our eyes meet, he stands up and gives me a double-arm flag down.

I climb the bleachers and take the seat next to him. "Putting the pep in pep rally, Keith?"

"I thought this would be a good vantage point from which to investigate suspicious activity." He points at the Jayla banner beneath the scoreboard. "We're looking for anyone pulling a paparazzi on our little Darling."

"I thought Jay's visit was—I mean, um. Jayla Heart's coming?" I nearly forgot that he doesn't know she's my sister. He thought I was joking when I offered to hook them up for an interview. "How do you know?"

"Zeff asked if I wanted someone from photography club to get pictures for the paper," he says. "Anyway, it works out brilliantly for us."

"Because you're such a huge Jayla Heart fan?"

Franklin nudges me with his shoulder. "Miss Demeanor is a Jay-Heart megaminion. If anyone's likely to get too close and camera happy today, it's her. She might be careless enough to blow her cover."

"You think Miss D might know something about the perp," I say, catching his drift. "Something that can help us."

Franklin looks supremely pleased with himself.

"But *everyone* fake worships at the altar of Jayla," I say. "Have you *seen* her fan page? People never pass up a chance to snap a few selfies with a celeb, even if it's just to make fun of her later."

"For research purposes, I have in fact evaluated the Heartthrobs page." Franklin scratches the back of his neck, which has turned suddenly and quite glaringly red. "But that's not the point. Miss Demeanor is truly obsessed. Just . . . be cool, okay? Don't give away our position."

"Covert ops. I like it." I put my sunglasses on and kick back, scrutinizing the crowd through dark lenses.

"Look alive, partner." Franklin points his half-full water bottle center stage. "Showtime."

Lav-Oaks administrators learned long ago that teacher speeches kill the pep rally buzz faster than cops at a party. After a blissfully short welcome and a useless reminder about switching off cell phones, Principal Zeff tells us to put our hands together for Vanitas.

The crowd roars as Cole, John, and Spence take center stage. Cole settles in behind the drum set, spins his sticks, beams at the audience. It's the pregame warm-up I've seen at every gig, every garage practice. But now, when he smiles at the crowd, I let myself dream—for one forbidden moment—he's smiling at me. *For* me.

He taps the snare to usher in John's opening guitar riff, and my heart rattles, aches, rattles, aches.

They play a five-song set—three covers and two originals. Every one of my senses is trained on him, eyes tracking the rapid *fling-bang* of the drumsticks, the bob of his shaggy head. Ears picking out the drumbeat above all other sounds. I feel it inside me, a deep metallic thud against my rib cage. And when I close my eyes, I feel his lips pressed to mine, taste his breath on my tongue, soft and warm and utterly unforgettable.

At the end of the last song, the crowd is on their feet. Bleachers rumble and shake, but I stay seated, my heart clinging to a memory that shouldn't belong to me, wishing like hell I could slip inside of it and live there forever.

Franklin touches my arm, spell broken. "All right, love?"

I'm still staring at Cole, and he's staring back at me too. Franklin must notice it, because he leans close and offers a supportive smile.

"You can't help who you love," he says, "even if the timing is horrendous."

"Even if people you care about get hurt?" I ask. I don't really mean for him to answer, but he does.

"It's not like you can switch off your feelings. Repression never helped anyone."

"That needs to be on a bumper sticker."

"You're in love with him," Franklin says matter-of-factly. "Don't try to outrun it. You can't." His eyes are full of regret, and I wonder how he came to know this particular wisdom, this hurt. I've been counting the days till graduation since freshman year, but now, for a moment, I wish I had more time. More time to know Franklin. Asher. Kiara. More time to be with Ellie and Cole and Griff. More time to be honest, to be me.

To figure out what that even means.

From behind his drums, Cole's still watching me, his gaze fiery and direct, and I know that Franklin's right: Not even with all the zombie survivalist cardio in the world could I ever outrun this. Could I ever want to.

It's a gruesome thought, love seeping into the chest, devouring the heart from within. But the image of it floods me, sends a current through every nerve. I almost rise out of the seat, rush down to the floor, fall into Cole's arms.

Love. Devouring. Heart . . .

The commotion at the side door distracts me, and the moment explodes, my nerves fizzling back to normal, heart pounding but still intact.

Saunters. That's the only word for my sister's approach, and I sink into my seat as the crowd erupts in a mostly mock cheer.

Jayla's smile is plastered on, beautiful and synthetic. If she senses the mockery in the air, she either doesn't care, or she's gotten really good at repression.

The phone buzzes my hip.

Griff: *check out olivia 2 rows down from me. closet angie-d fangirl, whut?*

I scope out the section of seats in front of Griff and Ellie. Olivia's on her feet, fist pumping, a solo standing O. Haley and Quinn flank her, but they're sitting down, laughing, shooting Jayla with their phones. They've perfected their fake fangirl squeals. Olivia, on the other hand, looks like she means it.

Me: *that's . . . unexpected.*

Griff: *only 1 being sincere for sis. told u she's shady as eff. I'm on her & team sprite like angie on a mattress.*

Me: *:-) good work, agent colanzi. vacarro out.*

When the noise finally fades, half the crowd buried in their devices, Jayla launches into a dramatic monologue of a scene from last weekend's episode. Only she reads *all* the parts, not just Angelica's, and despite her attempt at different voices, it makes no sense. The crowd goes crazy with laughter and more fake cheers, and my cheeks burn, and I'm pretty sure if Franklin didn't offer me his water, I'd burst into flames.

Official critique? My sister is one hundred percent, straight-up mortifying.

"Angelica Darling," she bellows across the gym, "takes a lot of things lying down. But treachery is *not* one of them, Mikayla McBride. You were supposed to be my confidante.

But now you'll be telling your secrets to the devil . . . in hell!" Jayla lunges forward, pantomiming an uppercut to an invisible opponent. Or possibly she's reenacting a knife fight, or maybe a hug. But before she can complete the scene, the lights flicker, followed by the unmistakable hiss of rubber wheels and the chirp of sneakers on the polished wood floor.

"We! Are! The point-zero-five percent!" Asher's got the megaphone again, and his minions—up from two to three today, Kiara included—form a line across the center of the gym. They've traded in the whites for blacks, each megaphoned and sunglassed.

The teachers are seated in the front row, and a few of them stand as if to put an end to the disruption. Zeff, smiling and curious, holds her arm out to stop them, her other hand raised in a pause: *Hold on. Give them a moment.*

Without missing a beat, Kiara steps forward with her megaphone, tall and proud after her brief suspension. "We are the few. The few who say *no* to Face-frack. *No* to perpetuating cruel celebrity gossip. *No* to electronic vanities. *No* to social-network brain rot and the government's plan to control us through personal-data acquisition and consumerist messaging."

That night with Prince Freckles at the prom, she was so nervous, decked out in her mermaid finery, sneaking a photo for her mother. But here, center of attention for a cause she wholeheartedly believes in, she shines.

"Think for yourselves." Asher rolls forward when Kiara steps back. "The founding fathers never intended for things to go down like this. The Constitution? They rocked it. We wrecked it."

"They rocked it," the others repeat. "We wrecked it."

"So honor our fab founding fathers. Unplug. Engage. And . . ." Ash lowers the megaphone and looks around. Kiara shrugs. He raises the megaphone again. "Where is Roman?"

"Guess he didn't get the memo about the time change," Kiara says.

"Are you sure we can't have cell phones?" Stephie asks. The whole conversation is unfolding via megaphones. "Hard to coordinate last-minute flash mob changes on handwritten notes."

"Texting *would* be easier," Kiara concurs.

"You guys are missing the whole point!" Asher shouts. Still with the megaphones. The crowd has gone silent—teachers exchanging confused glances, waiting for Zeff to shut this down—and suddenly Ash seems to realize that all eyes are on him. He clears his throat into the megaphone and, with his free hand, points toward me and Franklin. "Lucy Vacarro is not a perpetrator. She's a victim. All of you—the plugged in, the updaters, the uploaders—are victims. Only Face-frack is to blame."

"Lucy Vacarro is a slut!" someone shouts from a few rows behind me.

Jayla, who'd been stunned into silence by (e)VIL, whips her head toward the direction of my eloquent name caller. Still miked up from her monologue, she shouts, "Angelica does *not* approve of slut-shamers, you filthy little maggot!"

"Narc!" someone else shouts.

"Slut!" Pretty sure that was one of the vampire bros.

The chant's about to start; the anticipation of its arrival fills the room like a balloon ready to burst. Franklin grabs my hand, squeezes gently. "Shall we make a run for it, then?"

"The truth is out there, people!" Ash booms into the megaphone, hijacking the full force of the chant before it gets off the ground. "Open your eyes! Get *off* social media and *on* social reality! Friends don't trend! Friends don't trend!"

"Friends don't trend!" the minions chant. What they lack in number, they make up for in enthusiasm. "Friends don't trend! Friends don't trend!"

"Who are you, the hashtag police?" Jayla marches up behind Asher, spins his chair around so they're facing each other. The mock cheers are deafening, but Asher is positively star-struck. "Do you know what Angelica Darling says about that?"

That's my cue. Agent Vacarro out.

Franklin's still holding my hand. I return his squeeze and nod toward the exit.

"I don't particularly like police," Jayla says as Franklin and I weave through the crowd. "Especially ones with megaphones. Do you know what they say about little boys with big voices? They have teeny tiny—"

"And that's a wrap! Thank you, Jayla Heart." Ms. Zeff is on the scene, finally jolted into action. She takes Asher's megaphone and waves the group back to their seats. "Thank you, evil children, for that important reminder about balancing imagination with real life, online and off. Speaking of balancing . . . please join me in welcoming your Swordfish cheerleaders and the routine that made them famous for copyright violation on YouTube, 'Who Let the Fish Out (Woof Woof Woof Woof Woof)!'"

In the relative peace of the computer lab, I drop into a rolling chair and pull out my phone—it started buzzing with texts the second Franklin and I left the gym.

Griff: *are we dreaming this?*

Griff: *wait, where r u going?*

Cole: *wtf w/ evil? hollowell's insane! kind of awesome.*

Cole: *wait, where u going w/ FM? u ok?*

Griff: *zeff is all, wtf w/ this wtfery. so much for rah-rah civic engagement.*

Griff: *omg olivia asking ellie where u went. right now! she's like y did lucy just leave?*

Griff: *ellie goes, lucy's allergic 2 cheer routines. LOL! *dies**

Griff: *reply, girly!!!! hello!!!*

Cole: *:-(come back :-(*

I send a quick text to both of them: *bailed b4 things got more whacky. already in enough trouble w/ Zeff—time 2 lie low! @ comp lab. in good hands w/ our lead investigator.*

"Is (e)VIL trying to get me suspended?" I ask Franklin. He's in the chair next to me, for once not taking notes. "Or whatever it's called when you're about to graduate and they can't really suspend you?"

"I'm quite certain they're trying to help," Franklin says. "Their presentation against social media . . . it's as if they're trying to force a confession through group intimidation. A classic strategy, low-tech but impressive."

"So they're just *pretending* to interrupt Jayla Heart's show? Calling me out in front of the entire class?"

"More like going undercover to make a statement," Franklin says. "But yes, I suppose so."

"I just thought of something," I say. "Asher seemed pretty smitten with Jayla."

"I noticed that too," he says. "So?"

"What if Miss D isn't one person, but a group? And what if that group is (e)VIL, and they're, like, her secret force for social justice? What if *they're* the conspiracy? No one would ever suspect it." I spin around in the chair and stop to meet his gaze. "Think about it, Keith. It's the perfect crime."

Franklin's laughing at me, but his eyes light up so much when he laughs that I can't be offended. "Reel it in, Veronica. In case her name didn't give it away, Miss Demeanor isn't a force for social justice. Her column—and I use that term quite loosely—is largely responsible for your scandal."

"Sure, but it's not like she *told* people to go out and frame someone. They brought the scandal to her and . . . wait. What did I just say?"

"They brought the scandal to her?"

"Yes, that! Exactly!" I dig the iPad out of my bag and pull up Miss D's page. "You said if we identified Miss D, we might be able to ask her who posted the pics, to see if they got in touch with her or whatever."

"I think it's a good lead, yes," he says. "Potentially."

"Why not go straight to the source?"

"I don't understand."

"Give me five minutes." While Franklin sits quietly, I type another missive to our favorite gossip hound. Satisfied with the wording, I hit the send button, then pass the iPad to Franklin to show him the note. "Bask in the brilliance, Keith."

From: Lucy Vacarro

Dear Miss Demeanor:

Thank you for your Wednesday Words of Wisdom about the prom party photo scandal and the great framing of our time. Though I haven't been in touch since, I'd like you to know that your advice has given me both comfort and strength.

This might be asking too much, but I'm trying to be all bright side about this, so I'm sharing the idea anyway. Since you hold sway over the Lav-Oaks masses, and you haven't yet selected a photo for the #scandal contest, I'm hoping you'll consider this write-in suggestion:

Prince Freckles partying it up at the cabin in all his glittery glory.

Before you scoff at the idea of bestowing the great honor of Miss Demeanor page immortalization on a nonhuman, allow me to explain (and partially beg).

Though your advice to investigate the situation was intended for the wronged party, as the alleged wronger I've decided to take matters into my own hands (with help from a few loyal friends). Of primary import to our ongoing investigation, we aim to identify the individual who posted and tagged the party pics from my account. If you select the Prince Freckles shot as your winner, perhaps the proud photographer will step forward to claim her moment in the spotlight. It's a long shot, but sometimes even the most intelligent among us is wooed by the temptation of fame and glory—however fleeting—and my hope is that this person will be so blinded by the spotlight that she'll inadvertently out herself as the perp.

I appreciate your consideration and support.

Yours truly,

Harassed Yet Hopeful

"You're not basking," I say when he hands back the device. I can't read his poker face. "I thought there'd be more basking."

"I'm all for solving this mystery," he says, "and maybe you're on to something with the Prince Freckles idea. But . . . Do you really trust this woman? Girl? Whoever she is?"

"Think about it," I say. "She gives legit advice, couched in sarcasm. And yeah, she's all about the drama, but she doesn't attack anyone. Miss D isn't the one doubting me—my own friends are. Ellie. What does that say?"

Franklin points a pen at me. "Maybe Miss D *is* one of your friends."

"Back to conspiracy theory? You know, Lav-Oaks has a club for that."

The two of us laugh, but his idea isn't *that* crazy—it's crossed my mind. But Ellie's too serious to pull off Miss D's brand of snark, and Griffin isn't that sneaky.

"So maybe Miss D isn't one of your mates," Franklin concedes. "But she's still capricious. Someone that desperate for attention? Bit mental, no?"

"I like her. Officially."

Franklin sighs through his nose. "I still think the best way to deal with this is to put something in the *Explorer.* Get your side out there, take a stand on the issue."

"Here we go."

"No, listen! You won't help (e)VIL. You won't tell Zeff about the posters on your locker. You won't state your case." He rolls his chair closer. "You think this'll just vanish?"

"That's beside the point."

He holds out his hands, like, *Work with me here!*

"You're like them," I say. "Everyone who pretends to

fangirl Jayla Heart. All the stupid tabloids. The Juicy Lucy people. (e)VIL. It's all the same—everyone just wants a piece of drama pie."

"I hope you don't really believe that."

I lean back in the chair, close my eyes. "No, I guess not. I'm just . . . I'm spent."

The pep rally was a bust. My name's back on Zeff's radar for sure. Griff's still chumming around with Ellie, who's still ignoring me. Olivia . . . who knows what Olivia is, but she's definitely not on my side.

And no matter how hard I try to convince myself that it's wrong, that I have to let it go, I can't stop falling in love with Cole, again and again, each time harder than the last.

LOWDOWN DIRTY LOVE

No one ever accused Night of the Living Dog of being normal.

Sunday night, a thunderstorm rumbles in the not-so-distant sky, and Night paws frantically at the door—international dog lingo for *Walk me or you'll live to regret it.*

I put on Jayla's Broncos hoodie and hook up the leash, let him trot me out to the woods behind the house. "Colorado is a top-ten state for death by lightning. Know that, dude?"

Night ignores me, snuffles along the trail to his favorite tree just as the first raindrops plink onto the leaves. This is his spot—our spot—quiet, far enough from the surrounding houses that we're almost always alone. Despite the rain, I'm grateful for the escape.

Jayla's been pretty mellow all weekend, a forced smile that I shared tonight as we made a gourmet meal out of Ben & Jerry's Cherry Garcia, hot fudge, and crumbled pretzels. Pictures of her pep rally altercation with Asher leaked to *CelebStyle*, and even though it was all an act, and Asher was thrilled to go along with it, yesterday's headlines tell a different story.

JAY-HEART LOVES HER FANS, AS LONG AS THEY'RE "ABLE" TO LOVE HER BACK; ALTERCATION AT HOMETOWN HIGH SCHOOL REVEALS CELEB'S TRUE COLORS.

Since the story broke, she's been ignoring her phone, deleting nasty messages from her fan page.

After orbiting different suns for years, my sister and I suddenly have a lot in common.

I unhook Night's leash to let him explore, and beneath a canopy of aspen and ponderosa, I climb up on my favorite boulder, perfect for contemplating. As Night slops around in the mud, my thoughts drift from Jayla and Ash to Ms. Zeff, from Ellie and Griff to Olivia, but inside the brain of Lucy, all roads lead to Cole. Cole's sad-face text messages. Cole's drum solo. Cole's kiss . . .

When I open my eyes, he's walking toward me with Spike. It's like I've pulled him out of my daydreams, and he smiles when our eyes meet, rain darkening the shoulders of his blue-gray hoodie.

"Saw you walking this way," he says, unclipping Spike's leash. The Dachshund bolts down the path in search of his canine bestie.

I hop off the boulder, wipe my hands on my cutoff camos.

"You okay?" he asks. "I was worried. You took off at the pep rally, and . . . shit. Am I turning into stalker guy?" He goes all dad-voice, pounds his fist in his hand. "Dammit, Lucy, you haven't answered my calls or texts."

I laugh. "Maybe a *little* stalkery. Mostly angry dad, though."

"Okay, how about this?" With a huskier voice, he says, "You and Margolis seem to be getting close."

"Still kind of angry dad," I say.

"Help me out here, Luce." Cole's voice is back to normal, but a little nervous. "I'm totally jealous. Not a good look for me." He breaks into a grin, and I'm like, *Jealousy? Dude.* Totally *a good look for you.* But I update him on the investigation anyway, reassure him there's nothing going on with Franklin.

Which is so surreal that I stop midexplanation and shake my head. "Cole, this thing . . . What are we doing? We haven't even figured out who posted the pictures. And Ellie's a mess, and it's so—"

"Crazy. Straight up, mad-ass crazy." Cole steps forward, so close I can smell the rain in his hair, so close even Asher's surveillance drones would know, thousands of feet up, that there's nothing even remotely *just friends* about this.

"It wasn't just some random thing," he says, and I know he means the kiss. "Not to me."

"We were drinking."

"You think a few beers is why I kissed you?"

Maybe, maybe not. I couldn't trust my thoughts on prom night; the moment he showed up in my driveway in a tux, pinned me with a tea rose corsage, my logic board was fried.

Still is.

"Halloween," he says. "Sophomore year. You were dressed like one of those special infected things from your zombie game. Right?"

"The witch." I'm shocked that he recognized it then, that he remembers it now. "She kills you with her claws. One strike, you're incapped. Maybe dead."

"Yeah, the witch."

"But not, like, a *real* witch. The special infected are amped-up—"

"I wanted to kiss you," he says. His breath is powder soft against my cheeks. "That night. But I was with Ellie. And

I loved her—really. I took a cold shower and convinced myself I was freaking out."

The rain pelts our heads, our feet, soaking into the dirt.

"For two more years," he says. "I thought it would pass, like, cold feet—that's what John said. I put everything I had into Ellie. It was pretty good for a while too."

He told John about me? Back then?

"But it wasn't great," he continues. "Love and friendship? Yeah. I mean, you know—Ellie's awesome. But sparks?" He presses a hand to his heart and I know exactly what he's saying, because I feel it too. Now. At prom. Every time he's near, every time my name passes between his lips.

"Ellie and I both felt it," he says. "Knew it was missing. Why do you think we broke up?"

Night howls in the distance, and seconds later, he and Spike return, caked with mud and trouble, still chasing each other in hyper circles at our feet. Cole crouches down to wrestle with Night, to give him a big, wet-dog hug, and I think of Ellie, her too-cute status updates, the posed Facebook pics, the confident assurances that with Cole, all was happy and well.

For so long she was hiding doubts, dark and secret things she kept from even her best friend.

Just as I kept my own dark and secret things from her.

I see her face, her smile, her tears. She is simultaneously a soul mate and a stranger.

"I didn't plan it, Lucy," Cole says. He stands, unfazed by the mud on his clothes, and I know he's talking about the kiss again. "Every time I see you in those boots, I lose a few brain cells. Then all of a sudden we're under the stars, and I'm thinking about the crazy shit we've done, the laughs . . . We're all alone out there, and I'm like, this is it, dude. If you let her go now, she's gone."

I wasn't. I'm not. The forest is green and alive in the rain, the dogs curled up and panting at the base of the boulder, everything lush and beautiful as if it were painted just for us, just for this moment.

My eyes are on the dirt when I say, "You don't regret it?"

"On the deck?" he says. "I only stopped . . . I was worried I freaked you out. Like, maybe I was wrong when I thought you liked me too." He sighs, the rain tapping a gentle rhythm on the leaves above. "Maybe I'm still wrong."

My heart is thunderous, a raging storm that drowns out the warnings and the shouldn'ts and the can'ts, and I meet his gaze, hold it, look for the stars in his eyes.

I find them, glittery and infinite.

"You're not." The space between us is gone.

"God," he whispers, "I'm in so much trouble with you."

My skin is electrified by his touch, slick and muddy and

cool. The rain dampens our faces, leaves trembling overhead as his body shudders against mine, a moan soft and breathy in my ear, and I give in.

Just this once.

I make the silent promise and give in to four years of wanting. Four years under the sheets with the lights off, eyes closed in the dark hours of the dawn, thinking only of him, his hands, his mouth, his breath, all of it on me, covering me, enveloping me.

Just this once. Just this once. Just this once.

Love. Devours. Heart.

"Isn't there anything you can do?" Jayla's saying into her phone. She leaning against the kitchen counter, her back to me, shoulders high and tight. "Are you sure they won't reconsider? No. I know. It's just . . . Yeah. I'm sorry too." With a defeated sigh, she drops the phone on the counter.

"Jay?"

She whirls around, presses a hand to her heart. Her eyes are red, charcoal eyeliner smudged beneath them. "You scared me to death!"

"Are you crying?" I nod toward her phone. "Who was that?"

"No one." She swipes at her eyes, tired and crestfallen. "Just my useless agent. I'm thinking of letting him go, but it's *so* hard to find a good one." She slides a bottle of red wine from the rack on the counter, reads the label, puts it back, selects another. This one she uncorks. When she looks at me again, her eyes narrow suspiciously. "What happened to *you*? Why are you shaking? Where's Night?"

"Had to hose him off. He's drying in the garage." I tug off the hoodie and try to walk past her to the laundry room, but she stops me.

"Is that my hoodie?"

"Is it?" I look at the muddy blue-and-orange ball in my hands. "Sorry. Didn't know you were a Broncos fan all of a sudden."

Jayla reaches toward me, pulls a twig from my hair. She inspects it with great interest. "Explain to me, little sister, how one goes on a simple walk with her dog and comes back hours later with mud on her face and sticks in her hair and muddy handprints all over her shorts. *Boy* handprints."

"Oh . . . I ran into Cole." I comb my fingers through my hair, realizing what a bad criminal I'd make. A wet leaf falls to the kitchen floor.

With feigned indifference, I announce, "It's pretty muddy out there, Jayla."

Her eyebrows shoot up. "You and Cole were mud wrestling?"

"What? I fell! Night was running and I slipped and landed in this . . . um . . ."

"Tar pit?"

"Creek bed?"

"Cole's bed *whut?*"

"Jayla!"

"Lucy!"

My hand flies to my mouth, covers it instinctively. His kiss lingers, invisible evidence hot on my lips. I'm sure she can see it beneath the mud, read it as if the story's written in tabloid headlines all over my face.

She pours a generous glass of wine and hands it over. "Drinksies?"

I shake my head, and she takes a long swig instead.

"A bath, then." She tops off her glass from the bottle. "I'll run it. Drop those clothes in the washer and prepare to tell me your dirty little secrets. All of them."

Comfortably perched on the closed toilet, Jayla scrutinizes me over her wineglass as I recap the events of prom: Ellie's bird flu fake out, the dance, the party, the kiss on the deck, the argument. All the pictures, tagged and uploaded.

There's a hot washcloth over my eyes, the rest of me submerged in Jayla's luxurious imported lemon-ginger bubble bath, but I still feel her gaze.

"Lucy." There's a swallow of wine, then a sigh. "You *so*

lie. There's way more to this story and it's eating you up inside. A mother knows these things. Spill it, sister."

"Wait, are you a mother or a sister?"

"You think I'm judgy, right? That's it." More sipping. Sighing. "Luce. My whole life is one long tabloid joke." Her voice cracks on the last word. "I'm the last person to judge anyone. I just want you to trust me again. We're *sisters*."

The room is silent now except for the water—water dripping from my hair, water dripping from the faucet, water lapping the sides of the tub as the bubbles fizzle. I poke my toes out of the bath, wriggle them in the cool air above.

"Cole and I . . ." I say. "The pictures . . . It's not *exactly* how it looked. But . . ." Behind the washcloth, darkness is anonymity; in it I find the courage, for the first time, to confess. "There was more than one kiss on prom night. Um, kind of a lot more."

For the record, if you ever got sick, I would totally hold your hair back. . . .

Cole's voice was low and my heart was racing and I turned, just a little, and he pulled me the rest of the way. We were facing each other, so close I could taste him, but still I held back. We didn't kiss, didn't speak, barely breathed, and finally, despite the pounding in my chest and the buzzing in my head, I drifted off.

An hour? Maybe two? I'm not sure how long I was out,

but when I opened my eyes again, tangled up in Cole's arms, pale lavender light illuminated the room. In the sliver between night and day, the cabin was silent, the stars fading, the moment full of dangerous possibility.

One last chance before the spell breaks. Before the sun laces her fingers through the sky, paints the shadows gold and sends us back to real life . . .

Cole's eyes were closed, his lips parted, hair sticking up everywhere. He sighed in his sleep, and I drifted toward him, brushed my lips against his.

A second. Maybe three. His eyes stayed closed, but he stirred, his breath catching. My name was on his lips . . . *Lucy* . . . whispered into my mouth like smoke, like a ghost, and he pulled me to his chest, kissed me soft and forever.

I slipped beneath him in his bed that night, welcomed the weight of his body over mine, looked into his eyes as if the world were ending. Maybe it was. I wouldn't have noticed.

We didn't sleep after that. We held each other as the sun rose, said everything and nothing at all with one last kiss.

In all the stories about that night, the pictures that followed, the explanations and defenses, the recaps and apologies, the hints and fears and secret admissions, we never spoke of that moment. It was too intimate, too fragile. Too ours.

I know now that the pictures had already been taken by

then, that they'd already started telling their story. A different one with all the wrong lines, all the wrong scenes.

It wasn't like the pictures say.

Our story, soft and silent before the dawn, was so, so much more. And for days after—sometimes even still—I wondered if I'd dreamed it all along.

Still hidden by the washcloth, I tell Jayla my secrets, my truths, and by the time I get to the part about tonight, about the woods, I know that I'm a villain. That regardless of Cole and Ellie's precise breakup timeline, I deserve the scandal, the bullying that comes with it. That everyone is right about me. *Slut. Narc. Liar. Home wrecker.* Best friend backstabber and all-around bad person. I earned the Juicy Lucy page, the posters on my locker, the judging smirks in the hallway.

Heartless, someone called me the other day. A heartless bitch.

But that's where I get stuck.

If I'm so heartless, what's this bruised thing in my chest, full of fire and hope, banging so loud I can't sleep, can't think? What is it that aches when he kisses me, aches when I walk away?

I slide the washcloth off my face and meet Jayla's eyes, shame and confusion heating my cheeks.

"You're in love with him," she says. It's kind and contemplative, not a question. "Seriously in love."

I nod. "But it's, like, tainted. Like I cheated to get

him. And now I have to decide between my best friend and my heart. The girl I'm supposed to go away to college with and the guy who's moving to the other side of the country in three months. A girl who might never forgive me and a guy who might not love me back, no matter what I decide."

"What does Cole say?" she asks.

"He wants us to be together, but I can't do that to Ellie."

"You're already doing it, and that's not the point." Jayla sips the last of her wine and sets down the empty glass, closes her eyes. I watch her and wait, steel myself for the jabs about how I'm becoming more like Angelica Darling every day, how it sounds like a made-for-TV movie, how all I need is a drink and a few credit cards to make it all go away.

They don't come.

"What do I do?" I ask.

"Tell her." When she opens her eyes, they're clear and determined. "What happened, happened. All you have left is the truth. Ellie has to hear it eventually, even if she doesn't want to. For chrissake, Lucy. You and Cole are in love. You can't just walk away."

"But everyone—"

"All the haters and scandals in the world can't change your heart. You're already on the battlefield, right? So fight for it." Jayla picks up the glass and leans down to kiss my head, trailed as always by her pear perfume. "Fucking fight."

THE SHIT SHOW MUST GO ON!

MISS DEMEANOR

3,396 likes 👍

803 talking about this

<u>Monday, May 5</u>

Angelica Darling may be a schemer, but one thing
she's not afraid of is a little improvisation. When
conspiracy theorists stole her spotlight on Friday to
go all fanboy on the founding fathers? Angelica didn't
whither like a dainty flower. She rolled with it, pun

intended. I don't care what the tabloids say. Jayla Heart's a class act, and she deserves our fickle online loyalty, so head on over to the Jayla Heartthrobs fan page and thumb-thumb-thumbs it up!

If we've learned anything this weekend from Jay-gelica's grace in the face of being defaced, it's this: No matter what the soulless scandalhounds throw at us on our paths to self-righteousness, march onward we must. So even though it's Cinco de Mayo and it's time for a Monday-morning margarita (shout out to Mexico! Thanks for giving me the opportunity to misappropriate your cultural heritage in order to justify my drinking tequila before nine a.m.!), the show must, after all, go on.

I've got an important announcement.

Shuffles papers

The award (yes, OMG, finally!) for Miss Demeanor's final (you know you'll miss me) (try not to cry) (nothing says I'll miss you like anonymous cash donations to the bank account of my choosing) #scandal goes to a gent who puts the ass in class, and that's no insult. For his unwavering embodiment of class in a world of utter classlessness, and for so perfectly capturing the quintessential high school #scandal moment in all its glitter and desperation at the Lav-Oaks postprom party of the century, we've selected . . .

PRINCE FRECKLES!

Applause applause applause

Sadly, like all our equestrian-American brethren, Prince Freckles lacks opposable thumbs and is unable to sign into his Facebook account and claim his winnings. He's also unlikely to give two horseshits about winning a gold star of immortality on a cheesy, high school gossip column. After consulting with my wise adviser Jose Cuervo, I've decided to award, by proxy, the esteemed random photographer who *captured* the prince's special moment. Step forth and claim your fifteen seconds of fame, esteemed random photographer! You deserve every last second and not a moment more!

xo ~ *Ciao!* ~ xo

Miss Demeanor

LOVE IS IN THE AIR . . . AND IT TOTALLY SMELLS LIKE TEEN SPIRIT AFTER THE TEEN SPIRIT STEPPED IN DOG POOP

don't see any tarts."

In the cafeteria on Monday, Ellie gives me a frosty once-over. She meets my eyes for just a second; then her attention returns to her tropical-breeze sandwich—a combination of coconut, peanut butter, honey, and banana we invented last summer.

"What do you want now?" she asks coolly.

You're already on the battlefield. . . .

"Come outside with me." I take a deep breath, lean against the table to steady myself. "Those pictures don't tell the whole story, El. I need you to hear it from me."

She stops midchew, slides her eyes over the top of her sandwich to meet mine. "What if I don't care?"

"I know you. You *totally* care."

She doesn't deny it, and I press on.

"I screwed up. Majorly. And if you want to end our friendship, that's your right. But not until you hear me out. After that . . . I'm not transferring out of UCLA, but I'll leave you alone. We can get different roommates or . . . something." I throw it out there, hoping she'll throw it back. Tell me I'm crazy for even suggesting we'll be anything other than BFFs for life.

Ellie shoves the sandwich crusts into a paper bag. "I don't want you to transfer. God, Lucy. I thought we agreed that melodrama was Griff's job? Speaking of which, last period she started using a British accent. Any ideas?"

"She's got a little crush on our valedictorian."

"Shocking." Ellie rises, scoops up her lunch scraps. "Let's go."

Ellie walks in front of me to throw out her trash, and I'm so focused on her, so keyed up about what I need to say, that I don't notice the figure rushing me until we collide. With thuglike force, Quinn shoves a tray of garbage into my stomach. Spaghetti sticks to my Ani DiFranco shirt, chocolate milk covers my boots. The tray clatters to the ground.

Everyone around us whoops and claps.

"Eww." Quinn's fingers drip with chocolate milk, and

she flicks them at my face. "Nasty. Maybe if you weren't so busy watching other people's boyfriends, you could watch where you're going."

I blink the milk from my eyes. "I'm—I didn't—"

"Really?" Ellie steps between us, crowding up on Quinn. "You've probably been planning that trick all weekend, right? And that's the best you could come up with?"

I grab a pile of napkins someone left on a table and mop everything up, best I can. My shirt's stained with sauce, but due to their ass-kicking nature, my boots survive unscathed.

Perhaps there's a metaphor for life here.

Quinn doesn't answer Ellie's inquiries. She whips out her cell phone, thumbs flying over the screen as she walks away, vanishing back into the cafeteria hell dimension from whence she spawned.

"You okay?" Ellie asks me.

"As a cucumber." I take her elbow and steer us out into the sunny courtyard. We find a spot nestled behind a few ponderosas, a slab of red sandstone poking out from the ground. Neither of us sits.

"Quinn was at the party," I explain. "She's mad about the pictures of Olivia. Which I didn't post."

"I know." Ellie squints in the sun. I don't know if she means she knows why Quinn's mad, or she knows I didn't post the pictures. "I'm sorry you're getting so much crap about this, Lucy. It's not fair. People are harsh."

"They think I broke the cardinal what-happens-at-the-party rule," I say. "Not to mention the best friend's boyfriend rule."

"You kind of did."

"Ellie, I didn't plan it. I hate prom stuff. I just wanted to get through the dance and go home. But you know Cole—he made it fun."

She raises an eyebrow. "Uh, yeah?"

"Dancing," I say. "When he asked me about the party, I just . . . I went along. And I'm sorry about what happened, but you . . . How could you not tell me you guys broke up? How could you fake being sick just to get out of going to prom with a guy you supposedly loved for three years?"

Cole's words from last night replay in my mind, everything he said about the two of them knowing they wouldn't last, knowing there weren't any sparks.

As if she can read my thoughts, Ellie sighs, looking out across the courtyard. "Things with Cole were . . . fading. We broke up, completely mutual. And I'm sorry if you feel like I was keeping secrets, but that's my right. I knew we'd all be leaving for college anyway, and I wanted things to just . . . fade out. No drama."

"So why ask me to go to prom?" I ask. "Why didn't you both bail? Or just go as friends? It's not like you guys hate each other."

A magpie crosses overhead, and Ellie watches it, waits for it to disappear into a neighborhood across the street. "He wanted to go, and I just . . . I couldn't fake it. But then I had these jealous visions of him hooking up with random girls, which isn't even his style, but . . . you know. It was weird sending him off alone." She meets my eyes. "You're the only one I trusted to go with him. I thought you guys would have fun."

What did you think *would happen, El?* The thought comes, but I dismiss it. Ellie never knew how I felt about Cole. She never knew how I felt about practically anything important.

I never told her.

My eyes sweep her face, her stylishly tangled brown hair, the lone dark freckle on her left cheek, and again I feel that disparity, best friends and casual acquaintances. Soul mates and strangers.

"This whole thing is *crazy* embarrassing," she says. "I'm like the dumb wife, home cooking dinner while her husband's banging the secretary."

"Technically, you're the wife who kicked her husband out, ordered Indian takeout, contemplated banging the hot delivery guy, then lost your shit when you found out your husband—"

"Is this supposed to make me feel better?" she says. "You might need to work on your empathy skills."

Both of us laugh. It's short and a little forced, but it's there, the familiar smile in her eyes. I hate that I have to break it, this moment, this fragile peace. I wish we could sweep the whole thing out into the street, forget it ever happened. That I could be back with Ellie and the moms in time for our *Friday Night Lights* summer rewatch, just like we all planned.

But forgetting our fight would mean forgetting what caused it. Forgetting Cole. Forgetting the first kiss and the second and every one since, all the things he whispered in the woods last night, all the promises I've yet to give him the chance to keep.

Fucking fight.

I tell her the part about reminiscing on the deck, the kiss, the argument, crashing in Cole's bed. She's taking it all very calmly, like maybe—despite the secrets we've kept, despite the #scandal drama and all the ugly rumors—she understands.

Like maybe, when I finally get to the part about the pale lavender light of his room, she'll say Cole and I are meant to be together, that she always knew it.

She just needs to hear me say it out loud, the full confession. The darkest, deepest, truest words I know.

I'm in love with him, Ellie. I've loved him forever. I love him still.

But he's here again.

Straight out of my daydreams again.

And in his smile are a hundred regrets, none of them aimed at me.

"What are *you* doing here?" Ellie says to Cole. The air chills about ten degrees.

"Please listen," he says to Ellie. "I'm so, so sorry. I never meant to hurt you."

She grunts. "You sound like a boy band. Save it."

"I'm sorry," he says again, reaching for her arm. She doesn't shrug him off, but she doesn't return his warmth either. "I didn't plan for it to happen, El. I swear. But I can't stand here and say I regret it. The timing sucks, and the way you found out sucks, but it happened. You can hate me all you want, but don't hold it against Lucy."

Now she shakes him off. "That's between me and Lucy."

"*And* me," he says. "I care about you guys. Come on. We're friends, El."

Ellie relents. After a moment, the three of us sit on the rock slab, the dark red sandstone hot in the sun.

Cole runs his hand over the rock and laughs, and I know exactly what he's remembering.

Two summers ago, Red Rocks Amphitheatre, a beautiful Colorado sunset giving way to so many stars you could see them even over the stage lights.

"Radiohead?" I say.

Ellie can't hide her smile. "Are you guys ever gonna let this go?"

"You practically got us arrested," I remind her.

The three of us were prepared for a night of awesome—cooler of food and drinks, blankets, a thermos of cinnamon hot chocolate—but Ellie forgot the concert tickets. We didn't have time to go back for them, so Cole snuck us up to a rocky ledge where you're not even supposed to climb, let alone crash a sold-out show. We couldn't see the stage, but the sound was perfect; we spread our blankets on the warm rocks, lay there listening to Thom Yorke and watching the moon rise.

Everything was great until Ellie got up to pee, and then a security guard spotted us.

"'How'd you kids like to go to jail for the night?'" Ellie's voice is a gravelly impersonation now. "Climbing on these rocks is forbidden. You'd know that if you read the signs.'"

"I swear I didn't see any signs," Cole says. "That guard was, like, on a mission. I still can't believe we got out of it."

I smack his shoulder. "We? I'm the one who convinced him we were doing a geologic survey."

"Oh yeah," Ellie says, rolling her eyes. "That's why he let us off. It had nothing to do with you batting those baby blues, right?"

The three of us laugh again at the story, but in the way of all memories, it recedes quickly into the past, no more than a ghost.

Ellie hops off the rock, dusts her hands together. "I don't know what to say, guys. I know we were broken up, but come on. My just-barely-ex and my best friend, fooling around on prom night? It stings, okay? And I can't just pretend—"

"I'm in love with Lucy."

Ellie and I whip our heads up at the same time, matching dinner-plate eyes, my heart still raging its four-years war. *Take it. Leave it. Take it. Leave it. Walk away. Walk away. Walk straight into his arms* . . . .

"What?" I stammer.

"I'm in love with you," Cole whispers. "In case you haven't figured it out." His smile is both apologetic and hopeful, relieved and afraid. Two for her and two for me.

Ellie glares at me, tears glazing her eyes, our momentary understanding shattered. She's a ghost before I can even ask her to stay, receding back through the trees toward Lav-Oaks High.

"That's not how I . . ." Cole's words evaporate, and then he's gone, too, chasing after Ellie, apologies floating like birds on the breeze.

I'm sorry I'm sorry I'm sorry . . .

"I'm in love too," a voice says behind me. "Love's *intense*, dude."

I don't need visual confirmation. The pungent smell identifies 420. I turn, smile, focus on the bag of Doritos in his hands—a perpetual accessory he never leaves home without. I stare at the bright orange triangles on the bag, anything to keep the ground from spinning.

Last night, Jayla said that Cole and I were in love, but to hear him say it, to look at him and know that he truly meant it, to *feel* it . . .

I'm in love with you . . . .

"It's, like, okay," 420 says. He's rockin' a festive sombrero today, snug over his dingy orange cap. "Say you have Tostitos. And you really love them, their crispy, salty goodness."

Dear universe: Will this day get any weirder?

"But *then!*" he says. "Then you have Doritos." He holds up the bag and wriggles his eyebrows. "Cheesy nacho goodness, also crispy, but tangy too. Am I right?"

"Dude," I say. "I have no idea what you're talking about. But you're totally cracking me up right now, so thanks."

"Love's a funny thing. Dorito?" He holds out the bag, and I help myself. Doritos are kind of awesome. Maybe he's on to something. And *on* something. That's a given.

"Oh my God, are you guys smoking pot back here? Because if Principal Zeff catches you, you won't be able to graduate." Clarice jumps out from behind the trees like a DEA ninja, sniffing the air around us.

"I'm just high on life, Clarice." I wink at her.

"Clarice, dude. Deep down, you're a Doritos kind of babe." 420 offers her a snack, but she steps back like he's offering up a severed head.

"Go to class," she says, giving him a small shove. "I don't want to report you."

420 giggles. "Class. Yeah. Later, babes." He salutes us with orange-dusted fingers and shuffles along, stops to watch a bird on the path, shuffles along again. He turns left before he gets to the school and heads . . . somewhere else.

"Whichever way the wind blows," I say.

Clarice clucks her tongue. "You shouldn't be encouraging him, Lucy. Anyway, Marceau's looking for you. He says it's important."

"I pulled something for you." Marceau holds out a bouquet of purple-and-white flowers, his smile wide and proud.

He's, like, impossibly sweet.

"You *picked* them," I say. I take a seat next to him on a stone bench just outside the school doors.

"Picked them," he corrects. "They were behind the school."

"Yeah, it's totally illegal. Wild columbine is protected."

His smile falls. "Will they put me in Guantanamo Bay? I would go for you. It would be worth it."

I press the flowers to my nose and take a deep whiff, trying to break Marceau's adoring gaze. He reaches for my hand, and something flickers in his eyes, reminding me again of that night at the party, how he "missed on me" when he found me out back, how his eyes were full of adoration even then. He didn't seem jealous of Cole, not exactly. But maybe there was something . . .

"Marceau, that night . . . Did you take any pictures? I mean, at the party, after we . . ." I let the question die midair. *Stupid.* There's no way he did it. Besides, what's the point? Cole's confession ruined the last chance I had at patching things up with Ellie anyway.

Does it even matter who took those pictures now?

Cole's confession . . .

"Miss Vacarro, I've been looking everywhere for you." Zeff emerges from the doorway, clip-clops down the stairs to our bench. "Mr. Chantrelle, shouldn't you be getting to class?"

"Yes, madame." He presses my hand to his lips.

"Mr. Chantrelle?" Zeff says. "Class?"

"*Oui.* Yes, sorry." He rises from the bench and takes giant, backward steps all the way up the stairs, keeping me in his sights until the last possible second.

Zeff nods at my flowers, grabs them for a closer look. "Aren't these protected?"

"I tried to tell him."

"Okay. We don't need another scandal. I never saw them." She pitches the bouquet into the bushes behind us. "Good news, Lucy. The board would like to discuss your case at the final meeting tonight. You and your sister could come, if you'd like. The meetings are open to the public."

"We're . . . um . . . Jayla and I volunteer with animals tonight." I don't tell her that it's more like animal, singular, and it's my own dog.

Semantics, as Franklin would say.

"Oh, that's nice. Okay. Well, I want you to know that we're in your corner, and it looks like things are finally happening. I just need you to stay positive, focus on your schoolwork." She gives me an awkward head pat and hands over a copy of the meeting agenda. "We're going to resolve this. Make it go away once and for all."

LAVENDER OAKS CENTRAL SCHOOL DISTRICT: YEAR-END BOARD MEETING AGENDA

1. Cyberbullying: How to protect our Students
2. Postprom "Sexting" ("Sex" + "text" or compromising photos or texts that go "Viral") incident and copycat pages on The Facebook
3. Online Code of Ethics
4. Campus Cell Phone and Tablet Policy
5. "Netiquette" ("Net" + "Etiquette") training—mandatory for teachers and students?
6. Disciplinary action for vibrators

After school in the lab, Franklin's silent as he reads the painfully overcapitalized agenda.

"Did you know about it?" I ask him.

"No," he says, deep in thought. "But they likely meant 'violators,' don't you think? Talk about an unfortunate typo. I wonder—"

"Franklin! I'm not talking about vibrators!"

"No, I supposed not." Franklin pulls a pen from behind his ear, makes a few notes on the agenda. "This is fantastic. An official discussion of the issues."

"It's a discussion of me! This is, like, horrifying!"

"Relax. The meetings are rarely that dramatic." Franklin laughs. "Don't look so shocked. I cover them for the paper, which you don't know because you've never read it, you illiterate little beast."

I grab his pen and flick him on the knee. "Since you're so chummy with the school board, how do I get them to mind their own business?"

Franklin shrugs. "Chin up, Veronica. Vibrators on the agenda in a room full of suburban mums? Your name will be forgotten before it's even uttered."

WE INTERRUPT THIS NONSENSE TO SPREAD THE LATEST BUZZ ON THE DEADLY ELECTRONIC THREAT LURKING WITHIN THE PRIVACY OF YOUR OWN PRIVATES

MISS DEMEANOR

3,877 likes 👍

1,105 talking about this

<u>Tuesday, May 6</u>

What lurks in the dark recesses between the sheets? What seedy devil has called forth slippery things that go buzz in the night? Corrupting our daughters and giving our sons inferiority complexes?

Those pocket-size, battery-powered criminals are infiltrating, recruiting members, making promises they can't keep. Lock your doors and your drawers, for the esteemed board members of Lavender Oaks Central School District have brought to the ~~foreskin~~ forefront a grim situation, one that threatens to turn your wholesome children into a well-oiled gang of desperate, sex-crazed marauders (instead of the more typically disorganized desperate, sex-crazed marauders who go about their sex-crazed maraudery on an individual basis).

Who are these shady usurpers? These peer-pressuring, sex-positive, pleasure appliances gone bad? Undisciplined vibrators, folks. And they're no laughing, moaning, sighing, screaming, or otherwise emoting matter.

If you're unlucky enough to tangle with one of these pink plastic hellions, do not—I repeat—do not engage. Simply back away slowly in a nonthreatening manner and contact the authorities as soon as it is safe for you to do so.

Conversely, if you're the type of desperate lowlife who willingly harbors such electronic dangers in the privacy

of your own home and/or pants, please—for the sake
of the children—DISCIPLINE YOUR VIBRATORS.

This has been a ~~pubic~~ public service announcement.

(Honestly. At Lav-Oaks, the shit practically writes itself
these days.)

Buzz along now!

xo ~ *Ciao!* ~ xo

Miss Demeanor

STICKS AND STONES MAY BREAK MY BONES, BUT THE INTERNET? THAT SHIT'S FOREVER, MAN

Prince Freckles totally misses me, but instead of lunching with Franklin at camp equestrian on Tuesday, I'm called into Zeff's office, where this is an actual thing that happens:

"Miss Vacarro, take a cookie."

The cookies are legit double dark chocolate, and I take two this time, walking right into her trap. I'm utterly blindsided when she turns her monitor toward me and goes, "Talk to me about this 'Juicy Lucy' page."

Being the inspiration for a meeting agenda was bad enough, especially since copies—annotated and illustrated for my viewing pleasure—appeared on my locker this morning. But sitting through a special screening of my personal Facebook shame is, like, top-ten cringe-worthy moments in history.

Zeff's all over the Juicy Lucy page, pointing out pictures and commentary from yesterday's lunchtime tell-all with Cole and Ellie, a shot of me and 420 that suggests more than just an innocent exchange of Doritos, and an entire video of Marceau handing over the contraband flowers, which some enterprising Lav-Oaks student has remixed into a voice-over marriage proposal complete with orchestral soundtrack.

Somewhere out there is a therapist who's going to put her kids through college as a direct result of my senior year.

"I don't know who made it," I say. "Basically, I'm trying to ignore it."

Zeff nods, her face both stern and worried. "The board reviewed this page at the meeting and—"

"What? How?"

"We have a projector. Lucy, the parents are upset. Specifically, John Brandt's father and Griffin Colanzi's mother. Both are concerned about their children's futures."

I can only imagine Griff's mother at the meeting. I'm sure she had their full attention as she detailed all the ways in which I'm a horrible influence—she's room-commanding like that. Also, she has this total bitchface that makes babies cry and causes heart failure in small dogs.

"Mrs. Colanzi was upset that parents hadn't been notified about the viral nature of the photos earlier." Ms. Zeff leans forward, head in her hands. "I'd hoped to keep this thing better contained, but Facebook being what it is . . ."

"Griff's mother is a little crazy," I say, breaking off a piece of cookie. "You should see her at family dinners."

"I got that impression," she says. "Sane people do not wear lipstick that severe. Anyway, she wasn't the only one. It turned into a 'My Little Angel is the Best at Everything' free-for-all, and they all wanted someone to blame."

"Me."

"I kept your actual name out of it, but yes. 'The female student in the green sheets,' they called you. I'm sure some of the parents recognized you, though."

My cheeks go tar-in-the-summer hot. "Griff's mom."

"Griff's mom." Ms. Zeff flicks off her monitor and folds her hands on the desk between us. "Miss Vacarro, you should know . . . the other day in my office, when I showed you my Facebook? I was trying for a teachable moment. I was wrong to blame you. I didn't realize things had gotten so bad, that you'd been targeted like this."

Franklin's words echo. *Get your side out there. Take a stand on this issue . . . . You won't tell Zeff about the posters . . . . You won't state your case. . . .*

"Any idea who may be targeting you?" she asks.

I shove in a bite of cookie and shrug. It's not like I can show her Franklin's files, tell her about all the cross-referencing and our investigation. Not until we have proof. And with Ellie back in the arctic freeze-out zone again, I'm not sure it even matters.

She leans in close, lowers her voice. "Miss Vacarro, I'm in a jam here. The board's pushing me to do something about this, and I don't know where to start. You say you didn't post the original pictures—"

"I didn't."

"—and I believe you. But that leaves a lot of plot holes." She holds my gaze a moment longer, then sighs. "I thought maybe the adults could set an example, log out of Facebook for a while. But that won't fly. Don't tell anyone I told you this, but it seems that some of my esteemed colleagues are just as plugged in as you kids. They revolted when I suggested it last night."

"It's the baby pictures," I say. "Classic parental over-sharing."

Ms. Zeff's eyes light up. "I know, right? I'm so tired of baby pictures I could vomit."

I let out a halfhearted laugh, but it seems Zeff realizes she's crossing into the adults-trying-to-be-friends zone, and she stiffens. "Miss Vacarro—Lucy. I want you to know that I'll be announcing some new student policies tomorrow. We're also investigating the Juicy Lucy page to see if we can track down the owner." She looks to her darkened monitor, then back to me. "Olivia Barnes was in here yesterday, trying to convince me that you launched the page yourself to cover your tracks."

I stare, mouth open, cookie crumbs leaping onto my shirt.

"No, I didn't think so," Zeff says. "She's just rattled. She's as anxious to resolve this as we are. The pictures of her are quite embarrassing."

"I'm sure." I had no idea that Olivia's Cole crush was so *Fatal Attraction*. I wonder if I should put Night of the Living Dog on guard duty for poor Spike, just in case.

"I know I was wrong before, but now that all of this is out in the open, I have a job to do." Across her big oak desk, Ms. Zeff pats my hand. "Principals have to protect all students, regardless of fault. Sometimes that means doing things that make other students unpopular."

She means me.

"Couldn't you just wait on the unpopular-making stuff until after I graduate?" I ask.

She offers a sympathetic smile. "I wish I could. Unfortunately, you seem to be the source of this scandal, and those megaphone kids—what are they called?"

"(e)VIL."

Ms. Zeff laughs. "You think?"

"No, that's their call sign. Like, their acronym. Electronic Vanities Intervention League."

"Wow," she says. "That's . . . clever."

"Ash Hollowell? He's the leader. He's pretty smart. They all are. Crazy, but smart."

"I'm glad to hear you say that," Zeff says. "It makes what I'm about to tell you much easier."

She nods toward the plate of cookies. I shake my head, sink lower into my chair.

"Between you and Asher and his conspiracy buddies," she says, "the school's riled up. Teachers are complaining about the disruptions. And parents—as we learned last night—are getting pushy."

"But after exams and graduation, it'll blow—"

"It won't, especially if you're not willing to hand over names." She waits, giving me another opening, but I don't take it. Pointing fingers without evidence? That plan has *backfire* written all over it.

"I don't think you realize the seriousness here, Miss Vacarro. Your prom night escapades and the mess that came after—which you didn't deserve, but it's happening regardless—forced us to reconsider whether our current cyberbullying policies are effective. Most of those kids are minors. Parents could decide to get the police involved. I'm not trying to scare you. It's just the way it is in the age of social media." She pauses a moment to let that sink in. "Unfortunately, to show that we're being proactive, I need to make an example out of someone. You guys are the most visible."

"What kind of example?" I ask.

"Nothing too painful, I hope." She smiles without showing her teeth. "I'd like for you to do a group project. I'm allocating a ten-minute slot in the graduation ceremony, and I expect you to put your brilliant brains together and come up with a presentation about the dangers of sexting and cyberbullying."

"Um . . ." *Does not compute does not compute . . .*

"It's a cause they're obviously passionate about," she says, "and one that's come directly to your doorstep. Couldn't be a more perfect match."

"Oh, it could be." I picture Asher and his dossiers, white pants on the soccer field. Megaphones. "Ms. Zeff, couldn't I just, like, clean whiteboards? File people's . . . files? You have files. I've seen them. I can file them. I'm an excellent filer."

"I appreciate your enthusiasm, Miss Vacarro. I look forward to seeing you channel it into your presentation. I'll notify the others, and you can get started tomorrow after school."

"But how are we supposed to coordinate? They don't even have cell phones."

"And neither did I when I was your age, yet I survived." She gets that nostalgic look in her eyes that reminds me of Mom when she's talking about Texas barbecue. "Do you know we had to carry quarters so we'd always be able to use a pay phone in an emergency? And pay phones didn't have text. Can you imagine? The flip side is that there's no viral evidence of my personal indiscretions—not that I was indiscreet, but . . . anyway. I've already spoken with your sister about this. She's got no hard feelings toward Mr. Hollowell about the pep rally interruption, and she offered to host the group meeting at your house. Things are in motion, Lucy. Embrace the wave."

"But . . . wave? We're landlocked." I'm still stuck on the whole group project thing, but Zeff's face is all, *Are you really going to argue this, Miss Vacarro?* "Ms. Zeff, I do think cyberbullying is a worthwhile cause. I mean, anti-cyberbullying. But wouldn't you rather give that time at graduation to Jayla? You know how she moves a crowd. And there's supposed to be cameras and media and—"

"Let me be absolutely clear." Zeff leans forward in her chair, suddenly firm. "If you don't find a way to make this happen, you won't be graduating. Mr. Hollowell and his associates won't be graduating. And you'll all get to be very close friends in summer school together." She grabs the plate from her desk, the icy glare replaced with a fresh smile. "Cookie?"

GET GROUPTHINKY WITH IT

In conclusion, everyone is encouraged-slash-ordered to hate on Lucy for the rest of forever, and also, you should steal her lunch money and kick her dog while he's sleeping, and if she shows up at the twenty-year reunion, you should totally freeze her adult diapers."

Homeroom announcements the following morning, only slightly paraphrased.

"Hang in there, mate. We'll bloody solve this." Griffin offers a sympathetic smile, but I focus on my Converse, add a new skeleton to the pen-and-ink masterpiece I started at the beginning of the school year. Back then, drawing on my sneakers in homeroom was just a way to pass the time. Now it's like my personal Zen retreat where I go to sip green tea and listen to wind chimes and pretend everyone isn't plotting my make-it-look-like-an-accident demise.

Because . . .

LAVENDER OAKS HIGH SCHOOL CYBER SAFETY RULES (EFFECTIVE IMMEDIATELY)

1. Student Cell phone usage will be strictly prohibited during school hours. All students seen with cell phones—including at lunch and open periods—will have those phones confiscated.
2. Seniors will be required to attend an online Sensitivity and Anti-Cyberbullying training Session, to be administered repeatedly during lunch hours by a Local Law-Enforcement expert in Cybercrime.
3. All students are required to watch a Cyberbullying video at home, available on YouTube, and sign—together with their parent or guardian—a Pledge against bullying.
4. Any student caught engaging in bullying on school property, or using school computer equipment for said bullying, will be suspended and, depending on the

type and severity of the bullying, turned
over to the Police.

5. The students who launched and/or
continue to engage with the Juicy Lucy
Facebook page are urged to come forward
with a full confession. Otherwise, the
Page will be investigated and the students
responsible will be punished to the fullest
extent possible.

Strangely, Miss Demeanor's page avoids all the mud. Maybe because it's more of a conduit than an actual content originator. Or maybe Ms. Zeff is totally Miss D. Or maybe I'm getting a little too Asher Hollowell conspiracy cracked for my own good.

Griff's ditching first-period calc for a Black & Brew run with Ellie. When the homeroom bell releases us, we go our separate ways.

Moments later, the corridor goes total red zone.

The kids who aren't making lewd gestures and buzzings of the vibratory nature are cursing me about the new policies, taking up Quinn and Haley's slut-narc-slut chant with renewed vigor. A tennis ball bounces off my head. Catcalls pierce my ears. Someone flings an open water bottle, dousing my arm in icy liquid.

Bag clutched to my chest, I keep my eyes down, trace the familiar path to my locker.

Cole's there when I arrive, his arms loaded with torn-down posters and duct tape, my locker fully maroon again. I've been avoiding him since the thing with Ellie the other day, still overwhelmed, still shell-shocked and dizzied by his confession.

"Thank you," I whisper.

He smiles, and everything else just melts away. The pressure in my chest releases like a balloon set free, propelling me into his arms. He drops the papers and wraps me in a hug, rubs my back. His lips press the top of my head, *shhh shhh shhh, everything's gonna be okay,* and that's it.

Nothing.

Else.

Matters.

Not the snickers and *ohmygod*s that float down the hallway. Not the *click-clicks* of the cell phone cameras already breaking the new no-phone rules. Not the projectiles. Not Olivia, clucking at us from across the hall.

Sometimes the right hug from the right person at the exact right time makes all the wrong in the world disappear. . . .

And sometimes true love just can't compete with a dude and his megaphoned minions.

"Attention networked pod people. The corporate

social media empire thanks you for your service and your soul." Ash rolls down the hallway with determination and authority, legit hell on wheels, club members in formation behind him. They're dressed like Facebook—blue shirts adorned with a white, glued-on *F*. Knit hats stamped with the thumbs-up icon.

Kiara marches in step, megaphone at the ready. "Every time you upload a picture to the network, a baby seal dies. Thank you."

A few people laugh, but they're actually putting away their phones.

"Every time you tag someone in a compromising photo, a spot in hell opens up for new members." Tens flashes a wicked grin, the shells in his hair clicking as he moves. "Thank you."

A few more people vanish into classrooms or move along down the hallway, pretending not to pay attention.

"The battle for humanity will come down to the singular fight of our time, techs versus the tech-nots, machines versus hearts. Where do your loyalties lie, sheeple?" Kiara shouts. Well, she's not really shouting, but with the megaphone, it's loud.

"Tech-nots!" the (e)VIL members chant in unison. "Hearts over wires. Souls over clouds. Unplug, unplug, unplug!"

There's a knot of girls across from us, gathered around the water fountain with their phones still out. One seems to be typing a novel with her thumbs while the others giggle. Tens darts toward them, still chanting into the megaphone. "Unplug, automatons! Unplug!"

"Every time you perpetuate online drama and fuel the toxic waste dump of bad social karma, the terrorists win. Thank you." A long, beige slip of a guy with an army of freckles and a Mohawk the color of maraschino cherries—I've seen him around, but realize now he's the "Roman" missing from the pep rally—finishes with a bow.

Two of the science teachers poke their heads out of their classrooms, but if they're at all concerned about (e)VIL's latest demonstration, they're leaving it to Zeff, who's presently zipping toward us at lightning speed.

"Asher Hollowell," she says. "I do appreciate your dedication, but this is a school, not a movie set."

"I understand that perfectly well, ma'am. It's the school we're trying to reach."

She holds out her hand, nods toward the megaphone. "Hand them over. All of them."

"But—"

"Would you like to spend the rest of the week in detention, Mr. Hollowell? Copying the constitution by hand, perhaps?" She's acting all bad coppy, but her lips twitch with the ghost of a smile. Deep down, she's impressed.

Reluctantly, Ash motions for everyone to hand over the megaphones. His minions slink away to class, Zeff close on their heels.

Ash rolls up to me and Cole.

"That was quite a performance," I say. "What's up?"

"Revolutionaries to the Mockingjay." He gives a firm salute. "Sorry we couldn't debrief you guys on the mission, but we didn't have a nontech way to reach you."

The hallway is mostly empty now, save for us and a few stragglers swapping books at their lockers.

"Dude, you guys planned that?" I ask. "For us?"

He nods curtly. "Yesterday Zeff told me she'd be announcing the new policies. I figured you'd be targeted. She also gave us the good news about the project."

"Good news?" I say. "We have to do a presentation in front of the whole graduating class. Not to mention parents and grandparents. *And* the paparazzi—Jayla Heart will be there. If you look up 'total suckage' in the dictionary, there's a picture of this project."

"It's the perfect time to get the message out. Captive audience. Various members of the media regime." Ash pulls an old-school date book from the back pocket of his wheelchair. "Zeff said it's cool to meet up at your place later? I need the coordinates."

"Cool as it gets," I say, but I'm pretty sure the sarcasm is lost. I give him the address and cross streets, thank him for clearing out the networked masses. In a blur of blue and white and chrome, he vanishes down the corridor.

Cole's been dead silent since the first (e)VIL "thank you," and now he's reanimating, giving me a playful shove on the shoulder. "Looks like you have more friends at this school than you thought, Mockingjay. And also, I'm totally coming over later, because there's no way I'm leaving you alone with those fanboys."

"But . . . I don't have time for all this," I say, reality settling back in like a dark cloud. "I have to get my evidence. Even if Ellie never speaks to me again, I can't let this go on. Zeff's on my case. John's parents are pissed, Griff's mom . . . The whole school's getting sucked into the vortex, and everyone hates me, and I didn't even—"

"Hey, hey, stop." Cole brushes his thumbs under my eyes to erase the tears. "Take a deep breath."

"Cole—"

"Do it. You'll feel better."

I do as he asks. He's right, as usual. "Have you talked to Ellie since . . . the other day?" I'm still in friendship Siberia. I've called a few times, sent two texts and a link to Franklin's baby owl video—nothing.

"Tried. Still trying." Cole puts his hands on my shoulders, holds my gaze. "Don't worry. We're not giving up on Ellie. And you've got three other people working on the investigation with you. We'll solve this thing, okay?"

I take another deep breath. He's right again. Despite my pariah status, I've still got allies here. Friends. Cole.

"Griff and I are meeting with Margolis at three to compare notes," he says. "After that, we'll come by your place for a recap. And possibly to stop you from trading your possessions for a stake in an underground survival compound with (e)VIL."

"And a year's supply of dehydrated food," I add, just as the late bell rings. "You can't live in an underground compound without dehydrated food."

Cole smiles. "There's my little apocalypse survivor. Welcome back."

MY MOM'S HOUSE IS A COOLER
SECRET BUNKER THAN YOUR MOM'S
HOUSE

I'm just saying," Ash Hollowell's just saying. He's also brushing blue corn chip crumbs from his lap onto my TV room floor, something that endlessly delights Night of the Living Dog. "Star Trek technology is limited by comparison. They get around the galaxy way more efficiently in Star Wars. Take *Empire Strikes Back*. The *Millennium Falcon* hopped from Hoth to Bespin in, like, *ridic* time, *without* a functioning hyperdrive. What Trek ship does that?"

Tens rolls one of his dreads between his fingers, considering. "Doesn't the *Falcon* carry a Backup Class twelve Hyperdrive?"

"Yes, and that's an excellent point. Hyperdrive units are portable—singular intricate components. Warp drives have all those crazy-huge parts. Antimatter pods, dilithium crystals, warp core, cooling system. And how long does it take to get from Earth to Vulcan? Days . . . *with* warp drive!"

Kiara rolls her eyes. "Are you guys fracking lunatics from Arkham? Comparing warp technology to hyperdrive is like comparing Klingon to Wookiee. One's grounded in proper grammar and phonology—an actual language—while the other is . . ." Kiara lets out a hilarious series of Wookiee grunts.

"Shields up!" Ash covers his face with his hands. "Angry Federation-beats-Empire type has entered the conversation!"

With a freckled hand, Roman reaches across the coffee table for a corn chip, does a flyby on the guacamole bowl. Night tracks his every move. "Captain Janeway? You denying that Star Wars vessels—"

"There's nothing to deny. Hyperdrives have no basis in real science, no limits; they're utter magic." Kiara makes a starburst with her fingers. "*Poof!* Warp drive functionality is rooted in theoretical physics, which is why there are limits. Fact versus fiction. There's no arguing this, guys."

"An observation from planet Earth?" I flop into Dad's recliner and flip open an orange Shasta. "The antitechnology club is sitting in my TV room having a serious debate about two different technologically advanced societies that only exist in your minds at all because of our own advanced technology."

"I know," Tens says. "Meta, right?"

"If by meta you mean hypocritical, yeah." I turn on Dad's laptop and pull up the new official cyberbullying manual Zeff sent me, twice as long as the old one. My plan is to basically plagiarize, reimagining a few key points with PowerPoint animations. "Aren't you guys, like, hipsters?"

Ash nods. "I'm about half hipster, thirty percent nerd, fourteen geek, dash of headbanger." He throws a death metal sign and rocks out. "If you're into labels."

"I'm half jock," Stephie says, her swim team hoodie zipped over the Facebook tee. "Then equal parts hipster, nerd, and bookworm."

"Hipsters, gah." Kiara shudders. "I'm a cybergeek with a side of marching band groupie. I go total bookworm on the weekends, though."

Roman's Mohawk twitches. "And I fucking hate labels, so there's that."

"He's a hater," Stephie says. "That *is* his label."

"I'm a foodie and a coffee snob," Tens says proudly. "And a baker. I make tarts on the weekends for my parents' café."

"Those aren't labels, dumbass," Stephie says. "Those are activities. Labels are like: band geek, comic book nerd, art freak."

"I'm those, too," Tens says, and Ash beans him in the forehead with a chip.

"Wait," I say. "Not Black & Brew?"

"Seriously? How do you think it got its name?" Tens thumbs at his chest.

I blink.

"Are we challenging your Ass and Umptions today?" Roman laughs at my flabbergasted face. He's teasing, but my cheeks flame anyway.

Am I like this with everyone?

No wonder the whole school believes I posted those pictures. I might as well be wearing a shirt that says, *If you can read this, I'm already judging you.*

"Consider me challenged," I say.

"Hey! That's my line," Ash says.

Stephie punches him in the shoulder. "Challeng*ing*, maybe. Or just annoying."

"Lucy, we're not against technology," Kiara says seriously. "We're against *vanity*-based technology—which doesn't exist in these imagined societies—and the corporate regime that's co-opting it for their own gain. Not to mention bullshit labels, as Roman so eloquently pointed out."

Ash leans forward in his wheelchair to scratch Night's ears. "Corporations own the government. Agribusiness, big pharma. Like the FDA really cares about what's in our drugs, or how those drugs end up in the water supply. They're lobotomizing us." He taps the dog's head. "Mind control."

Night barks in agreement.

"Don't get me started on the FDA," Roman says. "Or the USDA."

"Not to mention the NSA and Department of Defense," Kiara says. "I'm totally applying DOD after college so I can, like, infiltrate."

Ash pats her on the shoulder. "Our girl here's a code breaker. Not to mention an ace hacker. Hardwired, of course. Wireless isn't secure."

She shrugs. "How else are you supposed to learn about the freedoms the government is revoking, one quiet infringement at a time?"

"Quiet infringements?" I say.

Kiara pushes my laptop closed, inspecting the side for what I assume is a hardwire port. "It's like you haven't even *read* the Patriot Act."

Tens and Roman chuckle, like, *Yeah, right! Who hasn't read* that *old classic?*

I look to Ash with a pleading gaze. "Rein in your minions, fearless leader?"

"Not until Kiara admits that hyperdrive technology is vastly efficient, thereby making the *Millennium Falcon* a much more elegant ship."

I slam my soda can on the coffee table in mock indignation. "Listen up, nerd herd. I was in the room at Comic Con when Neil deGrasse Tyson articulated all the reasons why the *Enterprise* wins the starship smackdown, so in all manner of superior space technology I defer to him, a legit astrophysicist, over a group whose primary mission in life is to unplug the Internet. Now please shut up about fictional societies and help me figure out this presentation or I'll activate the locator chip on the laptop and broadcast your shit to the man."

That locator chip thing? I don't even know what I just said. But Ash looks pretty impressed, and everyone cracks up, including me.

"You went to Comic Con?" Asher asks. "And stood in the presence of greatness like that?"

I shrug. "Truefax."

"Marry me?" he says.

"Only if we can update our relationship status on Facebook."

He winks. "We'll find a way to cross this digital divide, Lucy."

"Let's start with PowerPoint." I reopen the laptop and flip through the templates. "These backgrounds suck—we need to pick something semicool."

"Dude, no," Ash says. "PowerPoint is the devil's

playground. Bill Gates? Definitely working for the other side."

I blink and stare, openmouthed. It's getting to be my usual response with Ash.

"Allow me to demonstrate the proper way to do a group presentation." He snaps his fingers, and Tens, Kiara, Stephie, and Roman are on their feet, standing in formation.

"Point made," I say. "Let's put our nonlobotomized heads together and see what we come up with."

Ultimately, we compromise with a combination PowerPoint slide show and live-action interpretive dance on the negative effects of cyberbullying. We map out our bullet points, and I let them run through their moves, offer a few pointers on making it more obvious that they're supposed to be electrons bouncing up against humanity.

"Thanks for coming over today." I save the PowerPoint presentation and close the laptop. "Sorry I got you guys into this mess with my stupid scandal."

"Not your fault." Ash offers a sympathetic smile that his friends mirror. "And I don't know who's trying to frame you, but obviously they're in deep. That's why this presentation is so key. If we can reach just one person, stop this from happening to someone else . . . you know?"

"Tagging. God," Roman says. "Bad enough you can post pictures of anyone without their permission. Now there's facial recognition technology and location data . . . creepy." He shoves in another guacamole-covered chip. "Sanctioned stalking."

"And sanctioned bragging. Sanctioned bullying." Stephie nods at me, her blue eyes bright and compassionate. "You really are in a position to take a stand here, Mockingjay. Go all hashtag privacy rights on their asses."

I blow a frustrated breath into my bangs. "I'm not a poster girl, guys. I'm definitely not a revolutionary. I'm just trying to clear my name. Get Zeff off my back and prove to my friends that it wasn't me."

Kiara says, "If they're your friends, shouldn't they just *believe* you?"

It's a fair question, one I've considered. I know Cole believes me, but Griff? There's still a shadow of doubt in her eyes, and how could there not be? She's splitting time between me and Ellie, caught in the middle. And Ellie's back to pretending I don't exist.

"My friends are—"

"Who wants bundts?" Jayla sings her way in through the front door, Bundt Heads box in hand. I swear she's reading Mom's parenting magazine articles on how to relate to your ornery teen and her friends. She should've checked the freezer—we've still got a few dozen left over from the "you're not on the list" prank meeting.

I smile at her with gritted teeth. "I thought you were busy promising to stay at the mall and far, far away?"

"Whoa. You're . . . Ohmygod. The . . . Dangers . . . Aren't you . . ." Kiara's hyperventilating, and the guys are about three seconds from full-scale fanboy meltdown, all of them tripping over their sneakers and wheels to help Jayla with the box.

Before someone loses an eye, I stand and take the box from my sister, set it on the coffee table.

"This is top-secret, superclassified, doesn't-leave-this-room-or-I-kill-you information." I scrutinize each (e)VIL member, meeting their eyes in turn. "Jayla Heart is my sister."

Kiara still can't breathe, and the boys are practically squealing. It's a common reaction from those who haven't bought into the tabloid smears, but the show never gets any less barfy for me.

Still, Jayla seems touched. For all her marriage proposals and Heartthrobs fan page likes, Angelica Darling is mostly a joke. She acts all cool and bubbly, all *the show must go on*, but she *has* to know how people see her—the tabloid version. The Angelica version. That's who she is in their eyes, not even a real person.

I look at her now, her eyes misty, her smile almost shy, and my heart hurts.

Ash says, "Miss Heart. I truly apologize for the interruption at the pep rally. I hope the exercising of our First Amendment rights didn't upset you."

Jayla laughs. "Dude, not a problem. You guys rocked out there! I'm just sorry some jackhole sent pics to the tabloids—I hope your parents aren't pissed."

Ash beams. "They don't even know about it," he says. "As long as they don't check the secret cache under my SETI server . . ."

Stephie rolls her eyes. "Don't tell people the location of your secret cache, dumbass."

While (e)VIL continues with the being-enamored-with-Jayla portion of our meeting, my Mars Investigations team arrives, Spike in tow. He spazzes when he sees Night, and the two of them crash down the basement stairs in a blur, like, *Come on! Let's go do something naughty while the people aren't watching!*

Cole's got a folder—sorry, a *dossier*—full of printouts, photos Franklin enlarged on the school printer. Before he shares the details, he looks cautiously at Asher, waiting for my signal.

"Asher," I say. "Tens. Roman. Stephie. Kiara. What I'm about to share is, like the identity of my sister, highly classified. My friends and I are working undercover to investigate the scandal. If you're not interested, I understand, and you can leave now, no hard feelings. On the other hand, if you want in, you got it. Full security clearance."

I scan the ragtag (e)VIL members assembled in my TV room. How must I look through their eyes, a girl who until recently never spoke to them? A girl who spent more time making fun of their club, their mission, than she did finding out what they were about? A girl who never bothered to learn one simple thing about any of them—a hobby, a favorite book, how they spend their weekends?

Who am I to them? To anyone?

Labels float in the air before my eyes, angry black font on torn white paper.

Goth. Gamer. Ashamed sister. Bitch. Zombie freak. Bad friend. Loner. Slut. Narc. Slarc.

"Dude. Are you serious?" Ash pumps his fists in the air, like, *Rock on!* "I speak for everyone when I say, uh, yeah! We live for this stuff. And I'm not leaving my future wife out to dry."

Franklin says, "Congratulations on your engagement."

Cole and Griff simultaneously raise their eyebrows.

"Confidentiality is a given with us," Stephie says. "I don't even let my parents film the swim team meets. None of us have Face-frack or Insta-sham or any of that crap."

"Only my nana," Kiara says, and everyone laughs, and minutes later, we're huddled around the coffee table, bundts and corn chips everywhere, looking at a spread of party photos that just yesterday would've mortified me.

There's something about a real-life joint mission, a shared burden that lessens the sting in a way that all those hours surviving zombie attacks with my online gamer crew never has.

"After all the bloody cross-checking," Griffin says, fake accent cutting in and out, "I've determined that our mystery wing wearer is one of five girls. Olivia, obviously—best guess. Her friends, Haley and Quinn. Farrah, the zombie girl who was—according to the vampires—making out with all of them. And Clarice, president of SASA. John had wings for a while, but they were silver, and despite his eagerness to go all scandal, I don't think he's interested in 420 in a sexual or drug hookup way."

"Thanks for the analysis, Agent Colanzi." I look over the photos again, some of them circled in Sharpie where the girls appear with pink sparkly wings. "Guess they had a sale at the fairy store."

Kiara lines them all up, poring over each one with stern concentration.

"I'm telling you, Olivia makes sense," Griff says. "She's

majorly crushing on Cole, and she's been giving you shit hard-core ever since this happened."

"She also told Zeff I started the Juicy page myself," I say.

"No." Cole shakes his head. "She's acting crazy, but before all this, Olivia was really quiet and sweet. She's pissed, but I don't think she'd go to all this trouble just to out me and Lucy. Plus, that picture of her? Her dad freaked."

"Maybe it's a cover," Griff says. "It's not like any of us talked to the dad. Right?"

"Despite her atrocious accent," Franklin says, "Griffin has an excellent point."

She beams. "Thank you, Franklin."

"Well, it's not zombie girl," I say. "Cole and I saw her in the bathroom with one of the vamps at the same time our fairy would've been in the closet with 420."

"You guys. It's *her*." Jayla, who'd been quietly snarfing bundts until this moment, points to a picture of Clarice.

"Wait. She's right," Ash says.

"Dude." Tens shoves Asher's wheelchair. "You didn't even see who Jayla was pointing at. You're just in love with her."

"*You're* in love with her." Asher's face is the color of Jay's fuchsia tank top.

"Jayla Heart? I'm *totally* in love with her," Kiara says with a playful smile, "and I say she's right, too."

"You *guys*. Clarice?" I grab the picture for a closer look. Clarice is bent over the recycle bin, dropping bottles in by the fistful. There's a clear shot of the wings. Pink, sparkly. "No way. She's so, like, *proper*."

Jayla points to the photo in my hands. "Look at the wings. See how the top edge is scalloped? Three scoops there. Most of the others only have two." On the table, she pushes aside shots of Haley, Olivia, and zombie girl, all with two scoops. She grabs a picture of Quinn. "This one has three scoops, but only the tops of her wings are sparkled." She points to Clarice again. "The sparkles on the bottom set these apart. Now, look at the picture of the wings in Cole's room." She shuffles through the stack and locates it, holding the two photos side by side. "Same wings. It's totally her."

I take a closer look. As much as it pains me to say this, my sister's right.

"Clarice is a closet stoner?" Cole scratches his head. "Really didn't see that coming."

"She's legit," I say. "I've sat through her 'just say no' lectures—no way is she into that stuff."

Franklin taps a pen against his chin, leaving a blue smudge. "If that's true, what on earth were those two doing hiding out in the—oh. *Oh!*" His eyes go wide.

"You think they were hooking up?" I ask.

Jayla snorts. "Hiding out in a closet? You can bet they weren't doing an intervention."

Clarice and 420? That girl's whole raison d'être is to bust him. She's tried to convince Zeff to get a search warrant for his locker, filled his backpack with pamphlets, scowled and huffed at his constant cannabis cloud. That's just what the president of Students Against Substance Abuse does. And 420 . . . well, he's 420. He'd be the president of Students All *About* Substance Abuse if being president of something wasn't so mentally taxing.

"Lucy. You thinking what I'm thinking?" Jayla's eyebrows wiggle. "Season three, episode eleven?"

"Ohmygod . . . Barista Boy!"

Angelica had this crazy crush on her barista, but she couldn't let her fiancé know, and the barista always gave Angelica decaf instead of regular because she was so highstrung and bitchy to the baristas, and they'd always make fun of Lady Wiggles, Angelica's wallet-size dog.

But one night she got there just as the dude was closing up, and he made the coffee without charging her because he'd already cashed out the register. She was all appreciative—cue the witty banter—and in the very next frame, Lady Wiggles nosed her way into the supply closet to reveal Angelica and Barista Boy getting it on, complete with all the half-caff, extrafoam, extrahot, triple-shot innuendos you'd expect.

"Lucy?" Roman asks.

"Mocha what? What?" I blink back to reality. TV room. (e)VIL and Cole, Griff and Jay, the guilty-looking dog duo who probably broke something downstairs, all of us crowded around the table, everyone looking at me.

"I asked if you think they took the pictures," Roman says.

"No," I say. "But maybe Clarice knows something."

"Will she talk?" Franklin asks. "As I recall, your 420 interrogation didn't go well."

I scoop the photos back into the dossier. "I have pictures that place the president of Students Against Substance Abuse in a closet with the class pothead. I have a ten-minute slot at graduation with a projector and a captive audience. 420 might not care about his rep, but I bet Clarice does."

Franklin shakes his head. "More graymail, Lucy?"

"Superlight gray," I remind him.

"Right. In the meantime," he says, "any leads on the Juicy page?"

All of us mumble and shrug.

"I'll look into it," Kiara says. "No guarantees, but if the page is public, there might be an electronic trail." She turns to Asher. "Request permission to access social networks for investigative purposes?"

"Permission granted," he says.

"Permission to report findings to Lucy via secure e-mail alias, Code Name Hackalicious?"

"Permission granted," Ash repeats. "Anything Lucy and the others need. Oh, one final matter of great importance." He turns to Jayla with a serious glare. "What's a helpless kid in a wheelchair gotta do to score a ride in that Porsche?"

HIGH SCHOOL, THE MOON LANDING, AND OTHER CONSPIRACIES

MISS DEMEANOR

4,209 likes 👍

1,097 talking about this

Thursday, May 8

The moment you've all been waiting for—since you
forked over $100 of Daddy's cash for a memento that
will only torment you in the future as you drink your
depression numb and complain loudly about how
your life turned out and really, they should've voted

you Most Likely to Do JACK SHIT, but that wasn't a
category on the list—has finally arrived.

YEARBOOK DAY!

There's something magical about it, don't you think?
And by magical, I mean . . . I've seen you people
in real life, and your senior pictures aren't quite as
authentic as one might expect from the upstanding
students of Lavender Oaks. Back me up, (e)VIL.
You kids know photo manipulation when you see it.
Poreless skin and ultrawhite teeth, shadowy footprint
on the surface of the fake moon, could be a UFO,
could be a reflection. Feel me?

Shit. I just remembered (e)VIL isn't on Facebook.
All this carefully crafted conspiracy humor is lost to
the ether. No matter. For the rest of you, speaking of
manipulated photos, I'm compelled to report that the
Prince Freckles photographer has yet to come forth.
This is a once-in-a-lifetime opportunity for artificially
curated infamy, people. What are you waiting for, an
invitation? *Mi scandal es su scandal!*

Don't let me keep you, fishies. Run along to the

cafeteria and collect your yearbooks, write those
*keep in touch*es and *have a great summer*s until your
hands cramp. In twenty years, when the delicate arts
of handwriting and eye contact are long forgotten and
communication occurs solely via brainchip-to-brainchip
text, you'll have a lovely little keepsake of the good ol'
days. Or a doorstop for your space pod.

Either way, someone else's money well spent.

xo ~ *Ciao!* ~ xo

Miss Demeanor

HAVE A GREAT SUMMER! BON VOYAGE! TRY NOT TO SLEEP WITH ANYONE ELSE'S BOYFRIEND ON YOUR WAY OUT!

I'm sixty percent sure I'm ditching my yearbook anyway, but it's already paid for, so I brave the hostile territory of the cafeteria and get in line for the pickup.

Right behind Olivia and the sprite sisters.

The line moves at an agonizing pace, and the girls keep whispering and turning around and laughing, making a big production of it just in case I miss the point.

"Yes," I say. "You're all quite cool, and I'm a horrible person. Moving on."

"Did you hear something?" Quinn asks Olivia.

Olivia looks right at me, scans my zombie food pyramid shirt. The scowl looks funny on her sweet face, like she borrowed it from one of her friends and it's not quite her size. "Probably just the wind," she says.

"Why does the wind advocate zombies eating people?" Haley says, absently tapping her phone screen with a seashell-pink fingernail. "The wind is so, like, morbid."

I'm all, *Whatevs. You three would be the first to get eaten if I were in charge of feeding zombies,* but getting middle-schooled by Olivia and her friends stings. Kiara's creeping on their Facebook profiles, but she's yet to find any connections to the Juicy Lucy page owner. I haven't cornered Clarice, either—she's been too busy handing out flyers about staying sober at the upcoming graduation parties. *Avoid a scandal,* the flyer urges. *Party with pride!*

None of my allies are present either. Ironically, they're suffering through their mandatory cyberbully training today. Zeff let me out of it since I'm doing the presentation with (e)VIL, but word on the street is that Zeff's trotting out her personal Facebook feed again, complete with babies and inappropriate messages from her mom.

"Oh my God, prom pics!" Haley squeals when she reaches the table. The yearbooks are stacked in a pyramid, and on the other side, there's a file box with eight by tens of our unicorn pictures. In all the craziness that happened after prom, I forgot about them.

Say magic pixie dust. . . . Cutest couple ever . . .

I wait for the girls to finish collecting their stuff before I hastily sign for my yearbook, locate my prom photo. Anxious, I slide it from the box.

There's Cole, green eyes sparkling brighter than the unicorn's golden horn. I'm laughing at something he said, and he's got one arm over the horse's back, a hand on my shoulder, and it's almost the kind of picture you frame on the mantel to show your kids when you're fifty.

Almost.

If not for the angry black letters scrawled across my face.

#SLUT.

Everything inside me shrivels and aches. I tear the defiled photo in half and drop it in the trash.

"Don't throw it out," Haley says from behind me. It's obvious now that they knew, that they were watching me, waiting for the reaction. They must've planned it—probably got their hands on the photos earlier, left their mark. "Don't you want something to remember him by when he dumps you?"

"Hot tip for you, Haley," a voice says from behind us. I'd recognize it anywhere. "Cole and I broke up *way* before prom," Ellie says. "So I suggest you and your posse of haters recheck your facts and quit abusing Lucy. It's none of your business, anyway."

"It's our business," Haley says. "We have a right to know who's skanking around, trying to steal our boyfriends."

"None of you *have* boyfriends," Ellie says, grabbing my hand. It's so unexpected, I have to fight my instinct not to flinch. "We're all women, aren't we? We should be sticking up for our sisters, not perpetuating the patriarchy by tearing one another down."

"*She's* the one sticking things that don't belong to her into places where they don't belong," Olivia says.

"What happened to you, Olivia?" Ellie says. "Lucy's a person. She has a heart and a soul and she makes mistakes. You want someone talking to your little sisters like this? Or your mothers? What is *wrong* with you guys?"

"We're trying to help," Quinn says. "You should be glad."

Ellie snorts. "You're trying to cause drama, and it's pathetic. Show a little love and respect for your Lav-Oaks sisters. For yourselves."

I turn to Ellie with grateful tears in my eyes.

She drops my hand as the girls slink away, waves the air like it was nothing special. Nothing she wouldn't have done for anyone. "I can't stand seeing girls hate on girls. There's enough of that in the tabloids."

There must be something meaningful and important to say, something to make her stay. . . .

We're supposed to go to college soon. To buy coordinating bed-spreads and posters. To pack up the car with snacks and playlists and heart-shaped sunglasses in every color, Cali-bound, future-bound, best-friends-for-the-rest-of-forever-bound.

But all I come up with is, "Tell me about it," and then she's taking her yearbook from the stack, stuffing it into her backpack without asking me to sign it.

"See you around, Lucy."

On the downside, by the end of the school day, my year-book is MIA.

On the upside, I dug deep, and I've yet to unearth any regret about this. It was probably Quinn—she's in my physics class and could've easy swiped it from my backpack when I was at the whiteboard calculating the velocity of an elephant sliding down a seesaw at a forty-five-degree angle.

*Super*relevant.

The word of the day is . . . *meh?* By the time I stake out Clarice's locker after last bell, I'm feeling more curious and less graymaily than I was yesterday.

"I need your help," I say. "And before you refuse . . . 420. Photographic evidence."

Beneath her sleek black bangs, Clarice's eyes go wide, and an armload of flyers scatter at her feet.

"Relax." I crouch down to help. "I just have some

questions. I'm trying to figure out what happened that night and who started the Facebook stuff. It wasn't me."

"It wasn't *me!*"

"You might've seen something."

She holds my gaze for a moment, considering.

"Photographic evidence," I singsong. "Fairy wings, pot leaf hats . . . could be the biggest scandal to hit Lav-Oaks since the other biggest scandal."

She blows a breath through her bangs. "Fine. Because I respect Cole and I'm a huge proponent of truth, I'll talk to you. Confidentially?"

"Off the record," I say, which basically means it's not confidential but it's not going viral, either.

We grab her stuff and duck into an empty classroom, shutting the door behind us.

Clarice confirms that she and 420 were making out in the closet when Cole and I came in—they heard us arguing about Ellie, but didn't want to get busted. After we fell asleep, they saw their chance. 420 left first, and she followed a few minutes later.

"No one was around on the second floor," she says. "By that time, people were mostly chilled out in the living room and on the deck. Everyone was, like, wasted. Total *I Love You, Man* stuff, stupid parlor tricks."

"Olivia with the Mike's Lemonade," I say.

"Exactly. No, wait . . ." She shakes her head, presses her fingers to her temples. "That was later. I didn't actually see it. When I was in the living room, she was sitting with her girlfriends, all smooshed together in the big recliner. They were playing 'I Never.' A few minutes later, Farrah came in and told people that you and Cole were doing it upstairs."

"Doing it? God. Was there a stampede?" I say. "I'm surprised there weren't more pictures."

She shrugs. "Most everyone was so blasted by then, it didn't really register. Olivia and Quinn got up, just kind of giggling and whispering about it. But then Brian and Ryan got into a wrestling match on the deck with these two werewolves, and after that someone brought Prince Freckles inside, and . . . I don't know. I think people kind of forgot about you and Cole. Seriously, it's not like you really *were* doing it. You were asleep. It was just one of those 'what happens at the party stays at party' things."

"Can you say for certain whether anyone went upstairs after that?"

Clarice nods. "A few people. Olivia for sure, and maybe Haley and Quinn. I don't know them all that well, and everyone had wings, so . . . I just . . . People were kind of coming and going, and I found . . ." Clarice's face goes from pale to puce in a second flat. "I was doing something else. In the mudroom." She waits for me to get the drift.

Pause button on my own drama, because . . .

"You and 420, huh?" I say playfully. "He called you a Doritos kind of girl, right? In 420 lingo, that's practically a sonnet."

She blushes again. Despite our tense history, it's hard not to like this smitten version of her. "He's charming once you get to know him."

"How will you cross the drug divide?" I ask. "I don't mean that as an insult. But really. Clarice, you don't even like my boots. You're, like, hard-core straight-edge. And he's . . . more of a squiggle."

"Honestly? It's an issue." Clarice's voice is thoughtful, but her smile doesn't fade. "Look. I'm not one of those girls who thinks she can save the boy, or even make him change. I've been trying for years with no results. The thing is, all that time I spent lecturing him and following him around, I got to know him—even more than I got to know John. There's a lot more to 420 than just . . . Well, for starters, he has an actual name. Lucas."

Lucas. Such a little thing, knowing a person's name. A simple, everyday thing that changes my entire perspective.

Clarice smooths the back of her hair. "It's not perfect, Lucy. But you can't help who you love."

I text Franklin to meet up at the lab for the Clarice update, but we cross paths in the hall at my locker.

With Olivia.

"Oh, there you are," she says, all fake nice. She holds out a yearbook. "It was on the condiment table in the cafeteria."

"I didn't leave it in the cafeteria," I say.

Her face pinches. "Well, that's where I found it. Do you want it or not?"

Franklin's giving her this look, like he's trying to puzzle something out, and when I reach for the yearbook, he makes a move to do the same. I'm faster though, and the second it's in my hands, Olivia motors out of there.

"She's up to something," Franklin says. "Maybe you shouldn't—"

"People *signed* this? For me?" Every page, every inch of white space is covered with signatures.

But they aren't signatures. They're messages. Identical.

Have a #JUICY summer!

After all the name-calling, the spitballs, the Facebook page, this is the thing that breaks me, the final act that sends me over the edge. Tears slip down my cheeks unbidden, splashing onto the yearbook.

"Original," I choke out. All the lightness I felt with Clarice is slipping into shadow, all the camaraderie with (e)VIL a distant memory.

Franklin takes the yearbook, flips through the pages. "Bloody hell."

He slams the yearbook shut, and I grab it and chuck it into a trash can.

"We could talk to Ms. Zeff," he says, "ask if they have extras—"

"I don't want one. What's the point? No one will sign it."

Franklin's deep brown eyes are full of concern. "We're almost graduates. You can't let these petty acts of vandalism convince you that you're a bad person. You're not, Lucy."

"I hooked up with my best friend's barely-ex-boyfriend."

"One, I know there's a lot more to the story than that. And two, even if there weren't, that still doesn't make you a bad person."

"It just feels like no one's willing to stick up for me."

"Lucy, I was at your flat yesterday. The place was full of people."

I shake my head. "Ash and those guys just want someone to fight for their cause. You know? To make a point, like, 'Ooh, social networking is bad!' But what about *my* cause? Someone stole my phone, first and foremost. This is practically a criminal matter."

Franklin squeezes my arm. "Don't get mad at me for saying this, love, but you can't expect people to stick their necks out for you if you won't speak up for yourself."

"No one gave me a chance!" I break away from his touch. "They just attacked. Everywhere I look, people are whispering about me or throwing stuff. Since this started, I've had to cut gum out of my hair, wash ink out of my gym shorts, tear posters off my locker, pick noodles out of my bag. You saw the yearbook."

"I'm not defending their behavior. I just mean . . . you could've gone on record and said something in the paper, if not to Zeff. But you chose not to."

"I'm trying to figure out what happened first. I can't defend myself without evidence. Someone stole my phone and deliberately posted those pictures on my account. I'm trying to find out who. And every day, it gets a little more obvious that it's Olivia."

"Okay," Franklin says. "Let's say it *is* Olivia. Let's say you get your evidence—irrefutable, even. What then? All of this is pointless if you're not willing to take a stand. This is bigger than you, Lucy. It's not just about a stolen phone and a few embarrassing pictures. It's not even about Olivia and her friends bullying you."

"Then what?"

Franklin's pacing, his curls springing out everywhere. "It's about people using the anonymity of the Internet to make a public spectacle, to sanction harassment. Asher Hollowell's methods may be unconventional, but his point is valid. Social networking should bring people together, not serve as an online gladiator arena."

My mind drifts to Russell Crowe in his gladiator outfit, but even that picture of perfect badassery can't keep the knots out of my stomach. I want to do the right thing, to say what I need to say, to stand up for what's right—not just for me, but for everyone who goes through stuff like this.

But I'm not strong enough to do it alone.

"You have to trust people, Lucy. Maybe not everyone, but someone."

"I trust people. You, and I told (e)VIL about my sister, and . . . . *Hey.*" At the meeting yesterday, Franklin walked into my house, saw Jayla in the TV room. He wasn't surprised, and I forgot that he should've been. "You knew Jayla Heart was my sister?"

Franklin nods. "I've always known about your connection to Jayla. What kind of investigative journalist would I be if I didn't, you know, investigate?"

"But why didn't you say—"

"Bloody hell, Lucy, I'm not talking about trusting people with Jayla's identity. I'm talking about trusting your friends with the truth. We all want to help, but none of us knows what happened that night because you haven't told us."

"Trusting my friends?" I say. "You're only helping because I promised you the story."

"Yes, well . . ." He rests the back of his head on the locker and closes his eyes. "Perhaps I've changed my mind."

I'm not sure whether he's changed his mind about running the story or about helping with the investigation, but I don't stick around to ask.

I've got evidence to collect.

In the last stall of the emo bathroom, under cover of a wretched song about a woman named Sweet Caroline, I read Kiara's message on my now-contraband iPad.

From: Code Name Hackalicious

I've written up the details in a separate official report in case the authority figures need something more specific, but in laymen's terms:

We already know that the self-named creator of the Juicy Lucy page is Narc Alert—obviously, an alias. By comparing the time stamps (login/logout times, message and comment post times, date and page creation time) of Narc Alert and of the likely suspects from Cole and Griffin's lists—both on the Juicy page as well as on their own personal profiles—I was able to significantly narrow the suspects.

From there, it was a simple matter of

correlating common linguistic patterns, crutch words, slang usage, tone, average message length, and style on the Narc Alert page with the personal profiles of those on the suspect short list.

And ding ding ding! We have a match.

I've identified the creator of the Juicy Lucy fan page with a 99.8% confidence level: Olivia Barnes.

I will provide hard copies of all evidence in person. Please destroy this message on receipt.

I was never here.

—Hackalicious out

From: Lucy Vacarro

Hackalicious:

Your findings are both thorough and interesting. Thank you for your service. I'll destroy your message, per your request. We'll never speak of this e-mail again.

—Vacarro out

From: Code Name Hackalicious

By replying to previous message, you've created an electronic trail of our communiqué on multiple servers, thereby making it easier for the NSA to track, flag, and store indefinitely.

Please delete this and all related messages in your sent and received mail folders.

—Hackalicious out

From: Lucy Vacarro

Sorry! :-(I'm new at cyber espionage. Consider them deleted. Mum's the word. Um, words.

—Vacarro out

From: Code Name Hackalicious

!!!

Oh, right. God, this superspy gig has a lot of rules. I don't know how (e)VIL does it.

A new song floats through the XM feed, some girl dreaming about an eternal flame, and I delete Kiara's messages, trying to decide what to do with the information. I don't have enough evidence to prove Olivia stole my phone and posted the original #scandal photos, but I can at least prove she launched the Juicy Lucy campaign and turn her over to Zeff.

But to clear my name for good, I need more evidence.

Far as I know, the Prince Freckles #scandal award idea was a bust—no one's come forward to claim it.

I click over to Miss Demeanor's page and start composing a private message, explaining the situation with the Juicy Lucy page and asking if she has any information that might connect Olivia with the #scandal photos.

The note was supposed to be brief, a quick request, but once I start tapping in the words, I can't stop.

You have to trust people . . . . Maybe not everyone, but someone . . . None of us knows what happened . . . . You haven't told us. . . .

Franklin's voice is in my head as my fingers fly over the iPad. As if they're being guided by some otherworldly force, some instinctual reaction to Franklin's words, a full confession takes shape beneath my hands.

I admit everything. Cole. How I've loved him since that first time in the woods behind our houses, when he met me and Night. How every moment with him is this crazy adventure, a promise of sunshine and something more. How he smiles at me and I'm simultaneously lost and found.

I tell her about kissing him in his bedroom at the cabin, about our walk in the woods. How I'm so scared of losing Ellie, but that deep down, if it really comes to it, I'd choose Cole. How in so many ways, I already had.

I'm not a good friend.

I'm in love.

My heart is broken, but that's the truth.

And I'm still hiding, still doing exactly what Franklin accused me of. Staying in the shadows, too scared to take a stand.

My fingers finally stop, the iPad smudged and dim.

The confusion. The feelings. The mistakes. It's all there in the unsent note, the most I've ever admitted to anyone, including Jayla, including myself.

The message waits patiently, my thumb hovering over the send button.

Maybe it's because Miss Demeanor doesn't have a face. Maybe it's because out of all the people who've come into my life postscandal, she's the only one who doesn't gain anything by helping me. And maybe it's because, best of all, I won't have to see the judgment in her eyes when she finds out who I really am, no filter.

Maybe there are a million reasons to send it and a million more not to, but beneath a heartbreaking glam band soundtrack about roses and thorns, I hit the button, sending my deepest secrets through cyberspace to a person who doesn't even exist.

FANBOYS AND OTHER MINOR SCANDALS BY WHICH WE MEAN SCANDALS INVOLVING MINORS

What's wrong with you? *Move*." Haley bumps my shoulder as she stomps toward school on Monday. She's on her phone, and whoever's on the other end is no longer in the friend zone.

"I can't believe you guys did this without me," she says. "I thought we weren't *doing* the campout thing. Well, no one texted me, and I had to find out on Instagram! That's it. I'm deleting *all* you bitches."

The Lav-Oaks campus is dotted with the remnants of tents and campfires, and dozens of my classmates are hanging out in circles, playing guitars, singing, kicking around Hacky Sacks. It's a regular lovefest for everyone but Principal Zeff, who's frantic and overly pink in her beige sundress and white shawl.

"What's happening?" she's saying to 420. "Some kind of Occupy Lavender Oaks? The last thing this school needs is another scandal."

420 squints in the too-bright sun, nodding, but his nod looks more like a head groove to some nonstop Marley soundtrack playing deep within his soul.

"Do you people have any demands," she says, "or is this just a thing?"

"Thing, dude." 420 gives her two thumbs-up. Well, two thumbs kind of sideways, but I'm pretty sure he means up.

"Just . . . clean it up before the bell rings or you're all getting tardies. Lucy?" She smiles when she sees me, but it's a shark's grin, a warning. "I need to see you in my office. I'll let Mrs. King know not to expect you in home-room, okay?"

"No problem, Ms. Zeff." I have some information for her, too.

I don't see Ellie, Griffin, or Franklin in the campout crowd, but Cole's here with John, rolling up his sleeping bag and checking his gear like a pro. I've seen him do it a hundred times, all the mountaineering stuff spread out in his driveway before some new trek with his dad.

So this was the big prank.

John must've told him about it. Cole tried calling and texting me a few times this weekend, but I couldn't deal. I never heard back from my pseudo friend Miss Demeanor, neither a message nor a new advice column, and every time I saw Cole's name on my phone, I was certain she'd forwarded him my note, all the secrets I'm too scared—despite his own confessions, his own declarations—to say to his face.

Now that I see the tents, I wonder if he was simply calling to invite me.

I would've said no. I would've tried to talk him out of it too, despite his insistence that we've got nothing to hide, nothing to be ashamed of.

Still, when I see him packing up his stuff, sun shining on his messy hair, I can't help but wonder what things would've been like for us if I'd just been honest about my feelings all along, from the day we met. Would we have hooked up right away? Would we still be together now, high school sweethearts, crawling out of a tent together the morning after the senior prank?

Would we still be friends with Ellie?

The what-ifs fill my insides, tightening my throat with sadness for the real friendships lost and all the unknown potentials, and when Cole spots me and waves me over, it takes every bit of strength I have to turn and walk the other way.

Right smack into Franklin.

"Hey!" I say, relieved to see him. "There you are. I've been texting you all weekend."

"Oh?" His smile is low-wattage, his eyes unfocused. "Right, I had my phone off. I've . . . I've got to go, Lucy."

"Wait!" I grab his arm. After our argument on Thursday, he dodged me all day on Friday, ignored all attempts at communication. I felt so bad about how we left things that I hid out in my room all weekend, pulling back-to-back *Undead Shred* marathons and eating Cocoa Puffs straight out of the box.

"I just . . . I wanted to apologize," I say. "For how I acted the other day. I know you were just trying to help and I was a complete brat, and—"

"You're not a brat, Lucy." His eyes hold mine for a moment, and something in his face looks sad, full of regret, and then it's gone. He checks the time on his phone. "I really have to go."

"Close the door, Lucy." Zeff's all business, the calm of her beige sundress belying her frantic eyes.

"I'm glad you called me in here," I say, like, *Way to be proactive, Lucy!* "I have some information I thought you'd be interested in. It's about the Juicy Lucy page."

Her eyebrows raise. "Oh?"

I hand over the full report I printed out from Kiara, keeping her name out of it, as promised. "I did some sleuthing this weekend and identified the page creator."

Zeff scans the file.

"It's Olivia Barnes," I say triumphantly. If that doesn't deserve a cookie, I don't know what does.

But Zeff isn't offering up any congratulatory treats. She's frowning, shaking her head.

"This is all very interesting, Miss Vacarro, and I can tell you put a lot of work into it, but I'm afraid you can't prove anything. The Juicy Lucy page has been deleted."

"What? I was just on there this weekend!"

"As of this morning, it's gone. I suppose whoever created it realized someone was on the trail. Perhaps he or she decided to take our cyberbullying policy changes seriously. I can't say I'm sorry about that."

"But I have a report, and—"

"A report is not irrefutable evidence. Anyone could've typed up this information. Without the actual page backing up your claims, I'm afraid you don't have a case."

I flop into the chair. "Then . . . why did you call me in here? Did something else happen?"

From a drawer she procures a pile of magazines, spreads them out on the desk between us. They're tabloids—*CelebStyle*, *#TRENDZ*, all the usual suspects— each one featuring a variation on a theme.

By theme, I mean Jayla Heart, glowing in a tiny, sky-blue slip dress, her hand dangling like a carefree little bird from the driver's side window of her Porsche. The car is packed with half a football team. *Our* football team, according to the jerseys they're all wearing. I recognize a few of them as vamps from Cole's party, including Griff's Ryan/Brian boytoy.

Headlines: MINOR INFRACTIONS IN THE MILE HIGH CITY. DANGEROUS LIAISONS WITH DANGER'S DARLING. CARPOOL COUGAR LOVES BOYS WITH BALLS.

"I know you have your own scandal to worry about right now," Ms. Zeff says, "and there's nothing precisely *illegal* about an adult driving young boys in her car. . . ."

"But?"

"But it would really help me if you could talk to your sister and kindly request that she avoid engaging in social activities with students outside of our sanctioned visits and, of course, her personal connection to you."

"I don't really socialize with my sister," I say. "She's just . . . helping out at home."

"Where *are* your parents, Miss Vacarro?"

"They're on a couples . . . vacation. Thing. In California. They'll be back tonight."

"I hope so." The weight of Lavender Oaks's many scandals is heavy on her shoulders. She reaches across her desk for the familiar, encouraging hand pat. "Two more days of classes. Let's make the most of it."

Nasty glares aren't exactly traceable evidence of bullying, so I'm still getting plenty of those in the hallways, but otherwise? All seems quiet on the Lav-Oaks front.

It's the calm before the storm, the last desperate days of high school before finals and the crossing of the big stage, the bridge from childhood to adulthood. I mean, if you're into all that symbolism stuff. I would be, maybe, if Ellie and Griff were here to joke about it.

But my friends are keeping their heads down, all of us unsure about where we stand. About who posted those pictures, whose secrets were the most damaging, who was most in the wrong.

About where we're supposed to go from here.

After school I take the long way home, through the woods, and when I get to the house, I find Asher and Tens in front of the television, my sister between them, wildly slashing the air with her arms and legs. Night's pacing and barking, cheering her on as Asher brags about his high score.

Jayla's laughing, breathless, beautiful.

I drop my backpack in the entryway. "WTF?"

Three humans and one canine turn to face me, guilty grins across the board.

"Lucy!" Asher waves at me from side to side like I'm standing on a boat dock. *Bon voyage, sanity!* "We came by to go over some final moves for our presentation."

"Does our presentation involve Fruit Ninja?" I ask.

"Dude." Tens chops the air with his hand, dreads whipping around his face. "Your sister's teaching us."

"On Xbox?" I glare at Jayla. "Jayla! You're totally corrupting them! They don't do Xbox! It's connected to the network and . . . This is messed up on so many levels."

"Tell me about it." Jayla drops to the couch, panting. "I just got my ass kicked in Fruit Ninja by a guy in a wheelchair."

"Tried to warn you." Asher beams, giving the air a few ninja arm chops. "I got *mad* upper-body skills. Hand-eye coordination skills. Shit, big sis, I got skills you haven't even *dreamed* about yet."

Jayla raises an eyebrow, but before she can make an inappropriate cougar joke, I say, "Party's over, guys. And I'm sorry about . . ." I wave around at Jayla, Xbox, Fruit Ninja, the dog, my whole situation collectively, but they're all smiling.

I'm the dark cloud, swooping in to kill the buzz for no reason other than the fact that I wasn't part of it. "I'm just really tired. Talk tomorrow?"

They gather up their stuff and salute, fake chopping each other as they roll out the front door, down the sidewalk to Tens's car. He helps Ash into the front seat and carefully folds up the wheelchair, packs it into the trunk like he's done it a thousand times before and will keep on doing it for as long as Ash needs him.

Jayla pats the couch cushion next to her, which Night takes as an invitation. "How was your day? Any new scandals to report?"

"Now that you mention it, big sis." I dig Zeff's tabloids out of my bag and throw them on the coffee table. They slide across the surface, two fluttering to the floor, knocking down an empty wineglass.

"Oh, shit!" She picks up the top rag. "I can't believe they shot this! It was Saturday night. I went out after *Danger's*. Remember?"

"This is you going out? A fun Saturday with the boys?"

"I invited you, but you were being little miss mopey pants."

"These guys go to my school!" I say. "They're in my class!"

Jay shrugs. "They said they were eighteen."

"Zeff's pissed," I say. "They're not all eighteen. And even if they were, this is so . . . not appropriate."

"You're overreacting, Lucy."

"Don't you have a publicist or something? I mean, since this is so challenging for you, isn't it her job to tell you what *not* to do in public?"

Jayla waves me off. "Fired her. She was a helicopter publicist."

"Maybe because you need helicoptering?"

Jayla turns a wounded gaze on me, but her eyes go from hurt to hurtful in five seconds flat. "Lighten up, *little* sister. Maybe if you weren't so uptight and moody, you'd have more friends and bigger boobs."

She flips through one of the tabloids, forcing a smile at pictures I *know* she's embarrassed of. I almost laugh. It's something I'd text Ellie about, something we'd reenact at a sleepover with the stuffed animals in my bedroom.

Ohmygod, I'm so famous! Look at all my fanboys!

I drop into the chair across from her, head in my hands. "Why are you *here,* Jayla?"

It's not even a real question, just a tired, last-ditch insult, but as soon as the words are out, I feel the change between us, a shift and snap in the air like the instant before a lightning strike.

Night's ears perk, a low growl resonating behind his teeth.

I look up. She's crying. "Jayla?"

"They fired me," she whispers.

"What?"

"*Danger's* producers brought me into corporate for a meeting. When I got there, my agent was already in the room. He had a stack of paperwork in front of him. I knew it was bad news."

"What happened?"

"It was like *Intervention*. They accused me of partying too hard, missing work. I swear, Luce, they made it sound like I'm one of those crazies who freaks out on Twitter and goes all public meltdown. I don't even *have* Twitter! And okay, so I missed a few days and had to reschedule a few shoots. And maybe I did party a little too hard. But it's . . . Everyone does that stuff. It's, like, coping."

"Coping with what?"

Jayla wipes the mascara from beneath her eyes. "It's hard to explain. But one day you're normal, okay? Then you wake up with all this money, and you're famous, and there's a lot of pressure. . . . Hollywood isn't what I thought it would be."

"Poor little rich girl." I feel bad as soon as I say it, but Jayla's nodding.

"You have this dream. And you work your ass off, thinking if you can just get this one thing, your life will be perfect. Then you're lucky enough to get that thing, and your life isn't perfect, so you figure, well, I need a new dream. Then you get that one, maybe, work awhile for something more. More. More. And at every step, someone is there to stomp you down. To remind you that you're just a nobody with a nice ass, that you just got lucky." She kicks the table, scatters the tabloids. "But shit, that's why they pay us the big bucks, right? Real high rollers. Depressed, drunk high rollers. That's the Hollywood secret for you, Luce. And now I'm out of work, and I'm broke."

"Broke? But you're . . ." It doesn't make sense. My sister is Jayla Heart. She's Angelica Darling. She's famous. She's rich. She's the golden girl everyone loves to hate. "What about your credit cards?"

"Maxed," she says. "The only thing that still works is my debit, and that's almost done too."

iPhone, makeup, clothes . . . Guilt ripples between my shoulders. "What about your rental car?"

"Airline miles."

My eyes go wide. "The couple's retreat?"

"Already paid for. I was supposed to go with . . ." She taps her teeth. "Shoot, I don't remember his name. We dated for a month, but it didn't work out. I didn't want the trip to go to waste, so I told Mom—"

"What about your beach house? The condo?"

She shakes her head. "Everything I own is in boxes at Macie's house. She's the only person in the entire state of California who's still speaking to me. Well, not counting my so-called friends, the ones who only call when a new scandal surfaces." She nods toward the tabloids. "I'm sure I'll hear from them tonight."

"But . . . how can they just fire you? You're the star of the show." I cross the TV room and take the seat next to her, shooing Night out of the way. I don't know whether to hurt for her or to be pissed. To hug her or to lecture her. Is this how Mom and Dad feel? Is this why Mom hides the tabloids, pretends it's all lies? How much do they know? How much do they really see?

"They wrote me out of the script," she says. "Spoiler alert—Angelica dies." She reaches for me, her eyes wild and desperate. "You can't tell anyone. Not a soul."

"Talk to Dad," I say. "He'll help—"

"Of course I'll help, sweetheart."

My parents breeze through the doorway, happy and relaxed, bright smiles lighting up their tanned faces. Night knocks over a lamp on his mad dash to the door.

Jayla and I shoot up from the couch to hug them.

"You were supposed to call when you landed," Jay says, her voice all perky-perky again. "I wanted to pick you up."

"We took a taxi," Mom says. "Oh, sugar, it is nice to be home. The resort was beautiful, but boy was it hot." She fans her face, her big red Texas hair billowing around her like a cloud. If she or my dad overheard us, neither of them shows it, and Dad seems to have already forgotten that he offered to help with some unknown problem.

Mom scans the disaster of the TV room, cataloging the infractions. "See what happens when I leave you two alone for this long? Good heavens, darlin', it's like a tornado came through here."

Dad laughs. "What did we miss?"

Jayla and I stand in front of the coffee table, smooshing together to hide the space between.

Evidence from our two weeks of bonding rests on the surface behind us, damning and obvious. On one end, dirty dishes, half-finished Coke cans, cake crumbs. Ice cream spoons licked clean by the dog. Earrings, lipsticks, a tampon, a tissue covered in black nail polish. One sock. A hairbrush. A bottle of Aspirin. Two unpaid speeding tickets. A corkscrew.

On the other end, there's a stack of tabloids featuring Jayla car servicing a bunch of Lav-Oaks minors, a folder full of prom party pictures that would shock Mom's ladylike sensibilities and send her to the hospital, six incomplete PowerPoint printouts highlighting the dangers of cyberbullying, a second copy of Kiara's Hackalicious report, and a partially dog-licked bowl of crusty brown goop that used to be, in a galaxy far, far away, guacamole.

Jayla squeezes my hand, a silent plea.

I'll keep your secrets if you keep mine. . . .

"You didn't miss a thing," I say confidently. "Welcome home."

Later, when I'm deep under the cool sheets, my phone lights up the dark room. For a groggy instant I'm disappointed it's not Franklin, or at least an e-mail from Miss Demeanor, but when I see Cole's name, my heart soars.

"I needed to hear your voice," he says. "I miss you, Luce. I hate that we're tiptoeing around. I feel like I saw you more before me and Ellie—before all this."

"I'm . . . Everything's so messed up. I know I've been acting crazy. I just . . . I don't know what to do."

"You don't have to do anything. Just be Lucy."

"Even if I'm cranky and moody and demanding?"

"Wouldn't love you any other way."

I smile, the tightness in my chest loosening. "Here's a demand, then. Sing me a song. You said drummers get all the groupies, but I'm still not convinced."

"Oh, I can sing, Vacarro. I'm just waiting for the right moment to steal the spotlight from John."

"Think John's still awake? He did say I was hot, after all. Maybe I'll ask him to—"

"This is a B-side from Oasis," he says. "'Talk Tonight'? I always think of it as our song. At least, since that night."

"Dude. You gave us a song without consulting me?"

"Shit, girl. You're about to get a free concert in your ear, for which I'm asking practically almost nothing in return, and you're criticizing?"

"I thought our song was 'Reckoner's Encore'."

"Well, yeah. And 'Nothing Compares 2 U.' The Stereophonics version. If I told you I downloaded pretty much *all* those songs from prom and made a Lucy's Kickass Boots playlist . . . Is that creepy?"

"You're so concerned with not sounding like a stalker, not sounding creepy . . . why don't you just, you know, be less creepy?"

"I don't know how."

I match his laugh, and when it finally fades, his voice is in my ear, singing the opening verse.

I've never heard this song before. I've never loved a song more.

I wanna talk tonight . . . until the morning light . . .

And I'm right back in that lavender dawn, the moment full of all possibilities. At the end of the song he whispers good night, a love spell unbroken as I slip into the darkness. . . .

A text buzzes against my cheek, yanking me back. I squint to see the message.

Franklin: *i'm so sorry*

IDENTITY THEFT

MISS DEMEANOR
4,991 likes 👍
3,195 talking about this

Tuesday, May 13

My dear, loyal pretend friends.

I come to you from the precipice of 5,000 likes,
a white whale of a fan base I never dreamed of
reaching in all my one year of dreaming about this

page. Alas, on our final day of classes at Lavender Oaks High School, I'm writing with a heavy heart (and it's not because I'll miss the Jell-O).

Fangirls and fanboys. Minions and followers. Likers and oversharers. There's something you need to know. Something, I'm sure, you're *dying* to know.

Who is Miss Demeanor?

It's time to remove the mask.

I, the undersigned, do solemnly swear (on the U.S. Constitution shower curtain and coordinating Bill of Rights liner, which is a real thing that I own, along with a Declaration of Independence bedspread, because my immigrant parents are patriotic and educational that way) that I am the voice, the face, the mind behind your beloved/behated/be-totally-indifferenced Miss Demeanor.

Me.

Senior at Lavender Oaks High School. Valedictorian. Editor of the *Explorer*. Rogue Brit and secret admirer of American pop culture.

Franklin Margolis.

I started this column last year as a joint social experiment with Asher Hollowell, acting independently of his club, (e)lectronic Vanities Intervention League. He's given me permission to share the details of his involvement here.

Ash is a good friend of mine, something we've kept mostly under wraps in an effort to more effectively conduct our experiment. The idea came about one night during a Star Trek marathon that inspired a lively discussion about technology and its role in how we communicate and relate. Our central question was this: Do human relationships and interactions inspire and shape technology, or does technology shape us?

Together we set out to prove that people—specifically, our fellow almost-graduates—are more interested in perpetuating negative drama online than in engaging in important, interesting discourse about the news and events in our community and school, and that advances in communications technology— the Internet, texting, smartphones, and social networking—have done more to destroy relationships than to enhance or enable them.

Sadly, most of our assumptions were upheld.

Surprisingly, though, they were upheld not just by our subjects, but by me.

I fueled the drama, offering incentives for the #scandal page, asking you to validate me and profess your so-called love by clicking the like button. I posted gossip, reblogged negativity. I dished the dirt, doused it in gasoline, lit it on fire, and broke out the marshmallows, all under the guise of a legitimate experiment.

I was wrong.

I presumed that people use technology as a screen, allowing them to say virtually anything without consequence, but through the Miss Demeanor persona, I got to know students' issues in a way that writing for the newspaper never allowed. There's truth in all we say and do, even in our lies and exaggerations.

I never planned to out myself. After graduation, I was supposed to trail off into the sunset, go out with an air of mystery, become an Internet legend. But that was back when I was still treating this project as an effort to validate my own assumptions rather than as an objective experiment. I never thought this would change my perspective. I never thought it would be the catalyst to bring new friends into my life. And I damn well never thought it would be the thing that, through my underhandedness, would hurt those friends—especially the one I've grown to care about most.

Hurting her is my biggest failure, my deepest shame.

It's possible that my confession will earn more enemies than accolades, and that I'll regret going out like this instead of going out with an anonymous bang. Or perhaps a buzz? ;-)

Okay, no more jokes. My cynical heart being what it is, I'm guessing most of you stopped reading after "Franklin Margolis" above, and I'm typing into the echo chamber. But for those of you still with me, thank you for listening. I sincerely hope that those I've offended and hurt will find it in their hearts to forgive me, knowing that you've taught me much.

Mostly, that even as the guy with the highest GPA at Lavender Oaks High, I don't know jack.

With sincere apologies and a final online good-bye,

xo ~ *Ciao!* ~ xo
Miss Demeanor
Better known as Franklin Margolis

PANTS, SHIRTS, HATS, ACCESSORIES, AND ALL MANNER OF UNDERGARMENTS TOTALLY ON FIRE

They used me." I lean against Prince Freckles and breathe deeply, focusing on the soft sounds of the horses and the earthy smell of hay and oats. "I'm such an *idiot*."

"Shut up," Griffin says. "You're so not an idiot. Franklin and Ash are idiots. Honestly, I expected more from our valedictorian. Miss Demeanor? The whole thing is bloody—I mean, freaking—insane."

This gets a smile. "Does this mean you're not moving to London after college?"

"Hell no." Griff puts a hand on her heart. "From now on, the only Brit I'll ever love is Harry Potter."

I sit down just outside the pen, sketch two stick figures

in the dirt where I first had lunch with Franklin. It was only two weeks ago, but it seems like a year's worth of ups and downs have converged into one moment, today, our last day of classes.

"So what did you bring me?" I ask. Griff texted me just before lunch, *got something 2 cheer u up bigtime! meet @ stables?* "Please say it's the Daryl and Merle action figures from *The Walking Dead*."

"Not quite, weirdo, but now I know what to get for your birthday." Griff crouches next to me. She doesn't quite sit—no way she'll get her Calvin Klein cutoffs dirty—but the fact that she's enduring the horse barn at all shows her loyalty.

From her purse, she fishes out a silver iPhone. My iPhone. The one I lost at Cole's party.

"Where . . . ? How . . . ? What the . . . ?"

"This morning in gym," she explains. "The little Judas left her bag on the bench while she was in the bathroom."

"Olivia?" I ask, and she nods. "You went through her bag?"

Griff rises and dusts off her hands. "Hardly! The zipper was partway open. Like, a lot of the way. And I happened to see a phone that looked a lot like yours. When I saw the cracked screen, I knew for sure."

"What did she say?" I ask.

"I was about to rage on her," Griff says, "but I reined it in. I figured it would be better to talk to you first, see how you wanted to play it with Zeff."

"Good call." I flip the phone in my hands, trace my fingers over the familiar scratches and grooves. I'm not that surprised that Olivia turned out to be the perp—even before the phone, the evidence was pointing that way. But I guess there was a small part of me that hoped she wasn't, that hoped my suspicions would be proven wrong. I wanted to believe that decent people stay decent, deep down, even when bad things happen to them.

She *really* had a thing for Cole, more than I ever realized, and seeing him with me must've crushed her. Enough to make her post those mortifying hard lemonade pics as a cover. Enough to inspire her to launch the Juicy Lucy page, to turn the fickle mob against me.

The Daryl and Merle action figures might disagree, but it doesn't take a zombie apocalypse to bring out the worst in us, to chase off our humanity. Like the old song in the emo bathroom says—all we need is love. A secret, unrequited ache that goes deep enough to leave scars.

"Lucy. I hoped I'd find you out here." Franklin appears in the doorway, the sun lighting him up like some kind of poufy-haired angel. There's a deep apology in his eyes, but when I recall the message I sent to Miss D the other day, the confession that felt a lot braver when she didn't have a face—especially not Franklin's—my skin burns with the heat of a thousand lightbulbs.

The old, nonenvironmentally friendly kind that get, like, *super*hot.

Griffin levels an icy glare. "What are *you* doing here?"

"I was hoping I could talk to Lucy," he says.

"She's not interested," Griff says.

Franklin crosses the stables and stops before me, his eyes pleading. "You're my partner, Veronica. Don't shut me out."

"Was." I'm surprised at how much it aches to say it. "Guess (e)VIL was right all along. Vanity-based technologies really do kill relationships."

"Lucy—"

"I'm not perfect, okay? I screwed up majorly this year. And before all this happened, I was a total antisocial emo bitch most of the time. I get it. But you pretended to be my friend, and I believed you."

"It wasn't pretend. All that time in the lab, hanging out, working on the case . . . it was me. Franklin."

"But not Miss Demeanor, the one I was e-mailing for advice. I defended her—you—and you attacked her— you . . ." I squeeze my eyes shut so hard that when I open them again, I see stars. "That's so—"

"Meta?" He cracks a smile, but quickly drops it.

"*Really?*" Griff rolls her eyes. "That's pretty ridiculous, even for you."

"It was an experiment," he says. "Gone wrong. I never meant—"

"You set out to prove how meaningless relationships are by faking one with me." I slip the phone into my pocket and dust off my hands. There's a brush dangling from a nail inside the stall, and I grab it, get to work on Prince Freckles. "There was never any *Explorer* story, right? All your notes, your research, it was all part of your experiment."

He nods. "I misled you about my reasons for wanting the inside scoop on the Facebook scandal. But our friendship? That was real. From the first time we talked, I never saw you as just another variable. And Ash—he wasn't involved, as far as your story was concerned. He and I started this long ago. He wanted to help you solve this thing too. He believes in justice. And he really likes you, Lucy. He respects you."

"You both took advantage of me. You both lied."

He winces, but doesn't deny it. Instead, he turns to Griffin. "Do you mind if I speak with Lucy in private?"

She snorts. "Like *that's* gonna happen."

"I'm fine," I tell her. "Go. I'll catch up with you after."

Griffin huffs, but she does as I ask.

Franklin says, "You're right, I lied. I'm here to apologize for that. But you're a liar too." There's no melodrama in his voice, no accusation. Just fact. "Still trying to convince yourself that Facebook is the cause of your problems. Or cell phones or cameras or Olivia and her friends. Even your sister gets the blame."

"Jay has nothing to do with this."

Franklin shakes his curly head. "I've seen the way you treat her, how embarrassed you were during her performance at the pep rally. You didn't want me to know you were related—not because you thought I'd use you to get close, but because you were mortified of her."

I lower my eyes, focus on untangling Prince Freckles's mane.

"Why not add Cole, if we're making a list? He should've told Ellie no when she suggested you go to prom in her place." His voice is rising, emotion replacing his measured tone. "And Ellie . . . She's the one who kept secrets, then got upset when she discovered you liked her ex. There's also the school. Ms. Zeff. (e)VIL. Horses too. Right, Freckles? Bloody hell, he was at that party. He could've taken the pictures. Why not?"

Prince Freckles stomps his still-sequined foot. *Leave me out of it, dude.*

I'm silent, still brushing. It's one of those moments I'll reflect on later and come up with all the right things to say. All the best comebacks, the real zingers to put him exactly in his place.

But right now, all I can do is hurt.

He's right.

"You'd like to crucify everyone for living on Facebook," he continues. "Yet you shared more of yourself with Miss Demeanor, a fake online persona whose primary claim to fame is hashtag scandal, than you have with any real person in your life. You haven't even shared your feelings with Cole."

"I trusted *you*," I say. "Maybe not with everything, but with a lot. And look how that turned out."

The words find their target; hurt flickers in his eyes.

"I've been here for you all along, Lucy. I still want to help you solve this. And I still want to be your friend. You just refuse to let anyone in."

I clap the brush against the side of the pen and hang it back on the hook. "It's done," I say. "I know who did it. I have my proof."

Franklin raises his eyebrows. "Well, don't leave me hanging, Veronica."

"You won't be shocked to know it's Olivia." I tell him about Griff and the phone.

"Why didn't Griffin send me an update? This is a major breakthrough in the case."

"Why do you *think*, Miss Demeanor?"

Franklin's neck goes bright red. "Right. Well. Are you sure it's your phone? Lots of people have iPhones."

"Same cracked screen." I slide it out of my pocket and show him; then I remember he's not allowed to be involved anymore, and I put it away.

"What are you planning to do?"

"Confront her," I say.

"But it's still yours and Griffin's word against hers. I think you should—"

"Stop." I shake my head, erase my stick figure sketches with the heel of my boot before Franklin even notices them. "Griff and I can take it from here."

I'm so ninja style—minus the fruit—as I sit through our last art class, quietly rolling my final sketches into a long cardboard tube. Olivia's cozying up to Mr. Lopez today, no eye contact, no harsh whispers or smarmy remarks about me and Cole. But when the bell rings and she slips into the bathroom for a break, I follow her, quiet as a mouse, deadly as a viper.

Once she's in a stall, I lean back against the main door. I hold my breath.

And I wait.

Despite my impressive undead kill stats and my obsession with all things gore, I'm not a brawler; I detest actual violence. I'm not even much of a yeller. Sarcasm and avoidance, the dash of melodrama I inherited from my actress sister? Those are my weapons of choice.

I catch a glimpse of myself in the mirror and I almost laugh. Smudged black eyeliner. Dyed red hair. Nose ring.

Real intimidating.

There's the telltale flush, but before she opens the stall door, Olivia's phone rings. I hear the rustling, wait for her to dig out her phone and answer. There's a deep sigh, a pause, the hello.

And then she's crying, her voice broken and defeated as she tells her parents yes, it's fine if they cancel her graduation party; her friends will make other plans. Yes, she'll come right home after school, and yes, tomorrow's senior picnic is mandatory, but she'll come right home after that too. Yes, she knows she's still grounded.

I look at my cracked iPhone, the dead black screen smeared with fingerprints.

Oranges in a vase, sunflowers on the table. A basket full of puppies . . .

Olivia's paintings in Lopez's class.

When she lurches out of the stall, eyes red and smudgy,

I don't give her a chance to speak. I hold the phone up, wiggle it in front of her face.

"You're taking *my* picture in the bathroom now?" she asks. "Classic."

Her expression doesn't change, short brown hair sticking up like she couldn't be bothered styling it this morning. She ducks under my arm, heads for the sink.

When the faucet clicks on, I toss the phone into the sink, right under the stream.

"I'm not paying for that, I hope you know."

I hold her gaze in the mirror. She looks sad, maybe a little angry. The ghost of it still burns behind her blue eyes.

"I have irrefutable proof from . . . from an independent investigator that you created the Juicy Lucy page," I say. "They were able to cross-check the times of the messages and the linguistics."

Olivia's face rearranges into something closer to surprise, followed quickly by fear.

And then it crumples.

She turns to face me, takes a breath, looks at me like she's about to say something sincere, something important. But all that comes out is, "I deleted it."

She plucks my soaked phone out of the sink, drops it on the counter. "Pretty sure this is toast. God, you really *are* nutter butters."

Like I'm not even here, not even a blip on her radar, she goes back to washing her hands.

Olivia hates me for kissing Cole. She hates me for the picture that got her in trouble with her parents, even though I didn't post it. She just admitted to starting an online bullying campaign against me. She and her two best friends fueled it with new photos, captions, commentary, and lengthy discussions about my skankiness.

But one thing is suddenly clear: Olivia didn't steal my iPhone. She didn't take pictures of me and Cole kissing on the deck, embracing in his bed. She didn't upload incriminating evidence to my Facebook profile. Maybe one of her friends did it. Maybe Haley dropped the phone in her bag, set her up to retaliate for being left out of the senior campout. Maybe Griff just assumed the bag in gym class belonged to Olivia, but it was someone else's entirely. Someone we overlooked.

Maybe I'll never know who did it. Maybe it doesn't even matter anymore, because it's the last day of school, my friends are scattered, my reputation is shot, and the formerly kind and happy girl at the sink is graduating with her own scandal, her own disappointments and broken hearts.

"I'm sorry about the Facebook pictures, Olivia," I whisper. "I honestly don't know who posted them."

Olivia shrugs, meeting my eyes once more in the mirror. "What's done is done."

All the momentary fury I felt walking in here breaks on the shores of my heart, settling into a low, throbbing ache that no one can feel but me, and when I retreat to the gray-and-maroon halls to clear out my locker, to disassemble four years of pictures and quotes and magnets and long-lost, coffee-stained homework, I'm alone.

PRIVACY IS DEAD. GET OVER IT.

Does the phrase 'restraining order' mean anything to you?" I snap. "How about 'hungry German shepherd?'"

There's a dude with a camera sniffing around my garage when I get home, trying to get shots of Jay's Porsche through the dusty windows. He jumps when he sees me, mutters something about the wrong address.

Inside, the TV room is a cave, total darkness broken only by a single ray of light slicing between drawn curtains. Jayla's asleep on the couch, mumbling and murmuring, her thin body curled up and wrapped in one of Mom's afghans. Six out of ten manicured fingers poke through the crocheted holes.

On the table in front of her, there's a stack of tabloids, wrinkled with water stains. The top one is an old issue of *#TRENDZ*, and Jayla's on the cover, the Cali sun bright behind her. In one hand she's holding a to-go carrier with two coffee cups and a small pastry bag. Her hair is a wild nest, makeup smudged, something dark spilled down the front of her white blouse. Her expression is both shocked and annoyed, like she didn't realize she was being photographed until the exact moment the shutter clicked.

CAUGHT ON CAMERA: GET THIS GIRL TO MAKEUP, STAT!

Beneath the headline, in smaller print: *Your favorite celebs doing the walk of shame. Would you want to wake up next to them? Cast your vote on our Facebook page!*

There's a whole pile of old issues—*#TRENDZ* and *CelebStyle*—each one featuring a photo of her on the cover or in a sidebar.

None of them positive. None of them nice.

I pick up the stack and chuck them in the kitchen garbage, dump in a glass of water for good measure.

Back on the couch, Jayla's still asleep. Her skin is pale, the shadows under her eyes dark and deep, and the whole scene reminds me of last summer.

The last time I saw her in California.

Before that, I hadn't seen her since Christmas, and that was only for a day. When she invited me out to California after school ended, I couldn't wait to spend time alone with her. We'd have two whole weeks, I thought. Two weeks to catch up, to be together.

Jayla's life didn't stop when I arrived—shoot after shoot, dinner parties, bar meetings, agent calls. Most nights, she left money for pizza or Thai, and I spent my dinners alone, streaming *Buffy the Vampire Slayer.*

Two nights before I was supposed to head home, she promised she'd stay in. Only instead of spending the night alone with me, she insisted on throwing a party.

"I want you to meet my friends, Luce. You'll *love* them!"

All these fake plastic people showed up, half of them assuming I was a caterer or coat-check girl, some even stuffing money into my pockets. Jayla quickly disappeared in a cloud of drunk jokes and forced smiles.

Hours passed. Long, boring, uncomfortable, synthetic. Finally I decided to go to bed, and I pushed my way through the crowd to find my sister. She was in the kitchen, head thrown back in a laugh that didn't even sound like hers.

Everyone there was talking with borrowed voices, flaunting tried-on clothes and faces. When they saw me in the kitchen doorway, they smiled like sharks.

"Oh, Lucy! Everyone, this is my baby sister, Lucy!" She made a big deal, shouting across the whole apartment, but

I didn't budge. It took her a moment to realize I was upset, and when she did, she gave me this huge frown.

Come over here and hug me, I thought. *Put your arm around me and whisper that you'll send everyone home so we can hang out.*

But of course she didn't, and when it was clear that I wasn't moving from the doorway, she rolled her eyes. "What's wrong, Lucy? You don't like when the grown-ups have adult time?"

Her friends laughed, egging her on.

"Have a drink," she said, downing one of her own. "Maybe you'll learn something."

I knew better than to argue with her in front of her pseudo friends, especially drunk pseudo friends, everyone laughing at me like I was some poor little twit Jayla got stuck babysitting.

Wordlessly, I stalked off to the guest room, flopped on the bed. I just wanted to close my eyes, not open them until the party was over.

But I wasn't alone.

Someone had followed me, this bleach-blond wannabe actor I'd been half flirting with earlier that night—more out of boredom than intrigue. He sat next to me on the bed then, tried to kiss me. He was wasted, and I shoved him off. It really wasn't a big deal, but I was already annoyed and tired of drunk people, and the guy freaked, raising his voice.

It was all talk. He'd landed on the floor when I pushed him, and he was still there, holding his head, slurring.

Tease. Slut. Prude.

He got up slowly, stumbled to the door, yelled out a few more names.

Bitch. Dyke. Jailbait. Whore.

Jayla heard the shouting. When he opened the bedroom door to leave, she was walking in. He stumbled into her.

"What the hell's going on?" she said.

"Baby sister's a tease, that's what." He pushed past her, back out into the crowd.

"Lucy?" she said softly, and I thought she might hug me after all, might squeeze my hand and ask if I was okay. But then her face turned sour. "This party was the worst idea ever. I should've known you wouldn't be able to handle it."

She slammed the door, slammed me inside the guest room and went back to her party like I really was the poor little twit she had to babysit.

I packed the next morning, called a cab before she could stop me.

"What's your problem?" she said as I was hauling my suitcase out the door. "You're acting like he raped you or something. Grow up, Lucy." She laughed like the whole thing was a joke, like I needed to lighten up.

But she didn't get it. No, he hadn't attacked me. He was

just some drunk guy at a stupid party I didn't want to be at. He wasn't the reason I was leaving.

It was Jayla. The sister I no longer recognized as mine. I knew it that night, confirmed when she slammed the door.

Janey-girl was gone, and I never even got the chance to say good-bye.

Now, standing before our couch, I shove Jayla hard in the shoulder. "Wake up."

Her eyes flutter, sticky and uneven, squinting.

"There was a photographer outside. Should I let him in? Get a few behind-the-scenes shots?"

Her eyes finally focus, huge and blue, and for a second it's like she forgets everything that happened in the last few years. She's sweet and beautiful again, innocent, happy to see me. She smiles, stretches her fingers through the holes in the afghan, flutters them against my knee.

I want to scream at her. To cancel her graduation appearance, pack up her Louis Vuitton bags and get her on the next flight out. Back to California, to her fake friends, to anyone who wants her. I want to yell, demanding to know how the golden girl who had everything could lose it all so fast.

Reckless. Ridiculous. Impossible. Selfish.

The labels float before my eyes.

But under all the anger and denial and brattiness, the real truth rears its ugly head.

Jayla is alone.

Hundreds of thousands of Heartthrob Facebook fans, and she never once thought to talk to her own sister about how much she was hurting, about how dark her dreams had turned.

And her own sister—aka *me*—was too wrapped up in drama to figure it out. To offer one encouraging word. To draw her a hot bath. To bring her chocolate mini bundts with sprinkles. To challenge her to a game of Fruit Ninja.

To give her one sincere, everything's-gonna-be-all-right hug.

To forgive her.

"Die, beasty hellions!" I slam on the keyboard and lay waste to a rabid horde. The screen is doused in blood splatter. "That's right. I'm a *survivor*, bitches."

And a princess. Warrior. International girl of mystery. Back to the safety of online anonymity, where my toughest dilemma is choosing between a weapon that's sharp and one that's blunt, judged only by the number of walking corpses I slay.

No what-ifs and maybes.

No huddling around the coffee table, helping investigate a scandal.

No shades of gray.

No swapping videos of baby animals.

No drama, no #scandals.

No bundt cakes and nerd debates. No Fruit Ninja champs. No Keith and Veronica jokes.

"Kindly welcome your face to my shotgun! *Blam!*" I ice a few more zombies, exchange a round of digital high fives with my crew.

I'm toggling through my weapons when my e-mail notifier pings on the task bar, demanding to be clicked. It's from Miss Demeanor. Miss Franklin Margolis Demeanor.

Subject: EVIDENCE.

I pull out my flamethrower and torch another zombie, creep around in search of more carnage.

This is me, Franklin. Not clicking on your e-mail. Not clicking, not caring.

Movement on the screen—another horde. I light up a molly and toss it at a nearby gas tank, watch the whole shit blow up.

Survivor, that's me.

EVIDENCE.

Click-click BOOM!

EVIDENCE.

Rat-a-tat-a-tat! BOOM!

EVIDENCE.

EVIDENCE.

EVIDENCE.

EVIDENCE.

From: Miss Demeanor

Dearest Lucy,

If we were on the phone, here's the part where I'd say, "Don't hang up!" So, don't hang up.

I think I've got a way to identify the perpetrator beyond a shadow of a doubt.

Please hear me out.

I wasn't withholding information; I just didn't connect the dots until now. I only suggested tracking down Miss D that day at the pep rally because it seemed like a Keith Mars sort of thing to do. I didn't realize that she—that I—had real evidence.

But I do.

The morning after prom, someone sent Miss Demeanor a set of photographs from an anonymous e-mail account called #ScandalWhore. The person explained that she didn't have a Facebook account and requested that I post the photos directly to the #scandal page. It was both a red flag and against the rules, and I politely refused.

Obviously, #ScandalWhore later deduced that your FB password was stored on your phone, so she uploaded the photos taken with your phone directly to *your* account, sharing them on Miss Demeanor's page and tagging them with #scandal.

But there were also photographs posted that *weren't* taken with your phone (the ones of you and Cole on the deck and the ones with Marceau—your phone is *in* those shots). This person clearly took them with her own phone, then either sent them to your phone and uploaded them that way, or pulled them up on a computer screen and photographed them with your phone, uploading everything in one batch.

I never gave it a second thought, because we didn't have your phone to confirm.

BUT . . . clearing through the old Miss D e-mails tonight, I found the photos #ScandalWhore first sent me—the ones taken with her phone. They were original, unedited files, so they still had the associated metadata (technical details that cell and digital cameras store with the image file—file size, the time it was taken, location info, and the type of phone or camera used). I can't believe I overlooked this before.

I've attached those originals here.

With this metadata—particularly the cell phone details—you can *prove* it's Olivia with real evidence instead of hearsay. Then you can turn it over to Zeff, clear your name, and officially close the case.

I'm sorry. Until now, it didn't occur to me that the photos in Miss D's inbox contained data we could use, or I would've found an anonymous way to get it to you.

Hope it helps.

Yours truly,

Franklin

"Huh. Weird." Kiara frowns at the data onscreen, a jumble of letters and numbers that might as well be launch codes for nuclear missiles.

It took me a while to find her home number in the Internet wormhole of our student directory, but as soon as I tracked her down and explained the situation, and swore that I didn't hold Ash's secret Miss D experiment against her, and bribed her with Ben & Jerry's, she came over pretty much immediately.

Now we're huddled in my bedroom over the computer and a carton of New York Super Fudge Chunk. I swallow a mouthful and pass her the spoon. "Guess it's back to the drawing board."

"It's not that. It's just—check this out." With the spoon, she points to a line that looks like it might be a serial number. "The phone that took the picture of you and Cole on the deck isn't even available in the States. It's some super-high-tech conceptual thing. Crazy expensive. According to my research, it's still in beta overseas."

"Lucy Belle? You in here?" Mom pokes her head in the door, her smile widening when she sees Kiara.

I do a quick intro. "Kiara's helping me, um, study."

"For computer science," Kiara says, at the same time that I say, "Physics."

"Computer physics," I say. "It's highly conceptual. Lots of . . . computer . . . things."

"I'm really good with computers." Kiara's smile is frozen on her face, like, *We're not shady AT ALL!*

"Well, it's nice to meet you, Kiara," Mom says. "It's so rare that Lucy has friends over."

"Mom!"

"Don't be dramatic, sugarplum. It's true! Anyway, I just wanted to let you know that Dad's making brisket tonight, so if you have any room left after that ice cream, come on down. Kiara, you're welcome, too."

"Thanks," she says.

"Computer physics?" Mom crinkles her nose. "I don't think we ever had anything like that when I was in school. I'll leave you to it."

With Mom finally gone, I turn back to Kiara, my stomach as cold as our predinner ice cream. "The beta phone . . . overseas where exactly?"

She squints at the numbers again, toggles back over to Google. "It's Scandinavian. Finland."

I CAME TO BRING THE PAIN AND ALL I GOT WAS THIS LOUSY T-SHIRT

There's a text on my phone, news flash from Griff, and I'm sitting on our front porch pondering its blazing WTFery.

Griff: *breaking! new info on olivia sitch. ryan/brian remembered other party antics & is sending me pix. meet @ picnic early to review? meeting ellie after that. sry i can't hang. :-(*

There aren't any classes today, just a half day at Cosgrove Park for the senior class picnic. I didn't tell Kiara what her findings meant, and after a sleepless night, I've been dressed and outside for an hour now, staring at my phone, Night of the Living Dog panting softly beside me.

Incapacitated.

Until the bathroom confrontation yesterday, I believed

Griff's theories about Olivia, convinced myself that Olivia *had* to be at the heart of this scandal. When Griff told me she'd found my phone in Olivia's bag, I swallowed the tale, disappointed but not surprised.

And now that I have irrefutable evidence of the real perp, proof beyond that pesky shadow of a doubt?

It can't be.

Griffin is one of my best friends.

Why would she do this to me? To Ellie?

I hit reply: *good work, agent colanzi. meet under aspen grove @ north side of lake. 11AM.*

Cosgrove Park is a sunny green blanket dotted with classmates and Frisbees and dogs. It's a postcard, and half the class is here early, everyone excited to soak up the sun. To make those last-chance memories we're supposed to make before the glory days pass us by in the blink of an eye in the summer of sixty-nine, or however that song goes.

But what are my last-chance memories? How will I look back on high school?

Ellie.

Cole.

Franklin/Miss Demeanor.

Asher, et al.

My sister.

Griffin.

It's all too much, too unreal, a drama staged against this picture-perfect backdrop for entertainment purposes only. Maybe one of Jayla's people did it, some twisted Angelica Darling publicity stunt, and any minute now, they'll roll out the cameras and make a big announcement and we'll laugh and eat cake like we were always in on the joke.

Night blows a breath through his nostrils. Even *he* knows we're out of excuses.

With time to spare before Griff's arrival, I guide us to the aspen grove, away from the popular sun-swept meadows where most of the class is starting to congregate. Night stakes out a patch of grass next to me, and after spreading out my blanket, I tie up his leash and set up his water bowl.

"Brains! Braaaaaains!"

Three human shadows fall over my legs, teetering and moaning in the breeze. Tens, Kiara, and Stephie stare down at me, faces caked in undead shades of gray, torsos cloaked in ripped green T-shirts hastily scrawled: *L.O.H.S. Zombie Hoard!*

"So, the whole horde effect is kind of lost when it's just the three of you," I say, "and when you spell 'horde' wrong. Also, real zombies don't eat brains. Or talk. Why does everyone get that wrong?"

Tens leans toward me with his arms out. There's gray face makeup caked into his dreads. "Braaaains!"

"Do you know how hard it is to crack open a human skull without, like, a bone saw? Our jaws don't have the bite force to . . . Forget it." I shake my head. "What are you guys even doing?"

Tens, still holding out his arms, moans, "Senior prank! Praaaank!"

"The prank was the campout thing," I say. "On the school lawn?"

His brow furrows. "Last I heard, Margo Hennessy was telling everyone it was the zombie horde invading the picnic thing."

"She changed it," I say. "To the campout."

"Shit, dude. Why are we always the last to get the memo?" Tens says.

I hold up my phone. "Three guesses."

"Guys, who cares what the masses say? We rock the zombie horde prank." Stephie gives a defiant nod. "Lucy, we made you a shirt."

She hands it over, and I tug it on over my tank top. "So, I love it, but as a zombie fangirl, I'm compelled to set the record straight."

"Real zombies don't eat brains," Kiara says. "Got it."

"Real zombies don't exist, technically," Stephie says.

"But if they did," she quickly adds after seeing my death stare, "no brain-munching."

"Yes, and the spelling issue," I say. "With these shirts, and our current count of four, we're saying that we're a very small but dedicated group of people who collect zombies."

Kiara laughs. "I'm strangely okay with that."

"Me too, actually." I check out my new shirt. I kind of rock it. "Thanks, dudes."

Stephie and Kiara sit down on the blanket next to me, both of them reaching over to pet Night, but Tens is feeding him bologna, and until it runs out, Night only has eyes for Tens.

"Where's your fearless leader?" I ask.

Kiara nods toward a group of kids throwing pebbles into Cosgrove's man-made lake. I wasn't paying attention to them before, but now that I'm looking, I spot Ash right away. He's wearing a sandwich board decorated with silver spaceships.

"Lying low today," Kiara says. "He's trying to spread the word about this UFO hunter group his brother's starting at the middle school next year."

In addition to the sandwich board, Ash has a hat that's been user modified into a satellite dish.

"*That's* lying low?" I say.

"He thinks you hate him," she says.

"He's not the one who wrote the column. I mean, he lied, but, you know." I shrug. "Pot, meet kettle."

"That's what I told him when he asked us if *we* hated him," Stephie says. "I think he just feels bad. Like, he was supposed to protect you, and somehow he let you down."

I let out a sigh to match Night's. "This has nothing to do with him. I'm not even all that mad at Franklin anymore. I'm just . . . I don't like myself right now. That's what it comes down to."

Stephie frowns, blue eyes sparkling in her zombie-gray face. "Well, *we* like you, so there. And I think Franklin's Team Lucy too. He's moping alone under a tree, like, way on the other side of the park."

"And what are you even talking about, Lucy?" Tens asks. "You basically rock. And also, are you going to eat that?" He points at my lunch bag as a fake blood capsule explodes in his mouth, oozing down his chin.

"Pretty sure zombies don't like falafel either."

"You have a lot of rules in your fantasy world." Tens holds out his hand, and I surrender my lunch.

As Tens and Night wolf down my falafel wrap, I close my eyes, drifting off to the melodic sound of Ash ranting about the as-yet-fruitless search for extraterrestrial life.

When I open my eyes again, (e)VIL has taken their lunch-stealing horde mentality to another unsuspecting blanket of picnickers, and Griff is flopping down next to me, grinning in her aviator sunglasses.

She's a brunette again, with a shaggy bob that comes midway between her chin and shoulder.

I watch her a minute as she makes herself comfortable, trying to figure out where to start. So far, all I've come up with is, "Cute hair."

"I know, right? Ryan loves brunettes. Go figure." She pulls out her phone and starts scrolling, tapping, scrolling. "He sent me, like, five pictures. I'm telling you, Olivia is *way* sketch. And she totally had your phone in her bag! I don't see why we're waiting. When do we bust this bitch?"

"Can I see?"

She hands over the phone. The picture onscreen is just Olivia's bottle trick, same setup, different angle, and I realize now that this entire episode with the bottle probably lasted about eight seconds at the party. Eight seconds of her life, one stupid trick, one posing-under-the-influence dare that will now live on in infamy.

I flip through Griff's other pictures—there aren't that many. A few more Olivia shots from Ryan. A shot from today, some shirtless football guys playing Hacky Sack, which she must've taken on her walk over. A selfie of Griff in front of her bookshelf at home, still platinum blond. One of Franklin working at his computer.

We had a lot of fun together. The investigation, the Veronica Mars thing. Franklin, that first night on the phone, typing up his notes, advising me how to investigate. The day at my house, everyone in the TV room, all of us focused on the same goal. Everyone wanting to help me. To be my friends.

I swallow the tightness in my throat. "Do you still have the prom stuff on here?"

"Nah. I didn't take that many," she says with a shrug. "Remember? *You* were Ellie's Leading Lady in Charge of Uploadables."

"But you got a few, right? Like, the video of us in the bathroom? Because that was, like, private jokes. If it ever got out, it would make everything worse."

"Ya think?" Griffin snorts. "I deleted that stuff as soon as I realized what was happening on your Facebook. I didn't want anyone to find my phone and take that Cole stuff out of context." She leans forward to flick a grasshopper off her knee. Poor guy doesn't even see it coming. "You're welcome, by the way."

"Yeah, thanks." My insides are on fire, fingers gripping her phone so hard it might crack. "There's just one thing I'm not sure about. Metadata?"

Griff laughs. "Ground control to major freak show. I

have a theory that you've been spending too much time with (e)VIL. Nice shirt, bee-tee-dubs."

I smooth the fabric over my chest.

"Translation?" she says.

The Hacky Sack guys are on the screen again, and I click through the display options until the details come up. "Every digital picture captures information, and unless you tell it not to, it attaches that info to the image file." I point to the data on the screen. "Shows the date and time it was taken—fifteen minutes ago, for this shot. Geolocation data. Whether the flash went off. File size. And the exact kind of phone that took the picture. See all these numbers and letters?"

Griff swallows hard, and when she speaks, her voice cracks, words forced into a laugh. "Slow down, geek squad. Thanks for the tips, but—"

"If you're so inclined, you can Google these numbers to find the exact model of the phone, even down to the color, and the fact that this particular phone, for example, is still in beta and nearly impossible to get in the States. In fact, the only way to get one is to travel to Finland and bring it back, like your parents did. You know, I think you're the only girl at Lav-Oaks who's fortunate enough to have a phone like this. Lucky."

Griffin's face is as bleached as her former hair.

"With just a little sleuthing and technical savvy," I continue, "you can learn a lot about photographs—and their photographers—from metadata. I was surprised to learn it myself. But then, I was investigating a scandal that turned my life upside down, so you might say I was highly motivated."

"Lucy," she chokes, "I'm—"

"Don't." I drop my smile and all manner of politeness. "I mean, if you were planning to start with denial, let's just fast-forward to the part where you're explaining yourself."

Griffin pushes the sunglasses to the top of her head. "I never intended for it to get so out of control. It just happened. And then I couldn't stop it."

I knew that Griff was the perp the moment Kiara gave me the metadata report, the moment she said the photo came from an overseas phone. I knew she was the perp when I watched all the color drain from her face just now as I spoke, knew by the set of her mouth that she'd really done it.

But hearing her admit it makes me shrivel up anyway.

"Why?" I ask.

Griff takes a deep breath. "It basically started at the cabin. In the bathroom? You were saying stuff to me about trying to get on Miss Demeanor and—"

"I was teasing! We always joke about that stuff."

"No." Griff shakes her head. "It was laced with something. It fucking hurt, Lucy. You called me a slut."

"I didn't—"

"Not out loud, maybe. But you were thinking it. It was all over your face."

The grasshopper's back, flitting around on the blanket near Griff's legs, but she's not paying attention to him. She's got her eyes closed, her face still bedsheet-pale. "I was mad at you," she says, "and I didn't want to be. It was a party—prom!—we were supposed to have fun. So after all the excitement with John's speech and the pond, after everyone was back inside, I went looking for you again. I wanted to talk. That's when I saw you on the deck with Cole."

"And you took a picture of us?"

"*Lucy.* Not an hour earlier, you were all judgy about me hooking up with guys. Then I catch you making out with your best friend's barely-ex-boyfriend? That's some serious what-the-fuckage." She opens her eyes, stares out across the park. "I had my phone out, so I just snapped it, not thinking. Half the time my camera doesn't even work, but it did that time. I figured I'd give you shit about the picture later.

"Then *literally* a few seconds later you're making out with Marceau. And again I'm like, *Who's calling* me *a slut?* Then you come inside with a jab about me making out with Paul—my date, not someone else's boyfriend, by the way. Next thing, Cole comes down and tells me you're sick. I knew there was more to it, but I figured we'd just talk in the morning, sober up."

Night nudges Griffin's hand with his nose, like, *The last guy brought me bologna.* Griff ignores him.

"I'm hanging out with Paul," she says, "and suddenly people are saying you and Cole are upstairs doing it. I go check it out, never thinking it would go *that* far, but they're kind of right. I mean, you weren't *doing* it—"

"You think?"

"It looked bad, Lucy. You were all cuddled up. I couldn't even tell if you had clothes on. You know that saying 'seeing red?' I saw it. I whipped out my phone, only it was one of those times where I couldn't get it to work, and then I saw yours on the dresser. I grabbed it, took a few shots. You guys were the living dead—didn't even wake up. Someone else was coming up the stairs, so I just swiped the phone and vanished. My phone still wasn't working, so I just started taking random party shots with yours, passing it around to whoever. A little while later, Olivia and Quinn were laughing about you guys, joking that someone should take pictures in Cole's room and send them to Miss D's scandal thing."

"So you offered?"

Griff shrugs. "I told them to drop it, which they did

because they were wasted and Olivia has a crush on Cole and anyway, who cares? It was just a party thing. But the idea got in my head. I was so pissed about the stuff you said to me, and all the times you scoffed at me about hooking up or whatever, and I just . . . I snapped. I woke up in the morning hoping I'd feel better, but you and Cole were gone, and that made it even worse."

"I had to get out of there."

"Yeah, without even saying good-bye or trying to talk to me, after everything that happened that night. You just . . . you bailed on me. And you didn't call—"

"You had my phone!"

"You didn't even call me from your house to make sure I got home okay. That was the last straw. I wanted revenge."

I laugh. "Safe to say, you got it."

Griff shakes her head, her eyes red and glassy. "I didn't think about it like some big viral campaign. I swear I never meant for the Juicy thing to happen, or for you and Cole to get targeted like that."

"We were a Lav-Oaks Internet scandal, Griff. What did you expect?"

"I was venting. I wanted to embarrass you, call you out. And I thought maybe it would bring me and Ellie closer instead of me always being, like, the add-on friend. But it just got crazy."

Griff's crying now, and I know I should be angrier at her, that nothing she says can explain this, can make it okay. The only reason I agreed to meet her at the picnic early was to tell her off, to make a scene and stomp out in a blaze of glory. Friendless, maybe, but avenged. Right.

But Griffin's right too. She *was* the add-on friend, and I judged her every time, with every new crush and eye-candy target, her football boy hookups and fake British accent and hairstyle-of-the-month. I looked down on her. Not intentionally. Not with true malice in my heart. But the judgment was there nevertheless, and to deny it I'd have to bury myself even deeper in the sand than I already have.

Everything in me is exhausted and broken, and when I open my mouth again all that comes out is a whisper. "Should I tell her, or will you?"

"It was Griffin," I say.

Cole and I didn't have a chance to go private at the picnic, and now we're leaning on our boulder just before dusk, catching up while the dogs run in circles through the woods.

I tell him the whole story—Miss Demeanor's photo evidence. Kiara's metadata research. How I confronted Griff this morning, how she promised she'd tell Ellie. How she and Ellie were still BFFing around at the picnic all day, sharing drinks, reading under the trees. Hugging like everything was cool while I watched from the sidelines.

Griffin didn't tell her.

I gave her the chance to confess, and she snubbed it, because she knows I'm the girl who never says anything, not when it counts. Griff left me out to dry, to shoulder the blame for embarrassing Ellie and outing everyone at that party. Half of them are grounded for their last summer in Lav-Oaks, all because of pictures they think *I* posted. I'm lucky the worst I endured was posters on my locker, gum in my hair, chocolate milk on my boots. People could seriously kick my ass if they wanted to.

Because I'm the girl who never says anything, not when it counts. Right?

No. That girl is gone.

I have the evidence. And one last, epic chance to clear my name completely, to expose the perp to everyone: graduation.

I tell Cole my plan. "I have to do it," I say.

His eyes hold nothing but sorrow. "Maybe it sounds like a good idea in your head, but I really think you should drop it."

"And let Ellie think I posted all that stuff? Graduate as the class narc? The slut? The insert-favorite-name-here?"

Cole runs a hand through his hair. "Tell Ellie in private. Tell Griffin's parents. Do what you need to do directly. . . . I just don't see the point of making a spectacle just to call Griffin out. That's not you, Lucy."

"She called *me* out, and she totally screwed us over."

He levels those coppery green eyes on me. "Okay, what she did was seriously jacked. I'm shocked, honestly. But we're here, right? Together? Alone in our woods with two awesome dogs?" He traces his fingers along the fringe of my bangs. "All that stuff she posted doesn't change it. Doesn't change this." His lips brush my cheekbone, trail softly to the edge of my mouth, and there he stays, lingering, breathing.

I shiver and pull back. "Distractions won't distract me. I'm serious."

"So am I. Look, I know you dealt with most of the crap at school, and trust me, it about killed me watching it happen, not being able to stop it. But it's done. Our fifteen minutes of shame are over. Everyone's focusing on exams next week; then we're at graduation, and who cares? The bullshit of Lav-Oaks High is already a memory."

"But I *never* say what I'm feeling. Yeah, I'm snarky and opinionated, but I don't say stuff when it matters. I liked you forever, and I didn't . . . This is something I have to do. For me."

"I never said how I felt about you either. So for four years, we didn't say anything. And now there's just a few months left before we're both getting into cars, driving off in opposite directions."

I lean back against the boulder, looking around for Night and Spike. I spot them romping behind a tree, sniffing each other's butts, digging in the dirt, not a care in the world. "Don't remind me."

"I'm just saying. We lost four years by not talking. There's a million things I want to know about you, stories I need to tell you. We can't spend our last few months together obsessing about this scandal. About Griffin." His eyes are pleading, but he doesn't understand how important this is, what a Really Big Deal in the whole spectrum of my life.

If I let Griff get away with this, if I graduate with this scandal looming over me, I'll never be able to look at myself in the mirror. I'll never be able to trust anyone, including Cole, because I won't be able to trust myself. I'll spend the rest of forever walking under a cloud of shame and regret, wondering why—just once—I didn't do the right thing.

"You can't do this," he says. "It's cruel and mean spirited and it's nothing like the Lucy I fell in love with." Cole must see the hurt in my eyes, but he's not backing down, and neither am I.

"I have to do it, Cole. And there's nothing more to say about it."

He nods once, calls for Spike. We hook up the dogs in silence and lead them back into the world beyond the woods, and when the houses of our perfectly beige neighborhood come into view, he goes his way, and I go mine, only the dogs looking back at each other, wondering where the fun went.

ALL WE ARE SAYING IS GIVE (E)VIL A CHANCE

Nestled in my pocket on a flash drive the size of a Hershey's miniature Mr. Goodbar is all the evidence I need. My thoughts are drawn to it, heat-seeking, guilt-seeking, seeking anything other than crushing sadness.

After thirteen years of formal education and the last week of high school exams I'll ever take, I'm graduating today.

It's nothing like I imagined.

Here on the Swordfish football field, all decked out for the ceremony, I'm not waving at Griff and Ellie across the crowd, ticking down the hours until we celebrate our freedom, barbecuing and swimming and counting the stars. We were supposed to go with Cole and his family back to the cabin for the week.

Now Cole's going without us.

I'm not smiling at my parents, secretly proud with each cheesy photo they snap, secretly glad that my sister's here to share this day.

Instead, I'm sitting uncomfortably in a stiff metal folding chair between Pete Underfell and Kessa Vans, the three of us brought together by the alphabet for more than a decade of classes, assemblies, and ceremonies. I've watched them grow up, change glasses and hair colors and outfits and friends, but we've never shared more than a smile and a few polite words.

Next to Ellie's moms and the Fosters, my parents sit in the bleachers, faces still tanned from their time in Laguna but etched with new lines. Lines that weren't there until they came home from dinner last weekend to more photographers on the lawn, to Jayla crying in her rental car, locked in the garage.

She finally told them everything. Had to, really, and they wanted her to cancel her commencement obligations, to take some time to just be Janey again—*our Janey-girl*, they said—but she refused.

I don't want to disappoint Lucy.

She's kept my secrets, though, assuring my parents that my last weeks of school went just fine in their absence. Smooth sailing.

Even though, as Marceau can attest, we're landlocked.

My former best friends are in their chairs somewhere too, all the parents and grandparents and cousins looking on, no one meeting my eyes but Principal Zeff, offering her occasional smile, a double thumbs-up on acing my exams and surviving the scandal.

We've already crossed the temporary outdoor stage, and sitting here in my metal chair, I'm holding a rolled-up piece of paper that tells the world I made it. I graduated high school. I'm ready for bigger and better things, ready to be an adult. There's a couple of signatures and an official gold seal, so it must be true.

It's hot on the bright green field, hot under the black graduation robe, hot under the cap and the too-bright Colorado sun, and in my pocket, on that flash drive the size of a chocolate, I have everything I need to throw someone else to the gossip hounds.

Franklin's onstage now, telling family-friendly jokes and giving us the traditional valedictorian send-off, and I watch him, smiling, momentarily distracted from the burn in my pocket. His curly hair makes a fuzzy halo beneath his graduation cap, and he looks happy up there, like he was made to be this great orator, a leader of the people. In the final moments of his speech, I feel his eyes on me, his smile broad and genuine.

"I've always thought that the people who made a difference in this world were the ones who shouted the loudest," he says, "no matter who or what tried to drown them out. It's why I started writing, reporting. I wanted to be one of those loud voices, a voice from which people could learn. But sometimes the quietest person is the one who makes the most impact, just by refusing to give in. By refusing to be anyone other than herself, even if she's not shouting it from the rooftops. Or, you know . . . an online fake gossip column." The audience cracks up. "So as you leave the world of high school behind, no matter what challenges await you beyond, find your own voice. Trust it. Loud, soft. Online, offline. Find it, and don't let anyone silence it. Thank you for inspiring me to do the same."

"Thank you, Mr. Margolis," Principal Zeff says, applauding at the podium. Her voice is thick with emotion after Franklin's speech.

"Speaking of bright futures," she says, "it's my great honor to now introduce a very special speaker, a Lavender Oaks High School alum who really knows what it means to get out there and follow your dreams. Please join me in giving a warm welcome to our very own little darling, Miss Jayla Heart!"

There's an overblown cheer from the crowd, half a standing ovation, fake plastic glee rising above our heads.

The camera crews and photographers that had been snoozing on the sidelines for most of the ceremony now surge forward, each one jostling for the best angle as my sister takes the podium.

She smiles for a moment, waves to her fake fans, gives the cameras time to get her best features. The flashes continue as she flips through her note cards.

"So, I wrote this whole speech about following your dreams and reaching for the stars, but Margolis basically stole my lines. . . ." Jayla narrows her eyes at Franklin, then gives him a playful wink. "Angelica might have a few choice words for you, Margs. You're lucky this is a family event."

Everyone laughs.

"Can I just . . ." Jayla holds up her note cards, examining them as if they're strangers to her. As if she hadn't spent the last week crafting Angelica Darling jokes, reviewing them to cross out the R-rated ones. She fans them with her thumb, then grabs them in both hands and shreds. "Who needs notes? I'm a so-called adult living in the so-called real world, also known as Hollywood. Yes, I'll give you a moment to wrap your minds around that."

More laughing.

"But since I'm supposed to give you some wisdom from my post-high-school reality, let's start with the things I know. I know that on any given Saturday, most of you are laughing *at* me rather than *with* me. I know that unless you're a fourteen-year-old boy, you're not professing any real love on my Heartthrobs fan page. I know that people have turned my life's work into a drinking game, an Internet meme, a practical joke. I know that despite how hard I work, how much I try to find meaning in my career, I've spent more time on the *#TRENDZ* front page than I have on any awards shows, on any interview outlets. I know that like many of you, I had huge dreams on my high school graduation day, and I followed and achieved them. But now I can say this with complete authority: Dudes, being a television star is nothing like what you see on television."

People are still chuckling, but there's a whisper making its way through the masses, confusion laced with mockery. They don't know if this is supposed to be funny, if they're supposed to laugh, or if Jay's having a public, tweet-worthy meltdown.

The cell phones are out again, clicking and tagging, posting and sharing, a hundred silver devices turning my sister's honest words into another practical joke, another J-Heart tabloid smear.

I shrink in my chair.

"Advice from a so-called grown-up?" Jay says. "If you have a dream in your heart, no matter how impossible or silly or expensive or far-reaching, you *have* to go for it, to find a way to make it happen. Anyone will tell you that, right? That's what graduation is all about. Looking ahead. New beginnings. Finding your voice, like your esteemed valedictorian said." She holds up the torn pieces of her speech cards. "Like I was supposed to say. But no one ever tells you how hard it is when you get what you want. That even if your dreams come true, you'll still face a mob of people waiting to take them away from you, desperate to see you fail, ready to take pictures of the whole thing and tell the world how screwed up you are."

She turns a pointed smile on Quinn, sitting in the front row with her cell phone out.

"Thank you, Miss Heart, for that inspirational reminder." Principal Zeff is on her feet again, already applauding, giving Jayla a gentle nod. Translation: *Time to go! This school doesn't need another scandal!*

"Ms. Zeff, if you'll allow me just one more moment." Jayla's all poise and confidence, more real than I've ever seen her. "When the spotlight shines on you—whether it's because you're a celebrity or just a person following your own personal dreams—you don't get to choose which parts it illuminates, good or bad, false or true. But you *can* choose to remain true to yourself, to be who you are, no matter what people think. That's really the best advice I can give you. Stay strong, Swordfish. Stay real. And yes, you can quote me *and* Angelica Darling on that."

Jayla blows us all a kiss, and the paparazzi surges again, waving their camera crews forward as Ms. Zeff tries to usher them back to the sidelines. The spotlights are on Jayla, lighting her up like a fallen pop-culture angel, beautiful and broken.

Jayla and I lock eyes for one more second, but I look away before anyone notices, before anyone reads into it and makes the connection.

I have to clear my name . . . .

She steps back from the podium, turns it back over to Ms. Zeff, and takes her honorary seat at the side of the stage. The reporters follow her, clumped and bobbing like rotten seaweed at her feet.

"Ladies and gentlemen, graduates and families," Principal Zeff announces. "There's one more thing we'd like to share during our ceremony today. It's unconventional, but we believe it's an important message for everyone living in these digital times. Please welcome Lucy Vacarro and the student-run Electronic Vanities Intervention League: Asher Hollowell, Kiara Chen, Thomas 'Tens' Girard, Stephanie Wilcox, and Randall 'Roman' McCorkhill."

My classmates stir in their seats, but thankfully no one's hurling insults. Maybe it's the specialness of the day, the sanctimony of the graduation ceremony that's keeping them all respectful. Or maybe Cole was right—maybe this is already behind them, our fifteen minutes over, our lives moving forward whether we want them to or not.

Or maybe they're just too busy taking smooshed-face selfies in their caps and gowns to care.

I line up with my group, me with Dad's laptop at the podium, (e)VIL in formation behind me, heads down, awaiting their cue. PowerPoint is on the screen, projected for all to see, and I click the flash drive into place.

Error in connection.

My palms are sweating, my stomach a tangle of knots and weeds. I pop the drive out, push it back in. Relaunch PowerPoint as the crowd fidgets and groans.

This time it works.

Showtime.

The air around us has gone still in the heat, and a drop of sweat trickles down my back. Save for the paparazzi still bugging my sister, all eyes are on me, and I know the moment is here. My one last shot to rid myself of scandal.

I scan the crowd and find Griff's eyes. She's near the front, her face expressionless, arms crossed. A few rows behind her, Ellie watches me with the same bored, distracted look. Olivia's not too far away, looking sad and grim.

One section over, I find Cole, and in his eyes are all

the pleas from that day in the woods, the last words he spoke to me.

. . . nothing like the Lucy I fell in love with . . .

He's right. Revenge is nothing like the old me. But things are different now; we've all crossed so many lines that it's impossible to untangle them, to find our way back to the original starting points. I crossed lines when I kissed Cole, when I got into his bed that night, when I passed judgment on Griffin before any of this started. Griff crossed lines when she took my phone and uploaded those pictures. Even Ellie crossed lines, keeping her breakup from Cole a secret, urging me to go to prom in her place as if she really did have a simple case of the flu. When the scandal hit, she automatically assumed the very worst, that I'd posted pictures of me and Cole—and everyone else—just to avoid telling her face-to-face.

I'm not sure we can ever recover from that.

Cyberbullying: A Cautionary Tale, the slide reads behind me. The crowd goes silent. (e)VIL doesn't know I changed the presentation. I hope they understand.

My finger hovers over the button to advance the next slide. The one with Griffin's picture, a candid shot of her holding up her phone. Back when all of us were still friends. Back when I still had my own secrets, my own dark desires, none of them plastered all over the Internet.

"Miss Heart, is it true you're being fired from the show?" one of the reporters asks my sister, low enough that only those of us onstage can hear it.

"Is this your last season on *Danger's Little Darling?*" another says.

"Lucy?" Ash whispers behind me. "You okay?"

Roman leans forward, a flash of red Mohawk in the corner of my vision. "Start the show, Lucy. We're ready."

I nod, look from the paparazzi to my sister. She's waving her hands to shoo them off like flies, but they're relentless. A few seniors are watching them now, too, snapping cell phone shots of the whole scene, texting them off into cyberspace, ready for the next scandal or photo caption contest.

If they knew Jayla Heart was my sister, they'd be snapping shots of me, too.

One click. That's all it will take. One click and a few words to clear my name, to shift the blame to Griffin, to get off the stage before anyone realizes the scandalous Vacarro at the podium is the sister of the scandalous Vacarro in the honorary chair nearby.

. . . nothing like the Lucy I fell in love with . . .

"Any truth to the drug rumors?" The reporters are relentless. "Is rehab an option?"

"Lucy?" Ash asks again. Ms. Zeff is looking at me,

waving her hand in the international gesture for *roll the tape*.

I look out across the crowd once more, find Griffin's eyes and hold them.

It was laced with something . . . It hurt . . . All the times you scoffed at me . . .

"Any party plans this summer, Miss Heart?" That guy is loud, louder than the rest, and a bunch of students in the front row snicker. Their attention shifts from me and (e)VIL to my sister, and in that moment, in all that laughing and cell phone clickage, I know it's time to let my voice be heard. To stand onstage before this huge, captive audience and finally, without any more doubts and speculation, make things right.

I turn and catch Kiara's attention. "Message from the Mockingjay."

She cocks her head, confused.

"Change of plans." I explain the situation, my desperation fueled by the crowd's pressing impatience. The heat. The paparazzi machine-gunning Jayla. Griffin's eyes, now boring into my face. Cole's eyes, dim and disappointed.

"Leave it to (e)VIL." Kiara ducks into a commando roll behind the stage, narrowly avoiding the sound system. Tens follows her, also almost taking out said sound system, seashells clicking as he rolls.

"Fellow graduates," I boom into the microphone.

Certain I've nabbed their attention, I play a background track Stephie made with a few imposing, Borg-like theme songs and recite my canned intro about the dangers of cyberbullying, the difference between having fun online and having fun at the expense of other people's feelings. There's a whole pile of statistics and definitions, and while Roman, Stephie, and Ash perform their baffling interpretive dance of colliding electrons, I rattle off the facts, memorized from all my time bonding with Zeff's manual.

The entire audience—my classmates, our parents and relatives, the faculty, the administration, the paparazzi—is mystified and rapt, all eyes on me.

I take a deep breath, ready—after weeks of hiding—to drop the bomb.

"There's something you need to know," I say as the music fades. "Something I've kept under wraps for far too long." My voice echoes across the field. I look at Griffin again. Then Cole. Then, finally, at Jayla.

"Jayla Heart," I say. "Please join me again at the podium."

Her brow is pinched with confusion, but she smooths out her navy pencil skirt and rises from the honorary chair, crosses the stage to join me. The paparazzi follow, reassembling in a pile before us.

"Jayla Heart graduated on this stage seven years ago," I say. "Many of you didn't know her then, and unless you have older siblings, you probably weren't here to see it. But I was. She was going by Jayla Heart even then, but her real name is Janey Vacarro."

I pause, letting it settle across the field of caps and gowns before me.

"She's my sister," I continue, "and she's talented and beautiful. Whether you're a fan of the show or not, you should know that behind Angelica Darling's scheming, conniving backstabbery, there's a real person. An amazing person with the biggest heart of anyone I know."

Jayla's shocked into silence. I grab her hand and squeeze, don't let go. Not when my parents stand and applaud. Not when Zeff blinks at me through confused but heartfelt tears. Not when the media surges forward again, blasting Jayla with more questions.

"Miss Heart, are you bankrupt?"

"What can you tell us about your contract? Is Angelica off the show for good?"

Still grasping Jayla's hand, I twist her behind me, stand between her and the paparazzi piranha. Just when I fear I can't hold them off another second, I spot Kiara in the audience, standing on a chair in the middle of the crowd.

She's holding her megaphone, right on cue.

"Oh! My! God!" she shouts. "I can't believe it! Right here in Lavender Oaks! It's the Sarah Palin 2020 tour bus!

They just turned down Dorchester Street, flags a-blazing!"

The camera crew exchanges brief glances, then bolts away en masse, chasing Kiara and Tens onto Dorchester in search of the mythical bus.

Zeff seizes the moment and takes the podium from me and Jayla, rushing through her closing remarks, ending with an emotional send-off: "Allow me to be the first to officially congratulate you, Lavender Oaks High School graduates!"

"Lucy last name Vacarro!" From a chair in the back row, Marceau stands up to make an announcement of his own, one of (e)VIL's megaphones pressed to his lips. "Lucy Vacarro, I'm—"

But a cacophony of tubas and trombones drowns him out, blasting us with an off-key marching band rendition of Alice Cooper's "School's Out."

The crowd rebounds from the confusion and goes crazy, cameras flashing, parents cheering, horns blowing, black caps winging into the air like a hundred tasseled crows taking flight.

Freedom.

THE IMPRESSIVELY GRUESOME DEMISE OF ANGELICA DARLING AND THE UNEXPECTED RISE OF REALITY-BASED RELATIONSHIPS

A flirty tangerine dress is the only thing my sister kept from Angelica Darling's wardrobe collection, and it was *made* for Jayla. Stunning much?

Still, her eyes can't lie. She's nervous. A little sad, too.

"Sure you're okay with all this?" I zip her up and tie the halter at her neck, just below her messy-on-purpose updo. "We could go low-key instead."

"And cancel our joint party? Where there won't be any actual joints? No way." She turns to face me. "Seriously, Luce. I'm superexcited for you to see the episode—you of all people will appreciate the artistic vision. Besides, new leaf, remember? I'm done crying over one little canceled contract." She waves her hand, like, *Been there, done that, got the T-shirt, next?*

"You're beautiful. You know that, right?"

"I owe it all to Sephora," she says with a cute shrug. "And bee pollen smoothies. Also, wine is a factor—it's good for the heart. Now, turn around. People will be here soon and your hair is a hot mess!"

Despite the crazy-coaster we've been riding this month, and the ongoing paparazzi fallout from last week's graduation madness—including dozens of feature stories insinuating that Sarah Palin's team was covertly recruiting campaign aides from the Lav-Oaks graduating class— Mom and Dad wanted to throw us a combined *Danger's Little Darling* finale and grad party.

I'd been imagining something like this all year, only in my before version, the guest list was different. Jayla wasn't around in person, but Ellie and Griff were. We piled up on the couch, mowing down sundaes and poking fun at Angelica Darling, making outlandish predictions for next season.

In my before version, there was always a next season for the infamous Angelica Darling. Always a next season for me and Ellie and Griffin.

"Hold still." Jayla gathers my hair in one hand and reaches for a brush with the other. As she pulls everything into a twist, we meet each other's eyes in the bathroom mirror. "Congratulations, little sister. You survived high school. Now you can forget everything you learned."

"High school *whut?*"

Jayla smiles. "That's my girl."

"Hey. Mind if I borrow your girl?" Ellie joins the reflection behind us, the last person I expected to open my party invitation, the last one I expected to see.

"Ellie," I say. Her name is strange and foreign on my lips.

In my room, beneath my pen-and-ink series of celebrity zombies, Ellie and I sit on my bed.

She hands over a large brown bag. Inside, there's a white box stamped with Black & Brew's logo.

"You brought Tarts of Apology?"

"Chocolate espresso bean and lemon blueberry," she says. "I didn't want to show up empty-handed. Actually, I didn't want to show up at all."

My stomach twists.

"It's not that I didn't want to see you again," she says. "It's . . . I'm still reeling. Like, what the hell just happened?"

I lean back on my elbows and close my eyes. "Tell me about it."

"Griffin came over the other night," she says. "She confessed to posting the pictures on your Facebook. She said you had the evidence. Why didn't you say anything?"

Across the hall, through the closed door, I hear my parents getting ready, Mom sending Dad back to the closet. Again. "The *salmon* polo shirt," she says. "That one is orange."

"I had this big reveal planned for graduation," I tell Ellie. "But when I got up onstage, I kept looking at you guys and thinking about how things used to be and how screwed up everything got . . . how *I* screwed it up . . . and everything with Jayla and the paparazzi . . . Something shifted."

All along, I'd been waiting for summer to come and go, for Ellie and me to get on the road to California and our new lives. But now that high school's officially over, it doesn't feel right. Nothing feels right.

High school might've been about as fun as a zombie apocalypse, but I always had Ellie. Cole and Griff too. It wasn't supposed to end like this.

"Even when I saw the pictures that first day," Ellie says, "I never thought our friendship would be over. I mean, it was *super*painful, but . . . it happened so fast. The Cole stuff. The secrets we kept from each other. By the time Griff told me what happened, it was like it didn't even register. I guess I'm just . . . numb."

After that day at the picnic, I never thought Griffin would confess, but now that she has . . . maybe it *doesn't* matter. She may have been the one who made the evidence public, but she's not the one who created the evidence in the first place. I kissed Cole. More than once. And before that, I carried this spark, a red-hot thing that smoldered and burned for four years.

I love Ellie, but how could it *not* affect our friendship? There was always some barely concealed part of me that resented her, the easy way she had with Cole, the almost flippant shrug of her shoulders these last few months whenever she talked about the possibility of forever with him.

If Cole were *my* forever, I wouldn't have shrugged. I would've held on to it with everything I had.

"I've been in love with Cole Foster since he first moved here," I finally say. "The *whole* time. Prom was the first time we kissed, but it wasn't the first time I imagined it. Not even close."

Ellie's eyes widen, but just barely, as if her initial shock is immediately replaced with comprehension, how it all makes sense now, how she should've guessed it all along.

"That night, he kissed me on the deck after we'd been reminiscing. I kept telling myself it was just that—prom night, everything coming to an end, drinking, some momentary flash. But it wasn't. Later, in his room, I kissed him again. Not like the pictures made it look. But it wasn't innocent, either. I wasn't drunk. I wanted it to happen, Ellie."

Still Ellie doesn't speak, but no matter how hard I try

to convince myself that it's the right thing to do, I can't regret loving Cole, and I say as much.

"I know," she finally says. "Neither can I. I mean, things changed after the first year—like, we both knew it wouldn't last. But we had some good times."

We sit in silence again, not meeting each other's eyes. I can almost see the flickering filmstrip of shared memories between us, years of stories and moments whooshing by in a heartbeat.

Between them, secrets. Assumptions. All the unsaid things, just as much a part of our story as the rest.

"Where is my brown belt?" Dad shouts from the bedroom. Footsteps follow, Mom rushing to his side.

"Black belt!" she says. "You're wearing black shoes. Honestly, hun."

Ellie smiles. "Good to know some things haven't changed."

"Oh, yes, they have," I say. "Jayla sent them on this couple's retreat, and ever since they got back, they're all over each other."

"Seriously?"

"I've lost count how many times I've busted them making out in the kitchen. It's practically a health code violation."

"Eww," she says. "Thank God your parents aren't on

Facebook. The moms are all over it. It's gross." Then her smile falters, and she looks at me with watery eyes. "I was thinking we could . . . I don't know. Try. Not today, but soon. I don't want to start college like this. But I'm not . . . I still need time." Her voice is a fragile whisper. "I can't promise anything."

"I know," I say. "Neither can I."

"Fair enough." Ellie stands from the bed and smiles, and I swear it's like the sun rises in my bedroom, lighting up the undead celebs on the wall. Zombie Taylor Kitsch looks especially cheerful.

"Sure you don't want to stay for Angelica's official farewell?" I grab the Black & Brew bag. "It's supposed to be quite dramatic."

Ellie laughs, but shakes her head. "I'm helping the moms pack tonight. They're taking me camping this week—they say we have to bag at least three Fourteeners before I leave for California."

"Ellie." It's all I can do not to crack up. "You *hate* hiking. And the woods. And pretty much everything about being outside."

"Hey, we summited Mount Elbert! We *sang* on Mount Elbert, remember?"

"And the next day you refused to come out of the tent unless Cole promised that you'd never have to hike farther than the car. For the rest of your life. Remember that?"

She shrugs. "Eh, my plan is to fake an injury on day one, check into a hotel, and let them carry out their midlife crisis wilderness adventure without me."

"You've got it all figured out, huh?"

She taps her head. "Four years of quality Lav-Oaks education at work." Ellie gives me a quick hug. Not a bestie hug, not a *we made this mountain our bitch!* hug, but a genuine one nevertheless. "I'll call you when we're back to let you know I survived."

"I'll be waiting."

"Duuuuuude. Summertime, and the livin' is *eeee-zee*."

Under the brim of a new, bright red cap, 420 gives me his jack-o'-lantern smile and hands over a bag of Doritos, half empty.

"I think what he means," Clarice says from the porch steps behind him, "is thanks for inviting us. I brought fruit salad. It's the one thing I knew he wouldn't eat on the way over."

"Fruit and salad," 420 says, "are not one of the four major food groups of cheesy goodness."

"You're hopeless," Clarice says. But beneath her chunky black bangs, her eyes glitter.

Marceau shows up next, all sincere and adorable with a bouquet of store-bought, totally legal yellow daffodils. "These are for you, to say thank you for hosting me. But I didn't get roses because they are the flower of love and . . . we are breaking up, *chéri*."

I take the flowers. "Marceau, we never——"

"I don't want to crack your heart, but I cannot go on like this. Someone else is in love to you. And I cannot be the one who stands in the way of true love."

"Um . . ."

Marceau leans in and kisses my cheek. "You will find your heart to heal again."

He walks into my house, introduces himself to my family as my ex-boyfriend.

"Marceau!"

"He's right," a boy says behind me. "Someone else is in love to you."

I haven't seen Cole since graduation last week.

But I turn toward the sound of his voice, and here he is again.

Straight out of my dreams again.

He's tan from his week outdoors, scruffy around the edges. There's a small bandage over one of his fingers, a new hole in his olive cargo shorts, just beneath the left pocket.

He runs a hand through his hair, his perpetually perfect bed-head flopping back into place. "Can we skip the talking part?"

I nod vigorously.

He takes Marceau's flowers and sets them on the wicker table next to me, captures me in his arms. "God, I missed you," he whispers.

"Dude. I thought we were skipping the talk—"

His mouth is warm on my lips, apple-sweet and full of summer, and then he pulls back. "That . . . Wait. That felt like good-bye."

"You know what they say." I hold his gaze, count the flecks of gold in his eyes. "One person's good-bye is another's hello."

"Who says that? I've never heard anyone say that in my life."

"*You're* the one who said it felt like good-bye. That's, like, totally unromantic."

"Yeah, but it wasn't supposed to be good-bye. It was supposed to show you I'm seriously in love to you and also, I want to help you find your heart to heal."

"*That's* what you were trying to say with that kiss?" I frown. "Try again, drummer boy."

Cole grabs my shoulders and pushes me against the windows, takes my breath away and the last of my strength. His hands slide into my hair, our bodies so close I can feel the blue heartbeat just beneath his skin.

His lips melt against my throat, and I gasp.

"My parents are inside," I say.

"Your parents love me," he whispers, breath hot on my neck.

"That doesn't mean they're pro-PDA. Well, not when it comes to *me*. They don't even know about . . ." I close my eyes. "Any of it."

Cole shrugs. "We'll fill them in. Or . . ." He stretches his phone out before us, poised to snap a shot. "Selfie? We can put it online for old times, maybe tag Mom and Dad?"

I snatch his phone away. "Say it again and you'll be singing 'Nothing Compares 2 U' on your drive to Boston."

"You can't break up with me," he says, sparks lingering in his eyes. "Your contract is specific. I made sure this time."

"Ten minutes to showtime, y'all!" Mom ushers everyone into the TV room, leaving me and Jayla in the kitchen to wait for the next batch of microwave popcorn. When it beeps, I shake it into a bowl with cinnamon and sugar.

Jayla pops a handful into her mouth. "You're really something, Luce. Have I mentioned that?"

I roll my eyes. "It's just microwave popcorn with sugar, Jay. The whole salty-sweet—"

"No, I mean the guys. Cole. Franklin. Asher. Marceau. John. They're all, like, wrapped around your finger, yet there's no drama. Explain."

"I don't believe in love triangles. Totally unrealistic."

"Hey, Miss I Got a Perfect Score on My Calculus Exam, that's more like a love rhombus."

I laugh. "Either way. Four out of five are solidly in the friend zone."

Jayla chomps another handful of popcorn. "Angelica would totally sleep with all five, pick her favorite, and get the good one to ice the other four. In fact, she did that in season two, episode nine. Remember the lumberjacks?"

"Mmm. Who knew flannel could be so . . . inappropriate."

"Girls!" Mom yells from the TV room. "It's starting!"

Jayla and I settle in on the floor between Cole and Tens as the opening credits roll, the anticipation in the room as thick as the early summer heat.

Angelica appears onscreen in the opening scene, checking into a romantic hotel in Spain for a prewedding getaway with her third fiancé and Lady Wiggles. There's lots of walks along cobblestone streets, shared tapas, sunsets, tiny purses for dogs. But always in the background, hidden in shadow, a dark and brooding stranger. Meaningful glances full of not-so-subtle subtext.

Cut to the in-room hot tub and champagne bucket one fateful night, Angelica getting her man so drunk he can barely hold his head up.

Next scene, he's passed out cold in the four-poster bed, and she's donning a little red dress, silky as water, sneaking out with Lady Wiggles to meet Mr. Dark and Brooding.

Sadly and unbeknownst to our favorite schemer, this is the day of Pamplona's famed Running of the Bulls, and despite Lady Wiggles's frantic yelping, Angelica ducks down an alley near her lover's apartment and steps right into the path of the oncoming bull run.

That flowy red dress isn't doing her any favors.

Violins and tears, a life-flashing-before-our-eyes montage, the grief-stricken wail of a tiny dog, and before anyone can say *olé!*, Angelica Darling is gored to death, then trampled by the crowd in the bulls' wake. By the time the chaos clears, all that's left of Miss Darling is a scrap of red silk, fluttering dramatically down the cobblestoned streets.

Violins, slow and soft. Softer. Silence.

Fade to black.

The credits roll, and the room erupts, all of us giving Jayla a standing ovation.

Kiara is legit jumping up and down with glee. The only time I've ever seen her so spazzed out was right after graduation, when we'd deemed her Sarah Palin wild-goose chase a resounding success. "Okay, this is embarrassing," she says to Jayla, "but I totally promised my mom and my nana that I'd ask for your autograph. Is that . . . is it weird? Because if it's too weird, I'll just tell them no. Is it?"

"Hell no." Jayla beams. "I'm honored."

"Fascinating," Franklin says, still staring at the credits onscreen. "The emotion you brought to those final, knowing moments, death clutching you in his arms. That was bloody brilliant!"

"Definitely bloody," Stephie says.

"Will they let you keep the Porsche?" Asher asks.

Tens wings a corn chip at his head.

"What?" Asher says. "I'm just saying, that car is *hot*. It totally completes her."

"I'm not usually one for televised drama," Roman says, "but shit. Are the older seasons on Netflix streaming? I mean, not that I have Netflix streaming, or the Internet for that matter. I just like to be aware . . . you know, in case anyone asks and . . ." Roman rubs his Mohawk. "Are there any more Doritos?"

420 giggles. "Sorry, dude. Have some fruit salad."

"Luce?" Jayla smiles. "Honest critique?"

I rub my chin, strike an intellectual pose. "Blood. Guts. Fatal compound fractures. That might be my favorite episode ever."

Jayla throws a handful of popcorn at me, but her ear-to-ear grin softens the blow.

Neighbors. Friends. Aunts and uncles. Everyone's hugging her, patting her on the back, encouraging her. Mom pops a bottle of champagne, and soon there are congratulatory cheers for both of us, clinking glasses, tarts and mini bundts and fruit salad for days.

How much can life change in a moment? A week? A month?

When those pictures first showed up on Miss Demeanor's scandal page, blasted from my own Facebook account, I was certain my life was over. Certain I'd lost the few close friends I had, all my years of ducking the spotlight for naught.

But now I look around the TV room and kitchen, packed with people I never even knew before my private life got broadcast across the Internet, and I can honestly say I'm glad it happened. I wouldn't have planned it that way—I hate what it did to Olivia and the other seniors who got in trouble at home. I hate that things with Ellie and me are patchy at best, and that it'll probably be a very long time—maybe even never—before I speak to Griffin again.

But without the #scandal, none of the people in my house right now would be in my life. In my heart.

People like Franklin, who gave me a chance even when all the evidence was stacked against me, even when almost everyone else decided I was the worst friend in the world. Asher and the (e)VIL crew, kids I'd written off as a whackadoo fringefest for years, kids who in their own crafty way had my back the minute the scandal broke.

Jayla, happier than I've seen her in years, signing autographs, setting up Xbox for a Fruit Ninja rematch with Asher and Tens. Marceau, who may not be reporting back to Canada with an American girlfriend, but who'll have plenty of stories to tell anyway. Besides, he and Stephie have been cozying up all night, bonding over their shared fascination with the concept of fish sticks in a landlocked state, the great debate of clever packaging versus food shortage conspiracy.

And Cole. The one and only boy I ever truly fell for. Our first kiss was forbidden, and every one after a stolen secret, a whisper in the dark. A dream I didn't dare to hope for by light of day.

Yet here he is, smiling at me with mischief in his eyes, the unspoken promise of a summer of adventure, of nights under the stars, of walks in the woods. Of zombie game marathons and campouts with Spike and Night of the Living Dog. Of all the stories we still have to tell each other, all the memories we've yet to make.

Friends. With real faces and names, no mythical creature costumes required. With smiles I can see and laughter I can hear. Hugs and high fives and heartbeats I can feel.

Status update?

Totally real. Totally here. Totally content.

Vacarro out.

ACKNOWLEDGMENTS

The following real-life people have earned blinking gold stars and legit double dark chocolate chip cookies for their contributions to *#scandal*:

Alex, official consultant on all things zombie, author of (e)VIL's crucial hyperdrive vs. warp-core smackdown, and the most loving and supportive bestie a girl could ever ask for. Buddy, if *this* isn't nice . . .

Ted Malawer, superagent, honorary (e)VIL club member, and straight-up literary therapist whose guidance and encouragement I endlessly require-slash-appreciate; Michael Stearns, Immortal Death fan club president; and the Upstart Crow extended family here and abroad.

Patrick Price, rockstar editor and not-so-secret Jayla Heart fanboy who deftly guided these crazy characters and never once mocked my anti-smartphone status; Regina Flath, cover designer extraordinaire who brought to life that #scandalous kiss under the stars; and Bethany Buck, Mara Anastas, Craig Adams, Paul Crichton, Nicole Ellul, Michael Strother, Carolyn Swerdloff, Emma Sector, and the entire hardworking Simon Pulse crew.

Zoe Strickland, curly-haired intern of awesome whose smile brightens my writing days. All the best book boyfriends are for you, HT. Bee tee dubs… Happy Birthday!

Jessi Kirby, who fuels my creative soul with chocolate, wine, Tarot, the beach, writing advice, and friendship; Jackson and Dylan Kirby, who kicked my butt in Fruit Ninja and inspired those all-important scenes; Mike and Michele Knecht, who introduced me to the real Prince Freckles (totally love at first sight); Morgan Matson, who came up with the perfect title; and Jen Jabaley, Rhonda Stapleton, Heidi Kling, and Aprilynne Pike, whose early suggestions helped me shape a whacky proposal into a story.

Finally, hugs to Mom and Dad, Moma and Popa, and all the dedicated bookworms who continue to read my stories and offer high fives from around the world, online and off.

Status update?

Totally awed. Totally inspired. Totally grateful.

Ockler out.

SOMETIMES, THERE ARE NO WORDS . . .

READ ON FOR A SNEAK PEEK OF
SARAH OCKLER'S NEWEST NOVEL.

THE SUMMER
OF CHASING
MERMAIDS

SARAH OCKLER

AUTHOR OF #SCANDAL AND *TWENTY BOY SUMMER*

THE BEGINNING AND THE END

This is the part where I die.

Don't panic; it isn't unexpected. The sea is prideful, after all, and Death never goes back on a deal.

Granna always believed that the d'Abreau sisters were immortal, even after her daughter-in-law died delivering the last of us (me). But among our six bodies, she said, there were only five souls. Twins were special. A single soul dwelling in two bodies.

So Natalie and I—the twins, the babies—were blessed. Blessed by all who loved us. Blessed by the gods and goddesses, by the lore and the legends of Trinidad and Tobago, our island in the sea.

Our connection was unbreakable, and from the first time

we sang together in the bathtub, instinctively harmonizing at age three? Well. We were bright stars, Granna promised. Put on this earth to make music, to share it with the world. No matter that Natalie grew into a soft-spoken beauty with a voice as comforting as a warm breeze, and I became the raging storm, fearsome and bewitching. Our destiny tangled as our limbs in our mother's womb. We were the first to know each other, the first to feel our matching heartbeats. Together, we made magic.

Two bodies, four lungs, one soul.

The beginning and the end. Completion.

Natalie and I sang for Granna and our father. We sang for our older sisters. We sang at Scarborough in Tobago, for fund-raisers and festivals. We sang in Trinidad, our mother's homeland. We sang for the guests— always rich, often famous—at d'Abreau Cocoa Estates, Granna's farm and eco-resort, the place we'd called home after my mother's death. We sang for the men and women who harvested the cocoa pods, who came in for dinner covered in dirt and laughter, eager to listen. During Carnival we sang on top of the big music trucks that traveled through the streets of Port of Spain, Trinidad, as masqueraders jumped up around us dressed like angels and princesses and mermaids. We sang for home, Trinidad and Tobago, twin-island nation, the proud red, black, and white. For our mother's memory—though for Natalie and me, she never existed.

We sang for fun. For our lives.

That's what it felt like, the music. Like being alive.

So maybe I was a liar, and maybe I should've told her years ago, but I didn't. Granna, I mean. It's just that she was wrong about completion, so wrong about the connection and the stars.

The thing about souls was that Natalie really *did* have her own, like each of our four older sisters.

And mine belonged to the sea. Always.

I was born into the sea, born knowing this. Natalie had been born on the boat, but by the time my turn came, we'd been tipped into the water. My first breath outside my mother's body was salt water; the Caribbean Sea lay claim to my soul the moment it took hers.

I've never considered this soul more than a loaner, a broken-winged bird I've only nursed and borrowed. Granna might not believe it, but eventually, I knew I'd be called upon to return it.

One night last spring, just after Carnival it was, the moonlight sparkled on the waves not far from where our mother had delivered me, her last, and I came so, so, so close.

Then I escaped.

For a time.

Even a fool knows you don't cheat Death more than once. And technically, after my watery birth, that night last spring already made it twice.

There's peace in acceptance. Death in it, always. Inevitable. With the acceptance of one thing comes the dying of another: a new belief, a relationship. An ideal, a plan, a what-if. Assumptions. A path. A song.

Consider: Pregnancy dies upon birth. Plans die upon action. Dreams die upon waking.

Not to ruin the story, but if you've come this far, you should know how it happens.

The end begins, as all things must, in the water. Now.

Ropes of black hair twist before my eyes, swaying like reeds. One by one, red clips loosen from the braids, tiny jeweled starfish that

drip-drip-drop

into the deep.

My body is sinking, sinking, sinking. Cold . . . And a memory stirs. The warm sea pressing against me, leaking into my lungs. Stealing my voice.

No, wait. . . . That was then. The spring. That last time, when I came so, so close. *Then* was the Caribbean, my Caribbean. *Now* is the Pacific, and though it's late summer here, the Pacific isn't as patient, isn't as warm. My limbs will soon turn as blue-blue-blue as my silk dress.

It's midnight now, the in-between, and the only person who knows where I am is asleep above, in the berth of our boat, the *Queen of Cups*. He was dreaming when I left; I knew from his sleep sounds. Beautiful, he was, stretched out alone where moments earlier we'd been entwined.

When he realizes I'm gone, he'll search the water, dive beneath the boat. Frantic. Desperate. But he won't reach me.

There's blood in my mouth now, blood in the water, black-not-red at these dark depths. My lungs burn.

I'm ready.

But as my heartbeat stalls, as my limbs give their final tremble, as all around me turns to darkness, I can't help but wonder. . . .

If the sea had offered me one last chance—if I could've bargained with Death to make this broken wing mine, a soul with all its beautiful imperfections—would I have taken it?

Even after everything I'd lost?

SIX WEEKS EARLIER

CHAPTER 1

After spending the day in Aunt Lemon's gift shop with a sticky note in the shape of a crab stuck to my boomsie (and no one even told me until *after* I'd escorted a pair of surfers to our collection of mermaid dashboard ornaments, and then my cousin Kirby sent me the picture, all, *u got crabs!*), I decided a little alone time was in order.

If not for the crab incident, I probably would've just gone to Lemon's Summer Solstice party tonight like I'd promised. Instead, I was slithering around the Chelsea Marina docks, hoping to reach my boat before Kirby ensnared me in her net.

"Elyse!" Kirby shouted. "The party's starting!" In a gauzy white dress and fitted denim jacket, she stood like a beacon in the sand near the docks, hands cupped around her mouth. Her voice skipped across the waves. "Where *are* you? Elyse!"

She wasn't my blood cousin—Lemon was Dad's very best friend, all the way back from their graduate-school days in Miami—and before this summer I'd only seen Kirby twice: the first time five years ago when they'd visited the islands, and then again a year later when our two families met up at Disneyland, my first visit to America.

But I'd been in Oregon a month already now, living in her house, our toothbrushes cohabitating in the zebra cup in the bathroom, and still she couldn't get my name right. *Uh-leese,* it was like.

Close enough, maybe. It just didn't sound-feel-comfort like home.

Sing for us, Ay-leese. . . .

Ay-leese, stop drowning yourself in hot sauce. Give it to me!

Granna, you hear? Our Ay-leese, she got a boyfriend.

Ay-leese, breathe! Fucking breathe, Ay-leese. . . .

"But it's the solstice! And there's . . . cake?" Kirby's voice lacked conviction. She'd been searching the edges of the marina for twenty minutes, and I felt a little thrill that she hadn't found me.

Unseen in the shadows, I crept to the slip that held the old Albin Vega—last place on earth she'd check, since from a strictly "ownership" perspective the boat wasn't mine. I waited until Kirby finally retreated, white dress vanishing like a sail in the mist, and then I climbed onto the deck and ducked through the companionway into the saloon.

Freedom.

For a holiday that was supposed to, according to Aunt Lemon, "honor the full strength of the Sun God," the Oregon night was a bruise. I took in the blackness that seeped into the boat, the salty air, the mustiness that clung to torn seat cushions.

But for the damp suck of the sea, all was soundless.

The Vega rocked gently in the tumult, steadying herself, and my view of the sky—pink-purple-black through the starboard window—straightened.

Tipped.

Straightened again.

The ship was a castaway among the polished vessels surrounding us, a forgotten relic here in Atargatis Cove. I didn't even know her proper name. *Queen of* was all it said on the hull, once-gold letters peeling from the aqua-blue fiberglass. Could've been the *Queen of Hearts* or the *Queen of the Damned* for all I knew. But there was something special about that emptiness,

the unknown,

the unsaid.

Potential undefined.

She was abandoned, a fate we shared, which made her the perfect hideaway.

The boat jostled as a wave hit, and I took a deep breath, fought a shiver. *The sea can't hurt me here. . . .* I repeated the mantra in my head until fear left my limbs. Until I could breathe again.

I lit the big candle I'd brought from Mermaid Tears—Lemon's shop—to chase away the mustiness. OCEAN BREEZE, it said. It smelled like chemically enhanced coconut.

Soft yellow light flickered into the saloon.

Everything was as I'd left it. Straightened up, wiped down, cans of expired soup discarded. A fuzzy new blanket spread out in the V-berth, and another on top, for curling up. Scattered on the cushions, a few books Kirby had brought me from her volunteer job at the library. Some extra clothes, flip-flops, sunglasses I never seemed to need here in Oregon. My iPod. A box of crackers with the peanut butter already spread between them. A bundle of Sharpies, rubberbanded together, different thicknesses.

My shoulders relaxed. The Vega was still unclaimed.

I freed a mass of black curls from beneath the hood of my sweatshirt, and from a pocket in my denim cutoffs, fished out a handful of sea glass. Lemon was looking out for me this summer, so in addition to helping at Mermaid Tears, I tagged along on her morning beach combs. She collected glass to forge into sculptures, some for sale in the gift shop and others on display in the gallery above it. She valued each piece of glass like a gemstone, but she always let me keep some of the haul. I'd been saving it in an empty Costco jar that formerly contained a decade's supply of pitted olives—my hourglass. Once the glass reached the top, things would be right again.

Repaired, renewed, recovered.

Rejuvenated.

Restored.

All the *RE*s complete, and I'd be whole.

Fucking breathe, Ay-leese. . . .

My hand tipped into the jar, and I watched the colored bits clink and settle among the others, an inch of green-gray-blue rising like the tide.

Whole.

I didn't really believe it, but it sounded nice, like a poem. Even if it were possible, what then? Where would I go? Not back. Not forward. I was here, drifting on the current, eighteen years old and totally unmoored.

I pushed the jar back along a shelf in the triangular V-berth, way at the front of the boat, and settled into my favorite spot. My iPod still had a little charge, so I popped in an earbud and scrolled to a new playlist. Lemon had plenty of instrumental on her laptop—Native American wood flutes, classical, wind chimes, dolphin calls, ambient weirdness. On my first night in the States I'd desperately replaced my soca and calypso with it, erased even the reggae—anything that reminded me of home. Of who I should have been. Tonight I was onto Bach's unaccompanied cello suites, track one. Music hummed in my right ear as I cranked the volume, but I wasn't fool enough to sit alone on a boat with both ears covered.

A calm ocean could change in an instant.

Sing for us, Ay-leese. . . .

By the time my screen read "Suite No. 4 in E-flat Major," my heart rate finally mellowed, and I grabbed a Sharpie from the bundle. I found a clear spot among the tangle of words overhead—some nights my notebook wasn't big enough—and pressed the tip to the low ceiling.

> Words spin and spill
> ink from a ~~bottle~~ of ~~blood~~

Queen of lurched left, a game we nightly played, and I tightened my grip on the marker, waiting for her to settle. She perpetually lost. Her body was inked with the evidence.

> A smudge, a smear, a shaky line of
> ~~black~~ letters stands up erect and marches
> around my fingers, encouraging,

Back on the island of Tobago, 7,040 kilometers—no, make that 4,375 miles off the coast of my heartbeat—Dad and Granna had an old Albin Vega in the resort fleet, the *Atlantica*, a twenty-seven footer like this, one of three boats reserved for our guest charters. They'd taken the fourth out of commission in March, part of a long string of before-and-after afters that ended with me leaving for the States, but as far as I knew, the *Atlantica* was still going strong. It was the ship my twin sister Natalie had been born on. The one I'd been born next to.

The last thing my mother saw.

It was a dark and stormy night, our birth story. So they say.

inspiring,
yet ever

Now, out here on these chilly summer nights, the pale scar of the moon cutting the Oregon haze, I wondered if Dad was out on the Vega too. Lying in the V-berth, staring at the same moon, thinking of me as I thought of him. Of my sisters and Granna. The cocoa pods, red-orange-yellow, stacked in pyramids after first harvest, spicing the air with their intoxicating plums-and-tobacco scent.

Home.

Do you miss me?
soundless.

"Keep your skirt on! Let me check it out, make sure she won't sink." A male voice accompanied shadows through the companionway and into the saloon. The boat bobbed under new weight, and I yanked out my earbud and bolted upright, narrowly avoiding a head injury.

His image flickered in the candlelight. When he spotted me, he put one hand on his head, as if he'd anticipated the crash that never came, and said in a tone much softer than what he'd used on his friend, "Well. Hello there."

Unlike me, he was unalarmed, the ghost of a smile hovering on his lips. Something softened him around the edges—alcohol, probably—but his gaze was sharp and clear.

Toes to curls, a shiver shook me. This boy wore the ocean in his eyes, green-gray-blue, ever shifting, and I recognized him immediately. Knew before he said another word that he was as dangerous as he was beautiful.

Christian Kane. Official summer scoundrel of Atargatis Cove, fresh off his first year at Stanford. Aside from the upcoming Mermaid Festival and Pirate Regatta, the Kane family's annual return was the talk of the town. And this son, the eldest? Kirby had him to thank for the cake tonight.

Christian Kane had his own mythology, his own devoted following, much like Lemon's Sun God. Fitting that they shared a birthday.

I was frozen on the blanketed cushions as he scanned the scene: writing on the fiberglass walls and ceiling, damning black marker still clutched in my fingers. Somewhere beneath my elbow, two battered novels about the sea, ancient legends retold. A half-empty can of Coke on the shelf behind my head. A postcard from home, blank, tacked up on the wall. The yawning jar of sea glass, there next to the soda. Nautical charts and manuals once scattered throughout the saloon, now stacked neatly on the table beside the candle, held in place with a large rock carried in first by the tide, second by me.

This ship had belonged to no one. I'd been so certain. And rickety and neglected as she was, I'd called her my home away from my home away from home, my sacred space. Now Christian's gaze swept back to me and skimmed the unfamiliar legs stretched across the V-berth, brown skin made lavender by the moonlight.

When he finally looked at me full on, his stormy eyes changed course.

Confusion.

Surprise.

Intrigue.

The last was the most worrisome.

I tugged the hood up over my head, tied the strings across my seashell necklace and the scar gouged into the hollow of my throat.

Breathe. . . .

"Christian?" someone said, flirty and singsong. The breeze shifted, carrying a whiff of spicy vanilla perfume, and a girl crashed into him from behind. Her silver-tipped talons curled over his shoulders. "What's the deal? I'm freezin' my ass off."

Christian didn't take his eyes off me, just raised a curious eyebrow that lit a spark in my chest.

The girlfriend noticed me then, and around a faint smile, still watching me, Christian spoke plainly.

"There's a girl writing on my boat."

I basically ran.

simonTeen

Simon & Schuster's **Simon Teen**
e-newsletter delivers current updates on
the hottest titles, exciting sweepstakes, and
exclusive content from your favorite authors.

Visit **TEEN.SimonandSchuster.com** to
sign up, post your thoughts, and find out what
every avid reader is talking about!

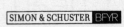

Margaret K. McElderry Books